KEEP AND BEAR ARMS

A NOVEL

Robert Isham Auler

KEEP AND BEAR ARMS

A NOVEL

Robert Isham Auler

Mayhaven Publishing, Inc.

Mayhaven Publishing, Inc.
P O Box 557
Mahomet, IL 61853
USA

Cover Art and Design by Jack Davis
Copyright © Robert Isham Auler
First Edition—First Printing 2008
2 3 4 5 6 7 8 9 10
Library of Congress Control Number: 2007931030
ISBN 13: 978 193227841-5
ISBN 10 193227841-9

Dedication

This book is dedicated to Rob, Jenn and James, my incredibly accomplished children; to Ray and Grace, my parents who would have loved reading it. And to Wm. E. O'Brien, the best teacher ever, who knew how to make a student want to write.

Acknowledgments

For her incredible encouragement and help, my friend, Judie Pearson; my publisher, Doris Wenzel, the tenth sister, whose vision and concrete support made this possible; to Anne Hawkins, whose experience and good taste made this a better book. Pete and Kevin King, superlawyers who represent people and helped me make this possible, and to John Johnson for his friendship and his considerable assistance. Paul Vallandigham supplied answers about guns and other technical matters. For Jackie who held the fort while I wrote. For a host of good friends who suffered through various early versions.

Thanks to three generations of clients, lawyers and judges, each of whom contributed small pieces to the composite. None of whom is a character in this book.

And for my black lab, Billie Holiday, who patiently waited to be let out when the words were flowing.

Prologue

Courtroom A
Moraine, Lincoln County, Illinois

The massive courtroom door squealed as it swung open. In the doorway stood a figure wearing a gray, hooded sweatshirt, draw-strings cinched over the face, eyes obscured by dark glasses.

A divorce case was underway and the wife's lawyer was locked on the husband. The ancient Bailiff lounged in his chair, on the edge of sleep.

A plastic cigarette lighter sparked and flame ran up a rag stuffed in a whiskey bottle. Orange light filled the rural courtroom, a glow from some smoldering nightmare. The burning bottle roared through the courtroom. Firelight reflected from Judge Harold Esker's glasses as the bottle smashed against the front edge of the bench. An orange demon billowed and rolled over the Judge. He twisted and fell writhing and screaming in a puddle of fire, robes flailing in outrage. Scores of unresolved cases the Judge had taken under advisement were transferred to a celestial court.

Panic drove the action. Frantic to get out, those in the courtroom threw chairs, climbed over desks and tables, stumbling through the smoke toward any exit they could recall. Screams filled the room, then the building. A stampede crushed through the side door into chambers.

The open courtroom door fed oxygen to the flames that raced up the rear wall and curled along the ceiling. Smoke belched into the hallway. A jumble of shouting and coughing incited terror thick enough to touch.

The State's Attorney's office emptied down the back stairwell. The Bailiff grabbed a fire extinguisher, then dropped it after peering through the door at the wall of fire.

A deputy who was in the hall guarding a teen-age prisoner rushed to the door, desperate to reach the Judge. A blast of heat changed his mind. Judge Esker lay unmoving, charred beyond recognition. A burnt sacrifice.

Within thirty seconds everyone had scrambled down the stairs, through the front entrance, into a cold April rain. Blackened people littered the courthouse lawn, screaming, retching, crying, and hacking smoke from froth-corrupted lungs. Sirens wailed and yelped. The Volunteer Fire Department arrived and attacked the fire.

Sheriff Marvin Burnett screeched to a halt, jumped from his squad car and ordered a cordon around the courthouse. Deputies swarmed through the crowd, holsters unsnapped, hand-held radios crackling. Bystanders gawked from the sidewalk across the street, but nobody seemed to know what happened to the figure wearing dark glasses and a gray, hooded sweatshirt.

Debris

Five hours after the firebombing of Courtroom A in Moraine, County Seat of Lincoln County, Illinois, the blackened walls and fallen ceiling still gave off heat like a barbecue pit. Upholstery springs from Judge Esker's chair jutted out of the charred remains. The smell of burned petroleum mixed with a stench that could only have been from a burned body.

In front of the Victorian bench stood Roger Fossum, an aging FBI agent based in Springfield. With him was Mark Ainsley, a senior staffer on domestic terrorism. His Washington team had landed an hour earlier in Champaign aboard a government executive jet. They were dressed in blue FBI windbreakers. Ainsley's looked tailored. He occasionally glanced at his wingtips, now coated with ash. An evidence van had arrived from Chicago, equipped with enough expensive equipment for a James Bond movie.

Prowling through the charcoal was Ainsley's traveling companion, Purvis Watson, a gray little man, the Bureau's top explosives tech. He was tweezing charred evidence into shiny new paint cans he would personally seal and transport to his lab in Washington. There would be no chain-of-evidence problem, no sampling errors, no escape for the volatile hydrocarbons in the debris.

Sheriff Marvin Burnett and four burly deputies stood in the center of the courtroom, frowning at the Federal agents.

Sheriff Burnett was a distant relative and look-alike of Smiley Burnett, the old western movie star who had begun his career as a radio personality in Central Illinois. The Sheriff had survived the Marine bombing in Beirut, and often made the voters aware of his close brush with death from governmental bungling. Now his territory was being invaded by the Feds.

The tech, Purvis Watson, was carefully poking through the wreckage.

Burnett checked his watch. "How long you think this is gonna take, Roger?" as if Roger Fossum were in charge.

Ainsley responded without looking at the Sheriff, "A lot longer than it did to cause this mess."

Burnett ignored Ainsley and asked Purvis Watson, "Gas in a bottle, right?"

Ainsley responded in a voice dripping with authority, "Sheriff, this is a Bureau matter. We're still processing the scene. Nobody's stopping you from pursuing leads, if you have any, but the collection of evidence is going to take some time. Mr. Watson needs a little space."

Burnett colored beyond his customary redness. "Well, get on with it! Out here, fella, the Sheriff is in charge of the courthouse. We're gonna need a cleanin' crew and some carpenters in here real soon. We got cases startin' up pretty quick or the speedy trial thing turns 'em loose..."

Ainsley interrupted, "Sheriff, we've got a capital murder here under your state law, and a dozen Federal crimes. There's a possibility this may link up with a terrorist group."

Burnett crunched his way over to Ainsley like a drill instructor bracing a recruit. "Possibility? Mister Amesby, shit got blowed out of a couple hunnert of my buddies in Beirut. We figgered out some Ay-rab done it with a bomb by the time the pieces come down! We don't need no expert t' figger out this was a firebomb thrown by some Moos-limic nutcase! Who the fuck else would it be? The Sierra Club? Now just how fuckin' long is it gonna take you? We'll prob'ly have the guy in jail before you fill up your little paint cans."

12

Ainsley's eyes narrowed but he choked back a reply.

Roger Fossum shouldered his way between them. "Sheriff, don't you have to put up some election posters or something? Courthouse security's your turf, right? Run along and ask your Bailiff how the guy got in here with a burning bottle."

Burnett's head jerked back. His shoulders had the look of a bar fight in the making but he said nothing. The deputies moved forward.

Ainsley turned on Fossum. "Stop making it worse!" Then he said in a condescending tone, "Sheriff, we have our work to do. When we get done you can have your courthouse back. Will you please come out in the hall with me and let the man take his samples?"

Skirmish over. No casualties.

———————————

At 3:15 p.m. Sheriff Burnett was getting into his squad car after consuming a double cheeseburger at his favorite truck stop on the hard road to Champaign.

As he turned the key in the ignition, the police radio crackled. The voice of the Chief Deputy boomed clean and clear, with no ten numbers or garbled mumbling, "Sheriff! We got him! We got Wally Aldin!"

Burnett snatched the mike and clicked the button, "No shit! You got him?"

The Chief Deputy responded, "Yeah...uh...ten-four. We got him about five minutes ago..."

Burnett pressed the button for several seconds to create an interfering masking signal and shouted, "NO DETAILS! I don't want you sayin' no details over the radio! Got that? No details! I repeat, no details over the radio! Come to the office right now! No details!"

He gunned his white Chevy squad car out of the parking lot, spinning gravel, heading toward the jail. Then he reached for his private cell phone, one containing the numbers for political contacts and a half-dozen waitresses who occasionally supplied the attention he seldom received at home. He hit speed dial and four rings later the voice of a local insurance agent answered, a man who brewed the politics of Lincoln County.

He said, "Sheriff, glad you called. Any progress in finding out who did it?"

Burnett smiled. "We just caught the bastard! Wally Aldin, the guy that runs the gas station store out by the Interstate. Can't give no details over the phone, but see if you can hurry up and set up a press conference for me, OK? Let's keep them Feds outta the feed trough. Call me and tell me where the press conference is at, and when."

— · — · — · — · — · — · — · —

At 3:25 p.m., Wally Aldin stood in front of the fingerprint table in the Lincoln County Jail, his sunken eyes boring into the booking deputy who was trying to complete the paperwork of arrest. Aldin ignored him, "Come on! Tell me what's your address!"

For the fourth time Aldin repeated his name. He maintained silence on everything else, except to ask whether his wife, Laura, had tried to contact him. The answer was no.

The deputy was frustrated. "Look, mister. I don't give a damn about your personal privacy right to remain silent stuff. I'm just tryin' t' git you booked. I'm just tryin' t' earn a livin' here."

Aldin looked at him with contempt. "Maybe you better start thinking about what you're doing for your money."

The deputy blinked. He stared at Aldin for a moment and gave up. "We'll try this again after you get a chance to cool off. Les! Git him outta here."

As he disappeared into the cell block, Aldin shouted back over his shoulder, "We will survive."

Stalemate

A gray insurgency was infiltrating Carl Hardman's dark hair and eye-brows, staging a revolution, but his blue eyes were youthful and clear. On a good morning he was six-two, still in reasonable shape from a youth spent playing shortstop, though every ancient sprain and bruise protested the thought of legging out one more base hit. He was glad he no longer required that kind of leg work to make his mark. He was considered one of the better lawyers in downstate Illinois. Trying cases was was his new game and reputation and demeanor settled most confrontations.

Carl's restored 1983 Jaguar XJ6 was prowling the Interstate toward Champaign, where the state university nestles in verdant flatland. Carl had driven the hundred miles from his home in rust belt Marquette County on the Illinois River at least once a week for the past five years.

In the early '60s he had left Chicago's gritty southwest suburbs to attend the University of Illinois, armed with a battered suitcase and a Sears record player. He had achieved high honors in philosophy followed by a U of I law degree. Champaign was the first place he had ever felt free and happy, but his vintage memories of Champaign were now soured by divorce and five years of truncated contact with his 11-year-old daughter, Susan. Her mother, Dani, had moved from Marquette County to Champaign putting space between herself and Carl. For Dani a return to the University was hope and refuge; it was where she had forged her intense political and social beliefs in the Domestic Theater of the Viet Nam war.

The prairie rolled by flat and black, threatening to become green. An occasional swipe of the windshield wipers handled the late April mist. Every barn and tree line was engraved with loneliness. Carl's mind browsed the bittersweet fragments of Susan's young life he had driven hundreds of hours to share. He passed places where he had pulled off and lowered the windows to let fresh air chase exhaustion. Gas stations rolled by, parking lots where he had surrendered for an hour of sleep. Grimy men's rooms. First-name cashiers selling plastic-wrapped sandwiches. On those trips he composed fast food reviews for an imaginary gourmet magazine.

The Jaguar's interior smelled of leather and wood. Its stereo was tuned to the Cubs losing their home opener to the Reds in the third inning. Zambrano, the starter, had gotten pounded and the bullpen was busy revealing its flaws. The baseball season always brought renewal, even though investing hope in the Cubs was contrary to the immutable laws of logic. He would have taken the day off to go to Wrigley Field except for Susan's science fair. He was several hours early and hoped he could convince Dani to let him take Susan to dinner.

The play-by-play of the Cubs game was interrupted, "Here is an update from WGN News. We are receiving reports of an arrest in the firebombing murder of Circuit Judge Harold Esker in a courtroom in downstate Moraine, Illinois. Sheriff Marvin Burnett has called a press conference for 4 p.m. Sources indicate there may have been terrorist involvement. WGN will interrupt the ballgame to keep you informed on this story as it develops." The game resumed with the eternal optimism of Ron Santo, the color announcer.

Carl muttered, "Wow!" He had been following the story. Moraine was less than 30 miles from where he was driving. The town was a failed experiment, sleepy and seedy, decades behind Millington, the industrial town in Northern Illinois where Carl practiced. Moraine had the Amish and apple butter instead of Millington's corner bars and home-style Italian food.

Carl had prospered in Millington. His commitment to his clients had never waned, but thirty years had slowly blunted his shock at the injustices within the legal system.

His ex-wife, Dani, had been a law student when she assisted him in winning a tough murder case that had made his reputation. After graduating from law school she had a stint in the Domestic Peace Corps, then returned to practice with him. After seven years they were partners. In another six they were married. Just like that. A merger finalized.

She was a marvel at researching and briefing, finding slivers of case law to jam under opponents' fingernails. Carl was quick in the courtroom and good with the clients. They had been an unbeatable team. Their practice had mushroomed. They remodeled the old Millington firehouse into a unique office building with the ancient brass pole still running down through Carl's office from the law library above.

But the law had slowly eroded their marriage, like acid rain seeping into their home and into bed with them. It had saturated their cabin when they fled to Wisconsin for weekends at the lake. Eventually it dissolved closeness. Disagreements over strategy or finances became pitched battles on the drive home; dinner was just another case conference. Conceiving Susan six years into their marriage had been a statistical miracle.

In his fifties he was mellowing. The system had grudgingly accepted him. There had even been a few feelers about a judgeship or a seat on the County Board.

The cell phone interrupted Carl's recollections. He pressed the hands-off answering feature. "Hello."

"Carl Hardman?" The voice was deep and well modulated.

"Who's calling?"

"Do I have Carl Hardman?"

Stalemate. He thought about hanging up, but his curiosity took over. "What do I win if I get it right?" He let the silence build. "Who are you and what's this about?"

"I'm calling to ask a question. Do you have any political or personal reason that would prevent you from defending somebody accused of murdering a judge?" The voice was calm and sounded vaguely foreign. Carl glanced at the radio and turned down the ballgame.

"Are you directly involved in that Moraine case? If so, you know how public a cell phone call is, don't you?"

"Directly involved? No, but I'm calling on behalf of someone who is. You have a reputation for defending people with...uh...unusual legal problems."

Carl smiled. "That fits a lot of my clients who haven't killed any judges yet. I guess it depends on a number of things."

"Like your fee?"

"Well... maybe I wouldn't put that first, but it'd be right up there in the top five."

"I will call you within five minutes and give you instructions where to meet. In the meantime, please do not call anyone about this matter." Without waiting for Carl's response, the phone went dead.

The call had an overtone of menace. Carl was seldom worried about his personal safety. He had represented a spectrum of people living on the far side of the line, many of them desperate or violent. Most of them still had a naïve trust that the American system of justice was as fair as their high school civics teacher had promised. What interested Carl was meeting someone who had signed off and had renounced the system. Despite his occasional disquiet about the fairness of the law, Carl considered himself in the exact center politically. But here was a case that intrigued him. He had heard about terrorists. He wanted to see one up close.

— · — · — · — · — · — · — · — · —

Exactly five minutes later, the cell phone played its little ditty. A surge of anticipation ran though him, the excitement of a new challenge. Before he could say anything, the same foreign voice asked, "Where are you?"

Carl glanced at a small town on the horizon. "On I-74, few miles west of Farmer City, headed east. Do you know where that is?"

"Yes. It would be very convenient to meet you soon. Can you take the exit at Mahomet? Can you do that?"

"Mahomet?"

"Yes. You know where that town is located?"

The irony struck Carl. The small bedroom-community of Mahomet, about twelve miles west of Champaign, had been so named for a century and a half, give or take. Now the new world reality had caught up, and it was apparently about to become a rendezvous, possibly with Islamic Fundamentalists. He wondered whether someone as toying with him. "I've been to Mahomet a number of times." The exit was only a few miles ahead. He had over an hour to spare before he needed to pick up Susan. "I can meet with you if it doesn't take too long. Where do you want to go? There's a Dairy Queen…"

"I am sorry, but I would prefer to speak with you in a more private setting. Please take the Mahomet exit and stop in the shopping center parking lot to the east of the exit. What kind of vehicle are you driving?"

"An old black Jaguar."

"We will meet you there."

"What are you dri…"

The cell phone went dead.

During the next few minutes, Carl's mind replayed the strange call, trying to identify the ethnicity of the caller. He didn't speak with an accent so much as his words and phrases sounded as if they came out of a language tape. Carl tried to ignore his disquiet at the man's refusal to meet in a public place, but curiosity overcame caution. He had always been able to drive his way out of most road emergencies. As a kid, he and his friends practiced spinning his old '53 Chevy on icy suburban parking lots at midnight.

He took the exit ramp and peered into a tired, small-town strip mall.

The few vehicles were full of groceries and kids. As he stopped in the middle of the lot, a red Pathfinder slowly appeared around the corner of the mall building. Caked with mud, the license plate was unreadable. It paused as if scanning for vehicles, then pulled up so its driver's window was less than two feet from Carl. The driver in the Pathfinder wore dark sunglasses and a canvas parka with a hood pulled over a Chicago Bears stocking cap, obscuring his facial features except for a heavy black moustache. An Illinois map was in his hand. Carl had an impression of medium-dark skin, but knew the gloom of the gray afternoon might account for it. The man rolled down his window and Carl did the same. Speckles of rain blew into Carl's face.

The man said, "We only have a few seconds. If anyone asks, I am seeking directions to a subdivision north of here. There is a county park called Lake of the Woods. Do you know it?"

Carl smiled, recalling a picnic with Susan the summer before. "Yes, I've been there."

"The western entrance is very near. I will leave first and travel north under the Interstate Highway. The entrance to the park is next to a small museum about the prairie, or some such thing."

"I know where that is, but it's not very private."

"We will not be going inside. Follow me into the park. It is empty because of the season and the rain. There is a good place to talk without being disturbed. It is impossible for anyone to approach without being observed. You will see."

The voice was different from the phone calls, but had a similar lilt. Before Carl could ask questions, the Pathfinder drove off and entered traffic headed north.

Carl paused, giving himself a last chance to change his mind. By the time he turned, the Pathfinder was several hundred yards ahead, separated by a Pepsi truck that had just exited from I-74. Carl passed the American Heritage Museum, a small building to the right of the highway. He exited and checked his mirrors. There were no vehicles behind him. He could see the Pathfinder slowly heading east on the narrow road that crossed Lake of the Woods Park, located on both sides of the Sangamon River. The road was the only connection between the east and west halves. Carl recalled the bridge as being near the ford where Lincoln and his Circuit-riding colleagues used to cross the river to hold court in Urbana and the other towns of the old Eighth Circuit. He felt the irony of meeting to discuss a controversial murder case where Lincoln the Lawyer had cast his shadow.

As they turned, Carl could see the covered bridge over the Sangamon, built to resemble an historic structure. The road ran along an embankment about ten feet above the flood plain. The mud flats were broken by patches of tall, brown grass and small pools tangled with branches. His window was down a few inches and he could smell the dank, black soil. The river was high with spring melt and fresh rain, but was still within its banks.

The Pathfinder drove into the bridge and swung to the left at the east end, blocking both lanes. Carl was forced to stop behind it. Within seconds a black Explorer drove up behind him from the west end. It, too, had mud splashed on the front end to obscure the license plate. The two vehicles now had Carl and the Jaguar trapped on the bridge. A fourth car, a battered blue Chevy Impala, stopped at the west entrance to the bridge, in the middle of the road. The driver got out and removed a jack from the trunk. He popped off the left rear hubcap and appeared to be trying to change the tire.

The man from the Pathfinder walked back across the bridge and stopped at Carl's window. "He wants you to sit with him in the Explorer." He kept walking as if he had issued a command that could not be refused. The man walked back to the Chevy and pretended to be helping its driver change the tire.

Carl overcame his queasiness and walked back to the Explorer. There were no other options. He tried to console himself that they wanted him alive and free, to be able to function as a lawyer. He made an effort to be casual.

The park appeared empty, but anyone approaching would see there

21

was no space to change a tire except in the roadway. That would permit a few seconds to end their conversation and make a quick departure to the east. Both sides of the bridge were protected by the river and mud flats. No approach could be made without being seen. It was a natural isolation.

Carl peered through the open window into the Explorer and saw a tall, muscular man sitting behind the wheel. He was wearing a heavy, olive-drab sweater that looked like a discard from some obscure army. Silver hair of medium length protruded from under the lowered ear-flaps of an orange hunting cap. His brow and nose were sharp and prominent. Heavy sunglasses veiled his eyes. An obviously-false black beard covered the rest of his face from his nose to his chest. In the back seat was a smaller man, wearing a ski mask and a dark gray parka. He was cradling a .45 cal-iber Colt automatic in his lap.

The man behind the wheel held a large, unlit cigar in his left hand. He extended his right hand to Carl who reached in and shook it. The man made Carl think of Castro. "Mr. Hardman, I apologize for the secrecy. This has come up very quickly and finding a secure meeting place has been a little…improvised. If we're not able to conclude an arrangement, not knowing my face should be a comfort to you."

Carl was impressed by the man's quiet tone. He had anticipated some surly fanatic. "I guess I should thank you for that."

"Please have a seat." This was the voice on the telephone calls.

Carl walked opened the passenger door and got in. He felt he had no choice. "Thanks. I have to be in Champaign soon. What do you want from me?" He forced a smile and wondered how much latitude he had.

The tall man leaned back and took his time striking a wooden match on a matchbox. He bent over and the flame licked the end of the large cigar. Then he sucked in the fire and the cigar began to glow as puffs of smoke surged from his mouth. Satisfied that it had a good start, the man spoke in a slow, seductively reasonable tone, "Mr. Hardman, I apologize for the cigar smoke. It is a very bad habit and I was taught tobacco is wrong, although it is a comfort at times like this. Bad times and bad company leave their mark. I suppose there are worse sins." He took a deep puff, obviously savoring it. "At any rate, I'm sure you must be prepared to distrust anyone accused of murdering a judge. You've been taught to believe people from the Middle East are primitive. Let me assure you the opposite is true. A large number of thoughtful and accomplished people have come to this country expecting to find justice, fairness...that sort of thing. Many of them have achieved material and professional success, but have never been accepted as real Americans. Some of them have given up on the system. They have returned to their roots...to old loyalties and beliefs they knew as children in the old country. The Federal government has now created a huge national police force capable of persecuting unpopular groups. Politicians suppress people simply by calling them terrorists. Please understand I'm not asking you to change your beliefs. What we want from you is your professional ability to secure a fair trial. We want you to defend Wally Aldin who was captured this afternoon."

"Does he know you're hiring a lawyer?"

"Yes, indeed."

Carl felt it was time to assert himself. "Ok, for now let's assume you're authorized to hire a lawyer, but whoever takes this case will have to hear it from Aldin."

The man nodded. "Mr. Hardman, he'll go along with our decision. He just needs to be told that we've spoken, and that we are with him."

"Who shall I tell him 'we' are?"

The man smiled. "Believe me, he will know if you describe me...even with the false beard."

Carl weighed the situation. He didn't need another long, stressful case. He was no longer attracted by publicity or even a large fee. The only thing that made him consider helping Aldin was knowing the first few days of a national-level case would be critical to its outcome. On balance, however, he felt too depleted to think about taking on another ordeal. "Any lawyer who takes this case is going to have to abandon his practice and spend months on nothing else. Most competent downstate lawyers would probably charge a hundred thousand dollars. A big time Chicago lawyer would at least double that. Aldin is in State court, at least for the present, but they're probably going to file a whole cluster of Federal charges. A Federal trial would undoubtedly require a fee double that amount. The Feds have no conscience when it comes to wasting a lawyer's time."

Carl had a feeling he'd said something the man behind the wheel accepted. The man in the back seat, shorter and heavier, nodded after he made eye contact in the rear view mirror. For a half-hour they discussed details of the arrest and what could be expected in court. It was clear the men were totally committed to defending Aldin. They promised to provide whatever it would take.

Carl felt the old excitement of a high-profile case but wondered whether he had another major defense left in him. On one hand, here were armed zealots who believed in things he didn't understand. Men who seemed intelligent, perhaps even cultured, but at the same time, menacing. On the other hand, there was a guy in jail facing a death sentence, who was about to be crucified in the national press. Aldin needed a lawyer who knew what he was doing if he stood any chance of living to old age. The death sentence itself was Carl's sworn enemy, but misgivings about terrorists gnawed at him. Nevertheless, rescuing unpopular people was what he did for a living and it had become a matter of personal commitment.

He decided to find a graceful way to gain time to think. "You probably need somebody younger, somebody with fewer personal and professional scheduling problems, but it's clear Mr. Aldin needs representation right now. I might be willing to hold the fort while you look for permanent counsel."

For several seconds the man said nothing. The dark lenses hid his reaction. Carl wondered if he had angered him. Then a smile. He nodded slowly and said, "That sounds reasonable. What kind of a fee would you require to represent Wally for...say a few weeks?"

Carl thought for a moment. It would require spending virtually full time in Moraine, staying in Champaign. He calculated and then mentally reduced the fee. "Tell you what. There's a lot of work that needs to be done quickly. It'd cost...say...ten thousand to do the arraignment, witness workup, maybe start working on the pretrial motions...suppression of evidence, and so forth. That's the stuff that needs doing right away. A lot of cases are lost because nobody gets to the witnesses and nails down their story soon enough. Now you understand that wouldn't begin to cover representing him in the entire case."

A nod.

Carl went on, "If I were to help Aldin, you'd also have to understand that I'm a conventional lawyer. I still believe in working within the system. You can't hire my conscience, just my ability to guide your...colleague...through the maze. I wouldn't be willing to help you attack the legal system itself."

The two men looked at each other. The driver said, "I thought you'd say that. But before this is over, I predict you'll see a lot of things our way. I'm impressed that you are not rushing to get in the spotlight. If you give us your loyalty, even for a few weeks, that's all we are asking now."

Thirty years of trying cases told Carl what a burden he would have to shoulder. His mind ached at the prospect. The time drain from his office would be monumental, but this was a legal crisis, equivalent to a "code" in an emergency room. Without prompt help, Aldin would lose whatever chance for life he still had. He thought for a moment then said, "Look, I'm serious when I say this. You need somebody younger, maybe someone who believes in your cause. Understand, if I get into this, it's only until you find permanent counsel. If you want me to do legal CPR until help arrives, I'll need ten thousand dollars, cash, up front. I'm in it for no more than a few weeks, and I'm going to prepare the case my own way."

The man said in his polished voice, "I suppose you take seriously the law requiring cash transactions of ten thousand to be reported. We don't want to put you into some sort of ethical bind so you'll feel you have to report this transaction. I'm paying you five thousand dollars to go to the arraignment. The man in the back seat is hiring you to prepare the motions you mention until we decide what to do about permanent counsel. We're aware of the Federal statute on proceeds of drug sales and other criminal activity. None of this has been stolen or raised in violation of any of those laws."

As the two men counted the money from thick rolls of hundred dollar bills, Carl noticed a large gold ring on the tall man's left ring finger, encasing a silver coin that appeared to bear a worn likeness of a Roman face.

The tall man read his mind. "That's the Emperor Hadrian. The coin is almost two thousand years old. You'll recall Hadrian built a wall to keep the barbarians out of the Roman Empire. I find that significant. It's what we have encountered in this country since your Homeland Security took over."

Carl didn't know whether to nod or point out that Hadrian's Wall was eventually abandoned as expensive and futile. But the irony caused Carl to shift uncomfortably and stare straight ahead, considering his last chance to avoid the burden he had been offered.

The men had finished counting the money and were waiting. They wanted a commitment. Here was a chance to help save a life by doing the things he had been trained to do. He was pensive.

They were waiting.

He knew the legal system would work overtime to convict an unpopular defendant, and Aldin was surely destined to be King of the Outcasts. On a personal level the case would play hob with his practice back in Millington, but his secretary, Sheri, had often nursed the office through long trials. What influenced him most, however, was realizing he would have to stay in the area, presumably in Champaign. Spending a few mid-life weeks on the campus of his old university would be sweet. Best of all it was a chance to be with Susan for more than a few hours of hurried and artificial visitation sandwiched between hundred-mile drives. That was the clincher.

Carl took a deep breath and said, "Ok. I'll do it."

The driver said, "Welcome aboard," and both men handed Carl the stacks of worn hundred dollar bills.

Carl said, "What kind of receipt do you want?"

Both men registered thin smiles and the driver shook his head dismissing the idea. He reached into to back seat and produced an expensive burgundy leather attaché case and clicked the latches. "Another little present for you." He opened the case to expose a piece of electronic equipment, marked JM-20F. "It's a sweep. A debugger. You probably think this is unnecessary, but before long you're going to understand."

He spent the next ten minutes instructing Carl on how to use it.

—— ·—— ·—— ·—— ·—— ·—— ·——

The man removed his false beard as he watched the Pathfinder clear the end of the covered bridge and watched the Jaguar disappear to the east. He looked in the rearview mirror and into the eyes of the man in the back seat, who had removed his ski mask. There was worry on the face.

"You have something on your mind?"

Startled at being read so easily, the man in the back seat said, "Begging your pardon…can we trust this lawyer?"

The driver stuffed his beard into the glove compartment and said, "I can understand your concern, but we didn't exactly pick his name out of the phone book. People I trust have given me a list of lawyers and doctors and accountants, over the years. Professional people who could help one of us if need be. I have spent a lot of time locating them and finding out things about them. Hardman has a good track record. He's a fighter. He doesn't abandon his clients like a lot of them do. I even got his cell number from a pizza delivery boy in Hardman's town. He seems to answer our needs."

"Back seat" pursed his lips and looked down. "Yes…perhaps…but he says he's just a temporary."

The tall man puffed on his cigar and smiled. "We can find a way to make sure he serves as long as needed. He won't find it quite so easy to quit."

Hit and Run

Sheriff Burnett stood on the bed of a blue Chevy pickup truck parked in front of the Lincoln County Courthouse and said, "Testing, one, two, three." He blew into the mike. A shriek of feedback suppressed the buzz of conversation among the reporters. Videotape began to crawl through cameras. Mobile television vans activated their transmission antennae, discharging the Sheriff's words into the sky, up-linked to Chicago, New York, Atlanta and the world. Photogenic young men and women pushed and shoved against the bed of the pickup, raising up their microphones as if asking for them to be blessed.

"Can you all hear me?" Burnett was still too close to the mike and the edges of his words were tinged with a squeal. Several of the reporters in the back nodded. Burnett lowered the volume on the portable p.a. system he had borrowed from the Little League diamond.

"As Sheriff of Lincoln County I hereby announce the arrest of the man who done the firebombing of the courthouse and the murder of Judge Esker." He paused and waited for approval. The press registered no emotion.

"Anyways, our office has in custody the one that done this deed, a Mooslem guy from Lebanon named Wally Aldin. That's where me and my Marine buddies got blowed up by them terrorists. He's been living here in

28

Moraine for about twelve years. He runs that gas station convenience store out by the I 57 exit. He was arrested through some rapid police work by our department as a result of some inside information we been collectin' on…possible terrorists. He's been filin' crazy legal papers in court cases around here for years. My deputies done some great police work under my direction. Questions?"

Burnett looked at the cluster of reporter faces staring at him. He could imagine what the press conference would be like when he announced for the State Senate.

There was a garble of shouted questions before one surfaced above the rest. "When was he arrested, Sheriff?" Channel 3 from Champaign.

"We picked him up about 3:15. You notice that's only a couple hours after it happened."

"What evidence do you have linking him with the crime?"

Burnett smiled. The question was from the talk show host of his favorite country music station, acting as a shill. "There was a search warrant and we got a gas container out of Aldin's car trunk. We found a whole bunch of guns in his doublewide, along with a lot of Ay-rab newspapers and a computer." He glanced at a list in his hand. "Some kind of book they say is pretty far out. We also got a shi…er, uh…a whole load of inside stuff we gotta check out. Prob'ly terrorist stuff. The FBI's here askin' for our help. We got this wrapped up for them. Which is more help than we got from them."

A young reporter with a big city haircut asked, "Sheriff are you implying the FBI has been a problem for you?"

Burnett humphed, shook his head and said, "Don't know as I'd say they was hurtin' much except we'd still be siftin' through the ashes this time next year if the Feds had their way. We went out an' got the guy what done the crime. Now the court system can get back to business."

The female anchor of Champaign's Channel 15 asked, "Is this Aldin the only person involved?"

"Well, for now, we don't have no other arrests pendin'. When we prove one of them groups put 'im up to it... Let's just let that go for now."

"What are the charges, and when will he go to court?" WGN-TV from the side of the pickup.

"Tomorrow at 1:30. Gonna be capital murder. Death penalty."

A buzz went through the reporters at the prospect of a long case oozing blood lust. Job security for months, maybe years.

"Look, that's all for now. We got work t' do. I'll call another press conference if we get a confession or if there's another break in the case."

He jumped down from the tailgate and walked away with questions bouncing off his back.

After listening to the Sheriff's press conference, Roger Fossum snapped off the radio in a small meeting room in Urbana's Federal Courthouse. He was livid. He turned to Ainsley and said, "What kind of asshole would give out details of the evidence yield in a press conference?"

"Watch your language Roger. Not all of us grew up in a locker room," Ainsley said with the disapproval of the recently-promoted.

Fossum said nothing. Ainsley had a degree from one of the big-time eastern colleges and somehow had lapped him, despite Fossum having fifteen more years of seniority.

FBI agents and secretaries from the U.S. Attorney's office were bringing in stacks of hastily-assembled computer print-outs, political literature, photocopies of court papers, all the material on Aldin anyone could find. Ainsley's eyes tracked Fossum. "Roger, sit down. You're making me nervous."

An insubordinate smile that could have passed for gas pains flickered across Fossum's face. Even a split-second hint of annoyance would have been unthinkable were it not for Fossum's impending retirement. He let out a quiet sigh. "I guess I'm a little steamed by that redneck sheriff.

Giving a press conference...going into the yield of the search warrant. The guy's a real hot dog." He leaned forward. "Ok, then, what do we have?"

"Roger, you've been working downstate Illinois for how long? Twelve years? Don't you have any ideas of your own? This country is swarming with people like this Aldin."

Roger idly flipped open one of the files. "We never had any terrorists around here before."

"Congratulations. Your fly-over territory just graduated."

Fossum sighed and slumped into his chair, adding one more rumple to his blue suit. "So what do we do?"

For the next hour, they discussed the spectrum of terrorist groups. Ainsley shifted the focus to Aldin and spread out a sheaf of photocopied legal documents faxed in from downstate county court files. They had rap sheets on him, none of them showing more than minor traffic offenses and a bad check charge. His immigration and naturalization papers had been requested and the CIA was searching for anything relating to him in his native Lebanon. Aldin's travel records were being assembled by Customs. Subpoenas for his credit card records were being drafted.

The civil records were interesting. Downstate courts had been flooded with bizarre pleadings filed by Wally Aldin in a variety of civil cases. Handwritten motions filed by him challenged the authority of the Courts and confounded standard legal procedure.

An hour passed and the air in the small room grew stale. Fossum stood watching the rain streak the window. He wanted to walk outside and let it run down his face. He longed for a year to pass and for retirement to arrive. He stretched before walking to the table and picking up the search warrant inventory. All it listed were a computer and some newspapers in Arabic, a gas can, and a number of firearms. And none of the guns were smoking. In fact, apart from the Arabic papers, there was nothing that could not be found in thousands of Central Illinois households. "Do you think we have enough to convict this guy? Sheriff Redneck assured everybody this is a piece of cake. I'm not so sure we've got this one in the bag. We're operating in a post-911 climate, but it's still pretty thin. And that Sheriff has certainly forced our hand. All this crap we've got…the crazy lawsuits Aldin's been filing…that's not going to prove he's a terrorist. Are we gonna find any real Islamic fundamentalist connections? Country types are skeptical about everything Washington does. People out here believe in black government helicopters and space aliens."

Ainsley frowned. "Just confine yourself to the facts, please. Get me a workup on any police contacts that don't show up on the rap sheet. I'll be staying out here until we get a handle on this thing. Have your report ready by tomorrow."

Fossum had become used to the gentle pace of pre-retirement. "Tomorrow?"

Ainsley's dark eyes demeaned him. "You're still capable of doing a report?"

Fossum wondered what would happen to his retirement if he told one of the stuffed shirts from Washington to go fuck himself. He decided not to find out.

Hitting Home

The Jaguar stopped in front of a family restaurant at the edge of Champaign. A sign said *Taffies*. Men in bib overalls stared through windows darkened by cigarette smoke, at Carl, who was making a cell call.

The phone rang as he waited for Sheri, his secretary of 30 years. To say she worked for him would have derogated their relationship. When she joined him in the late '60s she had brought with her experience from three law firms. Sheri wasn't good, she was indispensable. She ran the practice like a clan, mothering the three young lawyers who now worked for the firm, but cracking the whip when they began to pretend they were grownups.

The practice had matured since Carl's divorce. He had channeled his pain into a string of stunning personal injury and criminal victories.

Sheri had pushed him to rejoin life. She had subscribed to the *Chicago Reader* and had left the "Women Seeking Men" page on his desk with a few ads circled, her ribald comments scrawled next to them. Others she crossed out and marked with dire warnings and poison symbols. It had been good for a laugh, but eventually he called a few and quietly arranged dates on the weekends he wasn't visiting his daughter in Champaign. There had been beautiful women, predatory women, nice women and normal women. But none of them had a chance. Sex was permissible only if the woman had fair warning of his emotional unavailability.

His thoughts were interrupted. Sheri's voice said, "Hardman Law Offices." The tones were deep and husky, giving no hint she was ignoring retirement age.

"Sheri?"

Only a flicker of a pause. "No, Carl, Monica Lewinski. Who'd you think?" Sheri seldom permitted the illusion of anyone else being in control.

"Ok, Monica. Is anybody on the job up there?"

"Two of 'em never come back from the Courthouse. If they pull that stunt again, I'm sellin' their desks at a garage sale. The other one's had clients all day."

He could almost smell her chain-smoke through the phone. She would be leaning back in the ancient oak swivel chair she had rescued from some junk store. "You doing OK?"

"Me? The damn clients been gnawin' my ear off all day, but I don't let none of 'em get me goin'. Learned that a long time ago. You oughta figure that out one of these days, Carl."

He paused for a second and his voice became apologetic, "I think I'm about to do something stupid."

She listened for a couple of beats. Sheri could refine meaning from his silences. "When you start thinkin' I start worryin'. What'd you do, buy a barbecue joint?"

"Nothing that extreme. I got a strange call this afternoon. I've been trapped in a covered bridge, talking to a bunch of Middle Easterners. They want me to defend that murder case."

"The damn firebombing?"

"Yeah. I'm thinking of taking it...just until they get somebody else to defend him. I'd be down here for a couple of weeks. Probably need to rent a place in Champaign. Might be a little hard to find me for a while."

"Hell, you already took it. Don't shit me. You been needin' a little midlife pick-me-up. Go ahead, play counterspy or whatever. Do what you want. We'll figure it out."

He smiled. At an age when most women would be planning trips to the great-grandchildren she persisted in ramrodding his life, fueled by cigarette smoke and black coffee. Her dividend was the respect of everyone she knew.

"Can we hack it financially?"

"Carl, in case you haven't noticed, nobody's givin' no chili suppers for you. When are you gonna figure out you're ridin' the wave? Them kid lawyers are learnin' pretty good. You got those three death cases about ready to settle. You said yourself you'd just as soon coast for a while and try to spread some of the income to next year."

"Well, I've got ten thousand cash I'm depositing in a bank down here tomorrow. They'll transfer it to our account."

"You're such a damn boy scout! Most lawyers would just stick that cash in their pocket and nobody'd ever know different. Them terrorists ain't gonna tell the IRS."

"Well, I play it straight."

"Do what you want. We can run this end. You got every electric toy in the world, faxes, cell phones, laptops. It don't matter where you are. Same as here."

"Hmmm. Ok…I guess. I'm just holding the fort until they get some young hotshot, but I wonder what'd happen if I actually got involved in a two month trial down here..."

"Look, Carl. That's the thing. It's all about down there, right? You been burnin' up the road for the last few years, comin' home beat t' shit after seein' Susan. What you're lookin' for is an excuse t' see your kid like a normal person. Well, what's wrong with that? You paid your dues. Take the damn case an' rent a nice apartment down there. Just reverse your time. Come up here a day an' park your bod in Champaign the rest of the week. Some guys your age spend half their life on a lake or a golf course. Go and spend some time hangin' around the damn university. Hell, you send 'em enough money, they oughta let you live in the President's house. You can see Susan three, four nights a week, do stuff on weekends. Dani don't give you grief like a lotta women. It'd be good for you. The damn case...hell...you been gettin' stale. You need a little jab in the ass. Won't hurt the practice none t' get on TV, neither."

"You really think so? I mean, can you..."

"Yeah, Carl. Sheri can run your damn law practice."

His smile broadened. "By the way, you didn't get conned out of my cell number today did you?"

He could feel her temperature rise. "Carl, you gotta be kiddin', right?"

"I guess so. Sheri, you really could run the country. You know that, don't you?"

"Sure." She said it without inflection.

He was trying to pay attention at Susan's science fair. She had built a camera out of interlocking boxes that slid backward and forward to demonstrate focus and depth of field. The lens was a simple magnifying glass. It focused a lighted candle on an opaque piece of plastic in the rear box.

Susan had Dani's dark hair but, against probability, his blue eyes. She had a fierce intelligence from both sides. Susan was sitting with her partner, eyes glistening, her eleven-year-old face contorted with anticipation. She was holding her partner's hand as they judges passed down the row of tables.

They stopped and smiled at the girls and placed a blue sticker on the exhibit. The science teacher tried to say something, but the girls were squealing and dancing and hugging. Then Susan broke away and ran to Carl with her arms wide. "Daddy! Daddy! We won first prize!"

He thought, *No, honey, I won. You are first prize.*

36

Keep to the Right

On most days the Liberty Church was just a multi-purpose meeting room rented from the Fraternal Order of Eagles. It had cheap ceiling tiles, fluorescent lights, and casement windows. There were no pews and no religious symbols except for a plain, wooden cross about five feet high, kept in a closet between meetings. Folding chairs were arranged into rows eight across, and seven deep, but seldom more than two rows were needed. An electronic keyboard flanked a plywood lectern.

The group called itself a church, not unaware that section 501c3 of the Internal Revenue Code made many things possible through tax deductibility. Brother Bill, the un-anointed lay preacher, was an adherent of the racist Christian Identity movement, but he soft-pedaled this to keep his diverse flock in a consensus. Far beyond conventional fundamentalism and vigorously pro-life, it staged regular pickets of abortion clinics and worked hard for and against candidates. The paradox was its belief in political activism. Liberty Church shared its methodology, activist commitment to changing the real world, with Catholic radicals in Central America as well as Islamic fundamentalists, both groups it hated.

Rough bookshelves contained a tattered set of basic Illinois law books, many without covers, flotsam from a dead lawyer's estate sale. The floor was stacked with papers. Against one wall, tables were jammed with discarded computer equipment jerry-rigged with a maze of wires and manned by two dozen people in clean but inexpensive clothing. One or two men wore ties. The women were dressed as if for Sunday dinner at a franchise restaurant. There was no noise other than pages turning, computer keys clicking, and an occasional metallic squeak as someone shifted in his chair. All of them were working on their lawsuits, organizing protests or composing letters to politicians and editors. It was the Wednesday night legal clinic in which Brother Bill encouraged the flock to use the courts to clog the system that fostered sin and abortion and preyed upon the middle class. They drafted small claims cases, Social Security appeals, Workers' Compensation petitions, complaints to various agencies and pleadings in a jumble of lawsuits.

Finally Brother Bill stretched his beefy arms skyward, locking his fingers backward. Several joints popped. He scanned the flock with his penetrating gray eyes.

The rest of them stopped as if a school buzzer had sounded to end a test.

He smiled and said, "That sounds like an M-16, don't it?"

A woman with severe black hair pulled straight back into a bun looked up from Black's Law Dictionary. "Brother Bill, you're gonna get big, puffy knuckles if you keep doin' that."

He said, "Well, we'll have to pray on that."

Everyone relaxed and began straightening up their papers.

Brother Bill scanned the table. "Anybody got any questions about their research? We got time to talk about it."

Several seconds went past and pairs of eyes glanced around the room, reluctant to break the ice.

A man with blacksmith hands and a shock of white hair cleared his throat. "I don't get this here part about the Second Amendment. Where's it at in the Good Book?"

"Henry, it don't say nothin' about the Constitution in the Bible because the Bible come out a long time before the Constitution. But God made 'em both." Brother Bill talked down to him in a tone appropriate for speaking to a fifth grader.

Henry's face showed he was digesting the insight. He pinched his nose and wiped his fingers on the inside of his pants pocket.

Brother Bill continued, "They didn't have no guns back then in the Bible times, neither. That's why the Constitution just says you got a right to keep and bear arms, which includes guns an' other kinds o' things people need to protect their rights." He turned to the woman with the bun. "Alice, you got the refreshments tonight, right?"

Alice rose from the table and walked over to the last row of folding chairs where three boxes of donuts sat next to two twelve-packs of Diet Pepsi. She passed among them, distributing donuts and Diet Pepsi, the Liberty Church's parody of communion.

Sitting at the end of the table with his right leg stiffly extended, an arm-crutch leaning against his chair, was a tall blonde man with blazing, blue eyes sunken in a sickly, pallid face. The back of his jacket said *Southeast Asia War Games Second Place*. On his computer screen was a draft of an appeal to the Veterans' Administration regarding his service disability. He scowled and said, "Brother Bill, who are you kiddin'? There's no way the gover'mint is gonna pay attention to the Bible or the Constitution or their Momma's dyin' wishes. All this legal stuff don't do no good. If this here Liberty Church wasn't a good way to kill a Wednesday night, I'd be out tryin' t' thank the guys on my draft board for this here cane."

Brother Bill nodded. "Walter, you guys got the shaft. You know that. We all do. You was fightin' a war nobody was tryin' to win. They run that war like an experiment, usin' you an' the rest o' them boys for the rats."

Walter nodded his head and said, "Nobody's said nothin' here tonight about that towelhead that killed Judge Esker. That's a helluva lot more important to me than a bunch of damn lawsuits. What are we gonna do about him? Them liberal judges will cut him loose because he's a Mooslem or some other damn minority. I think we gotta start talkin' about doin' somethin' ourselves."

Alice laid down her donut. "What are you talking about?" Everybody stopped and watched. Alice had her own ideas and had been known to cause a problem or two.

Brother Bill intervened, "Well, Alice, I guess he's got a point. The Liberty Church is for the American way and that don't include no terrorists comin' over here an' eatin' good off of us, then killin' our public officials. Maybe it's time we done somethin' about it."

Alice stared at Bill. "That's the first time I've ever heard you say a good word about judges."

"Well, Alice, it's like an abortion of our Constitution, them murderin' a judge, and I know you don't believe in no abortions. Maybe he's right. Maybe we gotta stop things like this quick, so's they don't get drug out for years in the Courts, while some mouthpiece talks the Supreme Court into takin' away the death sentence. Maybe he's got a point. Maybe we need t' think on how we can do somethin' direct about this here Wally Aldin." Bill looked around at the faces. Several of them softly muttered "Amen."

Alice didn't give an inch. "I'm only here because of the murder of innocent babies. I don't have anything in common with people who advocate violence."

Brother Bill bristled. "You wasn't so particular about violence on that picket line over in Decatur that day. I seen you smack that abortion Doctor with your sign."

Alice looked away, "I know. But that was the heat of the moment. If I'm hearing correctly, you would…take action…against this Aldin person if you got a chance. That's calculated criminal conduct."

Brother Bill leaned forward. "We gotta stick together, Alice. The Feds want to break us up. The whole idea of the Liberty Church is we gotta make a common cause, like Benjamin Franklin said about all hangin' together or all hangin' separate."

Alice frowned, tossing the remainder of her donut into the wastebasket.

"If we bicker over ever' little thing, purty soon we'll be fallin' apart an' the Devil will win another round."

Most of the people in the room nodded and uttered a few more amens.

Brother Bill leaned forward on his elbows. "Let's sing *America the Beautiful* before we finish for tonight. How 'bout it, Dave?"

A pimply-faced boy of about eighteen rose and walked up to the electronic keyboard, hit the switch, and played the song from memory. Before the last words were sung, Brother Bill's eyes had misted.

Ainsley placed the delicate china cup in its saucer, careful not to spill the Kenya AA coffee. He did it silently, as if any tiny noise would cause the dozen or so men gathered around the gleaming rosewood table to punish him. He had flown back to Washington for this late evening conference, but hadn't slept on the way.

The Deputy to Someone in Homeland Security was talking. Ainsley was still trying to master the bewildering new hierarchy. He listened with simulated adoration, focusing his gaze upon a print of Van Gogh's *Starry Night* on the wall just past the head of the table. The Deputy was grilling Ainsley's superior about the Aldin case. The current topic was the hasty arrest and search of Aldin by the hayseed sheriff. It had yielded grounds for the Federal search warrant that had produced most of the evidence. But if the initial search by the Sheriff were held to be illegal, then the warrant itself might be quashed and the evidence suppressed, unusable in trial. A number of theories were advanced, precedents discussed, with no resolution of the problem of the search.

Then the Deputy leaned back in his chair and touched the fingers of both hands together, making a tent over his chest. He frowned and said, "The thing I don't get here is why?"

Everyone else in the room leaned forward and looked surprised. The Deputy caught the look and asked, "Why? Why would they attack a judge in a no-place county? Why would they waste a long-term sleeper agent on such a stupid stunt?"

Ainsley's supervisor leaned forward and said, "The psychological profile people think it represents a new phase. They see this as an attack on the heart of Christian America. Sort of a challenge to everybody who might think the Twin Towers attack was what we can expect. If no tiny little burg in the cornfields can feel safe…so the argument runs…there will be erosion of the commitment of the average American. The National Guard will want to stay home and defend family and farm. And we will be spread thin taking care of our rear to the point that we can't wage war in the Middle East. The psych boys think that's it. True terror spreading all over the U.S. so that nobody will feel safe going to the store. They think it's calculated to ratchet up the hatred for Moslems in the U.S. and that it will radicalize them all over the world. Same tactic the SDS used in the '60s."

The Deputy frowned. Clearly this was something he didn't want to hear.

The supervisor floated a trial balloon. "What about just taking Aldin to Guantanamo or one of the other installations?"

The Deputy winced. "Right! We don't have enough criticism for that kind of thing already? This guy is a naturalized American citizen. We're getting killed in court on the Padilla guy from Chicago. Do you want to risk the entire program for some crude firebomber in Mayberry?"

The supervisor caught the emotion and said, "Understand, now, this is just the theory of the psych boys. They could be wrong. There may be some hidden connection between this judge and terrorism. We can't know all the facts yet. We can certainly review the Gurantanamo option down the line someplace."

The Deputy grunted and a more satisfied look crossed his face. He emphasized the new political context in which domestic terrorism would be handled, aimed at avoiding another Ruby Ridge or Waco-type public relations nightmare.

Out of the blue the Deputy asked, "Mr. Ainsley, do you have anything to add?"

Ainsley almost knocked the cup from the saucer at the mention of his name. "Uh, no. I'm sorry. Well...nothing which differs from the points already made."

"So you agree there is a potential for embarrassment?"

"Yes, I suppose the premature arrest could create a problem, particularly if it comes out there was an arguably illegal search before the warrant was issued."

"Who is this Carl Hardman?"

"A State Court lawyer."

Ainsley's superior chimed in, "This Hardman has a decent track record. He's handled several challenging cases, but he's probably over the hill even if he's not out of his league."

The Deputy probed for the real point, the political one, "Why would they hire him? Is he affiliated with any radical or Islamic movement?"

Ainsley glanced at his supervisor who exhibited a blank look and said, "Perhaps Mr. Ainsley has some information about that."

Blindsided, Ainsley took a deep breath and tried to project confidence, "We've only had a short time to develop a file on Hardman. No arrests. No military record. No discipline by any bar group. He's admitted to all the Federal District Courts in Illinois, the Seventh Circuit and the U.S. Supreme Court although he's never had a case there. He's done about seventy matters on appeal, almost all of them in State Court. He seems politically stable, probably center-right economically, but he's a committed civil libertarian and openly opposes the death sentence. Moderately successful. In recent years he's done a lot of civil cases...injuries, products liability, that sort of thing, but he has a reputation as a pretty good criminal defense lawyer. His ex-wife is on the faculty at the state law school in Champaign, about 30 miles from where the attack took place. But there is no indication why anyone would hire a downstate lawyer when they could get a first rate lawyer from Chicago. That's reason enough to wonder if he's somehow linked to a terrorist organization. We could run a surveillance on him if that seems..."

The Deputy cut him off, "Absolutely not! Certainly not at this stage! When will you people learn the limits of domestic surveillance? How's it going to sound if somebody leaks the fact that we investigate the lawyers who defend the people we prosecute? Do you want to explain that to a Congressional committee? When will you learn?"

Ainsley hunkered down, "Yes, sir. I see the point."

The *Starry Night* print seemed at home in the silent room.

To avoid eye contact with the Deputy, Ainsley allowed his gaze to drift through the window, toward the lighted Capitol Dome.

The Deputy persisted, "Let me state this again so there can be no misunderstanding. There will be no probing the political background of the defense lawyer, unless, of course, the Bureau becomes aware that this Hardman is involved in a conspiracy or some other crime. I emphasize the difference between investigating Hardman's personal life and doing your job investigating violations of Federal statutes. Do I make myself clear?"

Ainsley looked at his supervisor to check whether it was clear. The supervisor nodded affirmatively but said nothing, possibly indicating that the meeting was being taped.

The Deputy wrapped it up quickly after reminding them that domestic terrorism is a war even more extreme than the Cold War. A war against the core ideals we live by; not just the content of our system, but the very methods by which we conduct civilized life. The Soviets had at least a recognized that control must rest in secular hands. Outmoded notions of personal rights would simply have to yield to pragmatic realities. This was said by the Deputy without any specific marching orders, without any limiting rules of engagement, with enough generalities going both ways to insulate him from later criticism. It would have been impossible for anyone in the room to miss the message.

Face Time

The prisoner interview room at the county jail in Moraine doubled as a storage facility for dead files. It smelled of disinfectant.

Across the table was a man of medium height in his mid-thirties. Slim, compact and fine-boned, with a well-defined, muscular chest. His face was a shade darker than was commonly found in Central Illinois after a long winter. Faded jail denims were a size too big and he wore plastic slippers that didn't match. His dark hair was longer than average. A clipped, brush moustache and heavy eyebrows contributed to his brooding look. Abnormally-large brown eyes stared at Carl, unblinking, festering with anger. Here sat Wally Aldin, instant celebrity, fresh meat for conspiracy theorists and debunkers alike. Dozens of governmental entities and a score of news organizations were scrambling to get Wally's inside story. An interview with him was worth tens of thousands and Carl was getting paid to listen to him.

Aldin waited for the deputy to leave before asking, "Why are you here? Who sent you?" His voice was distinctive, a little hoarse and grating, not inconsistent with Aldin's wiry appearance. What was remarkable was the lack of any accent. He sounded like Middle America.

Carl held up his hand for silence. He opened his briefcase, took out the device and began sweeping the area for electronic bugs. He went over

45

the table, the chairs, and then walked around the room giving special attention to light fixtures, wall sockets, and the telephone.

Aldin watched with approval. "Nice toy. You don't trust anybody, either?"

"I feel a little silly doing this, but maybe we're not just dealing with good old Sheriff Burnett. He probably couldn't operate anything more complicated than a toaster, but he may have a little help on this one."

Aldin stared and asked, "Worried about the Feds, huh?"

"They certainly must think national security is involved. If this were just a simple serial murder or a cannibalism..."

"I get the point. Who sent you?"

As he had been instructed, Carl looked around for any small defects in the walls that might harbor a pinhole video camera to read lips. He reached for a pad of paper and wrote on the second page "Tall man. Accent. Had a ring with a Roman coin." He flipped the top sheet over it, turning the pad toward Aldin.

Aldin lifted the cover sheet and peeked at the page, shielding the words with his left hand as if sneaking a look at a pornographic image. He wrote, "What did the other guys look like?"

Carl was taken aback. He wrote, "Second, heavy set, moustache, sunglasses. Third, ski mask. Another changing a tire. Didn't get a good look."

Aldin shielded his mouth and asked, "Which one did the talking?"

Carl wrote, "Tall."

Then Aldin seemed to relax. "That's good enough for me. Where do you stand?"

"Pardon me?"

"Where do you stand personally? What are your beliefs?" He pushed the legal pad over to Carl.

It is usually none of the client's business whether his advocate has a personal commitment to the bill of goods he is required to sell, but because of the overtones of state security he decided that he'd be upfront and candid.

If that ended in a breakdown of client confidence, so be it. Carl had tired of writing notes and said, "You really want to know? Does it matter?"

Aldin paused and studied Carl's eyes. "You bet it does! If there's a personal reason you're in this, that's one thing. If not...well..."

He composed his response before answering, "I suppose it depends on what you mean by 'personal reason'. I love this country and I've spent 30 years defending people from cops and bureaucrats who can't read the Constitution. If that qualifies as a personal reason, then the answer is yes."

A flicker of a nod. "Have you been in the military? Served in the Middle East? Lebanon?"

Carl sighed. He guessed that answering honestly might rupture any developing bond between them. "No, I've never served in the military. Most of the wars we've been in look questionable in retrospect. I've never been closer to the Middle East than Italy. If that's a problem between us, it'll just have to be that way." He stared back at Aldin. Carl couldn't interpret the smoldering look in Aldin's eyes.

Finally, Aldin said, "I'll accept that.

"Let's hope so, because we've got lots to do, even if I'm only on board until you get somebody else."

"What do you mean somebody else?'"

"I told your friends I'd hold the fort until they could get some somebody else, maybe somebody you'd be comfortable with.'"

Aldin soaked that one up for a moment. "They must trust you or they wouldn't have sent you. I don't put much stock in lawyers. They're just whores. A man ought to be able to go to court and explain his business without anybody getting between him and the way of right and wrong."

Carl was used to this kind of talk. He had long since decided it was part of a client's therapy. "Yeah, I know what you mean. Had a divorce, myself. Wasn't real happy with the lawyer."

Aldin registered mild surprise and perhaps a little disappointment, as if spoiling for a fight was now less possible. "Well, this isn't a divorce. Your government's decided I'm a threat now that they're the world policeman."

For just a second Carl wondered if it would be possible to return the fee and forget the whole thing. But where would a person like Aldin find anybody competent and willing to help save his life? What he got in return for his concern was another insult.

"So you're a hired gun, right? You're just a mercenary?"

Carl decided to lay aside his irritation and get on with the case. "Well...yeah...I guess you'd have to say I'm a mercenary. I get paid for doing this. I'm a mercenary except for the fact that I could make a hell of a lot more doing three or four rear-end whiplash cases in less time than you're going to burn up in the first week. So I'm either a pretty stupid mercenary or maybe there's a little whimper of principle down there someplace."

Aldin smiled for the first time. The taste of sarcasm appeared to be to his liking. "I guess if they picked you, you'll do. But I want one thing clear from the beginning." He paused and waited for Carl to say something. He waited in vain. Finally Aldin said with as much emphasis as he was able to muster, "I'm *not* testifying in this case, no matter what! Don't ask! And don't propose any deals that make me cooperate!"

Carl stared back. Many criminal cases involve technical defenses that rest on attacking the proof without the defendant testifying. Sometimes it works, more often it doesn't. Nevertheless it was Aldin's Constitutional right not to testify. His failure to do so could not even be mentioned. But a lawyer is a practicing pragmatist and everybody — the public, the press, the denizens of the court system — took refusal to testify as a sure sign of guilt.

Carl tried to maintain a blank look but it was running through his mind, *At least the guy's got scruples against perjury, if not murder.* "You certainly have an absolute right to stay off the stand. It says in the books nobody is supposed to hold that against you. Personally I think it cuts your chances drastically..."

"What?"

"Cuts your chances. Juries expect to hear the defendant deny he did

48

anything wrong."

"I thought we just went over that. I've got a right to maintain my silence, and that can't be held against me. Now you're telling me something else?"

"No, not officially. But after doing this for thirty years, I've seldom seen a jury acquit a person of a major crime if he didn't deny it." Carl thought that was the end of it, but Aldin was like a ferret.

"You're the lawyer. Just get me my Constitutional rights and things will be ok. You've tried criminal cases before, haven't you?"

Again a legitimate question, but Carl felt the sting of calculated insult. Not a good way to start. "Yes, Wally. I've tried hundreds of criminal cases. Several murders. I think I've got a pretty good track record, but that's for you to decide. If you're uncomfortable, by all means let's find somebody else right away instead of a couple of weeks down the line."

"No. If they picked you, you're as good as I can get short of someone….but what would a *Mowahhid* be doing practicing law? Taking money from honest people. Selling them back their rights."

It struck Carl that this was the first time Aldin had used a foreign word. He didn't know what the word meant, but decided it was neither the time nor the place to explore the matter. "Look, Wally, I'm running out of time here. I already know the practice of law is screwed up. What can you tell me about your case?"

Aldin seemed to shift gears. He became focused, angry. His brows furrowed. "I was served with a paper for a civil suit about 10 a.m. just when I was getting home from grocery shopping. Then the deputies came around 3:15 and arrested me leaving the house, getting into my car in the driveway. Apparently they came back later with a warrant and took all my guns and papers and my computer. That's it. Pure and simple. Bastards!" His eyes blazed.

Carl wondered if time would quench Aldin's fire. If it didn't, his decision to stay off the stand could be a blessing. "I need to get a look at the search warrant and the charges. We'll talk again after court." The strange sequence of events Wally described made no sense.

Aldin's fingers were gripping his chair. He said, "Yeah. Good idea. I'll see you in court at 1:30." With that he rose from the chair and strode to the door, knocking on it for the deputy's attention without acknowledging Carl Hardman's outstretched hand.

Carl thought, *Maybe he's just having a bad day.*

— ·— ·— ·— ·— ·— ·— ·— ·— ·—

It was late morning and Carl was aware of being watched by the two women who ran the Moraine County Circuit Clerk's office. The hairs on the back of his neck made him wonder whether there were other eyes focused on him as he flipped through Aldin's court file. He asked one of the clerks to photocopy a search warrant issued by the Federal Court in Urbana, not the local Circuit Court. The fact that it was Federal was very unusual.

The warrant commanded the seizure of any and all gasoline containers and flammable liquids along with any materials capable of serving as wicks, even matches and lighters. It authorized the search of Aldin's doublewide trailer and any vehicles possessed by him. Illinois criminal procedure demands the prompt filing of a Return on a search warrant, listing the things seized. There was none on file, but it was still less than a full day since the warrant had been executed. He carefully examined an Illinois criminal complaint charging the murder of Judge Esker. A state charge with a federal search. It was strange. He would have to examine the court file in Federal Court in Urbana for the original affidavits on which the Federal Judge had issued the search warrant.

Why wasn't it a state search warrant? Conversely, since the warrant was federal, why wasn't the prosecution being done in Federal Court? Were the Feds going to take over the case? That seemed plausible. Whatever the reason, it was a novel problem. But then again, Carl had read *Catch-22* during law school and was thereby equipped to practice law in the Twenty First Century

He closed the file and thanked the clerk who quickly flipped it open to check whether anything might be missing. He glared at her.

She narrowed her eyes. "We're very careful about anything that has to do with Mr. Aldin. He once ate the evidence out of the court file."

"He what?"

"Ate the evidence. It was a bad check case and he asked to see the court file. While the clerk was talking to someone on the phone, he ate the check."

"Well, I'll be damned!"

The clerk smiled as if she thought that was likely.

As Carl turned to leave the Clerk's office, he was ambushed by a still-photographer. His startled image was about to become an icon for the defense of Wally Aldin's life.

Preliminary Hearing

The oval balcony of the Lincoln County Courthouse formed a halo over the marble first floor lobby, calculated to impress as well as to serve as a forum for auctioning off the farms and homes of losers in the games of chance played in the courtroom on the third floor. Gleaming brass fittings smelled of fresh polish. An oppressive odor of smoke lingered in the air.

High above the formal front entrance was an arch with a large semi-circular transom window. Not even stained glass, just a half-moon of clear glass, divided into three pie-shaped wedges, giving a view of the open interior of the building. Obviously an effort to make the squat, Depression-era building a classic look.

The lobby had been hastily configured as an emergency courtroom to replace charred Courtroom A, still being sifted for evidence. The effect was strangely reminiscent of a movie set. On a folding stage, in storage since last Fourth of July, stood a walnut judge's bench that had been borrowed from a local antique store. Behind it was a black leather swivel chair that looked new. The files of the Circuit Clerk were stacked on a small oak desk. A scratched and battered captain's chair for the witness seemed precariously close to the left edge of the platform. American and Illinois flags stood behind the bench. Twelve plastic conference room chairs formed two rows to the right. Hastily-purchased portable screens formed a backdrop.

More than a hundred wooden folding chairs from a local funeral home filled the lobby. Taped to the rows were computer-printed signs that said PRESS, or LAW ENFORCEMENT, or BAR ASSOCIATION. Carl wondered whether ACLU or FAMILY OF THE STAR had been considered.

In front of the bench were two six-foot folding tables, each with three heavy oak chairs, weakened and scarred by decades of fidgeting lawyers. The hodge-podge of furniture looked like a rural foreclosure without the weeping children.

Three deputies armed with 12-gauge Remington pump shotguns leaned like gargoyles over the second floor balcony railing. Technicians were finishing the installation of a magnetic metal detector and an x-ray scanner at the main entrance of the building. Deputies whose VCR's at home still blinked "12:00" were being shown how to use the sophisticated equipment.

The room was surreal. The atmosphere was ominous.

Carl sat alone, his mind in turmoil. Was getting involved in this case a good idea? Rescuing Wally Aldin seemed improbable. He was already a pinball in a giant machine, the flippers being operated by unseen hands. But to Carl, the law had not entirely lost the majesty they draped over it in law school. He cherished the times he had watched good judges penetrate the forest of technical rules and find wisdom. He reveled in the collegiality of lawyers who had, like combat veterans, stories to share that only insiders could fully appreciate. But mostly he appreciated the civility of the law, the way it treated lawyers with respect. Conferences in chambers the public and the clients would never see; relaxed and mannerly discussions that often cut to the core and settled cases.

The rear door banged open and Aldin, flanked by three deputies, was hustled in. Shackles linked his ankles and chattered against the marble floor. Handcuffs held Aldin's wrists to a stainless steel chain padlocked around his waist. He was dressed in the bright orange coveralls issued to all the guests in Sheriff Burnett's jail. The wide lapels seemed a reverse fashion statement designed to humiliate the prisoner.

53

The deputies guarding Aldin scanned the lobby as if the County Recorder and the Traffic Clerk's offices might harbor terrorists. Carl worried that an itchy trigger finger could set off a colossal tragedy if somebody accidentally knocked over a chair or moved too quickly.

Aldin shuffled to the counsel table. No nod of recognition or greeting. He had the vacant look of the soldiers in the Hanoi Hilton, frozen in old newsreels.

"Hello, Wally. Welcome to Truth or Consequences."

"Huh?"

"Nothing. Just an old radio program from the 'Fifties. Anyway, this isn't gonna be very revealing. A Preliminary Hearing in this state is measured in nanoseconds. We get to ask about 3 questions and the only witness is some cop they call to read the police report. The rules against hearsay don't count. You don't get to face your real accusers at this stage."

"Well, how can that be? It says in the law books this is where they're supposed to show probable cause for holding me to trial!"

"It was supposed to be that way when Charlie Bowman, my old law professor, wrote the criminal code. But it hasn't been that way for a good 20 years."

"Make 'em come up with evidence! Proof! I don't want some deputy reading some other guy's report!"

"Don't get your bowels in an uproar. I'll object to the way they do it, but nobody's challenged the procedure in a generation. When I object they're going to look at me like I'm some punk just out of law school, but we'll protect the point for appeal if it's that important to you."

Wally turned up his nose. An appeal only happened after a conviction.

They were interrupted by a gush of spectators surging through the main door like passengers late for an early morning plane.

High above the large, formal front entrance was the Romanesque transom window. Carl watched the crowd. A man with haunted eyes in a gaunt face stared back at him from the second row. Nobody was bubbling with good humor, but this man had an especially strange, intense look. Possibly a relative of Judge Esker? Or maybe an agent from some clandestine government entity? Carl dismissed him as a distraction.

The CNN television truck parked at the curb was elevating a boom with a remote-control TV camera. It stopped remarkably close to the transom window, apparently able to zoom down from a bird's eye view, past the pigeon droppings, and focus on the inner workings of the justice system. So much for the rule against cameras in the courtroom. Like most careful rules of the judiciary it failed to take technology into account.

Carl smiled at the thought that the back of his head was about to go national. He went through his ritual of preparing for a hearing. He readied his yellow office docket control sheet for recording rulings of the court, hearing dates and deadlines. With the fountain pen he used at trials he wrote "Aldin" on the top line of a fresh legal pad. Now it was official. He was in court and he began to feel at ease. The pressure of clients and money and personal problems burned off like morning mist.

A few seconds later, Sheriff Burnett entered. He had appointed himself Bailiff for the trial because the regular Bailiff, Clancy Brown, would be a witness in the case. He smiled at the press and said, "All rise!" Chairs scraped against the marble and the babble fell to a murmur. "The Honorable Kirsten Harrigan, Judge."

Since the resident judge in this small county was the dead subject of this proceeding, another judge from elsewhere had to be assigned to the case, probably not chosen for sympathy toward people who went around incinerating her colleagues. He tried to remember if he'd ever heard anything about Kirsten Harrigan and drew a blank. He would have to make a few calls if she assigned the trial of the case to herself. She moved rapidly, with black robes flowing, trailed by a young, blonde court reporter. Judge Harrigan was in her early forties. She seemed youthful, with the slim, athletic look of a tennis player. Her frosted hair was short but looked as if it received regular and expensive care. She was brisk and businesslike.

She nodded to Sheriff Burnett who said, "Be seated." She opened the file and called the case, looking at Carl with a challenge in her eyes.

"Good morning, your Honor. Carl Hardman for the defense. I believe you will find my written appearance on file."

"Thank you, Mr. Hardman. So noted. And for the People?"

Carl noticed the county prosecutor, known as the State's Attorney in Illinois, had entered from the side and had taken his place at the other counsel table. He was tall, in his late forties, and dressed in a nondescript tan suit.

"Willard Gadsen for the People, your Honor."

"Thank you, Mr. Gadsen. This matter is set for initial appearance and because of the seriousness of the charge, for a preliminary hearing as well. Are there any other matters to be heard?" Her tone bordered on aggressive.

Gadsen spoke deferentially, "Your Honor...uh...the matter of a preliminary hearing is moot. The Grand Jury returned an indictment for three counts of murder and three of arson earlier this morning." He rose and approached the bench, on the way handing a copy of the Indictment to Carl before placing the original within the reach of Judge Harrigan. "As you know, Your Honor, but for the benefit of those in the courtroom from other states, in Illinois the purpose of a Preliminary Hearing is to determine whether there is some evidence on all the elements of a charge. If so, the case is bound over to the Grand Jury to consider whether it wants to indict. Well, in this case, since the Grand Jury has already returned an indictment, the Preliminary Hearing is rendered moot."

Judge Harrigan turned to Carl. "Mr. Hardman?"

Carl whispered to Aldin, "He's right." The ploy was classic. It avoided making public even the most superficial details of the police investigation. Grand Jury proceedings were supposed to be secret. The police report would have to be shared with the defense, but most judges in major cases issued gag orders silencing both lawyers while leaving it open for the police to leak the prosecution's version.

Carl mused for a moment and decided to feign shock. He rose and said,

"Your Honor, I'm from Millington and rarely get this far downstate. My client has asked me to vigorously insist on his innocence at the Preliminary Hearing and to require the authorities to offer some sort of evidence he had any connection whatsoever with this terrible crime. Back home we use a preliminary hearing to screen out cases so that people like my client can clear their names early on." Carl knew he was making an overstatement, but he wanted to proclaim his client's innocence for the benefit of the press. "Is it a common practice down here to indict a man so you don't have to offer even a scintilla of proof against him in a public courtroom?"

Gadsen was on his feet. "Your Honor! I object to Mr. Hardman making a speech. He knows perfectly well that an indictment moots a preliminary hearing. He knows that's a standard practice, and I don't see..."

"Perhaps I can shorten this up. I'm objecting to this local practice that thwarts the procedural guarantees of a public preliminary hearing regardless of how often it's been done in the past. I move to quash the Indictment for violation of Due Process under the Fourteenth..."

Judge Harrigan held up her hand. "Mr. Hardman, as we all know perfectly well, going directly to the Grand Jury and getting an indictment is an alternative procedure. Preliminary hearing exists to keep a defendant under bond while getting an indictment. And I suspect I know what you're doing in making your objection." She looked in the direction of the press. "Before this case starts to get out of hand, I wish to warn both counsel that I will strictly supervise discovery and that I will be very disappointed if I hear of leaks and speeches and grandstanding."

"Your Honor..." Carl tried to recapture the moment.

"Mr. Hardman, your objection is overruled. Unless you have any motions, I'm prepared to arraign your client on the indictment."

Carl made a show of pulling in his horns. "Your Honor, I'm just trying to do my job and protect my client in a difficult, high-profile case."

She presented an icy smile. "And you're doing your best, I'm sure. Can we proceed with the arraignment? Mr. Aldin, please approach the bench."

57

Aldin, still shackled, struggled to rise. He lurched forward, steadying himself against the folding table. He and Carl stood directly in front of the bench. One of the deputies was leaning over the second floor railing with his finger on the trigger guard of his shotgun.

The next few minutes were a perfunctory reading of the several counts of the Indictment, amounting to alternative ways to look at the same thing. They shared the common allegation that Wally Aldin had destroyed a courtroom and had snuffed out Judge Esker's life with a fire-bomb. And that he was being asked to pay the bill with his own life.

Aldin stared unblinking at Judge Harrigan while she read. Carl hoped she wouldn't interpret his client's intensity as threatening her.

When the Indictment had been droned into the record, Aldin was asked how did he plead and he shot back a venomous "Not Guilty!"

Judge Harrigan paused and stared icicles at him. She looked at Gadsen and said, "Recommendation for bond?"

He mused, then said, "At least a million dollars, Your Honor."

Carl felt Aldin's outburst had eliminated any chance of getting reasonable bail, but he went ahead and gave Judge Harrigan three minutes about how Aldin was a naturalized citizen and a local resident with a track record of coming to Court when required. He stressed that there was not one single fact in the record indicating any connection with this heinous crime other than the Indictment, and that she had not heard any evidence of guilt. He urged that a million dollar bond was absurd. He wanted to say that you could sell the downtown of Moraine without raising a million dollars. In the end he merely stated that the purpose of bond was to assure the Defendant's appearance at trial, not to punish him. Carl ended by saying that the Constitution guarantees that people like Wally Aldin are innocent until proven guilty.

Judge Harrigan had heard these arguments a thousand times in her short career. She managed an impassive stare until the noise coming from Carl's mouth stopped. "Motion denied. Bond set at two million dollars. Defendant remanded to the Sheriff. I'm assigning this case to myself for trial. Standard discovery hereby ordered in accordance with local rule. Any motions to be on file within 30 days. Settings to be arranged through my clerk. This matter is set on the docket call for a July jury trial. Counsel, this Court sees no reason why Central Illinois should go through the agony that seems to accompany high-profile cases in larger cities. We're not Los Angeles. The issues are straight-forward and this isn't going to become a side show. I will tolerate no delay by either side. Get your discovery done and get your motions filed and argued. We will be in recess." She looked at him, as if challenging him to say something she could spike back down his throat.

He paused and a wry smile escaped. "No, I guess you've overruled just about everything I can think of, Your Honor."

Judge Harrigan pursed her lips. She seemed on the verge of commenting but snatched up the court file as her chair rolled back toward the edge of the platform. Not a smile or a nod.

Sheriff Burnett lurched to his feet and said, "All Rise! The Circuit Court in and for Lincoln County is in recess." The Judge wasted no time disappearing into the Clerk's office.

Beefy deputies yanked Aldin to his feet. Carl interrupted, "Excuse me for just a minute, gentlemen. I need just a word or two with my client."

The deputy wearing lieutenant bars glanced at Sheriff Burnett who was slowly shaking his head in refusal.

"I gotta take him right back. Security. You can see him over at the jail."

So much for civility and simple common sense.

Carl watched Aldin as his quick, short steps jerked on the shackles and made him stumble. The press made a tangle of the folding chairs, racing out to circle Aldin before he could be spirited away. The room was all but empty. The court reporter was folding up her machine. She glanced at Carl, then quickly looked away. An experienced lawyer can tell a lot about what is being said about him in chambers by reading the faces of court reporters, clerks and bailiffs.

Perforations

Bullets ripped through a caricature of Hillary Clinton taped to a stack of railroad ties at 20 yards. Four semiautomatic pistols—two Glocks, one Walther PPK, and an old .45 Colt Combat Commander—fired until their slides locked open. The shooters popped out the empty clips, snatched loaded ones from their belts, jammed them home, released the slides to chamber the first round, then continued blazing away.

"Cease fire!" shouted a man in a fatigue jacket, fingering a stop watch. The time limit had been ten seconds. The shooters stopped firing with rounds still unexpended. The weapons were put on safety and holstered. All five walked to the target. They counted fifteen holes in the face and torso, remarkable rapid-fire pistol marksmanship at that range.

"Not bad. Not bad at all," remarked the timer. "I want you guys on my side when the shit comes down."

A thin smile was the only response from Brother Bill, who was holstering the Colt .45.

"Bitch got bad zits," said one of the Glocks.

"Them's nine-millimeter-short holes, four of 'em, right in the face," crowed the PPK. "I oughtta frame that target over my fireplace."

"First time you ever hit more'n one hole on a woman, Alan," one Glock said, clapping the PPK on the back with a hearty chuckle.

"Watch your language!" Brother Bill warned, reloading a clip.

They admired the target for another few seconds before taking it down. The PPK turned to Brother Bill and asked, "What you wanna shoot?"

Brother Bill said, "How 'bout a golden oldie? We haven't shot no Renos in about a month. I'd like t' punch a few slugs through her for old times sake."

The younger of the two Glocks walked back to his olive green Chevy Blazer and fished a fresh Janet Reno target from the rear cargo area. He walked to the railroad ties and tacked the corners with a staple gun.

"What's happenin' with that firebomber?" asked the second Glock.

Brother Bill said, "I hear the FBI jumped in the case before Burnett could even make an arrest. They're still studyin' on pieces of charcoal. That oughta take about six months, I suppose."

"Shit! Motherfuckin' Feds!" grumbled the PPK.

"Look, I don't like that kinda language!" Brother Bill was agitated.

"Sorry, Brother Bill. Keep forgettin' you're a man of the cloth, an' all."

"There ain't no Federal case against Aldin from what I hear," the beefy Glock said, shaking his head. "This here's Sheriff Burnett's arrest. But you're right. Them Feds was in there early. You know they'll be cuttin' some kinda deal for the bastard. Give him witness protection or somethin'."

"Yeah," said the younger Glock. "I seen that FBI guy, Fossum, goin' in the Courthouse after it happened."

"So what happens next?" asked Brother Bill as he tapped the reloaded clip to seat the cartridges into proper feeding position.

"Well, I hear Wally's got a good lawyer," added the beefy Glock.

"Who'd he get?" asked the beefy PPK.

"Some guy named Hardman from up at Millington. He done some murder cases before."

Brother Bill drew his .45 and chambered a round. "The TV said he was getting' smart with the Judge. A woman Judge, but she got on Hardman's case. At least, Aldin bein' a Mooslem, he didn't pick some Chicago Jew lawyer." He turned and perforated the former Attorney General of the United States six times.

— ·— ·— ·— ·— ·— ·— ·—

The video tape had reached its climax, a late-term abortion of a female infant. It was gruesome. Close-ups of the contorted face, then the tiny fingers interspersed with repetitive replays of the expulsion.

As the tape ended, everyone in the room was ready for action.

Women in the room cried openly. One was chanting the Rosary. A Charismatic man was speaking in tongues.

Brother Bill reminded them in ordinary English, "Remember, the bus leaves for the abortion clinic at 7:30 on Saturday morning from the Assembly of the Lamb. Also, there will be a meetin' after the regular Wednesday Law Clinic to discuss what to do about this Wally Aldin."

"I don't see what we've got to do with Aldin even if he murdered a judge," interjected the woman with the rosary.

Every eye pinned her to her chair. She shrank under the scrutiny.

"The point is, Molly, they're futzin' around with this case. Nobody thinks he's gonna get what he deserves. If we just let it go, it'll take a day short of forever, and somebody along the way will take the death penalty off of him."

A couple of *amens* from the group.

— ·— ·— ·— ·— ·— ·— ·—

It was a little after eleven. Carl was standing at the counter of the Federal District Court Clerk in Urbana, reading the Affidavit for Search Warrant for Aldin's property and vehicles. It alleged that a Lincoln County deputy sheriff had witnessed a gasoline container in plain view while serving a civil process on Aldin, who was alleged to have previously threatened harm to Judge Esker and the court system. The deputy claimed the gas can was located in the open trunk of Aldin's car. What angered and shocked

Carl was the allegation in the affidavit that invoked Federal jurisdiction because the firebombing supposedly occurred in a building allegedly involved in interstate commerce. Carl's eyebrows arched. *A county courthouse is a building affecting interstate commerce? That's a new one.*

The Affidavit alleged that the bombing had violated section 844 (i) of Title 18 of the U.S. Code. That section specifically made it a crime to damage any building involved in interstate commerce by fire or explosives. It also alleged a violation of section 924 (c), using a destructive device in the commission of a crime of violence. The third section, 844 (h) (2) made it illegal to use an explosive in the commission of a Federal crime.

In the last third of the Twentieth Century, Federal jurisdiction based on the power the Constitution grants to regulate interstate commerce had received steroid injections. The theory that almost everything affects interstate commerce was developed during the civil rights struggles of the 'Sixties to permit Federal injunctions requiring integration. While the goal was admirable and the relief needed, the aftermath was a massive shift of power to the Federal Courts. Seemingly every institution, from public schools and colleges to theaters and restaurants had been held by some Federal court to be involved in interstate commerce. But a state court house? That was a new one that defied the basis of Federal/State distinctions.

What amazed him, however, were the foundation facts supporting the claim of Federal jurisdiction. The affidavit alleged that civil litigation often took place in the Courthouse which resulted in financial judgments affecting interstate commerce; that the building contained vending machines dispensing beverages which may have moved in interstate commerce; finally, that the building was heated with natural gas that may have traveled in an interstate pipeline. Here was a solemn criminal pleading which reduced the plain language definition of interstate commerce to a parody. Under the same reasoning, any building in the U.S. would be subject to Federal search and seizure. A triumph of Orwell's Newspeak.

Has it really gone this far? Carl shook his head. He was shocked and apprehensive. *They may as well fold up the local cops.* He shook his head at the death of restraint. He was becoming more willing to oppose this assault on the Constitution, if not the English language itself.

Brother Bill was troubled. He had just left the Walmart, pricing a Remington pump shotgun, and was driving his Ford pick-up back to the farm. His scan for surveillance, once again, came up dry.

Added to his everyday suspicion was his new preoccupation with the firebombing case. Something just didn't feel right. The more he thought about Wally Aldin, the more he feared what he and his colleagues called the Zion Occupation Government would find a way to excuse Aldin from the consequences of his crime. Evil men were rewarded with new lives at taxpayer's expense in Witness Protection.

Bill was addicted to the History Channel, reliving the glories of America's wars, except for World War II, which should have continued until the Commies were routed. He had tried to enlist in the army after high school, out of frustration with the impotence of Carter's policies, but had failed the physical. Something about his heart, although it never gave him any trouble. Crushed with disappointment, Bill had dutifully returned to the family grain operation just east of Moraine to help his widowed father. Bill's personal life was devoted to studying his Bible and devouring the literature of Christian Identity and the Patriot movement. His days were Spartan except for the fellowship of others who feared God and feared for America.

His life was too full for him even to consider starting a family. Not that he didn't feel urges toward women, but to Bill sex was somehow contrary to the Good Book, no matter that the Old Testament was full of stories of men and women who went in for that sort of thing. Jesus was a bachelor.

The precious energy others expelled from their bodies, he would retain and try to channel it into his work.

—·—·—·—·—·—·—·—·—

Carl was at a loss. It was a Saturday afternoon, the first time he had to himself since the Aldin whirlwind began to blow through his life. He sat on a redwood bench in the shower of the rented condo, his feet being soothed by the jets of the shallow whirlpool. Staring back at him from the week's newspapers was the startled look he had flashed in the Lincoln County courthouse.

He was astonished at the fervor against his client being fanned by politicians and the media. Nobody had offered a scintilla of proof against Aldin, yet public opinion was ready to dismember him, preferably on the "Jerry Springer Show."

The odd federal involvement in a state case bothered him. Could the militia loonies actually be onto something about abuse of power? Carl drifted back to the 'Sixties when the U of I had been awash with SDS and a dozen other left wing groups. They all shared a common vision of runaway government squeezing young people into uniforms and stuffing their minds with propaganda. Now the fears of governmental abuse were emanating from the right end of the spectrum.

The whirlpool soaked away the aches of five decades and let his mind open up. How did the Government get so much power? A thousand government organizations, all sounding good, all aimed at protecting the country from some problem, but all they seemed to accomplish was new buildings filled with new bureaucrats sucking up taxes and leeching individual rights.

He took consolation from his status as a lawyer, an independent officer of the court who could fight from a protected position. Where he could oppose the deterioration of rights while enjoying a protected status. A war of ideas in a civilized country, where he would be honored even by his opponents. Not like the lawyers in countries where physical danger accompanied standing up to the system.

Carl clicked the button to shut off the whirlpool. He felt a twinge of regret that he would soon be replaced by someone who might not share his commitment to saving Wally Aldin. He was shocked to hear the doorbell. He had lived in the rented condo only a few days and couldn't imagine who knew about it. He shouted "Just a minute!" and quickly toweled himself dry and pulled on fresh clothes before answering the door.

She said her name was Laura.

Carl thought she was kidding. She identified herself as Wally Aldin's wife and asked if she could come in and talk about the case. She looked enough like Gene Tierney in *Laura* to star in a remake. He was seldom caught short, but he couldn't decide whether to tell her about her uncanny resemblance to a star she had probably never heard of, or just invite her to sit down in the kitchen.

"So you're Mrs. Aldin. Please have a seat. Want some coffee?"

"No, thanks. I serve people coffee all day." She smiled and the room seemed brighter. Her hair was long and straight, dark and lustrous. It bounced when she flipped it back from her eyes.

"Have you seen Wally?" Carl was trying to deflect the hormonal surge he was beginning to experience. Not the proper reaction to a client's wife.

"No, they say I can't see him except on visitor's day, and that's right in the middle of the Sunday rush at the restaurant, right after church. I can't get fired just to go to visit him. Wouldn't do either of us any good."

As she spoke, he was drawn to her youthful figure, her breasts stretching her dark blue turtleneck sweater. "I'm sorry. I don't have enough clout to get you a visit any other time."

"I didn't think you'd be able to. Seems like nobody can do much. They're all sorry, and they wish they could do something, but sorry doesn't cut it." Weariness rolled across her face.

"Are you getting any help from his...friends?"

Her eyes flashed. "That bunch? They're a strange group. I'm not even sure how to find them. I met Wally at my church. A Catholic Church. He let me believe he was some kind of Christian. When we met, he was a very nice person, just the kind of guy a girl could go for. Maybe not tall, but he was dark and handsome. And very smart. He charmed me. I fell for him big time. Things were going wonderful. Then those guys started coming around. From Chicago, some from New Jersey...wherever. They're strange. Sometimes they come and Wally goes with them and who knows where they go. They kind of smirk when I'm around, like there's so much I don't know. Pretty soon Wally started acting strange and kind of remote. I asked him where they went. He said it was none of my business. I cried for a week."

"Then?"

"I talked to the priest. He asked me what kind of religion he was. I didn't know, but I did know he grew up in Lebanon. The priest said there are Christian religions there—something called Maronite. Since they're Christian, sometimes the Church will let people marry if they promise to raise the kids Catholic."

"So he promised?"

"I did, but he wouldn't. He said our having kids just wasn't possible. It was hell for a while. I was so upset. We talked and we talked and we talked. Then one day he tells me he's from a different religion that's not really Christian, that his family has been in that religion forever. I was shocked because the way I grew up, mixed marriages were against the Church. He told me he really loved me, but it wasn't possible to ever have kids. I asked him why. He said his religion wouldn't let him bring children into the world and raise them in some other religion. I was so confused. Why was he going to the Catholic Church? He said that was ok. He could go to any of the Churches that believe in One God. But he couldn't join any...really join them. And his kids had to be brought up in his own religion. I assumed he was in the Maronite one. He never did say that in so many words. He just clammed up and wouldn't talk about religion any more. Finally I got tired of talking about it and we ran away and got married in Terre Haute by a Justice of the Peace. After we got married, he told me he's not exactly

Christian, but his religion believes in Jesus and lots of people from the Bible. Like…he led me on. So I was totally upset." She looked frustrated.

Carl had grown up with one branch of his family adhering to the strict old world Catholicism. "So what did you do? Are you getting along?"

"Just barely. Wally's a very smart guy. I was after him to go to college. His last job was running a convenience store where the hard road meets I-57. He used to make pretty good money, but he worked long hours. I think the store is owned by some of his friends. But he never was able to keep any money. I don't know for sure. Maybe he gambled. I don't think it was drugs. We used to have a boat and a van but they're gone now. I'm looking for a second job."

Carl asked, "So the two of you have financial problems?"

She looked at him with the sad smile of resignation so common in the Illinois prairie towns. The smile they wore after it dawned on them the high school prom had been the high point of their lives. "We had an appointment to go to Champaign and talk to a bankruptcy lawyer, Dave somebody."

"Was Wally in Court a lot? I mean getting sued over bills and so forth?"

"All the time. The deputy who serves summonses was like the mailman at our place. Wally…by the way, his real name is Walid. He thought 'Wally' would make it easier to get jobs and stuff. Wally was in front of Judge Esker about a week before the…" She started to cry.

Carl reached for a box of Kleenex on the counter. "Look…I know this has to be hard. You don't have to tell me all this stuff."

"No, I need to."

"How can I help you?" Carl really wanted to know.

Laura sighed and leaned back in her chair. "I was just wanting to know how the case was coming and what you thought was gonna happen to him. I know it's bad, but it'd help me a lot if I could kind of plan ahead. Is he going to...to be executed?" She was looking at him in a direct, country way. She expected him to know.

That look was always the hardest part. How could anyone predict the aftermath of a cyclone created by lawyers, judges and witnesses? He knew he had to blunt the question, make light of it. "Mrs. Aldin, I'm sorry. I have a non-competition clause with the Psychic Hotline. They don't practice law and I don't predict future events. I don't mean to be flippant, but whenever I start guessing it usually ends up wrong. Then I feel terrible and my client has double the grief. Anyway, I'm just temporarily in the case. His friends are searching for somebody to handle the trial."

She looked disappointed, but nodded. "Ok…I guess. I know this is a really tough case, but you seem like the kind of person who might be able to get Wally to cooperate, and everybody says you're a really good lawyer. I hope if they get some new lawyer, he knows how to handle him. Ordinary people don't know what's going on in law things. How are we supposed to get on with our lives?"

Carl didn't have a canned response. "I suppose you just put one foot after the other." He smiled to take the edge off the remark.

She went on to ask about court procedures.

Carl described the arraignment on the indictment, pre-trial preparation, and the trial. He explained the range of possible sentences, skating over the ultimate one. He covered the possibility of a second trial in the Federal system, explaining it would not be double jeopardy, primarily because the courts had said it wasn't. He was still mastering the art of putting common sense to sleep and swallowing nonsense written by the higher courts. But when he saw confusion register on Laura's face, he went on to explain the theory behind the parallel State and Federal systems of justice in America.

Laura sat without moving, her dark eyes fixed on him. Her eyes seemed. Was there a flicker of personal interest? Her attention was generating rollercoaster thrills and he was enjoying the ride. She couldn't be feeling what he was. After all, he was literally old enough to be her father, maybe even her grandfather if they were a little deeper into Southern Illinois. They talked about the law, about Moraine, about the Sheriff, about everything except her husband, his client.

She seemed willing to sit and talk all afternoon. Finally she half-heartedly asked about Wally and how he was doing.

"Do you miss him a lot?" Carl asked, part of him perversely hoping she didn't.

She paused and took a breath and let it out, "I miss the boy I met in church. I surely do. But Wally hasn't been that boy for years. He's bitter. He drinks. He lies and connives and hates. He's not the same sweet boy who wouldn't touch me until we were married. I think his friends have a lot to do with it."

He knew he should change the subject, but he was fascinated.

"Wally always used to treat me like I'd break if he touched me, like I was the Virgin Mary and he's not even Catholic. Anyway, to show you what he was like, we went to Chicago for our honeymoon. Wally's friends paid for an unbelievable room at a hotel called the Allerton, the same name as Allerton Park over in Monticello. It took forever to find the place, driving around with all those cars honking at us, but we finally got there. Neither one of us ever went to Chicago before, not even to go to a ballgame. We brought some hamburgers up to the room with us from a fancy McDonald's way up at the top of some shopping mall with all the stuff in the world! Did you ever hear of a place called Watertower?"

Carl nodded.

She went on, "Anyway, we got into the hotel room when it was getting dark. I never saw such a place. It was like an apartment, not a hotel room. It even had a living room and a little refrigerator with lots of stuff in it. I looked out the window and you could see a million miles and all the tall buildings were turning on their lights. Down below were streets and cars and buses and thousands of people bumping against each other. There were even horses and carriages, sort of like the ones the Amish have, only fancy. Anyway, Wally came up behind me and put his arm around me. He rested his chin on my shoulder and I felt light and airy, like I could fly right across to the buildings where there were people sitting at desks. He kissed my neck and I just stood there and let him touch me. He was so loving. His hands were all over me, like they were on fire and it was burning me where he touched. All the while I didn't move..."

Carl sighed and interrupted, "Look, Mrs. Aldin, you don't need to tell me these things."

She looked at him and her eyes were reaching out. "I really need for you to understand about me and Wally. You're the only person I can talk to about this."

He nodded as he felt his professionalism slipping away.

She began again, "Anyway, when he touched me I didn't tell him to stop or go over to the bed. My clothes were off, just dropped on the floor, and I was naked, leaning against the window, and he was touching me there, and all over my breasts. And he was behind me, and then I felt him inside me, and it went on and on in front of all of Chicago. Anybody could have looked up and seen me pressed against that window. I even left prints of my breasts on the glass. I had feelings...sexual feelings...I've never had before or since. It was like dying and going to heaven, flying off into space between the big buildings. I didn't care and he couldn't stop."

She looked at Carl with dark, misty eyes, seeking something from him. He didn't know what to say, but he knew he could not stop longing for more details. Several seconds passed until she said, "That's the Wally I married. The one you met is empty and sick and nasty, a man who lives with secrets. The one I loved in front of that window, he's gone. Now he's just a twisted person, not the same man at all. He's even hit me a couple of times."

Carl snapped back to the present, "Hit you?"

She looked down at her intertwined fingers. "It's probably my fault as much as his..."

"I don't see how..."

"Just take my word for it. I should have seen it coming, but that was back when I thought we could...maybe..."

"You don't have to put up with being beaten by anyone, and that certainly includes your husband. This is a new century."

"Yes, I know all that, but it wasn't really him. It was the person he's become. He's been warped, Mr. Hardman, twisted by his...sickness...or whatever it is."

Carl thought for a moment. The lawyer in him clicked into place and he wondered if Aldin might have some multi-syllable psychiatric disorder, one that could explain the horrendous murder. Mental defenses were notoriously unsuccessful, but if there were a recognized basis for becoming unbalanced and losing all sense of perspective, it would bear investigation. It might be enough to save him from the death penalty. After all, there didn't seem to be much left if Aldin refused to testify.

Laura was looking at him. "Did I say something wrong?"

"No, maybe you said something right. Has he been illogical or compulsive? I mean, has his personality changed to the place where he seems unable to control himself?"

She thought about it. "I guess you could say that. But if you're suggesting he's insane or something, you may as well save your breath. He'll never let you say that. He thinks he's a martyr or whatever. There's no way he's going to let anybody say he's crazy."

"What do you think about that?" Carl watched her eyes recall years of pain and worry.

"Me? Don't ask me. All he's done in the past three years is read and read. Books. Newspapers in some language that looks like scribbles and dots. He talks all the time about how he's just as much an American as the people who were born here, and how he has Constitutional rights to 'keep and bear arms.' If I never hear that again, it's too soon. He had a whole cabinet full of guns the FBI took. Not just shotguns, but pistols and rifles, high powered military-type rifles. All that started after 9-11. He says people treat him like a terrorist and he might have to defend us. People who stop for gas or for a donut. It's like he's thinking about it all the time, about people picking on him, being prejudiced against him. The last year or so, we've been strangers. He spends his time watching soccer on TV when he can find it. At least the guys in Moraine watch football."

Carl wondered how any man could ignore Laura. "That's pretty fixated, all right."

"I'm only here because of the memory of the man I used to know."

"I guess that puts a perspective on it. I'm still trying to figure out a defense and you may have helped. I'm glad you came. Please feel free to come back any time." *Day or night*, he thought, then tried to erase the thought.

Laura rose gracefully and started for the door. She stopped and extended her hand to him. It felt soft and a little chilled. "I've enjoyed meeting you. I truly have. You're not what I expected."

The clean smell of her hair stoked a response in him. "And what was that?"

"Well, you know the lawyer jokes." She managed a weak little grin.

"They're all true, alas."

Her rose-petal lips smiled. As she walked out the door his eyes memorized every movement so he could play them back. Forbidden delight mixed with memories of lost youth. He realized, if he withdrew from the defense of Wally Aldin, he would never see her again.

Feds

"Mr. Knight, I have a problem here." Purvis Watson was standing near the entrance of the building. David Knight, his boss, was leaving for his usual extended lunch. Purvis had been leaving e-mail asking Knight to discuss glitches in the testing of the Aldin evidence. He had asked Knight's Administrative Assistant to schedule some time with the boss. He had waited without response even though he had progressively added details to the messages to give them weight. The day before he had sent a draft report.

Knight blinked twice, as if caught shoplifting. He quickly examined his watch and said, "Hey, I know you've been trying to see me, but I'm really very busy right now. Gotta run."

He shouted across the street toward Knight's rapidly disappearing backside, "When can I see you?"

Without turning, Knight yelled, "Can't hear you! Just follow procedure."

That left Purvis shaking his head. He turned and walked back to his laboratory and focused on the computer screen showing the test results in the Aldin matter did not match what they expected to find.

—·—·—·—·—·—·—·—·—·—

The Deputy was livid. He spoke quickly and the meeting was over almost before the Kenya AA coffee was cool enough to drink. This time only Ainsley and his supervisor were present.

The Deputy asked, "What kind of rustic moron is that Sheriff? What's he got us into?"

Ainsley knew the content of the draft report laying in front of the Deputy. It was simple. Purvis Watson's findings of sample hydrocarbons from the courtroom failed to match the profile for the contents of the gasoline container—a disaster in the making. Fortunately Watson had not yet formally submitted his report, which would create a discoverable document. As long as it was just a draft, reality was still malleable, perhaps even deniable.

Ainsley's supervisor spoke when the Deputy stopped venting his irritation, "Sir, there's another way to look at this whole thing. Granted, the sheriff has handled this with the finesse of a bludgeoning. Nevertheless, a couple of facts remain: one, Aldin meets all the criteria to be the perpetrator; two, apparently the wrong container of accelerant was seized. Maybe Aldin threw us a curve and planted it, getting rid of the real one; three, we don't have a final written document setting out the test results, and there's no reason one has to be created; four, we don't need to be left holding the bag."

The Deputy perked up. "What do you suggest?"

Ainsley's supervisor quietly set out the solution Ainsley had given him. "We defer prosecution to the State. We haven't formally commenced a Federal case. We just leave it where it is. Out there they have some country music song about a dead skunk in the middle of a road. That's not a bad metaphor. Let's just let it reek."

The Deputy winced. Federal prosecutors are territorial. "Defer?" Then he sat quietly for a moment and asked, "Go over that in detail. Why do you think that's advisable?"

Ainsley realized he risked heresy, but grasped at a chance to receive credit for a solution. "If we're seen as being sensitive about Federal power usurping a State criminal function...all that State's Rights malarkey...surely it would be a plus with the public. We've been on the short end of a lot of bad press about Ruby Ridge, and Waco. This Sheriff has been crowing about his lightning-fast solution of the crime. Let him have the case. Dump the dead skunk in his driveway. If they get a conviction, we share the spotlight. If they lose it, we still could indict or we could simply let it drag on and on in front of a grand jury. But if you want my guess, I think they can get a death sentence out there in Illinois. The community is inflamed and the defense lawyer is over the hill. Even without lab evidence they've got three or four eyewitnesses who seem solid...and they'll be a lot better after a little prodding. The death penalty seems pretty popular out there in the wilds." Ainsley stopped to gauge the effect of his remarks.

The Deputy was thoughtful. Finally he said, "But what about the testing? Won't we have to give the testing to the state court?"

"Out in the corn they don't deal with our lab workups very often. I think we can just send the raw data in the discovery production. Just send in the numbers and make no conclusions—squiggles on graph paper without any technical interpretation. That would never pass muster in Federal court, but out in the sticks nobody will be smart enough to translate the data into English." Ainsley paused, to see if more was needed.

The Deputy sat and pursed his lips. Then he nodded his head approvingly. He said, "I see. Well, then, I suppose we don't need to discuss this again. We'll see what happens. We won't need any file memos on this discussion. Thank you both for coming up here." With that he turned and disappeared.

Frustration

The news stories about the firebombing case squirmed in the mind of Brother Bill every time he heard them. At first he resigned himself, suppressing his doubts and going along with the courts. Having faith. Sitting back and letting the system work. But patriots are not made for sitting and waiting. The public fury against terrorists stirred him. His mind writhed every time he read the paper or heard a radio talk show.

Bill sat in the kitchen of his weathered farmhouse and stared out of the window at the dark earth beginning to stir. Once again God was preparing to feed the hungry. The flatness was about to push a mist of green to the surface. In five months it would stand taller than a man, heavy with ears of corn. It made no sense that the bounty of the earth's best land failed to make him and his neighbors rich beyond words. There was something wrong with that. There was something evil about good American farmers grinding out record harvests, only to find themselves penalized by low grain prices and robbed by Arabs for the fuel needed to grow the crop.

His mind strained to understand this riddle. Brother Bill began to think about Hardman and Aldin. Why was Hardman doing this? Helping this terrorist. What was in it for him? Only money? For 30 pieces of silver Judas had betrayed the Master. How much was Hardman charging for betraying his country? Aldin was guilty and there was no reason to delay justice. The thing was over and done, except the needle in the arm, unless the lawyer could talk Aldin into accepting some sort of a plea just to stay alive. Maybe Witness Protection. It wasn't right.

A blend of outrage and fear coursed through him.

He began to plot.

The door to Mr. Knight's private office was open. Betty, his Administrative Assistant, was in the rest room. Since the door was open, Purvis Watson summoned his courage and walked into Knight's office.

Knight looked up, startled. He sat perfectly still.

Purvis stood before him and waited. Nothing happened for several seconds. Finally, Purvis said, "Mr. Knight, I really, really have to talk to you about this Aldin case. I have a big problem with it. I've sent you a draft copy of my report..."

"Now, Purvis, I wish to emphasize the channels your reports are to follow. Please review the procedures..."

"But Mr. Knight, it's not the same hydrocarbon..."

"Purvis, we run this laboratory in accordance with strict procedures..."

"What do I do about the fact that it's not the same..."

"Look, Purvis, I don't wish to be contacted informally about this sort of thing. You know how important this case is, don't you? You do read newspapers and watch television, don't you?"

"Of course I do. I'm trying to tell you it just doesn't match. This is a super important case, for sure, but it just doesn't match! The GC-IRMS is state of the art for testing petroleum hydrocarbons."

Knight held up his hand, palm raised in a stop sign against Purvis' words. He took a deep breath and said, "Well, then, test it again."

Purvis was exasperated. "But Mr. Knight, I've done the tests twice already and it just doesn't match."

"Please stop saying that! Look, Purvis, we have an obligation to enforce the law, here. We have a vicious killer who incinerated a judge. Do you want him to get away with it? Don't you want to be part of the team?"

Purvis reddened. "Mr. Knight, I've worked here 14 years and I know the importance of this case. You know I want to be a team player, but it just doesn't match. I wish it did, but it doesn't. What am I supposed to do?"

Knight squirmed in his seat and said, "Do the tests over again."

Purvis blinked. He had never repeated a test more than twice in all the time he had worked in the lab. "I already did it twice."

Knight boiled over, "Well, then, do it twice more, Dammit! Do it ten times if you have to, until you get it right!"

Purvis felt as if he had been slapped. Nobody had ever before suggested that he needed to improve his lab techniques. "Until I get it right? I'm sorry, Mr. Knight. I don't know what you mean? Did I do something wrong?"

Knight made an elaborate show of patience. He leaned forward, glanced through the door and found the outer office empty. "Listen, Purvis. You obviously aren't doing something right if you're not getting a match on the gas container and the charred debris. We know Aldin is the perpetrator, right?"

Purvis nodded without enthusiasm.

"Well, then, get with it and try harder to get a match on the accelerant. We're going to have to finish this in the next day or two. By the way, your report is to include only your raw testing data. New format for a case of this type. No conclusions. No write-up. Just data."

No conclusions? How could anyone in the court system profit from a report with no conclusions? Was this because of something he had done? Purvis was confused and embarrassed, but there was some other emotion mixed in, something Purvis had never felt. "I'm sorry, Mr. Knight. If I've done something wrong, I'm sorry. I'll retest the samples."

"Fine," Knight said, relieved. "Fine. Now get cracking." He picked up a document and began to examine it, as if Purvis had already left the office.

On the way down to the lab, Purvis replayed the conversation. He was confused. Confused and embarrassed. And what was this new emotion? Was it anger? On reflection it was more like disapproval. Yes, that was it. Purvis was surprised to find he disapproved of what his boss had said. Disapproving of someone in authority was a new and disquieting experience. He was angry about the implication that he had botched the tests, but he felt disapproval that Mr. Knight seemed to be asking him to make the test come out a certain way.

— · — · — · — · — · — · — · —

Carl was walking out the front door of his condo just before noon, debating whether to risk decorating his shirt with a Li'l Porgy's barbecue. Laura Aldin startled him as he reached his car. She was parked across the street in the 1988 Chevy Impala that had been the subject of the search for the gas container. She waved and smiled at him. "I was in town to go to the clinic. I just wanted to talk about the case."

It crossed his mind that most people would have called ahead, but he was thrilled she was there. "I was just leaving for lunch. I hate to have you waste a trip. Tell you what. If you're not doing anything right now lets eat together and we can talk."

She brightened. "Now there's an offer. Only if you let me buy."

He shook his head negatively and said, "We'll talk about business. That makes it deductible." Barbecue seemed a little sloppy for a pretty woman in a summer dress. "How about Katsinas? Ever eat there?"

"Do they have good salads?"

"A Greek salad to die for."

She got out of her car and smoothed the pastel flowers on her white summer dress, scooped at the neck to reveal just a hint of her athletic figure. Her dark hair was free and young. They got in his Jaguar and headed toward campus, chatting about how she was handling the stress of the case. They entered the restaurant and Carl seemed to know everybody.

The hostess showed them into a room decorated with white latticework and garden lamps. On the walls were smoked mirrors. The effect was comforting. They were given a table in a corner that allowed Carl to scan the room. He seemed completely at home.

Laura's eyes were on him. "You've been here before."

"Not since breakfast."

"This is your place?"

"I started coming here when I began coming down to visit my daughter. Since I took Wally's case, it's been like three or four times a day." Carl nodded at several tables where men were having lunch. "This is the center of town, at least for lawyers and sports nuts."

"It sure is different from the grease pit in Moraine."

The waitress took their order and disappeared.

"Do you take a lot of women here for lunch?"

"Only if they are beautiful and dress like a spring breeze." He knew he was laying it on too thick, but it was fun.

Laura's smile seemed close to a blush, if that was still possible in this new culture. She said, "Thank you, if you mean me."

"See those guys at that table? They're gonna grill me when I show up around five tonight, about who's the movie star I had lunch with. I guess that's why they call it a bar and grill."

Laura accepted the compliment, seemingly unaware of the pun. "What are you going to tell them?"

"How about you're Gene Tierney in *Laura*?"

"That was a really good movie. I saw it on cable once. Do you really think I look like her?" She touched his arm when she asked.

Was this an unbridgeable gap or had she entered a period in her life when older men seemed interesting? She was having a big effect on him. Part of it was sensual. Part of it was the open envy he could see over her shoulder. His buddies didn't have to know she was a client's wife and was untouchable.

81

They talked about food and movies, anything but the case. The food arrived. They both had Greek salads and he had an Italian beef sandwich. Then they settled into an update on the case. She seemed to follow every idea and strategy and as he talked, he noticed she was watching him. "What are you thinking about?" he asked.

"I could get in trouble for answering."

He said, "That warms my heart."

She laughed, "An honest, warm-hearted lawyer. Wow."

"I'm sorry. I shouldn't have said...."

Her eyes sparkled. "Don't be too sure."

Carl savored her look for a moment before reflecting, "I knew something good was bound to happen this year."

After they finished and were about to leave, he glanced across the room and was impaled by envious glances. As they arose she brushed his arm with her breasts. It was clear she could have avoided the touch.

Rewriting History

Carl let himself in by the side door of his office in Millington. Most lawyers like to have an escape hatch to foil clients camping out in the waiting room. The clutter was gone from his desk and stacks of papers had been removed from the floor around it. Files had been restored to the filing cabinets or had been adopted by the younger associates. Souvenir baseballs in plastic holders were lined up in a well-dusted row. The antique partners' desk had been given a coat of lemon and beeswax. Even the carpet smelled clean. Carl could hardly believe he was in his own office.

"Sheri!"

She appeared at the door, snuffing a cigarette before entering his office, to preserve the illusion that her smoke stopped at the threshold. "Here one minute and you're hollerin' at me already. What's the problem?"

"How am I supposed to find anything?"

"That's the secret, big boy. You gotta ask me or one o' the other secretaries...correction...the Administrative Assistants. That's what we got workin' for us now. Name don't cost as much as a raise."

He was pleased at the order she had brought to his office. "Where the hell is the last half of the pizza I left right next to the computer?"

"Smithsonian. They come for it yesterday."

"Thanks."

"Don't mention it." She sneaked a smile.

Carl sat behind the big desk and stared at the brass fire pole running down through a hole in the ceiling. It brought back the time when Dani had laughed and suggested leaving it when they bought the old firehouse. A trickle of bittersweet memory. He began to plow through an orderly stack of mail tagged with Post-it notes of different colors. Halfway through the stack he realized he had been thinking of Dani and the Aldin case at the same time. Did that mean anything, or were some of her vibrations left in his office? He decided to try his standard tactic for dealing with a dilemma. "Got a minute, Sheri? Sit down."

She did.

"I've got a problem with this Aldin case." For the next five minutes he outlined the tangled questions arising out of the seizure of the gasoline container from Aldin's car. It always helped him to organize his thoughts and see solutions when he talked out loud about them. He told her about the Federal search warrant. He told about the unanswered question of how, so quickly after the bombing, the Sheriff could have known there was evidence of Aldin's involvement. Carl wondered out loud who should help him with the Motion to Suppress.

Sheri didn't bat an eyelash. "Which of them kid lawyers we got? Is that what you're askin?"

"Well, you got any other ideas?"

"Why don't you get Dani?" She waited to see where the mortar round landed. He didn't react, so she continued. "You know she's the best at that kinda thing. I think it's a bunch o' bullshit that they let them bums go because some dumb cop screws up, but she's one of them big time liberals, Carl, an' I guess maybe you got a twinge o' that, too. Get Dani."

He had been thinking the same thing, but wanted to hear it from the only person he felt truly cared and understood. "You really think so?"

"Absolutely." She set her jaw.

"Yeah, but would she do it? I don't need another rebuff."

"Hell, don't ask me. I'm not her agent no more. Just ask her nice."

Special Agent Roger Fossum later wondered what might have been if he had ignored the telephone call and had left early for lunch. The caller was Purvis Watson from the FBI lab. They had gotten to know each other during a case arising from a crash on I-55 near Springfield of a semi containing a huge shipment of cocaine concealed in bags of quicklime to throw off DEA dogs.

While waiting to be called as witnesses, Fossum and Purvis had discovered they had a common interest in the Kennedy assassination. Over several years they had emailed each other with tidbits about JFK.

Today's phone call was brief.

Fossum said, "Special Agent Fossum."

Watson said, "This is David Ferrie."

Fossum felt a little jolt at the name of one of the mysterious figures in JFK's assassination. He picked up on the clandestine tone of the call. "Mr. Ferrie? I thought you'd be in New Orleans."

"No, I'm in a restaurant. Thought you might like to talk. Maybe we could meet at a...convenient place...near you. Nine cooks. Out in front." He emphasized the word "convenient."

Fossum tried to think of what Watson was referring to. Then it came to him. He must mean a convenience store. The simple code was probably an address. Nine probably meant Ninth Street. On the corner of Ninth and Cook there was a Shell Food Mart he remembered from his daily lunch-hour walks. Presumably the remark about "out in front" indicated a payphone. He thought he remembered seeing payphones outside the store.

The pause evidently disturbed Watson. "Are you still on the line? I can...uh...speak with you in ten minutes."

"Are you sure this is necessary?"

There was silence until Watson's worried voice said, "I hope not," and hung up.

—·—·—·—·—·—·—·—·—

Brother Bill pulled into the alley along the south side of a martial arts school across the street from Urbana Middle School on Vine Street, only a few blocks from the Federal Court House. It had taken him two days of lurking near the law school in the late afternoon until he was able to follow Dani Hardman and see where she picked up her daughter. There had been hours at the internet researching Carl Hardman before he located Dani's picture on a law school website.

Now it was 7:30 and the morning sun was shining through the back window of his pickup; plenty of light to make crisp, sharp pictures using a fast shutter setting. He unscrewed the red cup from his thermos and filled it with coffee. Sitting in his battered '92 Ford pickup shouldn't arouse suspicion since the alley was deserted at that time of day and the neighborhood was middle class.

He glanced around and saw children arriving, walking down Vine Street. He suspected they had been shoved out the door early so their parents could hold down two jobs and pay for expensive things they didn't need.

Bill opened a photo bag and took out a vintage Nikon F1 camera fitted with an inexpensive 500 millimeter Soligor mirror lens that he had picked up at a pawn shop in Decatur. The camera was loaded with 400 ASA T-Max black and white film. The 35-year-old camera rig fit nicely into a cover story, should he be challenged by the police. He always kept an ad running in the *Wooden Nickel* advertising paper listing cameras, electronic devices, and firearms for trade or sale. It was vague enough to explain having them in his truck or on his person. He had practiced a response that he was in town to meet someone interested in buying the camera, but this morning there was no policeman to inquire. It was a little disappointing how easily he could stalk the girl.

The main entrance of the school was not more than 40 yards away. The pace began to quicken. Cars stopped at the curb to discharge children.

He sipped the coffee and watched the steam drift into empty space.

Soon the vehicle he had been waiting for pulled up at the curb, a red Jeep Cherokee driven by the woman lawyer. Next to her was a beautiful, dark haired little girl, moving her head in time to some music playing in the car. It almost certainly wasn't a hymn.

The child opened the door and got out. Her face was profiled against the entrance to the school.

Click.

She was adjusting her book bag and speaking to her mother as the Cherokee drove off.

Click.

As she reached the door, she stopped in a beam of sunlight and turned to call to another girl coming up the walk.

Click.

Recall

Clancy Brown, Judge Esker's bailiff at the time of the murder, sat on a bench and sheltered a match with his hands as he sucked flame into a three-inch cigar butt. He tossed the match into a container of sand at the front steps of the courthouse. Clancy was well past retirement, and his right leg had an artificial knee. He was about to try to light the cigar a second time when Carl Hardman walked up the steps on his way to the Clerk's office to study the venire of potential jurors drawn from the list of registered voters. Clancy asked, "How you doin', Hardman?"

Carl stopped in front of Brown. He had often wondered whether the decrepit bailiffs of Central Illinois, typically retired town cops or former military, would be able to handle a family fight or an assault on court personnel. Clancy's feeble response to the firebombing had answered the question.

"Not bad, Clancy."

Clancy furrowed his brow, surprised Hardman knew him. "We met before?"

Carl said, "I saw your picture in the paper. You know I've got to interview you about the firebombing, don't you?"

"Mmm hmm. Sure. I guess so." He turned his back to the wind and had a third go at lighting the cigar.

Carl decided to be direct. "Why don't you tell me what you saw?"

A couple of puffs. The sausage-shaped butt glowed as if determined to stay lit. "Well, it sure was a mess, alright. I didn't see nothin' until after the bomb hit the bench. I was lookin' at the Judge and all I seen was this big ol' fireball. That's what it was, a big ol' fireball. Never seen nothin' like it. Thing went through my mind was how you squirt more starter on the charcoal when it ain't takin' fire soon enough. You know how it billows up? That big ol' yellow fireball rolled all around him 'til all you could see was the outlines of his face, with him screamin' and thrashin' around. An' the stink! Them fumes, an' the burnin' body..." Clancy stopped and looked down. He stared at the cigar for a second, then flipped it into the container of sand.

"Clancy, I know it's no fun to remember, but did you notice anything else? I mean, about the guy who threw it?"

Clancy's gaze was fixed on his feet. His head slowly moved from side to side. "Nope. Nothin'."

Carl waited a few seconds and was about to thank him when Clancy said, "Never seen nothin' no way. Nothin'. Mebbe if I was payin' attention, like I was s'posed to, mebbe I'd have spotted him an' mebbe I might've had time to holler so the Judge coulda dove under the bench or somethin'."

"Clancy, you're..." Carl started to say seventy-five years old, but caught himself. "...beating yourself up for something you couldn't have stopped even if you were sitting back near the door."

Clancy looked up, grateful. "I been blamin' myself, that's true. But it was up to me to make sure this didn't happen, an' I crapped out."

Carl didn't have the heart to push him. "So you didn't get a detailed look at the bomber?"

"Naw, but I didn't need to. I know Aldin pretty good."

Carl winced at Clancy identifying Aldin by name.

Clancy continued, "Used to be a nice kid when he was first over here from...wherever he come from...think it was someplace near Israel. He had a job at the drug store before his accident. Then he was limpin' around

89

town a lot until he got his settlement. Used t' talk about soccer all the time, an' I'd give him a hard time about baseball bein' the real sport. Never could understand what people see in that soccer. After a while, his money dried up. Then he got the job managin' the convenience store out on the hard road, and it kinda made him sour. I don't know. Sorta strange, with a chip on his shoulder. He's been in court lots, filin' them strange papers, goin' to trial on collection cases, pissin' off the Judge big time. But I never thought he was some kind of foreigner terrorist or whatever."

"But at the time of the firebombing did you recognize Aldin? Even though you knew him, did it actually go through your mind that it was Aldin?"

Clancy paused and looked around. "Can't rightly say. I was payin' attention to the fire an' the Judge. Aldin had on a sweatshirt an' them dark glasses. Couldn't see hardly none of his face 'cause the hood was tied closed. Came up over his mouth. Wish I could help there. Ever'body remembers seein' somethin' different that day."

Clancy seemed a decent sort. It didn't seem likely he'd invent detail just to please the prosecution. On balance, what he said was helpful. But at his age would Clancy tell it the same way twice?

"Take care, now. If you remember anything, please give me a call."

"I surely will."

Carl had the same feeling the last time he visited an aunt in a nursing home.

Curiosity fought with the butterflies in Fossum's stomach as he stood on Ninth and Cook in front of the Shell Food Mart. He could see the back of Abraham Lincoln's house less than a block away, now perfectly maintained by a branch of government. Fossum heard the pay phone ring. He picked it up and asked, "How did you get this number."

Purvis Watson responded, "I looked up convenience stores on the web and found one on Mapquest close to the Bureau office. I called the listed number of the store and asked the clerk to help me. I pretended to be from the telephone provider and asked him to go outside and get the number on the pay phone and see if the receiver had been torn off. Nice kid."

"Give me a number to call you. Let's get off these phones."

Watson said, "202 384 3022. Wait five minutes."

Fossum looked at his watch and wandered inside the store. He ordered a medium Coke and asked for seven dollars of his change in quarters. He asked the kid behind the counter if there was a video arcade nearby. The clerk brightened and gave detailed directions. Through a gentle rain, Fossum drove several blocks north to an Amoco station and parked under the canopy near the outside pay phone. He dialed the number, paying for the call in cash.

Only one ring and Watson's voice said, "This is a pay phone. Are you on one?"

Fossum could picture the little man mustering enough courage to violate Bureau policy. "Yes. Go ahead. What's this all about?"

A sigh. "Ah...I've never done anything like this before. You've got to understand why I'm doing this. I hope I'm doing the right thing. You seem to be an old-fashioned Bureau guy, like the ones I knew when I joined. I was convinced the only thing that mattered to those guys was the truth...."

"Get to the point. I'm standing in the rain. What's on your mind?"

Another sigh. "The Aldin case. I've been testing and testing. I've done GC-IRMS molecular isotope analysis, and no matter how many times I do the tests, the profiles for the accelerant and the gas container from Aldin's car don't match. Not even close. The accelerant is almost certainly 89-octane gasohol and some diesel fuel. Aldin's gas container had unleaded 87."

Fossum stood with the phone in his hand and watched a car stop, wait for a break in traffic, and enter the busy street.

"Roger? Are you there?"

"Yeah...I'm still here. Listen, are you really sure of this? I mean, we

91

all make mistakes."

"I'm sure. I've done the test repeatedly. I've torn down the apparatus and cleaned it. Taken fresh samples. I even asked another lab technician to do a blind retest for me. This is the most advanced apparatus for profiling petroleum accelerants. The test comes out the same every time."

"Who have you told about this?"

"Now you're scaring me."

"Look, I've gotta know if this is gonna reach me through channels."

"I went to my supervisor, Mr. Knight. He ordered me to retest everything and I did, over and over. Still got the same results. I told him again last week and he got angry and suggested I'd made an error. Then he told me I'd better just put the raw test data in the report. No evaluation. No summary. No conclusions."

"Shit!" Fossum stared at the traffic again.

"Roger, have I made a mistake in telling you this?"

"No, you've screwed up my life, but I guess you haven't made a mistake. Maybe you underlined a mistake I've been making for the last few years."

"Do you want me to get you the testing results?"

"Not yet. We'll talk here in one week, at exactly the same time. That ok?"

"Yeah...guess it's gotta be." A throbbing headache was fighting to establish its territory behind Roger Fossum's forehead.

Settling In

Carl was cooking a gourmet Italian meal for Susan. He was reasonably good in the kitchen, but seldom cooked for himself. They had decided to stay at his condo for dinner and watch a classic video from Susan's younger years, *The Mouse and His Child*, a magical, lost gem of a movie. He hoped she would still find joy in it and remember better times. It put him in a gentle mood to think of Susan, on the verge of asserting adolescent independence, but still a little girl.

Susan was suspicious of his cooking, especially since she had decided to become a vegetarian. While he was taking garlic bread out of the oven, she pried open his lasagna and investigated it for secret animal content. After the meal they talked at length, which seldom happened in their restaurant encounters.

He was truly relaxed as he listened to the things that she was willing to tell him. The fact that he could sit with the most important person in the world, safe and comfortable, made him feel his concerns were minor, that his professional struggles had given her endless opportunities. It was the payoff for being a lawyer. The cloister reserved for professionals. Protection from the street for himself and his family. That was what was in it for him, what kept him in the system. His profession, for all its faults, still operated within the basic rules of human decency. It was where talk settled differences, not violence.

She was talking about some pop group. He listened and nodded. Finally she became quiet. She looked straight at him and asked, "Daddy, are you really helping the terrorists?"

It was so unexpected he did a double take before answering. "Do you think I'm a terrorist, honey?"

"No, really. But are you helping them?"

"Of course not. Who told you that?"

"Nobody...I guess. It's just stuff from school. About you helping that guy..."

"Aldin?"

"Yeah."

"Well, he may have a few screws loose, but it's not right to call him a terrorist, at least not until he's had a fair trial."

"But he killed a judge, didn't he? That's what terrorists do, isn't it?"

Carl decided to go with the expanded version. She was very mature for her years. "Susan, you can't reason backward like that. There are lots of people who would like to kill a judge without being terrorists. Besides, nobody has proven that he did it."

"Like, who would want to kill a judge unless he was a terrorist?"

He could count on Susan to force him to think. "Well, maybe...the wife of the judge?"

She smiled. "No, really, Daddy. If they really hate each other they could get a divorce."

Her answer stung but he went on. "Maybe somebody got hurt badly by something the judge did in court. If such a person got even with the judge, it wouldn't make that person a terrorist, would it?"

"Is that what Mr. Aldin did?"

Carl always felt like a sellout when he had to say it. "Honey, I can't tell you what my clients say they did or even what I think they did. It's a secret lawyers have to keep, even from the people they love most."

"Oh."

He could tell she felt she should be an exception to that rule. He asked her in a conspiratorial voice, "Can you keep a secret?"

She said, "Yes!"

He said, "So can I!"

She punched his shoulder in fifth grade frustration. After that they watched the video. But it troubled him what he would say to her when, after the trial, he eventually had to answer her questions.

— · — · — · — · — · — · — · — · —

The 11 by 14 black and white picture was sharp. Very tight grain pattern, no camera movement. The smiling little face caught open-mouthed in the middle of a word.

Brother Bill examined the last print as he hung it to dry. There were two others. He leaned back against the darkroom counter and stared at the little face, framed by dark hair. The eyes sparkled. She was pretty. Her mouth was open, saying something to the woman in the car. What was it? He tried to mimic the shape of the word on the child's lips. Like an "O" but not quite. Lips more pulled back at the corners. What could the word be?

As he stared, his thoughts turned to the practical possibilities. What would be most effective? What would accomplish the goal of getting the lawyer out of the Aldin case? Would he have to harm the child?

He stared at the little girl. She was well dressed. She was from a world he didn't know. She probably had never waded in a creek or planted a garden. But it was obvious she was special to her parents. That meant they had a weakness to be exploited. A chink in their armor.

Brother Bill stared at the face in the picture, wondering what it would be like to have a child like that look back at him. He could imagine her walking up the sidewalk to Sunday School or to a 4H meeting, waving goodbye to him as he drove away. Envy crossed his heart, but he put it away quickly. His love was the Lord and His children, the patriots in this part of the country, who looked to him for the steadfastness he had learned at the knee of his own father.

As hard as it was to look at the picture and take action that involved this child, he could see no way to avoid it. The movement must be protected. Abraham didn't falter when he was called to sacrifice Isaac.

As he gazed at the dripping picture, the little mouth seemed to speak. The word frozen in the silver of the picture played in his head. It was "love." The child was saying goodbye. She was saying, "I love you, Mommy."

The next week was filled by Carl's preparation of the Aldin case while trying to keep up on his regular workload long distance. He canvassed Moraine and spoke with at least a dozen minor witnesses. He photographed the still-charred courtroom, the rest of the county layout, and Aldin's driveway. The case was constantly on his mind. He woke every morning with new ideas. Carl ignored the fact that he was already past the agreed time limit for his participation in Aldin's defense. He was absorbed by the legal issues and feared his replacement might not take the case as seriously as the dreadful odds against Aldin demanded. He worked with a sense that time was running out, even though he had heard nothing from any replacement lawyer.

A large Express Mail package arrived at his condo, containing ten inches of discovery material. Most of it was meaningless bureaucratic paperwork. There were a few ungrammatical reports and witness statements taken by deputies, and follow-up statements taken by the FBI, which made the same witnesses sound at least two standard I.Q. deviations smarter. Aldin's rap sheet contained a few minor speeding tickets, parking tickets, a contempt, a bad check charge and one conviction for hunting out of season. Near the center of the stack were unlabeled pages of graph paper and computer printouts. They contained squiggles, spikes, and numbers. It was gibberish to Carl. He made a note for the next lawyer that the documents were apparently some kind of testing, but didn't seem to have a covering report. Perhaps it was mistakenly left out in the photo-copying. It probably was a confirmation, matching up the gas container with the charred samples from the courtroom. It was the sort of loose end the next lawyer could look into.

— — — — — — — — — — —

Exactly one week to the minute since their last clandestine phone call, Fossum stopped at a McDonald's and dialed a pay phone number in Washington he had mailed to Watson on a slip of paper in a worn copy of Jim Marrs' *Crossfire,* one of the definitive books on the JFK assassination. The slip was inserted in a section discussing David Ferrie, the enigmatic figure Watson had mentioned in their first call. The slip could be explained away as a page mark he had used while reading the book on a recent trip to the FBI Headquarters. He was trying to quell a queasy stomach, worrying that Purvis Watson may have crumbled under the pressure. Maybe he disclosed the whole thing including the calls. Fossum was thinking about his pension.

He used a pre-paid phone card he'd purchased at a small local store in the rough part of Springfield. Such places had no video surveillance system.

The call went through at the same rate, the same sounds, the same volume as one Fossum had made moments before to the *Washington Post* classified section. A crude way to test for a bug on Watson's phone, but the only one possible on a pay phone. Fossum took a deep breath and placed his faith in Watson. The call was answered in half a ring. That helped. Standard advice on a bugged call was to let it ring a couple of times to avoid seeming eager or nervous. It gave time to get cranky recorders functioning.

"Hello."

"I'm returning your call at your request." Fossum said, to defend him-

97

self if he were being set up.

"Yes."

Fossum listened for the texture of anything on the line. Nothing triggered his suspicion. "You're in front of a drugstore, right?"

"Yes. How did you have this number?"

"When I was in D.C. the last time, I used to grab a newspaper there and I used the pay phone to call home because all I had was the Bureau cell phone. I wanted my wife to call me back because I ran out of quarters. I jotted down the number and put it in my wallet. Anything wrong with that?"

"No, of course not. The fact that you're being cautious makes me feel more like trusting you." His voice sounded relieved.

Exactly the response Fossum wanted. "Go across the street to the closest service station. Don't say the name! Call 217 529 4949 in three minutes." Fossum broke the connection, got in his car and drove two blocks to the Wal-Mart store. He walked to a bank of pay phones. On one of them he had placed an "Out of Order" sign a half hour earlier. He checked for anyone watching and tore the sign off the phone. In less than a half-minute the phone rang.

"Hello."

Watson sounded out of breath. "I'm too old to get places in three minutes. My boss, Mr....."

"No names."

"Ok."

"I got my copy of the material. It's as you say. No conclusions."

"I know. It's been on my mind that..."

"Keep this short."

"Ok."

"Now listen. I want a cassette in your voice telling me the history of this. Complete. Copies of your reports and testing. All contacts, all conversations and when. Destroy any notes you make. Send it by FedEx to A. J. Hidell, 24 Calzada De Los Reyes, Cuernavaca, Morelos, Mexico,

62131. If anybody can figure out your test results, he deserves a Ph.D."
Fossum paused. He repeated the address slowly. It was the retirement villa
of his old partner who had left the Bureau under a cloud and didn't figure
to be any help to the Government. It didn't seem like a set up, but Fossum
was only a year from retiring to a sunny beach. He had been as straight as
a piece of string for his entire career. It was tempting to reject Watson's
contact or report the little man, but for doing what? Placing truth and
honor ahead of letting some arrogant bureaucrat put his thumb on the
scales of justice?

"Are you still there? Is everything all right?"

"I sure hope so. You're being straight with me?"

"Straight with you? I should be worried whether I can trust you."

Fossum sighed. "I guess you can. I should just walk away from this,
but there are still a few things that turn my stomach. This smells more like
a cover-up than an investigation. I don't have any problem whether…that
person…did it. He fits like a glove and he's smart enough to plant a bogus
gas container where he knew we'd find it. But everybody's cutting corners
to get him. I just can't do that in a death penalty case."

"Nor can I."

"Leave it to me. We've got an extremely well placed source in this
case. Even that bothers me a whole lot. A few things shouldn't be corrupted. I think I can find out whether the defense has figured out the testing
problem. If they haven't, I'm gonna have to figure out something. Maybe
a little fundamental honesty. Who knows."

"It's in your hands."

"Thanks a lot! Now you just forget this until next week. Same time.
Same place."

Fossum listened to the dead phone for a full minute. It stayed dead.

———————————————

Carl's days at the condo in Champaign fell into a routine of waking, downloading work product on the case from his young associates, calling Sheri, and going through the accumulated phone calls. The virtual office. Cell phones. E-mail. Faxes replacing faces.

The Millington clients were making allowances because of the high profile case their lawyer was working on. Calls to insurance adjusters resulted in long-distance haggling over arms and legs and backs and necks. The stuff that pays the bills.

At noon he would head over to Katsinas' for lunch, then spend the afternoon at the mammoth University of Illinois Law Library. His day would end with Susan.

Carl was far from being a research gerbil, but he found renewal in reading the caselaw. It took him back to his law school days without the pressure of having a bell ring every fifty minutes for class. Reviewing the elements of murder and arson. Chain of evidence. Reputation evidence. Mental defenses. And of course, the legal war over the death penalty. But he knew the key to the case was the search of Aldin's car and home. The gas container was the only hard physical evidence directly related to the firebombing. The guns and political data were merely circumstantial, relevant only to motive or design.

Search and seizure is a frustrating topic. Cases seemingly identical on the facts reach opposite conclusions. Every Monday the U.S. Supreme Court reconsiders, refines, distinguishes and often reverses precedents defining the right to be left alone. Carl had never developed a feel for this slippery topic. At the law school there was one person who was a recognized expert on search and seizure, an expert who was the obvious choice to consult. The only problem, it was Dani. Sheri had suggested her weeks ago. He had not acted on the suggestion. Was it pride or stubbornness or fear of reopening old wounds? Or fear of finding they had never healed?

False Horizon

Hurshal Taylor sat behind his desk doing what he did best, oozing piety. His tangled, silver mane anchored small triangular reading glasses that were perched well down his lengthy nose, permitting Hurshal to unleash looks of disapproval over the top of the lenses. His red bowtie was perfectly tied, appropriate for a self-important country squire. Hurshal was a key eyewitness to the murder, since he was trying the divorce case in front of Judge Esker at the time the fire bomb was thrown.

Carl had decided to try to see him without an appointment. He had no illusions about getting much help, but he hoped to pin Hurshal down before Gadsen could prep him on his story.

Hurshal welcomed Carl a bit too courteously. A secretary served coffee without being bidden. Carl was invited to sit on a large, red leather couch. He had a feeling of being in the presence of the Dean of Students or perhaps the father of a girl on her first date.

"Kind of you to drop in. I suppose you're interested in what transpired during the murder? Poor Judge Esker. I used to play golf with him. Wonderful man." His manner was slow and unctuous.

"Yes, I understand he was a good person, and a good friend of yours, too. Nevertheless, I have to interview all the potential witnesses."

Hurshal nodded gravely and waited.

Carl consciously let a beat go by while they stared at each other, unblinking. Then he asked, "Did you do a lot of divorce work in his court?" Even though Carl seldom did cases this far south in Central Illinois, he knew Hurshal was a legendary small-town divorce lawyer who was often invited to lecture at family law seminars. Faking ignorance about Hurshal's divorce practice was calculated to take him down a peg and perhaps get him to reveal something out of irritation.

Hurshal's eyes narrowed. "I suppose I had as many cases in front of Judge Esker as anyone. I even get a few up your way once in a while." Tit for tat.

"What was happening in the case when the bombing took place?"

Hurshal affected a laconic yawn, which he politely smothered with his right hand. "Oh...I don't know..." He leaned back in his red leather swivel chair, knitting his hands over an immaculate white shirt. "...I suppose maybe we were about to expose the husband's meretricious relationship with his paramour." Hurshal smiled. He cherished archaic phrases.

"I see. Do you remember which peccadillo?"

Hurshal arched an eyebrow. Point for Carl. "Yes, as I recall, the subject was the husband's predilection for a mid-morning dalliance with the wife of the farmer whose spread adjoined the North Forty. He customarily did a little plowing in his neighbor's boudoir while his tractor languished." Hurshal tossed off the line like a tennis forehand, challenging Carl to return the shot.

Carl let his gaze drift over Hurshal's credenza, to a large, garish painting of a clipper ship in full sail, a calculated backdrop for Hurshal's expensive advice. The style was early Elvis-on-velvet, probably purchased at some struggling artist outlet. "Hurshal, what's the artist trying to say by having the horizon to the left of the ship a different angle than on the right? It looks like the two horizons would miss each other if the boat weren't there."

Hurshal swiveled and stared. "I don't know what you mean." His tone indicated that he certainly did, and for the first time.

Carl quickly feigned embarrassment. "Oh, it's probably just the angle from back here. It's a very striking image, with those bow waves and the porpoises, and all." He hoped Hurshal would remember the horizon whenever he noticed a client staring at the painting.

"Just what do you want to know about the bombing." Hurshal's tone had turned businesslike.

"When did you first see anything unusual?"

"I got a very good look at your client, counselor."

"You sound certain. The bomber was hooded and wearing dark glasses, wasn't he?"

"We all know Mr. Aldin very well. He's been a walking, talking obstruction of justice for some time."

"You were facing the husband on the stand when it started, I gather."

"At first, perhaps. But when you feel the heat of a flaming bottle whir past your head, it does heighten the senses. It invites further investigation."

"It must have been terrible watching your friend burning to death."

Hurshal's face lost the artificial smile. His sarcasm melted as the image seemed to be replaying. "It was horrible! Those flames...billowing up...." He swallowed.

Carl filed away a point for cross examination. If Hurshal watched the firebomb engulf the Judge, he couldn't have been watching the figure in the sweatshirt directly behind him. One or the other. By the time Hurshal turned, all he would have seen was the back of the bomber running away.

Carl tried to provoke a reaction. "I take it you tried to help Judge Esker?"

Hurshal looked guilty. His voice was uncertain. "I wanted to rush up there, but the heat was too intense. The smoke and fumes made it impossible to breathe. I ran through the side door into chambers to call for help."

"And Judge Esker was just lying there burning?"

Hurshal's eyes bored into him. "There wasn't anything I could do.

Getting help was the appropriate..."

"So you called 911?"

"That's right."

The answer eliminated any future claim by Hurshal that he followed the bomber to get a better look.

"Thank you, Hurshal. I suppose I'll get another chance to hear you tell it."

"I'm counting on it. Now, if you'll excuse me?" Hurshal shut off the chivalry and began to stare at the draft of a will lying on his reproduction Victorian desk.

—·—·—·—·—·—·—·—·—·—

At sundown Carl walked from the law library to the Illini Union to get something to eat. The evening was unseasonably warm. Champaign had a way of skipping Spring and starting Summer early. It was a long walk from the law school. He remembered how difficult it had been to span the sprawling U of I campus in the ten minute breaks between classes, even when his muscles were taut from summers working construction and playing baseball in the gritty suburbs southwest of Chicago. Now there was no hurry except that his life was drifting into its third movement.

His defense of Aldin was several weeks beyond what had been agreed. There had been no contact from anyone to relieve him. The fee had been used up weeks ago. Had Wally's buddies hoodwinked him? Self-interest should have made him withdraw from the case and head back to Millington, but the daily contacts with Susan were precious jewels. Research on the death penalty was generating a brief that might give Aldin a chance to live. Capital punishment was the lodestone drawing Carl to the case. Whenever he became irritated at Aldin, he visualized him with a needle in his arm. Turning him over to someone else would feel like abandonment.

Carl reached a semi-circular stone bench. The Senior Bench, they used to call it. He sat down and stared across the quad. A yellow Frisbee flickered through the cone of light from one of the pole lamps and a golden retriever leaped and made a clean catch. The dog ran it back to a young man in a Cardinals tee shirt.

He wished Susan were with him to watch the dog. He would always remember these weeks of semi-normality with her. She was slowly opening up, telling him things about school and innocent little teasers about boys in her class. She bubbled over with corny jokes. In a year or two she would almost certainly shut down communication. Teens are really in the custody of their friends. The thought disturbed him. Was Dani ready for it? Could she handle rejection by the perfect little doll she had created? A twinge of pain and remorse gripped him. Was freedom from a frozen marriage worth missing Susan on a daily basis?

He took a deep breath and forced himself to focus on the quad and the layers of memory that were painted over it. In the 'Fifties, these sidewalks ran through tunnels formed by majestic trees, all lost to Dutch Elm Disease. This quad had seen Spring Carnivals and mass water fights. JFK, running for President, had spoken from a stage not thirty yards away.

At the end of the 'Sixties, thousands of hippies openly smoked pot on Hash Wednesday, protected from arrest by their very numbers. One night a thousand streakers ran naked past the bench where he sat.

All of those things right here, stratified in collective memory.

Now the quad was normal and bland and the kids trudged past like automatons.

The next image was Laura, "a face that floats on the summer night." Her dark hair and eyes, her lithe body, her youth. Maybe youth was the real catalyst. What would it be like to be young, sitting with her on this bench in front of Frisbee dogs and students with employment worries?

He shook his head, disturbed by the imagined detail of her body. His daydream was stupid and pointless and unreal, the delusion of an aging mind. She was young and the wife of a client, but the fantasy was a lightning bug, drifting away only to spark again every few seconds.

He forced his mind to abandon Laura, replacing her with the girls of his college years. What disasters had overtaken them? Which marriage were they working on? That brought him back to Dani. A calm settled over him. Regret, not so much for anything he had done, but for third and fourth efforts he had never made.

Dani, in her late forties, was more than attractive. Aerobics and a vegetarian diet had stimulated a late bloom. Yesterday, when he picked up Susan, Dani answered the door in a leotard. She had little beads of sweat on her forehead, which dredged up memories of passion, not images of StairMaster. For just an instant, he thought he caught a look he remembered from bedrooms past.

People paid big money for his advice. How could he be so unsuccessful in making his own decisions? He explored a thought he had always suppressed. What would it be like to live with Dani and Susan again? Maybe not expecting as much this time. Maybe without the everyday grind of practicing law together. Maybe he could keep his practice in Millington, but have some kind of a family again. Somehow, some way. A partitioned life?

His head was spinning. It was a stupid idea, wasn't it? How could a man make a home in a halfway house? Was there an alternative to sitting on a stone bench in your fifties, fighting a fantasy about a client's wife while watching a dog play Frisbee?

— · — · — · — · — · — · — · — · —

Brother Bill stared at the three blowups leaning against the back of his couch. They were in sequence, documenting the little Hardman girl leaving her mother for a day at school.

It would be helpful to know her name if he had to call her over to his truck. He'd have to find out somehow. Maybe take a puppy to the schoolyard so the kids would come to pet it. He'd be able to squeeze her name out of one of them.

But what to do? How far to go? Was there anything less drastic? Bill did not seek violence, but he thirsted after righteousness, trying to follow the Word. The Good Book was full of bloody actions God commanded his people to perform.

Still, it was troubling to think of harming a child, one so pretty, at that. Nevertheless, she was a child corrupted by the money her parents earned whoring for degenerates. Still, she was not responsible for the accident of her birth. If she had been placed by the Almighty in a decent, God-fearing home out in the country, where she could smell the clean earth and be protected from the mongrelized city, if she could have been taught true values by someone like him, she would not have to be bait in a trap.

Something about that idea troubled him. He would have to think on it. No, better than thinking on it, he must consult the Good Book.

Needs

She had been Danielle Rovelli. In the divorce, she had considered dropping Hardman out of feminism or individualism or an urge akin to cleaning out a neglected closet. In the end she decided Susan shouldn't have to explain to her friends why Mommy's name was different from hers. Dani believed in many abstractions, including the right of women to procreate without the dubious benefit of modern wedlock, but when it came to saddling Susan with ancient prejudices, her radicalism faded.

For seven years Dani and Carl had tried to build a law partnership. They had won an impossible case at the end of the 'Sixties and that bond had slowly turned into love. Although the marriage had drowned in an excess of togetherness, professional respect remained.

After the divorce, Dani had been invited to teach at the Law School only a few years after her student activism had bedeviled the place. Now she was paid to infect future generations of lawyers with ideas that could have gotten her expelled. She was a true expert in the arcane mysteries of search and seizure. She lectured at bar seminars on suppression of evidence and she published in professional journals.

Dani was sitting in her office at her computer when the phone broke her train of thought. She sighed and picked it up with a resigned, "Hello."

"Hi," he said. His voice was tentative. "I was just thinking of you."

Carl's voice always caused a little flicker from the ashes. "Hi to you."

His response skipped a beat, as if he were debating whether to stoke the ember. "How are things?"

"Going pretty well. I'm being considered for Assistant Dean. The classes are full of bright kids who need to figure out there's more to life than clerking for a big-name judge, but what's an old radical good for?"

He chuckled. "Same old Dani."

She hadn't talked to him in over a year about anything more personal than visitation. It was unsettling, but she tried to sound casual. "Original article, not to be copied. What's on your mind?"

Carl picked up her tone and kicked dirt over the embers. "Business, I guess. Have you heard about my latest folly?"

"You joined the Al Qaeda? I think I read that."

"Mmmmm, something like that. I've still got a thing about guys who are getting measured for shrouds."

"And?"

"And so do you. I was hoping I could tap your brain on a search and seizure problem in the case."

She thought about that. The firebombing murder shocked and disgusted her, but she was committed to Constitutional rights for even the most reprehensible defendant. "What's the problem?"

"The key to this case is the search of Aldin's car. They seized a gas can."

"...and they claim he consented, right?"

"No, this is Moraine. They never saw the need to lie about consent. The police report states they were serving a civil paper on Aldin for contempt for some pleading travesty he committed in a civil case."

"In the state court? Contempt for filing a pleading?"

"What he filed would be a great story for a lawyer's luncheon if it hadn't pissed off everybody in the county, and I'm mystified about why the Feds are deferring jurisdiction. Because he's got a great chance of getting the death penalty in state court?" He was consciously pushing her buttons.

Dani thought, *Oh no! Here we go again.*

Carl picked up her ambivalence. There was a pause. "I'm asking because you're a hell of a lot better at search and seizure than I am. Correction, make that a hell of a lot better than anybody."

Dani wondered if that was the whole reason. Was there a more personal one? "Well, I won't argue about that. Sometime you ought to spend a few days in the library, Carl. It might save you from skin cancer. I can't imagine you picking up a lawbook in anger, but what about the kids in your office? Can't they punch out a decent brief?"

"Not like your briefs, Dani." His smile came through the phone.

She ignored the double meaning. "Well, I guess I could meet with them if you want. Maybe I can point them to some cases."

"Actually I was thinking of more than that. You and I really were a hell of a team way back when. How about it? Could you put our personal history on the shelf long enough to help save this guy? Aldin's friends promised a hotshot trial lawyer would take over but I haven't seen them or the lawyer. I need help with the Motion to Suppress. It's not like taking on a whole trial."

She didn't want to be pushed. She wanted to savor it, to roll it around in her mind and explore all the implications. She ended the awkward silence. "I won't say yes and I won't say no. Not today, anyway. Call me tomorrow if it still seems like a good idea. I've got to go."

"Fair enough. Talk to you later." He hung up first.

—·—·—·—·—·—·—·—·—·—

It was late in a Wednesday night Liberty Church legal study session. Brother Bill was in the bosom of friends and believers.

The documents they had printed from the Internet were lying on the table. In front of him was a printout of a militia web page, authored by someone calling himself "Patriot." Bill scanned to a section he remembered:

It is essential that our philosophy of command support the way we fight. First, to generate the tempo and the uncertainty, and fluidity of combat, command is to be decentralized. Local commanders must make decisions on their own initiative, based on their understanding of the strategic situation. Passing information up a chain of command and waiting for a decision to be passed down will not work and is wrong in principle. A patriot at the point of decision will naturally have a better appreciation for the problem than even someone with more experience, but a distance away. Individual initiative and responsibility are to be encouraged. Decentralized control is achieved through the use of mission tactics, which will be set out in detail later...

He had printed the web page to help decide how to deal with the problem of Carl Hardman and Wally Aldin. Why should some lawyer be permitted to rescue Aldin from the maximum penalty? Or worse, maybe Hardman was one of the terrorists. Maybe he was an agent of the ZOG.

He wasn't paying attention to the discussion around the table concerning whether Franklin Delano Roosevelt's War Powers Act still operated to suspend the Constitution. He was thinking about Hardman and the words "individual initiative" from the web page. Thinking of how it was his right and duty to take action. The web page did everything but say, "It's your call, Brother Bill Carmichael."

The discussion going on in the room had shifted to the fact the Federal Courts were presently operating under the law of admiralty, giving the President unlimited powers. He had heard all that before. What was on his mind was the problem at hand, the problem of Hardman. Would he find some loophole to save Aldin, and then make a fortune writing one of those tell-all lawyer books?

The more he thought about it, the more the problem cried out for decisive action. Brother Bill wished for the thousandth time he could talk to his dead father. The father who had stormed Omaha beach and had survived the Battle of the Bulge. The father who had felt betrayed in the 'Forties when somehow America was permitted to decay from the strongest nation on earth to one that didn't stop Russia from taking Eastern Europe and Asia. He had told stories of how we were sold out by Roosevelt and Alger Hiss at the Yalta conference. Sold out! The bloodstained winnings of a generation of American patriots handed over to Stalin. Bill wished his father could be there to tell him what to do.

He typed in the web address of the Patriot. The literature was a clear guide. He found the section on decision-making:

> Decision making is essential to the conduct of war. If we lack the will to decide, we have surrendered the initiative to our foe. If we postpone taking action, for some reason, that is a decision. Thus, any decision is better than no decision.
>
> Whoever implements his decisions faster gains a decisive advantage. Decision making is a time-competitive process.
>
> It takes moral courage to make tough decisions in the face of uncertainty—and accept full responsibility for those decisions—avoiding the natural inclination to postpone the decision pending more complete information or to kick it up a chain of command. To delay action in an emergency because of incomplete information shows a lack of moral courage. We must not squander opportunities while trying to gain more information.
>
> We must accept the risk. 'In audacity and obstinacy will be found safety.'
>
> All decisions are made in the face of uncertainty. Every situation is unique. There is no perfect plan and we should not agonize over one. Select a promising course of action with an acceptable degree of risk, and do it more quickly than our foe. A good plan violently executed now is better than a perfect plan executed next week.

That last part, the line about a good plan violently executed, stuck in his mind. Act decisively. Don't wait for a perfect plan. Don't wait for approval from someone more senior. Decentralization, that was the core survival strategy of the movement. Why should he ask anyone for permission to do what was perfectly clear? The only other thing that still had any bearing on his decision was the Good Book. He'd study on it tonight.

— · — · — · — · — · — · — · — · —

Dani was sitting in a lawn chair outside her house, exhausted from a forty-five minute workout. She was determined not to surrender her body to gravity any more than she would surrender her mind to TV. As the late spring evening faded, her mind was spinning a fabric from strands of memory.

She was trying to recall the texture of Carl's call.

The softened reminiscence of their best years, sweetened by time, suppressed any danger signals.

She and Carl had tried marriage the way students try a major for a few semesters. It had ruined a great friendship. They had ignored common sense by practicing law together day in and day out. After a decade of non-stop togetherness, all mystery had worn away. Their marriage declared emotional bankruptcy sometime during the Clinton years.

Dani had returned to Champaign-Urbana and the sanctuary of the University. The times cried out for women professors.

It was a natural fit. Academia welcomed her. She was thirsty for truth after two decades of polishing excuses for the misdeeds of the paying clients. Soon she was entrenched in committees and professional organizations and political campaigns and a rainbow of social causes.

It took her three years to recover from the divorce. For three years she avoided life. Then she met someone quite different, a photographer in the College of Fine and Applied Arts. He didn't like lawyers and was skeptical about those who incubated them. She had never before been with a

113

man who demeaned her professional world. She thrilled at the way he pulled velvety shades of gray from a piece of grade 3 photo paper, but found him lacking in commitment to real-world issues.

At that point Dani had abandoned the fairy tale ending. She had channeled her energy into the Montessori School and violin lessons and ballet classes. She hadn't been with a man in more than a year when Carl called. Dani wondered what it would be like to work with him again. Maybe even have some relationship apart from the law. Life was strange, wasn't it?

Brother Bill awoke at five to the Christian FM station playing from his clock radio. He had not slept well. He lay there troubled by the problem of the Hardman child.

On the one hand, it was clear the Lord's work justified sacrificing anyone. That was the lesson of Abraham and Isaac.

On the other hand, his conscience rebelled at the thought of touching a hair on the child's head. The Master always loved children.

He was sorely troubled.

Would it be possible just to threaten harm to the child? Would the threat be as effective as the deed? Were these lawyers capable of understanding such a threat would be his last desperate gift to them?

Carl always enjoyed the ride to Moraine. He had become accustomed to the road, to the beauty of the country. He had watched the corn seem to spurt upward before his eyes. He wondered how anyone from an innocent place like this could commit an act of violence. The farmers and small town people were decent. What would it be like to get to know them, to chat about their kids and high school football games, and who was going to Florida for the winter. He felt protected by their decency. Defending a criminal case here was paradise compared to big city practice, where

114

parking was nearly impossible and a three-block walk to the courthouse exposed lawyers to street crime. At least in Moraine he could relax and count on being treated with respect, if not honor.

It was a little after eight when he entered the courthouse, the dead hour after county workers show up, a time for viewing baby pictures and sharing coffee cake.

Carl had been procrastinating about interviewing the eye witnesses who worked in the Courthouse. Most would be hostile. He strolled into the charred end of the second floor and approached Judge Esker's former clerk. Since the death of Judge Esker, she had nothing to do but try to make order out of his undecided cases. Even if she were uncooperative, it might give him a clue as to what the prosecutor had asked her.

He had been told her name was Melinda. She stopped typing a docket sheet and stared at him. "I've been waiting for you to show up. Do I have to talk to you?" She sat back against her green steno chair. Her pink sweater was draped across her back, sleeves loosely knotted across her chest. When she crossed her arms, it made her look like a severe, four-armed deity.

He tried being friendly. "Melinda, now you know I have to ask you about the case at some point. Wouldn't you rather talk to me before you get on the stand? It might get you on and off more quickly."

She rolled that around for a second and said, "I suppose. But I'm not happy with this. Not happy at all."

"Well, I'll be gentle. I know it's your first time." He said it with a straight face. She didn't react. "What do you remember?"

"Nothing. Nothing, really."

"Well, let's talk about what kind of nothing. What were you doing when it started?"

"We were in the middle of a divorce. Judge Esker hated those cases. Just hated them. He got to the point where he lost his temper when they went on more than half a day. Well, anyway, this one was dragging on." She paused as if she were having difficulty crossing a threshold.

"Yes. Go on."

"Hurshal Taylor was cross examining the husband about his drinking. They were about to go over the guy's tax return. Well, the door opened with a big squeal! I looked up and the guy had a whiskey bottle with a burning rag. He threw it while he was running. I watched it fly through the air, but I couldn't do anything but scream. It almost hit Mr. Taylor. Then it broke on the front edge of the bench and exploded. A ball of fire just kind of rolled over Judge Esker." She swallowed hard before continuing. "It was like the fire was looking for him. He couldn't get out of the way." Her eyes were wide, on the verge of tears.

"Yes. Please go on. I know this isn't easy."

Melinda reached for a Kleenex and blew her nose. "It was horrible! He was covered with fire, like it was eating him. He was rolling around and screaming…" She stopped and dabbed at her eyes.

Carl knew he had to turn off the image of the burning judge. "Let's just concentrate on the person who threw the bottle, shall we?"

Melinda straightened up a little and took a breath. "He was dressed in a gray sweatshirt with a hood pulled up over his head. The drawstring was tied so you couldn't see his face except for his sunglasses."

"Anything special about the sunglasses?"

"They were dark. Very dark. Thick black plastic frames and dark lenses. I'll never forget that. Kind of like Buddy Holly glasses. Maybe Roy Orbison's."

"What about the pants?"

"I don't know, nothing special. Probably Jeans. Yes, I suppose it was Jeans."

"Look in your mind's eye. Anything stand out? A watch? Any jewelry?"

"Mmmmm. No, not that I can remember."

"Which hand did he use to throw the bottle?"

"I guess it was...yes...it was his right hand. Definitely." She was now exploring the image in her memory.

"You were sitting next to the Judge at the Clerk's desk, right?"

"Yes."

"So you and the Judge were the only ones facing the man as he came in?"

"Well, the husband on the stand, of course. I think Clancy, the Bailiff, was asleep. The rest of the people in the courtroom were facing us."

"How long was the man in the room?"

"It was really quick. He just opened the door, ran a few steps and threw it. Then he turned around and ran back through the door."

"How tall was he?"

"Oh, gee, I don't know. Average, maybe. Kind of slight. Aldin is kind of skinny."

Carl felt a twinge at her mentioning Aldin by name. "Did he say anything?"

"No."

"Can you remember anything else?"

"No, I was watching Judge Esker. It was horrible! Then I ran for the door into chambers. The courtroom was full of smoke and everyone was coughing and screaming and shouting. I didn't really see Aldin after the bomb exploded."

Melinda was depleted. She was obviously convinced it was Aldin who had thrown the firebomb and she could be counted on to tell Gadsen about Carl's questions. He decided to toss a red herring into the case. "So if you couldn't see any of the features of this person and he didn't say anything, how do you know it was a man?"

She blinked. Twice.

"Well?"

"Oh, it had to be!"

"Why? Your description could fit an athletic woman just as well, couldn't it?"

She wrinkled up her nose. "A woman wouldn't do a thing like that."

"Why not?"

Melinda was thoughtful. "Because it was Aldin. It was just the kind of stuff that sneaky little…well…anybody can tell you about the stuff he's pulled."

"Like?"

She became aggressive. "Like the fake heart attack."

"Pardon me?"

"The heart attack. The time he was being sued for a bill, something about fixing his boat. A lawyer from Decatur was trying the case for the boat company. Aldin always dragged out his court things. Here we were, having a jury trial over a bill for a couple of thousand dollars. Well, Aldin was about to make his opening statement and all of a sudden he fell over on the courtroom floor, twitching his legs and moaning. Everybody was very concerned. The lawyer was kneeling over him trying to see if he needed CPR. We called the ambulance and there was a deputy who was a paramedic. He checked him out. Finally they took him to Carle Clinic in Urbana, and they weren't fooled. They sent him home and we were back in trial the next day. The jury must have felt sorry for him because they came back with a verdict that he didn't owe the bill."

"He won?"

She gave Carl a sour look. "I guess you can call it that…if you don't mind cheating to win. I heard he was buying drinks for all the other deadbeats over at Terminal Moraine. That's Mr. Wally Aldin, and that's why I recognized him."

Midnight

Dani was letting her thoughts drift. Susan was sleeping-over at the home of one of her friends and Dani had the liberty of closing the *Pages for All Ages* bookstore at eleven. She stopped at Merry Ann's Diner to burrow into Iris Chang's book, *The Rape of Nanking*. Iris had attended University High in Urbana and so would Susan.

After a grilled cheese sandwich, she pointed her Cherokee toward campus and cruised down Green street. The atmosphere was sedate compared with her undergrad years. REO Speedwagon and Head East had been local bands at the Brown Jug and the Red Lion. John Belushi and Dan Fogelberg had played the Red Herring. Dani wondered whether there would be any legends arising from this crop of kids.

She thought about Carl and his request for help. Just thinking about terrorism made her angry. Why should she even consider helping? A lifetime at the bar answered her question. She had learned to control her fiery emotions. At least she had made an attempt. She laid out the reasons to get involved. The logical ones.

First, defending people in trouble, that's what lawyers do. They help people, even people they detest. They make sure the system is fair, even to its enemies. She had always been told this was the highest calling of the profession.

Second, she was very good at what was needed, and Carl wasn't. She had often wondered whether he had some sort of dyslexia when it came to search and seizure.

Finally, and most importantly, the overwhelming consideration was the death penalty. She was totally against it—for any reason. She felt any person who didn't actively resist the death penalty was like the Germans who smelled the death camps and ignored their own noses.

Maybe there were a few hidden reasons, but they weren't logical. Maybe she detected a personal note in Carl's call. Would that be so bad? They were adults and the divorce was over. Could they at least be friends? Were there any second chances in this new millennium? She didn't want to read too much into Carl's call because she didn't want to look foolish.

But was there more?

Only one way to find out.

Three a.m. is the time the universe selects for humans to lie in bed and explore the future; to fear and desire; to mourn lost possibilities.

Since taking the Aldin case Carl had fallen into strange sleep patterns, so exhausted he'd be cross-eyed by the end of the six o'clock news. Revive, read, work, then watch the History Channel or point the car toward Katsinas until midnight. After, sleep for a few hours and awake at three to keep his appointment with near misses and unreachable dreams.

This particular night he was serving a penalty for sharing an onion loaf with some guys while watching the Cubs blow a lead in the ninth.

Laura Aldin was haunting his dreams. She was nude at that hotel window, her breasts against the glass, in the throes of ecstasy. The dream was imprinted with jealousy and arousal and helplessness as she burst through the window in a slow-motion gush of glass shards, spreading her arms to fly, floating across the sky of Chicago while he stood in the street staring up at her as she disappeared in a rush of frustration. "Laura, but she's only a dream." He felt a surge in his chest and he found himself sitting up, fighting back acid reflux.

Wide awake and dosed with DiGel, he thought how little his fifties resembled the plans he had made. He still felt seventeen on the inside but he had explored life's cul-de-sacs. Physically he felt as if he had been ordered to carry handicap weights to compensate for the advantage of experience.

The television made strange, flickering patterns on the ceiling as it pumped an infomercial into the bedroom. He tried to recapture the spectral Laura of his dream. As he closed his eyes, her face floated back to him and flooded him with guilty pleasure. Carl had an urge to reach for the phone and call her. He flipped on the light and searched the Aldin file that was next to the bed. On the index sticker was Wally's home number. Laura's number. He looked at the phone and willed himself to overcome the impulse.

He searched for an antidote to Laura, something real and better and noble. A return to the promises he never meant to break. He thought of Susan and Dani.

Should he get up and turn on the computer? Read the new James Lee Burke? Review some pleadings faxed to him? It wasn't wise to lie there wide-awake and relive blunders and lost possibilities, but it was smarter than calling Laura Aldin at 3 a.m.

He picked up the remote and punched up jazz on the satellite dish. Classic jazz. Sarah Vaughn was singing *Midnight Sun*.

Laura was a dead end, the wife of a client, 25 years younger and vulnerable from her disappointing marriage. Even thinking about her was playing with fire. Going beyond thought could cost him dearly. But his right brain wanted her.

Forget it, Carl. At least try.

He thought about his life. Old age wasn't knocking at the door, but he could hear it coming up the front walk. If he stroked out in the next minute, who would know or care?

His last female companion, if that was the way you could describe a woman with whom he shared sex a couple of times a month, was a director in a video production house in Chicago. She was witty and knew the tough answers in trivia games. At thirty-nine she was smooth and tall and wore clothes like a model. Her legs were votive objects. She was the Art Institute and Russian Tea Time, or Gianni's before the Steppenwolf Theater. Not a ballgame and a hot dog. He was a release for her as much as she was for him, but a weekend with her was more a contest than a tryst. He was always ready to put a hundred miles between them by Sunday.

On this night, it was Laura. Badly-used innocence, prairie in her soul. The after-image of a pioneer woman who baked pies with a pinch of this and a handful of that. Eyes sparkling in a face innocent of postmodernism and French film. She was a Bourke-White photograph. He wanted to show her treasures from his childhood cigar box.

Carl shook his head and tried to sleep, but an endless sensory loop was playing. Her face, the lightness of her body and the sway of her long, dark hair; an over-the-shoulder smile as she walked away.

He dialed up the History Channel. Another Hitler documentary. The Second World War in syndication. He turned on the light and picked up the Burke.

At 5 a.m. the world was fresh. The rhythms of the country sounded in the chirping of the birds and the distant barking of farm dogs. Brother Bill watched deer crossing the fields in graceful stride, making for the timber along the river. He never could understand how anyone could kill such creatures for sport. They were God's gift to man, but only to assuage hunger, and in America people didn't need to be hungry if they would only help themselves. Killing anything without a good reason was wrong, especially killing a human. But if need be, he could take a life.

Suffer the little children to come unto me.

That phrase had prowled through his mind all night long. It remained as he drove to town to order fertilizer.

Suffer.

The idea of a child suffering was preying on him. Yes, this Hardman girl was worldly. She was over the age of seven, and was responsible for her sins. But she was still a beautiful little girl.

For of such are the Kingdom of God.

To think of her suffering set off strange feelings in Bill he didn't like, feelings alien to the Word.

Even threatening harm would surely hurt her. The parents would go into a panic and take protective steps that would infect the child with fear. She was not created to live in dread. She was created to enjoy the sunshine, carefree and joyous.

No, the child should not be the focus. The lawyers and Aldin would have to be the targets.

There would be no tender feelings generated in Brother Bill concerning the lawyer-whores who were doing their best to betray right and truth. He would do whatever would be needed to remove Hardman and his ex-wife, even permanently.

———————————

How much after midnight it was the man couldn't say. One hour tended to grade into the next after hitting a couple of bars. He stared with hollow eyes. He had merely increased the sum total of wrong in the world. What about the lawyer? The Arab?

Merry Ann's

The fluorescence of Merry Ann's Diner was spilling onto the street. Carl pulled the Jaguar into the lot.

Merry Ann's is too sophisticated to pretend to look like a retired railroad car. Campus professionals mix with drunks and pierced young people. After midnight it is a nexus of textbooks and laptops, of faltering careers and marital disasters.

When Dani walked in, Carl was digesting the *Tribune* sports section. He almost spilled his coffee on the box scores. It wasn't often he was totally at a loss about anything. Almost never was he out of words.

She was dressed in a blue Nike running suit. Her face displayed a little lipstick and blush. Dani didn't need much to enhance her dark attractiveness. She walked up to Carl and asked, "Private séance?"

"No, of course not. Good to see you." That sounded weak to him and he searched in vain for something else to say.

She smiled. "Always good to be seen."

He said, "I'm surprised to see you...as if you couldn't tell."

"I should be surprised to see you. This is one of my regular stops. Now that Susan has a life of her own, it's usually the third shift."

He seized the moment. "I'd like it if we could sit and talk. Just talk about things when we're not handing over Susan at the front door."

124

She said, "Yes, I think it's time for that."

"This place OK?"

"Champaign is Champaign and grease is grease. Not a lot of options after midnight. We can shift to a juice bar if we're still talking when the sun comes up."

He looked at her to see if she were kidding. "I guess I don't have anything definite to do until the day after tomorrow. We can drive up to the Palmer House for breakfast if you'd like."

A subtle emotion crossed her face, something like nostalgia. "I guess Champaign will do. We need to talk about what you have in mind for me. You know, Carl, we aren't exactly operating in a vacuum. There's Susan and there's still some baggage we haven't unpacked. How would we cope with all that?"

He reached for his coffee and sipped it the way a smoker would light up while formulating an answer to one of life's important questions. Finally he said, "Damned if I know."

She waited.

"I guess I ought to start with the easy stuff. We're both lawyers and we both have a few ideals that don't get split up in a divorce. There's a guy facing the death penalty and neither of us wants to see that happen. I'm still waiting for some genius to show up and enter his appearance. Until that happens, I'm stuck with it."

She nodded.

"Moving right along, you're extremely good at what you do and I'm never going to learn search and seizure. After an hour in a library, I'm wanting to go out in the hall and talk about baseball or the rhubarb crop. And there isn't anybody I trust as much as you."

She nodded. "Thank you."

"Now we're down to 'all that'." He killed time with another sip. "Frankly, my dear, I don't know."

She leaned back against the booth, folding her arms across her chest.

The waitress plopped down a mug of coffee and two containers of cream. Dani waited until she was gone. "Carl Hardman admitting he doesn't know? Now there's a sound bite."

He refused to take the bait. She had a way of provoking to mask her feelings. "You and I both know when you say things like that you're hurting. Is there something bad going on in your life?"

She dumped a second cream into the coffee. "Not exactly cappuccino."

He went on, "Being honest with you, my life hasn't exactly been euphoric since you and Susan left."

She said, "That sort of thing happens after a divorce."

Carl let it bounce off. "I've met myself coming and going to Champaign to see her. I think I've been a good father under the circumstances."

"Correction. You've been a champion dad. I haven't erected any barriers to that. A lot of women make the child a battlefield."

He nodded. "Agreed. I guess that's number three, right? How many ex-spouses can agree on that many things?"

She said, "Add one more. You've been on my mind just like I've apparently been on yours. The only difference is you haven't seen me drive past your place at midnight."

"Does that mean you haven't or just that I haven't seen you?"

She cracked a smile. "I'll never tell."

"So are there any other things we can get together on?" The double meaning was not far below the surface.

She ignored it. "I'm not going to tell you life has been perfect. I've had a couple of male friends who treated Susan well. For a while I thought they might be possibilities, but I managed to run them off somehow."

He resisted an impulse to call them fools. Instead he countered with his own recent history. "I won't kid you, Dani. I've met some women since we split up. There have been several of what we've come to call 'relationships'. I guess that's a better word than the old Anglo-Saxon terms."

"You do seem to find a way to reduce things to their essentials."

He smiled and continued. "Anyway, you asked what else, and I'd have to say I'm not emotionally involved with anybody." He stopped and looked at her for a second, then shook his head. "Why try to bullshit you? There hasn't been anybody I'd be willing to nurse through stomach flu."

She laughed, "Always the true romantic."

"Well, doesn't it come down to that? If there's no chemistry, what keeps middle-aged people together in the face of snoring, bad backs, and sagging body parts?"

She nodded. "Of course, you're right. I've always believed that. It's called 'love,' Carl. One of the philosophical concepts you were never very good at articulating."

He pursed his lips, acknowledging her point. "Doesn't ostensive definition count? Doesn't doing it beat talking about it?"

She said, "I suppose a woman needs to learn about men if she's going to keep from going nuts. Like accepting that Paul Newman's getting old."

The conversation was overheating. Without admitting it they both realized the need to change the subject. He asked about Susan's recital. They made plans for visitation. Then they talked about friends they no longer knew. An hour went by then another. They were having fun and filling in gaps. The old problems seemed to have rounded edges. As the night drifted on they both understood the rendezvous had to come to an end. But how to end it?

Finally, when Carl started telling her a story about one of the judges they knew, she reached across the table and took his hand. "Carl, I have to go. You can sleep all day if you keep the TV reporters out of your bedroom. I've got 35 law students to entertain in about five hours."

He nodded, but seemed unhappy the conversation had played out. "I guess we never did cover the rest of the things we agree on."

She said, "Life's long," and got up and left.

On the way she dropped a five dollar bill on the cash register and smiled at him as she disappeared into the prairie night.

127

Milwaukee's Famous

Two men at the bar wore baseball caps that said "Burn Gasohol." They were eating greasy cheeseburgers at the Terminal Moraine. Behind the bar a busty redhead in her early forties was flirting with them. Clusters of small town types filled the tables. The painted windows created a level of murkiness that gave no clue as to the time out in the real world. Most of the illumination came from Bud Lite signs. Alan Jackson was singing "Don't Rock the Juke Box".

At the end of the bar, Harvey Barnes was drinking his lunch. He was wearing a cheap blue blazer over a frayed white shirt. His maroon club tie, hanging slack from his unbuttoned collar, was from the collection of Sam Walton. He was studying the *St. Louis Post Dispatch* sports pages.

Carl had no trouble picking him out, having checked the composite picture of the Lincoln County Bar Association in the Courthouse. It crossed his mind that Harvey may have taken the "bar" a bit too literally.

Carl sat down next to him and was drawn to the road map of small veins on Harvey's nose as he continued to stare at an article about the stratospheric price of scalped tickets for the upcoming Cubs-Cardinals series. Harvey said, "Pisses me off."

Carl wasn't certain whether it was said to him or was part of some ongoing soliloquy. "Pardon me?"

"Pisses me off. I coulda had tickets for tonight's game two months ago. Now I'd have to sell my car to get 'em."

Carl decided to play along. "What are they up to?"

"Lower level boxes maybe three hundred."

"Well, there's always TV."

Harvey shot Carl a disdainful look. "Yeah, and a porn flick is as good as a woman."

"I gather you're a serious baseball fan."

"That's like saying Clinton likes girls."

"Cubs or Cards?"

"My daddy and my momma got married before I came along. Cubs, of course."

The female bartender stopped drying a glass and gave him the finger.

Carl smiled. "Me too. When do you think we'll trade Lee?"

That was too much for Harvey. He winced. "You tapping into my nightmares?"

"No, but I need to tap your memory. I'm Carl..."

"I know who you are. You want to talk about my testimony, right?" Harvey abandoned the paper and swiveled around to face Carl.

"Right."

Harvey sucked in breath and let it out slowly. "I may as well tell you what I know. I'd expect as much if I were the poor bastard in your place, but I'd just as soon get my prostate checked."

"I've been known to probe on cross-examination, but not that far."

Harvey laughed and said, "Ok, you got me. Here or back at the abandoned shoe store where my alleged secretary plays computer games?"

Carl thought for a second. A lawyer behind his desk is like an Admiral on the bridge. "This is ok."

"Fine, always like to talk right here in my office. Teri, Hon, gimme another Bud. You?" He nodded at Carl.

"No thanks. Just a coke."

129

She asked, "Pepsi?"

"Fine." Carl reached into his inner suit coat pocket and pulled out two folded sheets of yellow pad. "Mind if I take notes?"

"Wish you would. I'll probably need to go over them to remember what I said."

"You having a hard time with this?"

Harvey took a large swig and savored it before swallowing. "Yeah. I guess so. The death scene was lifetime stuff. And I'm not real happy about being on the spot. I've tried a few criminal cases...not like you, maybe. I heard you were pretty good in your day. Well, anyway, I've been there. The bottom line is I can't make a positive i.d. on him. That's what you want to hear, isn't it?"

"You get right to the pay dirt, don't you."

"Well, there's no use beating around the bush. Now that's the good news. The bad news is maybe by the time you go to trial I'm gonna be a lot more certain."

Carl's eyebrows went up. "Why's that?"

Harvey dumped the rest of the draft down his throat. A few drops ran down his chin and landed on his shirt. He didn't seem to care. "Ever try to earn a living in a burg like this? Want to eat lunch here at the five-star Terminal Moraine every day?"

"I'm not a big city type, remember."

"Look, you're outta my league. I'm making the payments and that's about it. If they cut me out of a few appointed cases and guardian fees, I'm fucked. And Aldin's not exactly Mr. Wonderful."

"Why do you say that?"

"He's screwed over just about everybody at one time or another."

"Like?"

"What would you call it if a guy gets sued by Mastercard and removes the case to Federal Court?" Harvey flashed him a look that claimed one up.

Carl blinked. "He did what?"

"Removed it. He removed the damn thing to Federal Court, claiming prejudice as a member of a minority group. You remember, they told us about that in law school. I never actually saw it done before. Really it's kinda neat. You just file a Petition in Federal Court alleging prejudice in the state court or some Federal remedy or diversity or something. It's automatically removed to Federal Court and nothing more can be done in state court. Play your cards right and it could take forever to wade through Federal procedure before it gets sent back to state court." Harvey obviously enjoyed telling the story.

Carl vaguely recalled the removal right, which he hadn't thought of since law school. "But isn't removal pretty limited? I mean, there aren't very many reasons to remove something."

"You got that right. You and I'd probably get sanctioned for dumping a garden-variety collection case into the Federal system. But what can they do to Aldin? He hasn't got a license to lose."

Carl was amazed at his client's creativity. "I guess you're right. What happened after he removed it? I mean, there's gotta be a day of reckoning there someplace, even in Federal Court."

"Yeah, but that's gonna require a Petition for Remand in Federal Court, and what collection lawyer is gonna go through all that bullshit just to collect seven grand for Mastercard and get paid a third? Some collection drudge wouldn't know as much about removal as Wally. And besides, when Wally lost, he'd be a cinch to appeal and that'd last another year. The credit card company wrote the damn thing off."

Carl grinned. "You've got to hand it to him. That's pretty slick."

"Slicker'n owl shit. That's for sure. But I'm just thanking my lucky stars I wasn't involved."

"So you're worried about what happens if you don't go along with the program?"

"Yeah, but I'm still enough of a lawyer to remember what I ought to do. Maybe if I drink enough of this stuff I can forget it."

Carl felt sympathetic but had to press him. "You know I've stuck my neck out about a mile coming in here trying to get Aldin a fair trial. Doesn't look like he's gonna get much of a chance to pass on his genes the way this Judge has been staring at us."

"Krucifyin' Kirsten? Judge Harridan?"

Carl groaned. "Harridan? Is that what they call her around here?"

"Yeah. She comes over from Decatur when somebody bumps ...uh...when somebody used to bump Esker off a case for prejudice. Guess somebody bumped him real good this time. We wondered if you checked her out while you still had a bump coming. But if you'd bonged her, they'd have found another one, I guess. Might have been worse, but I don't see how."

"I made a few calls to some lawyers over there and nobody warned me. Maybe they weren't exactly terrorist sympathizers." Carl drank from his Pepsi and crunched an ice cube. "So what do we have here, then? What can I count on when the chips are down?"

"You can count on me being there with my necktie all the way up. Beyond that, I'm saying I don't know how much I'm gonna remember. It was kinda quick and we were all trying to get out of there. Not exactly a line up. The sweatshirt and glasses covered most of his face. But I gotta live here after the case is over. I guess you can count on that."

Carl didn't respect the remark but didn't want to lock horns with Harvey, hoping his better instincts would eventually prevail. "Listen, I'm not hard to find. Think it over. You know as well as I do that the identification in this case sucks. No way anybody could possibly know who did it. They've got Aldin fingered for being a pest, bothering the local court system."

"Pest? That's like saying Michael Moore's a Bush critic. Aldin is a cham-peen pettifogger. Big time! The stuff he's pulled...hell...nobody in town can stand him. Did anybody tell you he figured out that he gets a continuance if he sues his own lawyer? One time he sued the bank lawyer for fifty million in Federal Court for trying to repossess his car. Got the case continued for a year."

Harvey went on to describe how Wally had spiraled down and down into his guerrilla war against the court system.

"Why do you call it a guerrilla war?" Carl was straining to see it from Wally's perspective.

"You gotta read the pleadings he files. They're from Middle Earth. He owed Sears about four grand on a credit card and promptly filed a small claims complaint against them for fifteen dollars, claiming a defective hammer or something. The paperwork went on for about 10 pages of blather about the hammer being made in Communist China. But he stuck in a Demand to Admit right in the middle, demanding Sears admit he'd paid cash for the hammer and didn't owe Sears any other money, and that his Sears credit card had been canceled five years before..."

Carl picked up the thread. "...and he served this small claims lawsuit on the Sears corporate offices with the Demand to Admit sandwiched inside, and somebody probably gave it a once over and decided it was a whole lot of paper to read for a fifteen dollar lawsuit."

Harvey picked it up. "Exactly. The complaint probably got coffee rings and finally got handed up the line like any other letter bitching about Sears' products. Nobody bothered to read the Demand to Admit contained in some stupid complaint for fifteen bucks. If they did, who the hell in the Sears middle bureaucracy would know you've only got 28 days to deny the allegations in a Demand to Admit or they become true?"

Carl's smile betrayed a grudging admiration. "So he gets a bunch of bogus facts admitted in the Small Claims suit and uses them to win the bigger suit. By the rules of the game, the fact that they aren't denied in the fifteen dollar case makes them true and he wins the big collection case. Pretty smart."

Harvey nodded. "And pretty sleazy. I told you it's a guerrilla war to Wally, just like the Middle East. He doesn't give a shit. He thinks cheating big corporations is patriotic. Funny what you can believe when you want to keep your own money in your own wallet."

133

Carl winced. "Nevertheless, you're a pro and you've got to admit the identification is pretty thin."

"It may be thin, but it remains to be seen whether I've got to admit it. That's the present state of the market. Ask all you want, that's what I've got right now. Wanna talk baseball?"

Carl got up and threw four singles into a puddle on the bar. "Another time, thanks."

Welcome Aboard

The phone rang at 7 a.m. and Carl answered, "Hello" with a voice edged with phlegm.

"You're lucky you didn't get custody. Girls need an hour in the bathroom every morning. You'd be awake by six."

Instantly he was lucid. It was Dani.

"I guess I wouldn't be able to stay up all night working if that happened."

"A likely story. You probably ran the last blonde out at 4 a.m."

He wondered why she was playing with him. Then he remembered she had said she would get back to him about helping with him on the suppression of evidence. "If there was a blonde here at 4 a.m., I hope she was doing something useful about search and seizure."

"You get right to the point, don't you, Carl? Once a bullshitter, always a bullshitter."

"Dani, I..."

"Stop before you screw it up. I'm going to help if you still want me."

His spirits leaped. It was like someone volunteering to help move heavy furniture or chop wood, but it was more than that. He let hope drift into speculation. "Sure I want you. I mean...I want you to help me."

"Well, fine, but I'm gonna have to do it my way..."

He thought *So what's new?*

"...and we'll need a few law students. I think I can draft a couple of good ones who need some real-world experience for their resumé."

"You don't know how much this means to me!"

"I'll pretend I do. Now let's get to work. I'll meet you at the library at 3:00 sharp."

"That's fine. Give my little girl a hug."

"Our little girl."

With that she hung up.

— · — · —— · —— · —— · —— · —— · ——

The Motion to Suppress was short and easy to prepare, consisting of three pages, it challenged the seizure of certain tangible objects from Wally Aldin's person, vehicle, and residence. It alleged state and federal agents had conducted an unconstitutional search, the illegal fruits of which were then used to secure a search warrant. The motion stated that most of what was important in the upcoming trial — the gas container and any other items seized which could connect Aldin with the crime — should be suppressed and the prosecution barred from using them in evidence.

The motion was succinct. What would take weeks, however, would be the brief. Dani succeeded in enlisting law student volunteers eager to bloody themselves in a real case. They downloaded, indexed, checked to determine whether their cases were still good law. They even read a few old fashioned printed books and law journals.

Dani worked side-by-side with the students. The library was not Carl's natural hunting ground, but this particular afternoon he was seated in one of the alcoves behind a pile of books that kept getting taller. Dani was across the table, whispering and pointing to a section in the old Supreme Court *Spinelli* case that still had vitality. The young woman who hunkered next to Dani's chair was dressed in designer Jeans and a Banana Republic sweater. Carl thought how different she was from the 'Sixties-

136

Dani who took off a semester from law school to help him defend a murder case. Now Dani was the voice of experience as well as a mother and a supporter of the symphony and a teacher of wide-eyed young people who idolized her.

As if sensing his thoughts, she looked up from her conversation with a quizzical expression and said, "What?"

He shook his head and buried his gaze in the yellow pad where the argument on the Motion to Suppress was being hammered into shape.

— · — · — · — · — · — · — · — · —

It was a warm morning. Carl was finally on his way to file the Motion to Suppress at the courthouse in Moraine. The drive put him in a good mood. Thin layers of mist loitered in the fields. He stopped twice to point the Nikon out the passenger window and take pictures before the sun burned away the humidity. A little after eight he saw the huge concrete silos of the grain elevator east of Moraine. They reminded him of medieval battlements. Carl had called the Circuit Clerk the previous afternoon to make sure the office would be open to file the motion at eight a.m. The woman's voice on the phone had been cold and she had implied he must be an idiot for not knowing the office hours.

As he drove into town, his thoughts were interrupted as he began to notice an unusual number of people on the sidewalk. Some were walking toward the courthouse, some standing on lawns, looking in that direction. At first Carl thought nothing of it, but as he drove further, it was plain that something was going on.

In front of the courthouse, a large crowd was watching several dozen people waving hand-lettered picket signs. As a child of the 'Sixties, he had watched peaceful protests many times, but these people seemed angry. Ominous. The signs said things like *Death To Terrorists* and *Avenge 9-11*. There were a number of others, but when he slowed to read them, a woman shouted, "That's him! That's the lawyer!" The crowd began to surge and men stepped into the street in front of the Jaguar. They were shaking their fists at him.

He promised himself that in the future he wouldn't be quite so open about when he planned to come to Moraine.

Angry shouts from men and high-pitched screams from women fueled the turmoil. About a dozen demonstrators were surrounding the car and hundreds of bystanders seemed on the edge of becoming involved.

His first impulse was to keep driving; to keep the wheels moving slowly and expect the men in front of the car to use common sense and get out of the way. They had nothing like that in mind. The continued progress of the car infuriated them and they began to pile on the hood. One man with wild eyes was slamming an arm crutch repeatedly against the driver's window. Carl winced with each blow, but the aluminum crutch wasn't heavy enough to smash the glass. This seemed to infuriate the man. Pounding the flat of his left palm on the windshield was a large man lost in fury, shouting something about the Lord.

Carl began to realize the situation had the potential for somebody sustaining a serious injury. Probably him. He checked his seat belt.

Panic seized him. He couldn't believe this little American town could harbor dozens of zealots threatening his life. The bystanders seemed ready to join in. It shook him to the core. How could ordinary Americans from the heartland permit a stranger in their town to be beaten or killed? He had a flashback to Spencer Tracy in *A Bad Day At Black Rock.*

Carl looked out the passenger window, desperate for help. He saw a beefy man wearing a tan uniform with a star on his chest. The face came back from the arraignment. It was Sheriff Burnett. Carl had spent a lifetime believing in the law and its power to separate right from wrong. He expected to see the Sheriff wade into the crowd and try to disburse the angry mass, or at least use the radio attached to his belt to call for help.

Instead, the Sheriff crossed his arms and displayed a smile that made Carl feel a chill run up his back.

Now the men at the driver's door were surging against the window, blocking Carl's vision. Others were yanking the handle of the passenger doors. The car began rocking from side, each sway becoming a little more extreme. If they kept it up, the Jaguar would roll on its side with Carl in it. He could still see through the windshield because the men on the hood had stepped back a few feet to avoid being turned over with the car.

Ahead was a space a few feet wide. He was about to hit the accelerator when two TV cameras appeared and filled the space he was aiming for. They squared themselves, blocking his last chance. He saw the blinking red lights on the cameras and fury overcame him. If he had to hit anybody, it would be the ghouls who were marketing stupidity and prejudice.

It was fortunate Carl wasn't twenty years younger, when the consequences of impulsive acts didn't play out so clearly before decisions were irreversible. His mind projected the edited version that would play on millions of TV screens that night. He would be the cold-hearted defender of a terrorist mowing down helpless journalists and ordinary country people with an imported luxury car.

As hard as it was, he took his foot off the accelerator and resigned himself to being turned over in the car, possibly beaten. At least Aldin wouldn't have to pay the price for his escape. He began to wonder how easily Jaguars caught fire.

Just as he was reaching to turn off the engine, he saw the man with the arm crutch being jerked back from the driver's window. Then a man's back filled the space and he heard a loud voice shout "FBI!" several times. Each time the rocking of the car lessened, then ceased.

The voice shouted, "Get away from the car! NOW!"

Carl watched as the faces in front of him began to change. Bewildered glances shifted from Carl to the FBI agent. Then sullen resignation and retreat.

The agent looked down at Carl and shouted, "Listen to me! Drive slowly...SLOWLY...out of here! I'll be right here until you get clear!"

It didn't take any persuasion for Carl to follow the order. He switched into low gear. His legs were shaking and he didn't want to accidentally run over anybody.

The car began to roll forward and a path cleared as the agent continued to shout at anybody whose body language seemed to imply resistance.

The crowd was now focused on the FBI agent, coating him with a creative gush of profanity. He jogged briskly alongside the car as it emerged from the crowd, holding the driver's door handle. A few men and one very large woman continued to follow, but kept their distance. The woman was shouting, "God will get you!" over and over. The man with the crutch screamed "Fuckin' Feds!" as he was left behind.

Standing clear from the crowd was Sheriff Burnett. His smirk had vanished, but what distracted Carl was the only face in the angry crowd not distorted with surly shouts. This face was gaunt and agonized. Its owner was standing still and was staring at Carl. It was a face he had seen in Court several times. Although the man's mouth was closed, the face was reminiscent of Edvard Munch's painting, *The Scream.* It was puzzling and upsetting. Why did this man keep turning up?

The FBI agent slapped the rear door several times and Carl came back to the problem at hand. He popped the lock. The agent yanked the door open and rolled into the back seat, leaving the door open until Carl's rapid acceleration made it swing shut. He hit the lock button as they turned the corner.

Carl could see the agent in the rear view mirror. He was deep into middle age and was out of breath and red in the face. It surprised Carl that he had risked the crowd's fury.

Carl drove several blocks before he stopped the car. He took his hands off the wheel. They were shaking violently. He turned and faced the agent, searching for words. "Who are you?"

The agent barked, "Fossum. Special Agent Roger Fossum, FBI."

Carl opened his mouth to thank him.

Fossum's scowl stopped him. "Don't say anything. Don't. I think you're slime, but the law's the law. That asshole Burnett would have let them have you. He probably thought he was getting votes from those morons."

Carl said, "Anyway…whatever…I want to thank you."

Fossum opened the door and as he stepped out he said, "For what? Doing my job? Dealing with crazies is a big part of it, anymore. If I were you, I think I'd find some other place to be until these jerks get hungry and go home. Be more careful driving into riots!"

And he was gone.

Carl took the hint and didn't linger another minute in Moraine.

Brother Bill was in anguish as he sat on his back porch and watched the stars. He unconsciously swatted at mosquitoes swarming from breeding pools left by the summer rains. But it wasn't mosquito bites that upset him. The problem of Aldin and the lawyer would not let him sleep. He had decided several days ago he simply could not threaten or harm the child, Susan. He hadn't the courage to take action against a pretty, white little girl. He felt ashamed that his moral fiber had weakened.

That had made him review the options for direct action. Picketing was one of them. If a demonstration turned ugly, that was often useful, and that's the way it turned out.

Now the problem had become even more complicated. The demonstration that morning had been frustrated by the FBI. How did they know? Was he under surveillance?

Late in the previous afternoon, he had received a call from Henry, of the Liberty Church, telling him that he had heard the women in the Circuit Clerk's office talking when he had been at the counter filing a small claims lawsuit. They said Hardman, the lawyer for the murderer, was going to be filing something early the next morning. Armed with this, Bill had called an emergency meeting to plan a demonstration for eight the next morning. The news of it had spread quickly in Moraine.

The turnout had been impressive. All the members but Alice had kept their promises and were formed up in front of the main entrance. The crowd was growing and seemed ready to support the picketers.

When the lawyer drove up, it all began to move very quickly and it would have ended with a solid blow against evil, but for the FBI agent.

He had stepped out of the crowd to save the lawyer. How could one man have put fear into the hearts of the Liberty Church members? They had faded and turned back.

After it was over, Bill had found himself standing on the sidewalk within earshot of Sheriff Burnett who was cursing the FBI to one of his deputies. He had called on his radio, ordering his patrols to find the lawyer and follow him.

But what sent a shock through Bill was what the Sheriff said next. He said to the deputy, "If the fuckin' FBI is gonna stick its nose into these demonstrations, we're gonna have to shut them down first. The publicity. We can't have no TV showin' us up."

Bill knew another door had closed. Demonstrations were no longer an option. Righteousness would have to find a new way.

What to do? He knew from the readings on the Internet the movement was decentralized to protect it from infiltration. He believed it was up to him to take action, and to live with his decision, but he felt a numbing hand holding him back. It must be Satan standing in the way of God's plan. How could he find reassurance, find the power to act? Where could he find an ally to give him strength for his mission?

Although it was his call, there were others who could understand and who might have ideas on how to accomplish the mission. For many years he had been drawn to the Christian Identity movement without trying to reconcile its teachings with his conventional Christian fundamentalism. He had attended patriot convocations and camps. He had met many people from all walks who shared his terror that America was disappearing all around them, being melted down by internationalists and liberals and

142

races of many shades. The immediacy of the Aldin case was a weight on his chest.

There had to be someone who could supply him with certitude and moral reinforcement.

He remembered David Koresh and a dozen other martyrs. They were all gone. Then his mind turned to someone who had lived his life nearby, someone who knew Central Illinois. Matt Hale, head of the World Church of the Creator, now rotting in a federal prison cell for planning to murder a federal judge.

Matt Hale! Yes!

The World Church had crumbled after Hale's imprisonment.

Brother Bill knew Hale was unreachable, but there remained at least one of the members of his Church, a young man with fire in him and an unflinching commitment, ready to combat the things they all hated. The name came to him. P. Michael Madden. He was as close to Matt Hale as anyone could be. He would know what to do.

— · — · — · — · — · — · — · — · —

Carl awoke dizzy with the sensation of rolling back and forth in the Jaguar, with women screeching and picket signs smashing the windshield. Cold sweat beaded on his face. No longer were his dreams infused with the temptations of Laura. This was the third night since it had happened, since being attacked by the crowd — the third night he had awakened in terror.

He finally decided he had to cut and run or face squarely into the gale blowing through his mind. It made his stomach squirt acid when he thought about forcing himself to drive down that street in Moraine again and again until the case was over. It was clear that he would have to overcome this emotional barrier every time. In his mind, Moraine had transformed from a sleepy burg filled with quaint people into a brooding wilderness as dangerous as any big city slum.

But the remaining eye witnesses still had to be seen. Carl had to suck up his courage and get it done.

Tracking down Steven Yoder, the husband on the stand at the time of the firebombing, proved more difficult than Carl had expected. Central Illinois has a heavy growth of Yoders, a fertile offshoot from Amish roots. They seemed to have had a fetish for the first name of Steven.

Finally he located the right one, but only after breaking through the emotional barrier and driving to Moraine to check the divorce files. The clerk had informed him over the phone that it was against policy to give out information except in person. He knew the policy wouldn't apply to lawyers calling from offices down the street in Moraine.

He phoned Yoder about 4 p.m. The call was answered on the tenth ring.

"Hello." The voice seemed listless.

"Mr. Yoder? My name is Carl Hardman, and I'm..."

"I know who you are."

Carl was about to invent some stratagem for defusing anger when Yoder volunteered, "I'm probably one of the few guys in this county who'll buy you a beer."

Carl was surprised. He moved Yoder out of the Amish category, past Mennonite, and into the great, unwashed mass of small town Illinois beer drinkers. "Well, that's refreshing. What brand?"

Yoder chuckled. "You can meet me out here and you got Bud or I'll meet you in Tonada, and you got two choices."

"How about your place?"

"Know how to get here?"

"Follow the horse turds in the road?"

Yoder laughed. "No, them's the real Yoders from Arthur, still drivin' them Amish buggies. My people escaped. You in Moraine?"

"Yeah."

"Go north on the street right in front of the courthouse. Keep goin' four miles, take a left on the first blacktop after the bridge. Second house on the right. Big red barn."

"See you."

"Right."

The Jaguar loafed along at 60, ironing out the imperfections in Lincoln County's principal north-south blacktop road. Farms here were large, usually at least a section. The idea of owning a square mile of some of the richest land in the world would have seemed incredible to the persecuted European ancestors of these people. Millionaires walking around with cow manure on their pants, driving rusty pickups to the brokerage in Champaign or Decatur.

Carl checked the cruise control to make sure he wasn't risking a stop by one of Sheriff Burnett's henchmen. Carl dreaded the naked authority of a rural cop at home in the middle of nowhere.

An Eagles' tape was playing on the Jag's stereo system. *Take It Easy*. A corner in Winslow, Arizona. He tried to remember how Winslow had looked on a drive from Salt Lake City to Phoenix. *Blue Highways*. Drifting for a couple of weeks after the divorce, pretending it could be a lifetime.

He crossed an ancient iron bridge a single span wide. It groaned at the weight. A creek snaked its way through the fields before disappearing into a grove of secondary-growth trees. He looked across the field and saw the red barn Yoder had described. A minute later he stopped the car in the farmyard and was confronted by a chubby black lab barking hoarsely but wagging its tail.

A tall, heavy man with a dark crew cut leaned out the back door of a square, two-story frame house in need of a fresh coat of white paint. He looked at the dog and shouted, "Billy! Get back here!"

The dog ducked his head, retreating behind the man, and sat quietly.

"He won't hurt you. Named him after my ex brother-in-law who's a noted son of a bitch. I used to have a pit bull. He'd be through your window by now." Yoder, dressed in blue bib overalls, walked up to the car with a bowlegged gait that could only have been developed by walking with each foot in a different furrow.

145

"You said 'used to,' didn't you?"

Yoder laughed. "Very used to. The pit bull was screwin' the neighbor's collie bitch out on the road when the school bus come along and busted his leg. He only lived a couple of years after that, but it sure cut down his interest in sex. Some kinda message there for a divorced guy like me."

Carl cocked an eyebrow, not knowing how much rustic leg pulling was taking place.

Yoder read the look. "No shit. It really happened. Want your Bud inside or out?"

"Your choice."

"Then grab one of them lawn chairs. I'll be out in a minute."

Carl eased into one, hoping the flimsy aluminum frame would support him. He waited. The quiet was impressive. A few sparrows chirped in the lazy afternoon breeze. The rusty windmill twirled slowly.

Yoder appeared with a six pack of Budweiser, tore two from the plastic web and popped them open. He sat down carefully opposite Carl, sucking suds from his fingers. "Lucky to have these chairs from Wal-Mart, I guess. She got first pick of all the household shit. Only weighs one-twenty, but she had to have the strongest ones."

Carl closed his eyes and leaned back in his chair. "I lived through a divorce, too."

A glow of comradeship crossed Yoder's face. "Your wife use Hurshal Taylor?"

"No, some little jerk from back home."

"You're lucky you didn't have to defend yourself against both of 'em."

"I don't think I follow that."

"Taylor and his buddy Judge Esker. The Ex-Lax twins. Clean you out faster'n the IRS."

"Tell me about that."

Yoder drained his can and crushed it. He tore off another and popped it open. "Fuckin' leeches. I was gettin' reamed without no KY Jelly when the fire bomb went off. You never seen nothin' till you watched them two splittin' up a guy's money in court."

"You felt Judge Esker was going to rule against you?"

He chuckled an ironic little laugh. "Felt? Hell, the Judge was already askin' my lawyer how much I could borrow, an' what was he proposin' for permanent alimony. Alimony! Shit, she's a healthy 36 year old. She got a J.C. degree in nursin' while I was workin' two jobs. What the fuck does she need with alimony?"

Carl said, "I don't do much divorce work."

"I know what was comin' down. Your client done me a huge favor. I just got the divorce last week from that travelin' judge, the one from Champaign they sent in. Once we got out from under Esker, the new Judge was sorta reasonable. Anyway, it's over."

Carl was surprised by the negative comments. Yoder was the first person in the County to criticize Judge Esker. He was even more surprised anyone had something good to say about Aldin, even if it turned out to be backhanded gratitude. "So you feel Esker and Taylor were a bit too chummy?"

"Shit, everybody knows that! They're asshole buddies from high school. Played on the same football team. Used to go golfin' every Saturday mornin'. I'm not blowin' no smoke. There's this men's group on the Internet. It gives you the names of the judges and lawyers which screws men the worst. They keep track of complaints an' do some kinda checkin'. Anyway, Esker gets a black hood award from this men's group. You know, like the black hood them English judges used to wear when..."

"Yeah, I know, when they passed a death sentence." Carl was excited to have found an ally, albeit somebody with an ax to grind, who was looking directly at the bomber when he entered and threw the bottle. Maybe Yoder's disdain for Esker and Taylor would produce uncertainty. Maybe Yoder could neutralize Taylor's positive identification.

"Mr. Yoder..."

"Steve. Want another one?"

147

"No thanks, Steve. Gotta drive through enemy held territory. Don't want to end up in Sheriff Burnett's clutches. Anyway, the whole thing happened directly in front of you, right? You were looking straight at the guy who threw it. What did you see?"

"I seen Aldin run in there with that firebomb an' throw it. I seen it hit the bench."

Carl's hopes plummeted. "You say you saw Aldin?"

"Well, yeah. Didn't know at the time, but when he got arrested, I guess I just assumed..."

"Don't assume, Steve. Maybe the Sheriff was assuming when he had him arrested. You think you were getting screwed by Judge Esker? Well, try facing a murder charge where everybody assumes you're the guy inside a hooded sweatshirt."

Yoder nodded gravely. "Well, when you put it that way..."

"Look, Steve, what we need here is to cut through the bullshit. Just what did you actually see, as opposed to what you assume?"

Yoder leaned back and looked up through the maple tree into the blue sky as he drained the second can. "Twenty-four beers in a case. Twenty-four hours in a day. You think that's a coincidence?" He crushed the empty, dropped it next to the chair, then leaned forward and pursed his lips. "I see your point. I guess I don't really know what I seen that day."

Carl was apprehensive. He didn't want to be accused of fostering perjury. "Understand, I've got to defend my client. One of the ways is to point out that people jump to conclusions even when they want to be fair."

"I get the drift. Honestly, I guess I was buyin' in to what everybody said, and that ain't right. I see your point."

Carl exhaled in relief.

"Lookin' back, it happened real fast. Maybe count to five an' he's gone. Whole thing was over. There was screamin' an' flames, an' smoke an' the stink. Jeez, did it ever stink! Don't mean no disrespect, but it was like a bad barbecue where they burn the steaks."

Carl's stomach lurched. "Tell me any details about the bomber. Height, weight, which arm he threw with...whatever."

Yoder popped a third Bud. "Let's see...right handed for sure. Height? Mebbe...oh...around medium. No way to get closer than that. Kinda slight, on second thought. That's about all. Just a sweatshirt an' sunglasses."

"Any chance you noticed anything about the sweatshirt?"

"Nope. Wasn't no school name on it. Just a Sears sweatshirt."

"Sears?"

"Yeah, you can get 'em there. Prob'ly other places, too. Had a couple like it. She took them, too, whatever the fuck for, I swear I don't know."

"But you say the sweatshirt was from Sears?"

Yoder leaned forward and stared at the Bud that was cradled in his hands. "Sure looked like the ones I had. I dunno."

"Did the guy say anything? Make any noise?"

"Nope. Just threw it."

"What kind of throw?"

Yoder looked up. "What?"

"What kind of throw. You know. Like a baseball throw? Did he lean back? You know, like they teach you in Little League, 'rock and fire'? Guess that's a bad pun. Did it look like a man's throw?"

Yoder said, "I see what you mean." He thought for a while, then said, "Looked like somebody that's played baseball. Wasn't no pussy kinda throw. He let 'er go pretty good. Had to. They make them whiskey bottles pretty strong. I smashed a few in my time. Takes a pretty good whack."

"So what was Taylor doing while the guy was throwing it?"

A rueful laugh. "Motherfucker was countin' his fee. He was right in the middle of borin' me a new asshole. We was talkin' about my tax refund an' when was I gonna get it."

"So he was staring at you?"

"Fuckin' A. Had me in missile lock."

"Did Taylor ever look back at the guy with the firebomb?"

Yoder gazed at a red-tailed hawk circling high above. He took a swig, then looked directly at Carl. "You know what? I can remember seein' the firelight on his face when the bottle hit. Yeah! That's as clear as day. No way the bastard looked back until Aldin...the guy...was runnin' out the door. Taylor was lookin' at the Judge the whole time."

A surge of hope ran through Carl. "What happened then?"

"We run."

"Everybody?"

"Yep. My lawyer, Harvey Barnes, he was leadin' the way. He run like a rabbit. Taylor was right behind. There was screamin' an' hollerin' like you never heard. I was right next to the bomb, an' it like t' scorched my hair off. Never got no burnin' gas on me, though. Too bad it missed Taylor on the way up to the bench. Mighta got 'em both, like a billiard shot."

"Anything else?"

Yoder's calloused right hand crushed the can and dropped it alongside its companions next to the chair. "Nope. I'd like t' help you, but there really wasn't much to it. Only took a few seconds."

"Anybody from the sheriff's office or the prosecution talk to you?"

"Huh-uh. There was this Fed, though. Fossum. Not a bad guy. Not pushy like most cops. Told him to go fuck himself."

Carl looked up at Yoder. "Why?"

"Look, I ain't no hero. I just mind my own business. I don't wanna get crosswise with them terrorists. They're all over. They can knock a buzzard off a shit wagon at 100 yards with them assault rifles. Besides, the Feds never done nothin' for me."

Carl got up, suppressing several thoughts. He handed Yoder a card. "We'll be in touch with you about testifying. You take care, and call me if you think of anything more. Thanks."

"Right. I'll do 'er"

Carl and Dani were enjoying the truce between them as they walked slowly through West Side Park at the annual Taste of Champaign, browsing food booths ranging from the University's large Asian community to the best of the local barbecue joints. The crowd sported tee shirts with Greenpeace and Malcolm X and a dozen more icons; Birkenstocks and running shoes; beards and bald heads and long hair; young families and yuppies.

Carl had decided not to tell Dani about the attempt to overturn his car. He held his breath until the story stopped replaying on TV. Apparently she had somehow missed it. He marveled that she could be so wrapped up in her academic life that she would be oblivious of a juicy piece of news. Or was it because she was so wrapped up in Susan's life?

He had thought about it, and if it seemed Dani might be at risk, he would immediately get her out of danger, even if it meant having to do the Motion to Suppress without her.

Susan was thirty yards ahead with several of her friends, pretending she had no parents. Dani and Carl walked slowly among the booths displaying paintings and photographs and every kind of craft. Dani was telling him about her research.

"You know, Carl, it's almost impossible to get the trial courts to follow the case law on bad searches. They look the other way. There's precious little encouragement coming out of the appellate courts, either. If they don't want to follow the law, I wonder why they just don't do away with the remedy of suppressing evidence. It'd be more honest than pretending there's an 'exigent circumstance' or some other lame excuse every time they want to disregard the Constitution."

Carl appreciated her intensity. This was a passion for her—the rights of the people.

She shifted gears. "The thing that really bothers me is it always seems the person we're saving is from the lunatic fringe. I know...I know...the law is blind. If the least of us doesn't have any rights nobody does."

He nodded. What she was saying eased his conscience a little. It was

151

plain she knew there were crazies out there. She had signed on to try to get Aldin a fair trial despite the passions of the public. She was a lawyer and an adult, and had entered the zone of risk to try to save a life. He felt it was time to try to separate the client from his enemies. "You know, you're a little overboard on Aldin. He's strange, but he's very bright. And he has a point about prejudice of the weirdos out there in the community."

She flared. "Imagine that! The gall of these people! Hating intelligent terrorists!" Her fire was still there. It was her best and her worst feature.

In the swirl of people behind them was a tall, heavy man. He looked like someone who used his muscles to make a hard living. His pace matched theirs, but they took no notice of Brother Bill.

Dani went on, making no effort to hide her agitation. "You know what would really bug me? If by some miracle we saved him, he'd be out there with his buddies planning to blow up the Courthouse with us still in it."

Carl let her burn off her frustrations.

She shook her head and continued, "I'll do what I promised, but it's tough being a lawyer when we have to try to save that cretin."

Brother Bill was listening, pretending to examine a display of carved wooden eagles.

Dani ran on. "If there were any justice, we'd be able to get Aldin's evidence suppressed without helping his screwball cause."

Brother Bill had been watching the way they touched. He longed to have a woman, a partner to share his commitment, but when he heard Dani's comments about the movement, his mind clicked into alarm mode. That she knew she was aiding evil, that alone was enough to confirm his plan. He put down the wooden eagle, turned his back on Dani and Carl, and was swallowed by the crowd.

He didn't notice a dark, squat man with a heavy moustache, who had been standing in front of the next booth, eating a *gyros* and watching the Hardmans. Now the was watching Brother Bill Carmichael.

House Odds

The hearing on the Motion to Suppress was a zoo. Television trucks created Moraine's first-ever gridlock. Reporters and photographers swarmed like fruit flies on a warm banana. There was no place to walk. Carl thought about George Wallace's shooting. Anyone who hated lawyers could easily do a copycat performance. Carl's gaze rested on the face he had seen at the arraignment and in the crowd when he had been attacked The same gaunt eyes radiating an overpowering emotion that seemed to be reaching out for him. Was it hate? Pain? Carl looked away.

Dani, dressed in a pearl-gray suit, looked calm and cool to everyone but Carl. He cleared the way through a thicket of microphones. Shouted questions followed them up the stone steps and through the metal detector.

Once through security they were alone in air conditioned silence. The movie-set courtroom was empty, but the second floor balcony sported at least a half-dozen armed deputies, double the number which had success-fully guarded the arraignment. Their weapons had escalated from shot-guns to M-16 assault rifles. Carl shuddered as he imagined some mistake, some misinterpretation, that could send high-powered rifle bullets rico-cheting off the marble floor. What terrorist risk in this county courthouse could justify ill-trained, over-armed rural deputies with no clear idea what they were doing? He wondered whether the hearing of a Motion to

153

Suppress had ever turned into a bloodbath.

Dani opened her briefcase and began to marshal the stacks of photo-copied cases on the folding table, ready with precedents to plug any hole.

State's Attorney Gadsen wandered in, impeccable in a dark gray pin-stripe double-breasted suit and maroon tie. Carl leaned over to Dani's ear. "He looks about a thousand bucks better than he did at the arraignment. Bet his wife found a sale."

She whispered, "When's the election? He looks like he's ready."

The rear door of the courthouse opened and a swarm of deputies hur-ried Aldin into the building. Leg irons had been abandoned in the interest of speedy entrances and exits. Aldin was wearing a blue suit fresh from the rack at J.C. Penney, thanks to Dani. His white shirt sported a bright red knit tie. The flag effect was hard to ignore.

No sooner had Aldin reached counsel table than Sheriff Burnett, having appointed himself Bailiff for the duration of free publicity, called out the opening of court. Judge Harrigan breezed across the marble floor from the Clerk's office and took her seat at the bench. The reporter and clerk fol-lowed quickly. The Judge called out, "Please be seated," in a brusque tone.

Dani whispered, "Sounds like we get three minutes of undivided fair-ness."

Carl muttered, "Nobody wins a suppression at the trial level, I guess."

Aldin frowned at them.

Judge Harrigan intoned, "People versus Walid Aldin. Please announce your appearances."

"Willard Gadsen for the People, Your Honor."

"Carl Hardman and Danielle Hardman for the defense, Your Honor."

Judge Harrigan wasted no time on courtesies. "Proceed with your Motion to Suppress. Opening statement for the moving party."

Carl had been hustled through hearings by Judges many times. He decided to set his own pace. He shuffled papers and waited until the quiet begged him to speak. Perhaps a slower pace would lull the Judge and make her a little more willing to listen. If she expressed anger or impatience, at least it would help show bias in the record on appeal.

A motion to suppress evidence is an exercise in stretching the law beyond the common sense of the citizens. The motion is decided by a judge, not a jury, and asks the Court to deprive the prosecution of the evidence seized in violation of the Constitution. Whether this deters police misconduct is subject to great skepticism. Cynics have suggested punishing illegal searches by depriving the police of donuts for a month might work better.

The lobby-courtroom crackled with tension. Every chair was taken. The faces were frozen with anticipation.

Carl took a deep breath and began, "May it please the Court. Counsel."

Gadsen said without looking up, "Counsel."

Carl went on, "This was a search pursuant to a warrant issued by the Federal Court in Urbana. Why was the the federal court invoked instead of this court? Initially, a warrantless search took place within an hour of the commission of this crime. Nothing was physically seized at that time, but the deputy sheriff went on the Defendant's property and made observations of a gas can in the Defendant's trunk. He thereby seized information the Defendant had a right to expect to be private. The deputy promptly turned that information over to Federal agents who secured this search warrant using that same information as the probable cause. The Federal warrant was served, and a computer, personal papers, an empty gasoline container and weapons were seized from Mr. Aldin's residence. He had an Illinois Firearms Owner's I.D. card giving him a legal right to possess those firearms. The papers and computer were not contraband."

Carl paused and took a drink from his water glass to let his argument sink in. Judge Harrigan's pen was tapping against her legal pad instead of making notes.

"This Federal search warrant is based on an absurd claim of Federal

Jurisdiction over this very Court! According to the Affidavit filed to secure this warrant, Moraine County's judicial sovereignty vanishes in a facetious argument that this Court is a business involved in Interstate Commerce. The political independence of the State of Illinois dissipates like a handful of dust in the Federal cyclone known as the Commerce Clause. The warrant is absurdly over-broad. It states that this very Courthouse is involved in Interstate Commerce because it issues verdicts that produce money, that it burns interstate pipeline gas and dispenses interstate cans of soda pop from vending machines. We may as well fold up Federalism, Judge. You're now just a glorified storekeeper under this legal theory, subject to the Federal power to regulate interstate commerce. In addition to violating the Fourteenth Amendment, it also violates the Ninth."

Judge Harrigan's eyebrows rose. Nobody cites the Ninth Amendment, which guarantees that states retain all rights not delegated to the Federal Government. It is regarded as a relic in contemporary legal education.

"This case cries out for this Court to reassert its jurisdiction. I call the court's attention to the comments of Justice Rehnquist in December, 1998, criticizing the increasing Federalization of traditional State criminal matters including crimes of violence." Carl sounded like a states-rights politician. He cited older foundation cases defining the Interstate Commerce Clause, then continued his attack on Federal usurpation. He believed his argument, but at the same time he knew it was hopelessly out of fashion.

Carl went on to a more conventional approach, that the search warrant was premised on facts that could only have been seized in violation of the defendant's rights.

The way search warrants were designed to be issued, a neutral Judge is supposed to pass on whether there is probable cause to invade the privacy of a citizen. However, there had emerged a myriad of exceptions to the requirement for a search warrant. A car could be in the next state by the time a judge could issue a warrant. This case, Carl argued, presented no such emergency. The deputy sheriff was parked at the end of Aldin's driveway, and there was no indication Aldin was trying to leave.

Carl pointed out that the facts recited in the Federal warrant were contaminated because they were gathered illegally by the deputy serving the civil summons who took the opportunity to give Aldin's car a once-over. The result, Carl argued, contaminated any warrant that might be issued, just like picking a rotten apple and storing it with the good ones. Carl looked up and caught Judge Harrigan with a glazed look in her eyes. He paused and then stated, "The arrest of Mr. Aldin and the search of his car were clearly illegal, your Honor." Carl stopped talking.

Judge Harrigan glanced at her watch.

A lawyer is a practicing pragmatist. If an argument is falling on deaf ears, simplify it and save it for the appeal. He had been hoping to educate the press, but not at the expense of eliciting open boredom from the judge.

"You may call your first witness, Mr. Hardman."

"Thank you, Your Honor. Call Deputy Walt Strader as an adverse witness." This permitted cross-examining the deputy.

A young, blonde giant strode toward the bench with a subpoena in his hand. The way his muscles rippled threatened every seam of his cheap brown suit. He took the oath, settled into the witness chair, and scowled at Carl with a look appropriate for barroom confrontations. The preliminary questions were answered with minimal information and less civility.

"Deputy, you made the arrest and served the search warrant, am I correct?"

"Not exactly. I was in on the arrest. The search warrant came later."

Carl was on his feet in front of the witness chair, taking easy, slow strides as he talked, hoping to reduce the deputy's hostility. "Not exactly? What do you mean?"

"The Sheriff's Department is a team effort. The team made the arrest." We all did it. The standard explanation for war crimes and gang rapes.

"But you were in charge when the gas container was initially discovered, weren't you?" What Strader said about a team effort was still echoing. What did he mean? Why insist there were others involved? Carl could see Strader's hands clenching and releasing, as if squeezing a rubber ball. Ripples ran through the muscles around his jaw. Why the tension? Had the question touched a nerve?

Strader snapped, "I was in command."

"Oh...command. I see. Well, what did you command your troops to do?"

"The subject was observed when he came out of his doublewide into the driveway about 3:07 p.m. We had reliable information that the subject matched the description of the subject that murdered Judge Esker, and that he had a gas can in his trunk."

Had a gas can? Carl's mind was trying to wrap itself around this information. "Did you search the car?"

"We did an inventory after the arrest. See, when you make an arrest, you gotta tow the car for safekeeping. You gotta inventory the car so nothing gets stolen and we don't get blamed."

"That's the reason you searched the car?"

"Inventoried it."

"Let me understand how this worked. You searched his car to safeguard it although it was parked in Aldin's own driveway, and this was so you could make sure nothing got stolen because you were gonna tow it out of his driveway to some other place where it would be safer, right?" Carl braced himself for one of the several objections that never came. Gadsen was asleep at the switch.

Strader answered, "Yeah. He'd just opened the trunk."

"And when you arrested him, he closed it, right?"

"The subject was requested for his keys so's we could do the inventory."

"Requested? With handcuffs on him and two or three deputies holding him down?"

Strader's nostrils flared and his suit strained at the armpits. "We asked him the first time."

"Well, don't keep me in suspense. What did he say? Was it like 'Sure, guys! Whatever you want. I'm just dying to cooperate ?' Something like that?"

A few smirks from the audience.

Strader scowled, "He didn't say nothing like that. He used profanity."

"I take it you interpreted this profanity as a negative answer to your...request...to search his car and house?"

Strader was glum. He thought several seconds and stared a hole in Carl before saying, "I guess."

"So you took his keys away from him and opened his car for your search or your inventory or whatever you call it, right?"

"We have a right..."

Carl had given up on being nice to Strader. "Answer the question, Deputy. The Court will decide who had a right. Did you unlock the car and look inside?"

"Yes, we did. That's pursuant to section..."

"Your Honor, I disclaim the last portion of the answer and request you to instruct the witness to answer factually and leave the legal arguments to the lawyers."

Judge Harrigan said, "Just answer the questions, please, Deputy. I realize this is a trying experience, and that you must feel strongly about a Judge being murdered."

Carl reeled at the remark. "Thank you, Your Honor. Now, Deputy Strader please tell us what you found."

"Located in the trunk of the subject's 1988 Chevy Impala was a red plastic gas container."

Carl walked over to the prosecution table and reached into a large cardboard box. He withdrew a red plastic container with a molded label saying it was approved for gasoline. He stuck an evidence sticker on it and passed it to Strader. "Please examine what I've marked as Defendant's Exhibit 1."

Strader made a great show of studying the container. Finally he conceded, "Yeah, that's it. Got my mark on it. See that 'WS' at the bottom?"

159

"What did you do when you seized the container?"

"We didn't seize it. We just put it in a plastic bag."

"Then what?"

"Called the Sheriff. Then he said..."

Gadsen interjected, "Objection, hearsay."

To stop Judge Harrigan from having an excuse to start ruling against him, Carl said, "Withdrawn. Deputy, just tell us what you did after you talked to the Sheriff."

A large question mark seemed to form over the Deputy's head. The muscled shoulders were knotted with frustration. "After he said..."

"Objection." Gadsen was leaning back in his chair.

"Sustained, Counsel." Judge Harrigan spoke to the witness in a soft, kind voice, "Deputy Strader, let's try it another way. What happened to the container?"

"When we got back to the Sheriff's Office, there was these guys from the FBI. I give it to one of them. Guy named Purvis Watson."

"And they took it away? For testing?"

"Yeah, I guess so."

"Have you seen it since?"

Strader looked at Gadsen who nodded. "Sure. I seen it in the State's Attorney's office."

Carl and Dani's strategy was to unravel the thread backward from the Search Warrant and show that it rested upon evidence that had been illegally seized. There had to be more to the story than Strader had revealed.

"Deputy, I'm clear on what you did, but now let's go back to the beginning. What reason did you have for waiting in front of Mr. Aldin's home to arrest him and search his car when he got into it? Was it because you already knew there was a gas container in the trunk?"

Gadsen stirred and seemed to be searching for an objection.

"Well, yeah, we knew he had it. He'd have to. No time to get rid of it. And he fit the profile of a...screwball terrorist who'd throw a firebomb."

"You knew he had the gas container? How did you know that?"

Strader looked uncomfortable. He stammered out the answer. "S...sh...Sheriff told...ah....us Otto'd seen it."

Gadsen somehow let the answer slip by without a hearsay objection, although it was arguably an exception to the hearsay rule. But with this Judge, Carl was lucky to avoid the issue. He could feel a door opening. "Otto? What's his last name?"

Deputy Strader displayed the deprecating smirk country people have for outsiders. "Otto's his last name. Amish name. They're Mennonite now. Half the county's named Otto."

"How did Mr. Otto know about this container?" Carl was now inviting hearsay but Gadsen was whispering to Helen Powell, an Assistant State's Attorney, and missed his chance.

"It's Deputy Otto. He was servin' a civil paper on Aldin an' he seen it. Around 10 o'clock."

Was this the key he'd been searching for? Otto's earlier observation of the gas container explained why Strader would contrive an arrest so that Aldin's car was involved, knowing it contained the damning gas container. Carl dug further. "A civil paper?"

"Yeah, Aldin got his bathroom wallpapered with writs we served on him over the years. No kiddin'. We seen them when we searched the place. Otto was out there servin' a contempt citation on Aldin for some crap he pulled in one of his civil suits."

"So you weren't surprised to find the gas container in Aldin's trunk because Deputy Otto told the Sheriff it was there? That was your state of mind?"

Strader looked toward Gadsen who apparently was aware that state of mind is an exception to hearsay.

Carl looked over at the prosecutor. "Am I missing something, Deputy? You're staring at Mr. Gadsen. Can't you remember the answer without his help?"

Gadsen glanced up at Carl. It would have been impossible to nod or blink advice to the witness without the entire courtroom observing. Strader was on his own. "It was in his trunk when we arrested him."

"Yes, you've made that point several times. But you knew it was going to be there when you watched Aldin go to the car, didn't you, Deputy?"

Strader shifted from one large buttock to the other. His forehead began to shine with perspiration. "Well sure. I knew Otto seen it."

"And where's this Deputy Otto right now?" Carl, of course, had not subpoenaed him because his name had just surfaced.

"That's him runnin' the magnetic scanner," pointing to an older man in a tent-size tan uniform. Everyone turned to look at Otto.

"Did you search...or inventory...anything else?"

"No, I took care of Aldin so he wouldn't give nobody no trouble. I didn't do nothing more." He had a look that begged to be let off the hook.

"No further questions."

Judge Harrigan asked, "State?"

Gadsen looked like someone eager to close the bag before the cat got all the way out. He said, "No questions."

Carl looked toward the entrance and said, "Call Deputy Otto as an adverse witness."

Heads swiveled and focused on the bulky figure standing next to the scanner. He was about six feet tall and overflowed his khaki uniform. Obviously in shock, Otto stumbled through the crowd and stood in front of the witness chair, raising his right hand and blinking at Judge Harrigan through horn-rimmed glasses. The clerk administered the oath as if she were announcing stops on a city subway.

Carl began, "State your name, please."

"Uh...Jacob. Jacob Otto."

"To save time, you are a Deputy Sheriff of Lincoln County and your duties include serving civil papers, am I right?"

Gadsen stirred with the automatic reaction of a lawyer hearing leading questions, but let Carl shorten the foundation material.

"Yeah. That's right. I been servin' process for the last five years, mebbe. Now they got me on that magnet scanner thing."

"Do you know Wally Aldin?" Carl gestured at his client.

Otto smiled as if everyone must surely know how often he had served summonses and writs on Aldin. "Yeah, sure. I know him pretty good."

"Calling your attention to the 12th day of April, this year, did you have occasion to see Mr. Aldin?"

"Was that the day...uh...I think so. That's the day he bombed..."

"OBJECTION! I disclaim that volunteered statement!"

Judge Harrigan said, "Sustained. Deputy Otto, please confine your answers to the questions. Proceed."

"Yeah, I guess so. You're gettin' at the time I seen the gas can in his trunk, right?"

"Tell us what you were doing that brought you into contact with Mr. Aldin and the trunk of his car."

"Well, we was...uh...Sheriff said go out an' serve him with a paper we had there. I was gonna get around to it the week after. See, we try to serve them rural papers by quarters of the county to save gas. The Northwest Quarter, where Aldin's doublewide is at, that's the third week of the month. But Sheriff Burnett says go out 'an serve him. So I did."

"And violate your established policy of economy? Didn't the Sheriff realize this would waste gas?" Carl wasn't sure Otto caught the ironic tone.

Gadsen, however, did. "Objection to what the Sheriff thought. Calls for speculation."

"Withdrawn. Deputy, just tell us what instructions you thought you were operating under."

Otto sneaked a look at Sheriff Burnett who was at the Bailiff's desk. The Sheriff glared back. It was a signal Otto clearly received, but clearly didn't understand. Did the Sheriff think he was he saying too much? Not enough?

Carl spotted the exchange, rose to his feet, and walked to the side of the courtroom farthest from Burnett. If the Sheriff planned on playing winko with the witness, he'd force Otto to swivel with every question to get Burnett's signals.

"Now, Deputy, calling your attention to the morning you learned of the firebombing, what were your instructions concerning Wally Aldin?"

Otto started to turn but thought better of it. He seemed perplexed trying to guess what would help or hurt. "Uh...well...the Sheriff just got back from the fire a half hour before an' he says, 'Jacob, go on out an' serve that Rule to Show Cause on Aldin. See if you can look around while you're doin' it.' "

Carl's heart leaped. "Look around?"

Otto waited to see if Gadsen objected. No objection came. Gadsen was rummaging in his briefcase searching for Otto's report. "Yeah. He wanted me to...er...he wanted me to see if I could get a look inside Aldin's car to see if he had a gas can."

Again, Gadsen was slow. The answer came in without objection, one of those brass rings that come along during a trial. "You're telling us this was done right after the explosion, before Aldin was arrested and before the search warrant had been issued by the Federal Court?"

"Yeah. That warrant wasn't issued for...oh...mebbe half a day. Couldn't of been. Some of the stuff I seen went into the Complaint for the search warrant."

"Like what?"

"Like the gas can. I guess it wasn't really no can. It was that plastic container." He pointed to it.

"Where did you see this container?"

"I seen it in his trunk."

"The trunk of his car?"

Otto looked at Carl as if he were a little dense. "I seen it in the trunk of his car."

"What time?"

"About 10:30...maybe 10:30."

"And you knew before that you were looking for a gasoline container?"

Otto's exasperated look implied Carl was too dumb to live in the country. "Well sure. What else would he be carryin' gas in?"

Carl ignored the jibe. "So your state of mind when you served the civil paper was that you were expecting to find something Aldin had used to carry gasoline."

"Yeah. Like I said, Sheriff told me to watch for a gas can while I was servin' the paper. Said to wait 'cross the road in them trees. I had a 4x scope from my rifle with me. I was lookin' through it and I seen him pull up into the driveway and open the trunk to take out some groceries." Otto radiated pride at his top-notch police work. "Anyways, it seemed like a good time t' serve the paper, while he had the trunk open. So I drive up there, no lights flashin' or nothin'. Aldin, he's just comin' out from his doublewide, headin' back to the car for another bag. So I pull up an' get out with the Rule to Show Cause. He walks over t' get it, like usual."

"Like usual?"

"Yeah, I serve a lotta papers on Aldin. He...uh...gets sued a lot, and he sends out a lotta civil papers of his own to serve. I know Aldin good."

"Go on. Tell me about what you saw."

"So I says, 'Good mornin' Wally.' He says, 'Whatta you want now, Jacob?' I says, 'Got this here paper from the Hospital.' He says, 'Oh no! Not another one! I paid those bastards.' An' I walks up to next to the car, kinda halfway to the trailer, you know, so I could see into the trunk."

Carl nodded in mock admiration. "Very clever! So you used the Rule to Show Cause to get a look in his trunk?"

Otto smiled back. "Yeah. I could see in there real good. Right next to the rest of the groceries, there it was, that red gas can...er, that plastic container right over there on your table."

State's Attorney Gadsen squirmed in his chair and flipped some pages

165

on his yellow pad.

"Then what?"

"Pardon me?"

"Then what did you do?"

"I figgered I seen enough, so I took off."

"Did you go over to the car and look at the gas container or touch it or help him carry the groceries or anything?"

"Huh uh. Didn't see no point. All I was supposed...uh...I just served the paper."

It was evident Otto had been sent out to search Aldin's vehicle under a subterfuge. A cute way to get a peek in the trunk, but how did the Sheriff know there was a container to look for? Had there been a tip? Was someone supplying information to the authorities?

"Mr. Hardman?" Judge Harrigan's bored tone cut through his thoughts. "Are you finished with this witness?"

He realized he had been staring at Otto for several seconds. "No, Your Honor, I was just awestruck at how Sheriff Burnett knew there was going to be a gasoline container in my client's trunk."

She scowled at him. "Ask a question or tender the witness."

He smiled, trusting the point had been made despite her effort to ignore it. It was clear he was talking to the Appellate Court. He wasn't going to get any relief from this judge. "Certainly, Your Honor." He smiled and nodded politely. "Deputy Otto, let's go back to the beginning. Was it kind of like Sheriff Burnett called you into his office and told you to try to sneak a look in Aldin's trunk because he had a gas container and somebody had to see it to supply information for a search warrant...was that pretty much the way it was, Deputy?"

Otto swallowed twice and his eyelids blinked visibly, enlarged by the thick glasses. "I guess so. All I know is the Sheriff calls the shots, an' he decides what I'm supposed t' do with my time. He says serve a paper, I serve it. What I seen was in plain view while I had a right t' be on his land, so what I seen was perfectly legal."

"Perfectly legal," Carl said with irony as he picked up the gas container to justify approaching the witness. "That's interesting, Deputy Otto. Perfectly legal. How did you know that? Was there some discussion with Sheriff Burnett...or possibly with State's Attorney Gadsen, before you went out to look for this gas container...about how to make it perfectly legal?"

Otto looked trapped. He pulled in his chin, as if some ancestral turtle-reflex had clicked in. "That ain't right. The State's Attorney wasn't there."

Carl lowered his voice a notch to soothe Otto. "All right, then, the State's Attorney wasn't there. But the rest of it's true, isn't it?"

Otto strained to keep from looking toward Sheriff Burnett. "I dunno. I can't remember. So what if he did? He's the Sheriff. He got a right t' tell us what's a bad search. That's his job."

Pay dirt. Maybe. Carl had established that law enforcement had some unexplained, undisclosed reason to believe Aldin possessed a gas container and then manufactured a legal pretext for Otto to peek into Aldin's car.

"How did the Sheriff know Aldin had a gas container in his trunk?"

Otto knit his brow and thought for a second. "He didn't say."

"How did the Sheriff know Aldin would be driving home with groceries in his trunk to unload?"

Otto squirmed. "Heck, I don't know. He just told me Wally'd be comin' home and to wait for him to open the trunk."

Carl stared at him. It still didn't add up, but it was clear that Deputy Otto had spilled all the beans he had. "Your witness."

Judge Harrigan said, "We'll be in recess," and stalked off the platform.

Carl sat down and stared at his legal pad. Dani had written "You're still good" on the margin. He wondered how broadly he should take that.

— · — · — · — · — · — · — · —

After they reconvened, it was State's Attorney Gadsen's turn. Seated next to him was Assistant State's Attorney Helen Powell who was equipped with photocopies of cases and copious notes. She was whispering advice as Gadsen sat nodding. The press had filtered back into the room and the remaining seats in the gallery were filled by the general public, including the man with the gaunt face and the haunted eyes. Every time Carl saw him, some energy was transferred from him, but once again there was no time to muse on why.

Gadsen began a meticulous re-examination of Otto's testimony. He asked whether Otto had been asked to do any of a number of clearly improper acts such as breaking in, peering through the windows of the doublewide, or stopping Aldin on some trumped-up charge. He got the negative answers he expected. Gadsen established the boundary line for Aldin's property was the edge of the rural road. While staking out the house, waiting for Aldin to return, Otto's car was across the road, off Aldin's land, behind a tangle of scrub trees. Gadsen established that it was sometimes necessary to hide and wait to serve a civil paper because of Aldin's talent for summons-dodging.

At this Carl winced. The examination was repairing many of the holes he had opened. Nevertheless, Gadsen didn't touch on Sheriff Burnett's remarkable foreknowledge of the gas container and how the Sheriff knew Aldin would arrive with groceries to unload. He didn't attempt to explain how the Sheriff got this information in a constitutionally permissible manner.

Gadsen spent a half hour questioning Otto. By the time he finished, Otto looked wilted. The final question was whether Otto had any reason to hate Aldin or to fabricate any testimony about him.

Otto shook his head vigorously. "No. Huh-uh. Wally's maybe a little far out sometimes, but he an' my youngest boy kicked the soccer ball around sometimes. Wally didn't know how to play baseball. I never had no bad feelin' toward him. I'm just tellin' what happened. Just what I done."

Gadsen rolled that around for a few seconds and apparently decided it was an ending. He said, "No further questions. Your witness."

Carl glanced at the legal pad Dani shoved in front of him. It contained the same question that had been troubling him. It said, "Who told the Sheriff?" Carl asked him.

Otto tried to shift to a more comfortable position as he stared at Carl through his owl glasses. "I said I dunno."

Carl walked around the folding table and was tempted to lounge against the front of it to relax the witness. Then he remembered how temporary and insubstantial it was. "Do you feel anything at all for him?"

Otto rocked back and forth a couple of times, weighing his feelings. "I guess I feel sorry his life's gone bad. He was just another guy. Then he went sour on ever'thing."

"You want to be fair to him?"

"Sure." Otto seemed to mean it.

"Well, then, tell us how just a few minutes after the explosion the Sheriff happened to know there was a gas container in his trunk?"

Otto's eyes flickered to the Sheriff. Carl caught him shaking his head a few microns left and right. "Your Honor, I wonder if the Court would instruct the Sheriff that as the acting Bailiff of this Court, he shouldn't be sending signals to the witness."

Judge Harrigan saw no evil. "If I had noticed such a thing, I'd certainly do so, Mr. Hardman. Now proceed."

"Well, Deputy? Do your conscience and your memory let you recall by what miracle you knew you'd find a gas can in the trunk?"

Otto sucked in a breath and shrugged his shoulders. "I dunno."

Carl had hit the high water mark with Otto. He said, "No further questions," as derisively as he could.

Gadsen passed on asking further questions. Another recess.

Swine Before Pearls

The defense had been given a small, windowless janitor's closet just off the lobby of the Courthouse to confer with Aldin. Earlier in the morning Carl had swept the room for electronic eavesdropping devices. Mops and pails stood in one corner. A cheap metal desk, with only three legs, rested its fourth corner on two outdated, red volumes of the *Illinois Revised Statutes*. Dani looked at them. "At last they've found some use for the law in this county." She ran her finger over the seat of a folding chair and examined it before sitting down.

Aldin, still shackled, sat down next to her. "Wouldn't want you to get dirty." He glared at her.

Carl interceded. "Let's stick to business, Wally. Do you have any idea how the Sheriff knew about the gas container in the car?"

Aldin simmered for a few moments, then said, "Haven't got a clue."

Dani drummed her fingers on the table. "Did you tell anybody you had this gas container?"

"Now wouldn't that be kind of stupid? I mean if I'm some big time terrorist, would I be running around telling people about my tools?"

Carl glanced at Dani. She caught the hint to let him pick up the questioning. "This isn't an I.Q. test, Wally. Just answer the question so we can help. If somebody's been giving information to the Sheriff, it's really

170

important. How did Sheriff Burnett know to send Otto out at just the right time to confirm you had a gas container? So what's the answer? Did you tell anybody?" Carl let the question hang in the space between them. "Even some of your...friends...or colleagues?"

Aldin exploded. "I knew it! I knew you'd be trying to get me to sell out my..."

Carl cut him off. "That's not it at all! We're just trying to find out if there's a leak!"

Dani slapped down a handful of photocopied cases. "Look! Finding out how the Sheriff knew about your little gas can is absolutely essential! For the first time this morning we find out that Otto was told to serve a civil paper on you as an excuse to look for the gas can. That's probably plain view. But where it could get dicey is how Sheriff Burnett knew you had the damn thing in the first place. This was within a few hours of the fire. Did they have your line tapped? Is there an informer in your...?" She paused as if ridding herself of a bad taste.

"What does all this have to do with my being innocent?" Aldin said it as if he were trying to goad her.

Carl stepped in. "Wait a minute! You say you believe in the Constitution. They can't use the stuff they found in violation of your rights. We're trying to suppress illegally seized evidence"

This time Dani tried to cool the confrontation. "Forget the comeback, Mr. Aldin. Just tell us if you can think of anybody who'd tell the Sheriff what you had in your trunk."

Aldin slipped back behind his stony face. "I told you I was innocent. There's nothing anybody could tell. I'm innocent. The Constitution says so. What's the use? There's nothing anybody can do about this. It's predetermined. They're going to kill me."

Dani lost it. "Well, that's enlightening! If you can't help with how Sheriff Burnett knew..."

"I told you up front I'm not testifying. That stands. Whatever happens, happens."

Carl was trying hard to restrain himself. "Look, Wally, I only agreed to do this case until you got a permanent lawyer. Where the hell is he? If you don't want to cooperate with us, why not fire us and get somebody you agree with?"

Aldin was silent for several seconds, then said, "They picked you out. Ask them."

Dani looked at Carl. She shrugged in disgust and said, "Thanks for your help, Mr. Aldin. Now if you'll excuse us, we have some work to do." For the next fifteen minutes Carl and Dani went over the testimony while Aldin sulked. Dani pointed out it was their burden and the Sheriff was the only one who knew how he found out Aldin' car had a gas container in the trunk. He had to be confronted. He had to be called. They ignored Aldin while they worked.

—·—·—·—·—·—·—·—·—·—

A knock on the door announced the resumption of the hearing. They gathered up their papers and exited the room. A wave of fresh air relieved the stuffiness of being closeted with their client and the cleaning supplies.

Judge Harrigan entered and everyone dutifully rose.

Carl noticed there was something missing. Then it dawned on him nobody had officiated over the entrance of the Judge. No Bailiff. No Sheriff Burnett. The Bailiff's chair was empty. The Sheriff must have guessed who the next witness was likely to be. "Your Honor, may we approach the bench?"

Judge Harrigan nodded. Carl motioned for Dani to accompany him. They took up their stations next to Gadsen. After the court reporter was ready, Judge Harrigan leaned forward and said, "Keep your voices down," to make sure the truly important parts of this open and public trial didn't leak out.

Carl spoke in a hush. "Your Honor, I was about to call the Bailiff,

Sheriff Burnett is my next witness, but looking around it seems he's not here. Does Mr. Gadsen know where he is?"

Judge Harrigan shifted her gaze to Gadsen who was perplexed or did a good job of pretending. "Search me, Judge. I haven't seen him since we went into recess."

The Judge turned back to Carl, "Mr. Hardman, do you have him under subpoena?"

"No, Your Honor. The last witness suggested for the first time..."

"We operate under a few fundamental rules here, Mr. Hardman. One of them is we subpoena our witnesses so this won't happen."

"Judge! How could I subpoena him? I didn't even know he was going to be a witness? How could I guess the Bailiff of this court was going to take a powder? I didn't even know..."

"Anticipate and prepare your case, that's how, Mr. Hardman. You're asking me to continue this proceeding until you can locate the Sheriff?"

"Yes, Judge. That's the way it shapes up." Carl looked at the court reporter to make sure she was transcribing the exchange for later use on appeal.

"Well, I'm not inclined to have much sympathy for you. I've got a full courtroom here and everyone's ready to go, except for you. I'll give you ten minutes to locate him. Perhaps he's in the building. We'll be in recess for ten minutes."

The audience began to buzz and the reporters surged forward, scavenging for remnants of what happened at the bench. Carl and Dani broke in opposite directions. She started a search of the building. He headed for a phone to call the Sheriff's office. Aldin sat under guard at counsel table with a sullen stare aimed at the empty bench.

The time went by in a flash. Carl was still on the phone when Dani appeared at the door of the Clerk's office and said, "Carl, they're coming back. He's not in the building and I didn't see him outside. Any luck?"

"Nope. They claim they're trying to reach him on the radio but there's some malfunction."

"Malfunction, my ass. We've been had." She slapped the counter.

They hurried across the vestibule. Judge Harrigan entered without fanfare. Carl remained standing, trying to appear calm. "Your Honor, the Sheriff seems to have defected. He's not in the building and he's not reachable through his office. His testimony is crucial to the Motion to Suppress. How did he have unexplained information about the gas container being in the car? The critical piece of the puzzle is how Sheriff Burnett could have known there was a gas container in the trunk. How was he able to instruct Deputy Otto that a gas container was in the trunk? How could he have acquired that information legally? The arrest, the inventory search, the issuance of the formal search warrant…all of those things depend on how Sheriff Burnett could have gotten this key information without violating the defendant's rights. I move to continue this hearing until we can subpoena Sheriff Burnett."

"Denied. You scheduled this hearing. You're an experienced lawyer. When Deputy Otto raised the point, you could have requested the Court to order the Sheriff to make himself available after the break. Be ready next time. Now call your next witness."

Carl looked at Dani who was staring daggers at Judge Harrigan. He turned to the Judge and implored, "Your Honor, you are crippling Mr. Aldin's defense with this ruling! This is a capital case! We claim surprise! The last witness raised, for the first time, Sheriff Burnett's fascinating precognition that there was a gas container in Aldin's trunk. As the Court knows, if the Sheriff relied on an informant there must be a showing of the reliability of the informant. If he found out through bugging or some other breach of the defendant's rights..."

"MR. HARDMAN! I have RULED! Now PROCEED!"

Carl saw it was hopeless. "In essence, your Honor, this Court is ordering me to rest. I have no other witnesses other than Sheriff Burnett."

"Then you rest?"

"I suppose it amounts to that."

She glowered at him as he took his seat at counsel table. He hoped the point was clearly preserved for the appeal.

Gadsen said, without being asked, "I don't think the State needs to call any witnesses, Judge."

Dani looked at Carl. "Argument." She stood and addressed the Judge.

The next hour was a blur. An erudite blur that swirled like a mist around the bored expression of Judge Harrigan. Dani dumped bucketfuls of pearls in front of her, but none were acknowledged by questions from the bench or even facial reactions. Dani began by citing the foundation cases on search and seizure. She traced the requirements for warrantless search. She hammered on how the Sheriff could not have legally obtained knowledge of the gas container. She cited cases holding that the burden of proof had shifted to the State. Because of Aldin's ethnicity, had he been singled out for some impermissible wiretap or surveillance?

Judge Harrigan didn't react. Not even with mild curiosity. The look on her face was consistent with killing time by counting the audience. She even smiled at someone sitting in the front row.

Dani concluded her masterful summary by saying that nowhere was there any authority for the Court to presume the entire chain of events in Aldin's case began with anything other than illegal information the Sheriff relayed to Otto. The Judge's face was a blank. Dani sat down, looking as if she had tried to deliver a pizza to an unoccupied house.

Gadsen rose and began to address the Court.

Judge Harrigan held up the palm of her hand. "Counsel, I don't think you need to respond. Motion denied."

Dani whispered in Carl's ear, "This is a case of Fourth Amendment Lite."

He said, "We live in post-Constitutional times."

—·—·—·—·—·—·—·—·—·—

Carl tried to explain to Aldin what had taken place, but he wasn't interested. He was absorbed in glaring at the Judge. The next five minutes were spent discussing scheduling. Judge Harrigan didn't even ask about Carl's availability when she set the trial in July. He knew he'd get no slack, so why ask for it?

Aldin was led out the back. The courtroom rapidly emptied and the press surged through the front door and circled the building to the rear entrance, hoping to catch a comment from Aldin while he was sufficiently upset to lose control.

Dani looked defeated. She slowly shook her head from side to side. "At least when I'm teaching this stuff I can punish a blank stare with a flunk."

"Well, I suppose any judge might get a little worked up over the incineration of a fellow judge."

"I got myself into this, but I'm beginning to get seriously ticked off. This guy is getting railroaded even if he's an Islamic terrorist." She looked disgusted.

"You keep saying that. I don't think he's a terrorist. He's screwed up, but he's closer to a classic anarchist."

"They throw bombs, too. Comes down to the same thing, doesn't it?"

"I'm not so sure it does for good old Wally. There's something very strange about this Islamic angle. His wife told me they met in a Catholic Church and he led her to believe he was a Lebanese Christian. Have you ever heard an Islamic fundamentalist who'd be caught dead in a Catholic Church? And why isn't Wally ranting and raving about Allah and about the U.S. being the Great Satan? Does that figure?"

She thought about that. "No, but is there a rule against having enough sense to keep your mouth shut? Maybe he's thinking that stuff."

"And maybe everybody's wrong about the guy. Maybe he's not an Islamic terrorist."

"As for meeting her in Church, where the heck else is he going to

176

meet a nice girl in Moraine? The Mosque? Closest one has to be in Champaign, right?"

"Well, Urbana, I guess, but what's to say he hasn't been."

"What's to say he hasn't been burrowing into our culture for years, kind of a deep agent for the Al Qaeda? What they used to call a 'sleeper' back in the Cold War days."

Carl didn't have the energy to argue with her. "I don't know. But it just doesn't feel right to put him in a box and label it 'Islamic Terrorist.' I've got to think about that."

"No rule against thinking. But don't let it cloud your mind. We're here to fight the death penalty, not to get him elected President of the Rotary Club." She had that little set to her jaw. There was no point in discussing Aldin any further.

"How about a beer?" He smiled and said it seductively.

She shifted out of high gear and began to coast. "Only if we can get one outside this burg. Any saloons on the way back to civilization?"

"I think I can find one." *And then I'm going to find out more about Wally and Islam.*

Druze

The bell for the change of classes rang at 10:50 and Carl found himself in Lincoln Hall swimming against the current of students rushing to their next class, often blocks away, on the sprawling University of Illinois campus.

He stepped into the shelter of a doorway and watched the students stream by. They looked different from the ones he remembered. More conventional, less scruffy. He remembered this same hallway filled with army fatigue jackets festooned with political buttons. These kids looked like throwbacks to the '50s. Perhaps it was a trick of age.

Several minutes went by and the flow reversed. Classrooms began to fill with an incoming herd.

He walked along the hallway where philosophy professors maintained their offices, searching for the professor who taught Comparative Religion. Carl scanned the printouts taped to the frosted glass in each door, many decorated with graffiti. Halfway down the hall he found "LEBOUT, FRANK" with one office hour listed, Thursdays at 9 a.m. This was Friday. He cursed under his breath until he noticed there was a light on in the office. He knocked.

A squeal of casters followed by footsteps. The door opened a crack and a chubby face peered at him through coke-bottle lenses. The man was large and appeared to be in his late forties, wearing a rumpled green corduroy jacket over an open-necked, light-blue shirt. He seemed startled to see an adult at the door. It took him a second to ask, "Are you looking for someone?"

"Are you Professor Lebout?"

The man looked as if he might deny it. "What is this about?"

Carl said, "I apologize for interrupting you. I notice you have an office hour on Thursday. But since that's almost a week off, I was hoping…"

"Come in." Lebout opened the door and walked through the cramped office, past metal shelves jammed with tattered books and a scuffed briefcase, to a metal office chair pulled back from a metal desk. Untidy stacks of paper were on the verge of an avalanche. A Mac Powerbook was open. Lebout walked over to an institutional oak chair, sporting a decal with a U of I serial number. He picked up a sheaf of exam booklets decorated with red markings and jammed them into the briefcase. "I'm sorry for the mess, but as you say, I wasn't expecting anyone until next Thursday." He gestured for Carl to take a seat and lowered himself into the office chair. "What can I do for you?"

Carl sat on the edge of the straight chair, testing to see if it would handle a non-Thursday guest. "I have a few questions about religion."

Lebout leaned back, as if relieved that Carl wasn't from the accounting office or the Campus Parking Division. "Well, I've spent the last 20 years studying religions. Ask away."

"I ought to tell you first that I'm a lawyer." Carl waited for a reaction. None came. "Once upon a time I majored in Philosophy in this building. Dr. Gottschalk was my advisor. These offices haven't changed much."

A smile from Lebout. "It's nice to meet a former philosophy major who's employed. I remember hearing about Gottschalk. An innovative mind. He was Chair for some time before he retired, wasn't he? As for the facilities around here…you can bet we aren't on the list for upgrading

179

very soon. I suggested we should rename the Department *Linguistic Engineering* or some such. That ought to improve our position on the funding list. Now as you were saying about religion?"

"I'm defending a man on a murder charge, who's supposedly an Islamic terrorist."

Lebout grimaced. "The firebombing of the judge?"

Carl tried to read him and answered tentatively, "Yes, that's right."

"I followed it in some of the newspaper stories. It's very unlikely he's an Islamic terrorist. He has a Druze name. I should have guessed somebody would want to know about him."

Carl's eyes brightened, but he was tentative about pressing Lebout. "Wally Aldin is a Druze name? Is that good or bad?"

He leaned back in his chair and nestled his hands across his lap as if to start telling a long story. "Both, I suppose. First, I'll bet his real name isn't Wally, it's Walid, am I right?"

Carl nodded. "What is a Druze?"

Lebout let out a little chuckle. "The Druze? Well, that's a good one. Not much call for information about the Druze, or the *Mowahhidoon* as they prefer. One thing for certain, they aren't Islamic fundamentalists." Lebout stared at Carl, the glasses reducing his eyes to beads. He went on, "And the last name is almost certainly al-Din...small "al" hyphen capital 'D'. Baha al-Din was a famous Druze...correction, *Mowahhid*...that's the word they prefer for an adherent. Anyway, he died in the first part of the 11th Century. After his death the movement or religion, or whatever it is, became closed and secret and cancelled all evangelistic efforts. Basically, nobody knows exactly what they believe, except for occasional statements or articles by a Druze...that's the name the rest of the world calls them, and they grudgingly accept it. 'Druze' is a word derived from a fallen preacher named Dazair who was killed because he was empire-building for himself. Calling the religion 'Druze' is like calling Southern fundamentalists "Bakkers" after the TV. preacher who lined his pockets selling salvation."

Lebout paused as if waiting for appreciation of the point.

Carl nodded and smiled.

"Philosophy teachers don't get much call to consult about problems in the real world. Then, again, we have to be philosophical about such things." He chuckled as if this were enormously funny.

Carl forced his smile to widen and said, "Well, this is a chance to help with a real problem with life and death consequences. I'm interested in what you say about not being an Islamic fundamentalist. It's terribly hard to understand my client and his motivation. He's apparently been his own worst enemy for years. The legal system has him down as a bad guy because he's an Islamic terrorist."

"As I said, that's certainly most unlikely."

Carl perked up. "Tell me more."

"The Druze religion, properly called *Tahweed*, is an enigma. It is so secret scholars have only second-hand reports of its inner mysteries. I don't know anyone who claims to have looked at the *Tahweed* sacred texts. There are somewhere between low hundreds of thousands up to maybe a million Druze worldwide. They've become a successful minority by learning how to merge into the dominant culture, even taking on the outer cloak of the major monotheistic religions. They have no churches of their own. They keep their secrets and seldom truly convert to other religions without keeping a Druze point of view at the core."

Carl said, "Go on. This is the first good news I've had in weeks."

"Your client's first name should be familiar to you. It's the name of the political and military leader of the Druze during the Lebanese civil war, Walid Jumblatt. The popular press at that time wrote about him constantly and called him Wally. He's very modern. Rides motorcycles, dresses in stylish clothes from the West, and he's something of a playboy."

Carl sat mesmerized. "I guess I asked the right person."

Lebout seemed pleased. "They've always been one of my favorite mysteries."

"So what kind of Muslims are they? Sunni? Shiite?"

"Neither. Like most things Druze, they are but they aren't. Most of the literature seems to agree they probably were an offshoot from Islam in the 10th Century, not unlike the Protestant offshoot from Catholicism. The Druze honor the Koran, but believe it's just the outer wrapping of mystical and secret messages. Certainly this is totally inconsistent with the Islamic fundamentalism we have today. Tampering with the accepted, literal meaning of the Koran is a capital offense in an Islamic republic. The Druze reject the five pillars of Islam...reciting the creed, praying five times a day, donating to charity, fasting during the month of Ramadan, and making a pilgrimage to Mecca. Moslems find this shocking. The Druze themselves believe their religion goes back to ancient Egypt and some claim it traces to the Pharaoh Akhenaten who introduced monotheism and tried to convert Egypt from the panorama of gods they recognized. In another paradox for a group claiming to be strict monotheists, they appear to believe an Egyptian Sheik, Al-Hakim, was the most recent incarnation of God."

Carl was swamped with information. He was trying to organize it so he could recall it later, but there were several points crying out for more detail. "You said they adapt to the dominant religion and culture where they live." Carl was hoping for a clue to Wally's meeting Laura in a Catholic church.

"Yes, indeed. They are fiercely monotheistic. In fact that's one of their criticisms of Christianity. They feel it is nearly polytheistic in practice, with the veneration of Mary and the Saints. They don't believe God has a son or has partners in any Trinity. Nevertheless, they believe the Christian, Jewish and Moslem God is the same one they recognize. Sometimes they even refer to themselves as Unitarians. The Druze can attend services of the local monotheistic religions, but keep their own counsel about what to believe. This happens to work out quite well as a survival strategy. They are so flexible the Druze who live within the borders of Israel even serve in the Israeli army and have recently achieved high rank."

"That's completely opposite of the official picture of Aldin. I've been waiting for him to criticize America like the fanatics you see on T.V. He has a Catholic wife who told me she always thought he was some kind of Lebanese Christian…"

"Maronite? That's the principle Christian group in Lebanon."

"Yes, I suppose so."

"The Druze have had good relationships with the Maronites over the centuries, give or take a few civil wars and foreign invasions in which they found themselves cornerwise to each other. Odd thing about the Middle East, there are so many splinter groups you can have five or six sides in a war. One of their traditions holds that Druze are three of the lost tribes of Israel. Druze forces did resist some of the Crusades, allied with the Muslims. That never went over very big with the Pope."

"So it's possible for a Druze to take on a Christian religion…sort of like wearing the local style of clothing? Marry a Christian woman and not exactly level with her that he's a Druze?"

"They are very reluctant to marry outside their religion, though they have been known to marry outside their faith if love or hormones over-come tradition. They are very reluctant to be candid with anyone not a Druze, even a non-believer wife…maybe especially a wife. Being from the Middle East they have never exactly been feminists, although Druze women enjoy religious equality. It's certainly true having children with a non-Druze would be strongly disapproved. If they had a non-Druze child, where would the soul come from? One of their main tenets is an absolute belief in human reincarnation at the moment of death. Sort of taking the course over again for thousands of years until the soul is perfect enough to reunite with God, and they believe there is a finite number of souls. That's why they don't believe in converts. There is an inner circle within the religion that keeps the real secrets and guards the sacred texts. The rank and file can only be elevated after a lot of study and pious living. Many scholars think that's why there is an apparent reluctance for the

183

ordinary Druze to aspire to become part of the *Uqqal*, which is a sort of *illuminati,* if you wish…that seems to be a popular term in the current best sellers. There would be too many demands on their personal conduct if they wanted to be initiated into the inner truths." He smiled as if cherishing a taste for sin was a universal principle.

"How do they feel about violence? Murder and so forth. Terrorism."

"Well…that's a little hard to say. They're excellent soldiers, believe in self defense, and are fiercely loyal to their group. They have a five star flag with five colors. Each represents one of their beliefs. Not a national flag. They are tough fighters when they find themselves threatened. As for murder, I suppose it goes on in every society no matter what the moral code proscribes, but it's clear their moral code is similar to the Judeo-Christian one. And which one might that be? One that seems wide enough to encompass Ariel Sharon, Bush, and Albert Schweitzer."

"A point well taken. Tell me, is there anything else that's a characteristic of the Druze I should know about?"

"Hundreds of seeming paradoxes. They share belief in seven major prophets including Adam, Abraham, Mohammed, and Jesus. Some of the minor ones include Daniel, Aristotle, and Plato. How's that for variety? One belief stands out, however—they are very fatalistic. Similar to what we would call predestination. They don't fear death because it's just the passage to a nice, clean, new body and a fresh start. They are quite different from Islam in other important ways. The only hell is separation from God and the despair it would bring."

Carl pursed his lips and thought about that one. How did it play in Wally Aldin's case? Would a firebomber be more or less likely to murder somebody and risk the death penalty if he believed he would instantly be reborn—and that hell was out of the picture?

"Oh yes! I ought to tell you about a couple of other things. The tenets of *Tahweed* require a truthful tongue and opposition to falsehood. Of course, that only applies to fellow *Mowahhidoon.* Dissembling to a non-believer is not a sin. Also, as I said before, a Druze must cheerfully accept whatever comes from God. And last, he must protect other Druze, no matter the cost."

Lebout glanced at his watch.

Carl noticed. "I think I'm intruding on your schedule. May I come back again?"

Lebout smiled as if a breeze from the real world had been refreshing. "I'd like that."

Civil War

Harry Monahan, a law school classmate of Carl's, practiced in Soy City, located about fifteen miles from Moraine. He had been Carl's study partner in the hated Income Tax course. Were it not for Harry's ability to read the Internal Revenue Code without falling asleep, both of them might be permanently fertilizing some rice paddy in Viet Nam. Carl hadn't seen much of him over the years even though only 100 miles separated them. Harry was more at home at Civil War re-enactments than U of I football games.

On Friday evening Carl was sitting in Harry's office. Carl had been surprised when he ran across Harry's name on a computer search of Wally Aldin's nefarious legal doings. It was a personal injury claim Harry had litigated for Aldin in Reavley County, the next county west of Moraine. Harry would be a person who could be counted on for the truth, and to keep his mouth shut about what he said.

Harry locked the office door and extracted a six pack from the battered refrigerator in the copy room of the strange little law office, converted from a defunct Dairy Queen. Harry's preoccupation with the past accounted for him leaving the huge ice cream cone over the entrance, painted with a sardonic sign saying, "We'll Lick 'Em One And All."

Harry liked to fondle the Union Army memorabilia strewn around his office. By the time they had discussed the successes and disbarments of their classmates, three Heineken empties were already ballast in the wastebasket.

Harry snickered when Carl asked about Wally Aldin. He popped the cap of another beer, leaned back in his chair and launched into a description of Aldin's strange niche in the ecosystem. He had come to Moraine just prior to the Gulf war, and Harry had met him soon after.

What brought them together was an auto accident with the customary back and neck injuries, but it was a head injury that had escalated the settlement. Wally presented with a puzzling constellation of memory loss, headaches, and personality shift. At least that's what the insurance company paid for. Doctors hired by State Farm disagreed, but Wally was so convincing the company paid well to limit the risk.

Harry got him a decent settlement which let Aldin coast through the next few years in relative prosperity. This was devastating in the long run. Wally ignored Harry's suggestions as to conservative investments and rushed out to buy a new van and a boat. He must have thought the remaining fifty thousand dollars would last forever. Aldin claimed he couldn't do physical activity because he was too dizzy and weak. His unemployment ran out and he tried a variety of things, including Social Security Disability, to no avail, and finally went back to his old job at a convenience store and gas station on the Interstate.

As the years passed, Wally's rainbow of physical and emotional problems became more vivid. He began to drink heavily. At local taverns he constantly complained about governmental indifference and prejudice against Middle Eastern people. Barroom reaction was seldom sympathetic. He kept the local Congressman up to date on every slight to his dignity. He developed a taste for pestering public officials and for litigation.

None of it resulted in any solutions.

The inevitable backlog of bills accumulated. Soon the credit card companies featured him on their public enemy list. The banks shunned him like a leper.

Harry said Wally used to rant and rave about the inadequacy of the settlement whenever he met him on the street. He drifted back into Harry's office seeking advice about his financial condition and his disability claim, which had been rejected twice. "I did one of the few smart things in my young life, Carl. I told him I was on the board of the bank and had a conflict of interest because he was delinquent on his home loan. He was giving off beeps from outer space or something. I just knew all I had to do was listen to one confidence and I'd be socking the tar baby. Pretty soon all my fingers and toes would be stuck to Wally. The appointment was over just like that. Wally looked at me as if being on a bank board was worse than treason. He snatched his papers and stalked out, but I kept up on Wally from courthouse gossip and from what passes for a local paper around here."

Monahan went on to describe how Wally had spiraled down into his obsession with his guerrilla war against the court system.

"Why do you call it a guerrilla war?" Carl was straining to see it from Wally's perspective. Carl finished his second beer and placed the empty in the wastebasket.

"Guerilla war? Well...how about Wally's mortgage. I told you he was delinquent. His doublewide was about to get foreclosed for missing six payments. He went to the bank with a buddy...a young, good looking guy...so they asked a cute little secretary to see the original mortgage. While the other guy distracted her, Aldin dabbed a little White Out on a couple of words in the fine print so the damn thing read just the opposite. When they sued him the bank made a Xerox copy of the mortgage. The law firm the bank uses...I'm not involved because I was on the board...attached the mortgage to the complaint without anybody reading it. You've hung around a few law offices. Did you ever see anybody read the fine print of a mortgage before they really had to?"

Carl smiled and shook his head in agreement.

"Anyway, they filed a Verified Complaint swearing the mortgage copy attached was true and accurate even though it read just the opposite of what it did when everybody signed it. Aldin filed a Verified Answer admitting the document accurately stated the agreement. Of course, under the rules, the court was bound to accept the accuracy of the altered photocopy of the mortgage. The Judge held the bank had no right to foreclose. Wally's still on the property and the bank is still sucking wind. For the last year, the State's Attorney has been trying to decide whether they can charge him with anything."

Carl was blown away. "Unbelievable! I just can't imagine anybody doing that!"

Harry was blasé. "That's only because you and I have careers to protect. If we even thought about doing that shit, we'd be back working for a living. What can they do to guys like Aldin? Put them in jail for contempt? Hell, he'd open a grad school for the rest of the prisoners. Watch yourself with Wally Aldin. You think you're gonna run his defense? Wake up. He'll smile and pick your pocket."

— — — — — — — — — — —

Carl had heard enough. At first the stories about Aldin's judicial sabotage had seemed mildly amusing, little more than ingenious mischief. As they accumulated, though, Aldin began to seem fixated on destroying the Courts. His skillful and deceitful war against the system had merely exploited its weaknesses. Anyone wanting to paint him as a terrorist could make a case that he had finally snapped and had resorted to violence. Gadsen was probably working overtime to find cases that would let him introduce Aldin's legal vandalism as evidence of motive.

In the twenty minutes it took to drive to the jail in Moraine, Carl had time to think. Any grudging admiration for Aldin had worn off, and he was angry and perplexed at how to handle his client. His anger took the edge off his apprehension at driving down the street where he had been

189

surrounded and terrorized.

He now had insights about Aldin's Druze background that explained why he would be wary and distrustful, but there was the disturbing record of abuse of the law. How to approach him? Threaten to withdraw? Sympathize with his Druze-born distrust? He couldn't decide, and that made him frustrated. Finally, he concluded that letting Aldin know he had researched Druze beliefs would set off a firestorm.

When he entered the jail he said, "Thank you" to the deputy. He kept his temper until the door closed and then he slammed down his file on the green Formica table top.

Wally Aldin met his stare evenly and said, "Mornin', Counselor. Trouble in the stock market?"

Carl suppressed an outburst. He almost told Wally Aldin about the riot and the risk he had run just to have the dubious privilege of defending him. Instead he choked back the temptation. Aldin's life was more seriously at risk than his own. He decided to keep his personal fears bottled up and concentrate on the defense. He said, "Jeez, I wish just once I'd get a nice clean case without having the client screw it up."

Aldin looked up with a slow stare. "You saying I'm gonna make you earn your money?"

It was time to establish who was in charge. "Let's start with the guns." He paused to see if Wally would be defensive.

Aldin was silent and stared back.

Carl went on, "What about the guns? Why did you have them?"

Aldin said in a falsely pleasant voice, "It's the American way. Everybody has a right to keep and bear arms. It says so in the Second Amendment. Or did you skip that one in law school?"

Carl decided to skip the argument that the right was intended as a basis for an organized state militia. He asked, "Ok, I'll concede the right to hunt, although I personally think it's barbaric. Shotguns and squirrel rifles, but what in the world do you need with a Kalashnikov? Or with seven high cal-iber pistols? That .44 Magnum would bring down an elephant, and there haven't been any around here since the Mastodons."

Aldin shook his head. "You just don't get it, do you? Are you one of those so-called liberals? Nobody's got a right to do anything unless it helps the environment?"

"I'm just pointing out to you that having a Russian assault rifle isn't going to get you any brownie points in the eyes of the Judge and Jury."

"Am I running for something? Do I only have the right to keep and bear arms if somebody else thinks it's a good idea?"

Carl sighed. This was going to be uphill. "I'm only pointing out that keeping an arsenal to shoot cockroaches or burglars or whatever, lets them brand you as a terrorist."

"Well, that's what you're trained to prevent, isn't it, counselor? You're here to get me a fair trial. Have I got that straight? Saw that in a couple of movies." Aldin leaned back, in a defensive posture, arms folded, a cynical smile. Dark eyes spoiling for a fight.

"I got an earful about some of the stuff you've been pulling in your court cases."

Aldin rolled his shoulders. A wan smile was his only response.

"Don't look so pleased with yourself. You've got the entire courthouse terminally pissed off."

Aldin leaned forward, elbows on the table, chin on his fists. "You know, I'm just beginning to wonder what the hell business it is of yours what I do in some civil case?"

Carl exploded, "What business is it of mine? Which one of us has to get you a fair trial? You're slightly less popular around here than the IRS. Did you really fake some kind of heart attack to con the jury?"

A smirk crossed Aldin's face. "I've been sick since the Lebanese Civil War. You think it was a sort of picnic over there? I guess if I've got a health problem, it must be my heart or something, right?"

Carl let a couple of seconds go by. "Look, are we gonna screw around or play baseball?

"I think I told you I don't know how to play baseball."

Carl sighed. "I've got a stack of bullshit pleadings you filed. Absolute crap! You really think the court system is illegal? That's the stuff those right wing militias believe."

Aldin dropped the flippant manner. "You can scoff at what an ordinary person has to do to defend himself. Try it some time without your fancy title."

Carl thought about that and decided he owed Aldin a sympathetic ear. "Ok. I take it back. I'm willing to listen."

Aldin looked at him for a second and said, "Yeah, I'll bet."

Carl sighed and leaned forward, trying to break through to Wally. "Let's just start over and try to stick to your legal problems."

Aldin smacked the table with his palm. "That's just the thing! You just don't see it, do you? I'm going to be convicted no matter what I do because I'm not like the rest of you. They don't want to live up to the things they say they believe. I'm being executed for my beliefs in..."

"WALLY! I'm here to try to defend your LIFE! I don't care if you believe in the Single Tax or the mystical number seven! You can advocate a nut diet for all I care. We've got to get focused on defending this murder case."

Aldin fixed him with a look of hopelessness. "You really don't get it, do you?"

"Don't get what?"

"I'm going down no matter what. It doesn't make any difference if you're as crafty as Jerry Spence or Johnnie Cochrane. I'm going down, so you can clear your conscience."

"Why do you say that?"

"It doesn't matter. That judge's been sent to get me. She's just a hit man...uh...woman. No way I'm getting a fair trial outta that bitch! She's got orders."

Carl felt a wave of despair wash over him. How could he explain that Judge Harrigan wasn't a secret agent of some clandestine agency, that her bias was only runaway indignation? Did it even matter? A weight was pressing upon Carl. He shifted to a practical question, "What did you go through in the Lebanese Civil War?"

Aldin sat brooding, seeming uncertain whether to answer or deflect the question. Finally, he leaned forward. A troubled look passed over his face. "I was just a kid. My father was killed in Beirut by a mortar round that landed in the market where he was delivering produce from our farm in the mountains. I was with him, but I was in the back of the truck and the shrapnel from the round didn't penetrate. I had to load his body into the truck and drive him back home. When I got older I was in our militia, and we were in lots of firefights. That's how I was in buildings that got blown up. RPG's, mostly. They're not very accurate, but when they hit a building they have a tendency to make it fall down on top of you. First time that happened I was 16. After the third time, when I got out of the hospital…it was really just a tent with a nurse…I was having a hard time breathing. I was weak and wasn't worth a damn as a soldier. One of my uncles lived in New Jersey and he pulled some strings to get me over here. I couldn't speak English very well, only what I learned in school, but you learn pretty quick when you get dropped into a new country. My uncle worked in a convenience store. There were lots of guys from Lebanon in New Jersey. They were good at business and they started buying stores out here. They needed somebody stupid enough to run a store and live with these rednecks and put up with their bullshit. So here I am. Mr. Stupid!"

Carl's eyebrows went up. "That's quite a story. You've seen a lot of life, haven't you?"

Aldin just stared back.

"If there were some way to get this across to the Court…some way to tell your story about what you've been through…I think it would matter."

"You're saying it would make the jury believe I didn't do it?"

Carl felt the small breakthrough was about to seal up. "Not exactly. …not even approximately. Your background won't be relevant on the guilt phase…"

"What?"

"The guilt phase. The trial. Where they prove you did it."

Aldin frowned. "Where else would it be…relevant? Is that the word? What else would it be relevant to?"

Carl wanted to swallow the word, but he spat it out, "Sentencing."

"Sentencing?"

"Yes…sentencing. Where we may be trying to save your life."

Aldin shot out of his chair. "Why you son of a bitch! You've already got me convicted! What are you doing to me? I should have known! You're selling me out!"

Carl grimaced. "I'm not selling you out. I'm trying to do one of the jobs a lawyer has to do. That's to plan for anything that can happen, and getting convicted by this judge is certainly a very real possibility. If you won't testify…"

"So that's what this is all about! You're trying to get me to testify! I will not do that! I told you I'm innocent! It even says so in the Constitution! Now get me a fair trial. Get me some of that 'innocent until proven guilty' I've got coming. I held up my hand and swore allegiance to this country, and that's my right."

For the next half hour, Carl Hardman went over the case with Wally Aldin, but there was never any wavering. Aldin flatly refused to testify. He smiled the mirthless little grin Carl had come to expect and said, "You and I both know if I get up there and deny I did it, they'll question me about the Middle East and the people who are helping me. No way! No way! I'm not doing anything that will harm my friends."

A weight descended upon Carl. In his heart he admitted to himself that Wally Aldin had killed Judge Esker. He desperately wanted out of the case, despite his obligation to help this sad, self-destructive man.

Patriot Plots

East Peoria, Illinois, is in a different world from Moraine, less than 90 miles away. The people make earthmovers and belong to unions. They live within sight of the Illinois River and its endless stream of barges moving the commerce of the world. People with hard surfaces and sharp edges. East Peoria has a casino and a gentleman's club with exotic dancers. Richard Pryor grew up in a brothel across the river. Its most recent gift to the world was the Reverend Doctor Matt Hale. His World Church of the Creator crashed and burned in a Federal Courtroom in Chicago, not over its racist-right diatribe, but in a misbegotten legal stand over the name of the "church" in a copyright suit by some other group foolish enough to retrieve the polluted words.

Hale, a law school grad, had been rejected by the Character and Fitness Committee of the bar. Something about his racist expressions casting doubt on his respect for the law. License denied by the Illinois Supreme Court, the Reverend was belched back into the lay population, unless his self-anointed clerical status counted.

The Rev. Dr. Hale had been convicted of soliciting the death of the Federal Judge who upheld the copyright claim in defiance of the Rev. Dr. Hale's legal theories. In the wake of this strange legal event, one of the adherents to the *World Church*, Benjamin Smith, had gone off on a shooting spree across Illinois and Indiana that ended in the death of three and the wounding of another half-dozen. He died by his own hand, trapped in a swarm of squad cars. Smith was the only casualty who was not a member of a minority group.

— — — — — — — — — —

Brother Bill had agonized over the fact that he simply could not harm the child, Susan, but as the days passed, he now agonized that his decision was mere weakness. For Brother Bill, the God of Righteousness and Judgment was the driving force in his life. He listened for messages and watched for signs. When they failed to appear, he was in turmoil. This was what moved him to point his car northwest to East Peoria. Bill remembered the brotherhood he had felt with people at various patriot convocations, people who were united in resisting the Zion Occupation Government's plans to turn America over to international control.

He parked near a small supermarket and looked around for anyone following him. He went inside and lingered in the back, pretending to shop, but watching through the front windows. In 15 minutes, all he saw was middle-aged female customers streaming in and out.

A teenager was stocking produce. Bill assumed a look of urgency and said, "Excuse me! I have a disability and I have to use a restroom right now! Where is it?"

The young man looked as if he were about to recite some rule about rest rooms being reserved for employees, but the magic word "disability" had leverage. Nobody ever got in trouble for letting a disabled person do whatever he wanted. "Right through those swinging doors. Men's on the right."

Thanking him, Bill hurried through the doors and looked over his shoulder. The young man had resumed stocking tomatoes. There seemed to be nobody else around. Bill cautiously walked to the back door, looking for a security alarm. Finding none, he pushed the panic bar and stepped out onto the loading dock. It was deserted. He walked down the steps and headed toward the end of the strip mall, pausing occasionally as if to check his watch, but scanning for anybody following. There was nothing but dumpsters and cardboard boxes. He walked around to the front and strolled into a pizza place.

In one of the booths was a man in his late twenties, with short-cropped hair and intense grey eyes. They held their stare as Bill crossed the room and took a seat in the next booth, sitting back to back with the man, only inches between them. If anyone was watching, it would be difficult to prove any contact between them. The arrangements had been made only two hours earlier from a payphone call to a person in Hale's family.

A waitress with a cadaverous look, reflecting the new Midwestern passion for meth, wandered over and Bill ordered a small pizza with onions and sausage and a Coke.

In the adjoining booth, P. Michael Madden, one of the few remaining faithful of the World Church was working on an Italian Beef sandwich. They had been at several of the same convocations: Branson, Missouri; Rosholt, Arkansas; West Harrison, Indiana. Bill had marveled at the inspiration he had received during these weekends. While he considered himself a believer in old fashioned, fundamentalist Christianity, he was inspired by the political and racial ideas he heard that explained the direction the world was taking. For the first time he heard of the "Mud People," descended from Eve's coupling with Satan that produced Cain, father of the darker people of the world. Not merely different races, they were truly non-humans given by Satan the power to interbreed with white people and to contaminate the Children of God with non-human genes. This message had been hard for Bill to reconcile with the teachings he heard in church, but these new ideas had power. Their believers did not apologize. They did not flinch at the reaction of big-city-liberals and other traitors to America.

Bill was in awe of their commitment to their beliefs, no matter the cost. Mired in doubt and indecision about harming Susan, he needed an inspiration, an infusion of will, an end to his paralysis.

He had come to East Peoria ready to listen.

Madden pretended to be wiping his lips with a paper napkin to screen his words, "Are you sure you weren't followed?"

Bill whispered, "Can't know for certain. They're very good, but I've doubled back a few times, checked for helicopters, and I went out through the back door of the grocery store."

Madden said, "Good."

"Do you think it's safe to talk here?"

"It's as good as anyplace. Headquarters is only a couple of blocks away, and I eat here a lot. Keeping to a few places gives you a pretty good notion of who belongs and who doesn't. If they want to take us now, we can't stop them. But for some reason...make that *no* reason...I think they've let up since they put Dr. Hale in their steel box. They're foolish enough to think that will stop us."

Bill felt a tiny tightening in his stomach at the word "us." He had never reconciled his respect for the selfless commitment of Hale with his inner qualms. "Ok, I guess it's safe enough. Want me to sit with you?"

"No, back to back is safer, and we can keep our voices down. Now what's on your mind?"

Bill felt as if he were on a train, crossing a frontier in some old movie. The train was in motion and he was helpless to stop it. "I've got a situation..."

"Yes? Go on."

"It's bothering me."

"What kind of a situation?"

"You know the murder of Judge Esker?"

"In Moraine? By that sand-nigger?"

Bill took another step by rejecting his reaction to the word. "Yes, that's the one."

"They'll find some way to let him go, or they'll put him into Witness Protection."

Bill was shocked that Madden grasped so quickly what had taken him weeks to understand. "You see the problem, then."

Madden put his hand to his mouth and mumbled, "And the solution."

They talked for the next hour about how to do it, about how Bill could become the instrument of Justice. When they finished, Brother Bill was refreshed in spirit. He had a plan and someone to turn to for inspiration and reassurance.

A Modest Proposal

No other legal matter is quite like a capital murder case. A life being bartered for a life. Such transactions develop quirks. This one was no exception. The clock radio went off at six, playing a song that must have been from the *Worst of Sonny and Cher* album. When Carl finished his shower, he noticed a blinking red light on his answering machine. He pushed the playback button. A female voice said, "Please call Mr. Gadsen. 485 2671." That was all it said. Call him. No explanation. Just call him.

What the hell's this about?

Carl punched in the number and after one ring Willard Gadsen answered his cell phone. He invited Carl to meet him for breakfast. A meeting away from his office, outside the glare of TV lights and the web of courthouse gossip.

At eight on the dot, the Champaign oldies station went to local news and Carl twisted the key to shut down the Jaguar. He was parked in front of a '40s gas station in its second life as a restaurant, one block from the Courthouse Square. The distinctive Standard Oil torch had been painted over and the word "Eat" had been superimposed. There was no restaurant name on the building to separate it from its past. Locals called it the Grease Pit.

As he got out of the car, he was conscious of sweat forming on his brow. His hands were clammy and he was alert for any threat. There was none.

Was that the reality of Moraine, or an illusion of safety and normality Hitchcock would have directed?

Carl walked through the front door and a small bell tinkled. The decor was straight out of a craft mall. Every wall was cluttered with cute little sayings painted on wooden plaques. The scorched odor of soybean oil from donuts being deep fried competed with the sour smell of hi-test coffee. At a large round table, five men in coveralls were engrossed in a local card game called *Pitch*. All the eyes in the place followed him. Generations of inbreeding had strewn the town with cousins and nephews or closer relatives no one mentioned. They all looked similar.

Along the windows a half-dozen plastic booths looked as if they had been rescued from a dead McDonald's. Willard Gadsen was alone in the last one.

Carl tried to ignore the sullen stares as he walked through the room. His memory was working overtime, trying to recognize a face or two from the riot. He could feel the tension rising.

Willard was dressed in a white shirt, open at the neck. He was lounging in the booth with his right leg up on the seat, affecting indifference. He motioned for Carl to sit down opposite him.

Carl loosened his tie and unbuttoned his collar, preparing to play whatever game Willard was dealing. A surly, gum-chewing waitress stopped and wordlessly stood with her ballpoint threatening a plain pad of white paper. Willard said, "Glazed, Deena. Black, Carl?"

"Sounds good."

Deena disappeared without any change of expression.

Carl broke the ice. "I assume we're not here to do a food review."

A bemused look played across Willard's face. "You get right to it, don't you?"

"Well, we're going to have our mouths full of carbs in a few minutes, if she can spell."

Willard sighed, sat up a little straighter, and took a swig from his coffee mug. "I'm wondering if you've thought about how this is gonna come out."

Carl's expression remained impassive.

Willard waited for a response just an instant too long. When none came, he continued, "You know, I kinda feel like I've been doing ok for a country boy up against a pro like you, especially when we're fighting over a death sentence."

Carl couldn't resist. "It's always hard to beat a country boy in his own chicken yard, especially if one of the chicken's is wearing a robe."

Willard smiled. "Gonna take a while for us 'round here to catch up with a new century and all those liberal ideas, like due process, I guess. Nevertheless...I've been thinking about your client and trying to soften my heart a little."

"It sure escaped my notice until now."

"Yeah...well...whatever. But if you're interested in talking, I think I've got a little latitude I can extend."

The idea of a soft hearted prosecutor in one of the small Illinois farm counties aroused suspicion. But he listened with a glimmer of hope "Yeah? What're you offering? Death by cholesterol?" He pointed to a plate of donuts Denna as dropping onto a table next to him.

"Glad to hear you admit what's at stake here. I'm talking about keeping your boy alive."

It flickered through Carl's mind that Gadsen's offer had to be the result of some political calculus, but what that could be that made no sense. He could not suppress a look of puzzlement. "So tell me what brought on this attack of conscience."

The plate of donuts slid across the faded green Formica. Gadsen chose one and took a bite. Carl wondered if he was hungry or just needed time to invent an answer.

Gadsen carefully examined the donut in his right hand, as if debating how much to disclose. Finally he said, "Well, over time we all mellow, I guess. I was thinking about your client during church, and I decided to extend an offer. Aldin wasn't such a bad guy until he went crazy and declared war on the Courts. Maybe he felt justified in some twisted way."

This sounded too sensible to be coming from a small town prosecutor with a career-builder case. Carl began to look for the hook. "So what's your thought?"

"Life." Willard took another bite, chewed slowly, and swallowed, allowing the word to stand on its own. "Life, pure and simple. He gets to live. He can save his life. Plead him guilty. We won't recommend the death sentence...even recommend against it if the Judge gets bent out of shape. You know, Judge Esker had personal scruples against the death sentence. He was a decent, Christian man, a Methodist. We could point that out to the Court as a reason...if your boy pleads guilty."

Carl felt as if a dam had broken and all the pressure had been released. He hadn't been conscious of the numbing feeling welled up inside, but he tried to keep from showing his relief. "Well, that's interesting. It's certainly something to think about. I'm going over to see him, and we'll discuss it. But what about the Feds? They've still got a shot at him. They might feel they have to try him on a terrorism thing. It could get politically uncomfortable."

Willard swallowed some coffee and leaned back. "Thought about that. I've cleared this with the Feds. Talked to a supervisor in Justice and with the Fibbies. They cleared it with Homeland Security."

Somehow that didn't set right with Carl. A tiny alarm was going off. Why would the Homeland Security and the FBI give up on a juicy political case like this? Why would they be willing to just fade away while some local prosecutor would be seen to have caved in? He decided to set aside his misgivings and not poison Gadsen's offer by questioning it. After all, life was life! The death sentence was his enemy and here was a chance to defeat it. A guaranteed win. On a personal basis, an exit strategy.

"Well, give me some time to think about this and talk to my client." Hope was filling him with warmth. He even felt hungry enough to grab the last two donuts and wrap them in a paper napkin. He got up and reached for his wallet.

"Can't let you pay for it, Carl. After making you an offer like this one, these days they'd appoint a special prosecutor and accuse me of accepting a bribe."

Carl laughed. He threw down a couple of dollar bills. "Here's for Miss Personality. Might be enough for a new wad of gum."

Carl was elated as he walked into the jail and asked to see Aldin. While waiting to be admitted to the County Board room, he began to dream of how to use the time that wouldn't be lost in hopeless weeks of trial. A lawyer seldom realizes the extent of his tension until some event cancels a trial. A winter storm that closes down the Midwest or getting fired by a client retrieves a chunk of life. Saving Aldin from a lethal injection seemed like a big win, especially for a client who had spent a decade sporting with the legal system.

Carl walked into the County Board Room. Aldin, as usual, was ushered in and took his usual place lounging on a swivel chair.

"Morning, Counselor. Is the Land of the Free still in business out there?"

"Wally, let's play later. I've got some great news for you!"

Aldin raised an eyebrow.

Carl relayed Gadsen's offer to drop the death sentence for a plea. He explained the possibilities of parole many years down the line. Aldin turned and stared out the window without a flicker of gratitude or even curiosity.

Carl was perplexed. Then his mood changed to irritation. "Are you listening? I'm trying to tell you we can save your life!"

"Are YOU listening? The answer is NO! Under the Constitution I'm not guilty, and this illegal court can't prove I'm guilty. You told me, yourself, the State has to prove me guilty beyond a reasonable doubt, and that I don't even have to offer any proof if I don't want to. Well, I don't want to. I'm not testifying, and I'm not pleading guilty."

Carl's shoulders sagged. For a moment he wondered about Aldin's competency. "Let me get this straight. You're refusing to deny committing this crime. You expect the presumption of innocence to win the case. You're turning down a deal that would save your life. Am I right, or did I forget some important piece of stupidity?"

Aldin flared. "Call it what you want, but I'm not pleading to anything! I'm innocent! Do you know that word? Get your ass in there and defend me!" With that Aldin got up and walked over to the door and hammered on it with the flat of his hand, shouting for the deputy to take him back to his cell.

As Aldin disappeared, Carl shouted, "Get somebody else! I've done all I can."

Aldin didn't even look back.

Carl fumed his way out of the Moraine County Court House. He intentionally cut across the lawn and kicked the "Keep Off the Grass" sign as he did a bee-line for his car. As he opened the driver's door he noticed a black leather attaché case in the back seat. He knew he hadn't given anyone a ride. He opened the back door and examined the briefcase. It bore no identification tag or monogram. It was not locked. As he popped the latches, he was astonished to find stacks of worn hundred dollar bills, each stack circled with a rubber band. He looked around. There was nobody within a block. He picked up one stack and riffled through it. There were fifty bills in each package. And there were twenty stacks.

———— · —— · —— · —— · —— · —— · ——

Brother Bill put down the binoculars. His pickup was parked a block west of the Courthouse behind a hedge with an opening allowing a line of sight to the building. He was as alarmed as if waking to a sound in the night. Hardman had reached into his briefcase and was holding up a wad of money. It confirmed Bill's suspicions. Big money from someplace was buying this lawyer. Where did money like that come from? It had to be terrorists. Bin Laden? Maybe one of the offshoots of that strange Saudi ruling family. Maybe it was part of what Saddam Hussein looted from his people. Bill didn't know. But he was certain it smelled of evil and was being used to buy a way out for a fanatic who had assaulted America.

Bill did not panic. He did what he always did when he needed an answer, look in the Good Book. He reached in the glove compartment for his *King James Bible*. He grasped the spine in his right hand while praying for guidance. The *Bible* fell open. While his eyes were closed he placed his finger on a verse in *Joshua VII*, the chapter following the conquest of Jericho, which was accomplished by strict obedience to God's commands. After the miraculous collapse of the city's wall when the trumpets sounded, God had ordered the devastation of the city. He had forbidden Joshua and his men to loot the corrupted wealth.

Bill's eyebrows went up. The verse under his finger was about the Middle East, the same part of the world that spawned the likes of Wally Aldin and his terrorist buddies.

Joshua VII was the story of the woes that befell Joshua's people after one of Joshua's men violated God's injunction to take nothing from the evil place. The traitor was Achan, the son of Carmi. In the verse under his finger Achan admits looting a "…goodly Babylonish garment, and two hundred shekels of silver, and a wedge of gold of fifty shekels weight…" and hiding them under his tent.

The image was obviously the filthy money in Hardman's briefcase, his loot for trying to free the enemy. The garment was the cloak of Justice.

Brother Bill's finger pointed to Verse 12, "Therefore the children of Israel could not stand before their enemies, but turned their backs before their enemies, because they were accursed: neither will I be with you any more, except ye destroy the accursed from among you."

His mouth dropped open. Destroy the accursed among you! Achan, the son of Carmi! Even the name Carmi was the name of a town in Illinois an hour's drive away. Yes! It was a sign! Hardman must be destroyed along with Aldin. It was confirmation of the plan he had made with P. Michael Madden!

— · — · — · — · — · — · — · — · —

Another car was parked on a side street, a half-block behind Bill's pickup. The car was a nondescript, green Nissan Pathfinder, several years past its prime. Its occupant, the tall, dark man, had chosen the location to monitor the Jaguar and to observe Carl's reaction as he returned from the Courthouse and examined the contents of the briefcase.

The pickup had slowly pulled into his line of sight and had taken up a position permitting the pickup's driver a direct view of the Jaguar. Years of war and anticipating treachery had developed a sixth sense. The man watched as Brother Bill looked through his binoculars at Hardman crossing the Courthouse lawn, opening the car door, examining the money, and scanning the area with a perplexed look.

This is the man who followed Hardman and his wife at the festival.

The tall man in the Pathfinder watched Hardman drive away and watched the person in the pickup put down his binoculars and open a book. He took down the license number of the pickup. Then he reached into his jacket pocket and withdrew a *Romeo Y Julieta,* removing the band and putting the cigar in his mouth, moistening it, preparing it slowly, making it ready to light after giving the pickup time to get several blocks away.

Pressing Matters

It was the third inning of a warm Saturday afternoon, and eleven year old girls can become bored with baseball even if the players are handsome. Carl and Susan were sitting in the bleachers behind third base. He had been enlightening her with the fine points of a double steal.

Susan squirmed in her seat. Carl was about to point out the restroom when she said, "Daddy, why are you helping a bad man?"

The question hit him like a slap. He said, "What did you say?"

"Why are you helping a bad man?"

He asked, "Who do you mean?"

She said, "Wally Aldin, the man who killed the Judge."

Oh boy! Here it comes, he thought. "Why do you believe he killed a Judge, Honey?"

"Well, didn't he? Everybody says he did."

Hearsay apparently didn't seem a problem for an 11 year old who believed in multiplication tables because everybody told her they were true.

"My job is to make sure nobody gets to do anything to Wally Aldin unless the jury is reasonably certain he killed Judge Esker. I'm supposed to point out all the reasons why it's not for sure. It's kind of hard to explain, Susan, but I'll try. Do you remember the time you came home from school crying because some little girl said you pulled her hair?"

It was obvious she remembered. Her face clouded over.

"Do you remember how mad you were when the teacher didn't even ask your side? She just got angry and sent you to the office?"

"Yes! And I didn't even do it! Frankie Krasnowski pulled her hair when we were in line for the slide. He ran away before she turned around, so she thought I did it."

"Well, in court we try to keep people from deciding before they hear all the facts. That's what lawyers do. They try to get the jury to go slow until everybody gets a chance to tell what they saw."

She thought about it. A couple of pitches went by. Then she turned and said, "I guess you should be really sure. That's fair. But did he really do it?"

The only thing Carl could say was, "He says he's innocent, and by the rules of how we decide those things, he is. But what will the jury believe? Who knows?"

She smiled at him, the smile that kept him going. "I bet you know, Daddy. You already told me it's a secret."

He smiled back, "Yeah, something like that."

The Jaguar pulled into the driveway of the Condo. He had just dropped off Susan, and was half hoping that Dani would invite him in. But her car was gone and Susan called out from the front door that her mother had left a note saying she was picking up some dry cleaning and would be back in a few minutes. He decided not to linger.

As he reached his condo, he shut off the engine and crossed his fingers that its cranky electrical system would start again next time. As he looked up, he saw Laura Aldin sitting on the front step. She was wearing the same summer dress that had captivated him, but this time seeing her only produced confusion. His mind was on Dani, and he felt guilty for what he had felt about Laura the last time they were together.

She seemed to pick up on his emotion. "I hope I'm not intruding. I

209

was in the neighborhood and decided to stop. We haven't had a chat for some time…about Wally. What do you hear from him?"

A legitimate question from the wife of a client. "He's confusing and frustrating, and he's a mystery to me. But you knew that already. The bottom line is he refuses to help himself. Thinks he knows better than I do how to try his case. I can save the man's life, but he doesn't seem to care. Won't testify. Won't even consider a guilty plea that would eliminate the death sentence."

She looked at Carl and shook her head. She seemed upset. "What's that about eliminating the death sentence?"

Carl said, "We've got an offer to plead guilty and accept a life sentence. Of course life doesn't mean life. In this state he'd be eligible for parole in…

"No death sentence?"

"No, it would be a negotiated plea that the Court would almost certainly go along with."

She looked troubled.

Carl said, "I know the prospect of serving decades in jail isn't pleasant. Apparently it's unbearable for him. He refuses to go along with it. Says he wants to go to trial. He's a hard case, for sure."

Her troubled look faded. "Now you're getting the flavor of what I've been living with. He's a strange person. I've often thought he had a death wish."

Carl stood on the sidewalk, looking down at her. The scoop neck of her dress was revealing, but this time he was embarrassed to find himself looking. He turned away and asked her, "Has he ever talked to you about his life in Lebanon? Maybe about his personal beliefs?"

She said, "No, that's what I was telling you before. He led me to believe he was a Christian of some kind. I don't know…he never talked about his beliefs…I just don't know."

Carl wanted to avoid this conversation. He wanted to savor the time with Susan and keep alive the flavor of Dani. And talking to Laura like this was interfering. A part of him was inflamed by her, and he resented that. He decided to cut the discussion short and give himself time to think. "Mrs. Aldin..."

"Laura."

"Ok...Laura...I'm having kind of a bad day. I don't mean to be inhospitable. I'd invite you in, but maybe that's not a good idea right now. Can we follow up on this later?"

Laura looked at him, perplexed for a moment. Then she rose and said, "I'm sorry. I guess I've intruded."

"Please...don't feel that way. I guess some of the problems I've been dealing with are getting to me."

"Don't worry about it. I'll call next time before coming by. Thanks so much for caring." She smiled weakly and made him feel as if he had crushed a flower.

— · — · — · — · — · — · — · — · —

As Dani and Carl walked out of the Art Theater in downtown Champaign, the crowd was subdued, except for a few college students who were agitated by the rerun of *Fahrenheit 911* and were cursing Bush.

They walked along Church Street, down Neil, to the outdoor tables at the *Cowboy Monkey*. They found a small table and ordered two Heinekens. Neither had spoken since the movie.

Dani said, "That film is scary. I haven't talked politics with you in...what...five years?

He wanted to keep from being dragged into a political quagmire on a warm summer night. "I guess politicians are all the same."

"Surely you can see that Bush is a tool of the oil people."

"Aren't all of them puppets dancing on somebody's strings?"

She asked, "So what do you think about the war?" She obviously had more on her mind than a movie review. Was this a test that had consequences in their personal relationship?

"Dani, this war isn't much better or worse than the average war, and we grew up in a century with hundreds of them. I remember being a little kid and I was eating a BLT with my grandparents when all of a sudden I heard 'boom! boom!' I ran out of the house. Kids were coming from all over the neighborhood, headed for the house across the street. An old guy lived there, name of Pikula...something like that. Anyway, he's got a double barrel shotgun, shooting it up in the air. All the kids are scrambling around for the empty shotgun shells. I'm looking up in the sky for Russian planes. I remember saying, 'What are you shooting at?' He just said, 'The war's over! My son can come home from Korea!' I can remember looking at him and thinking 'What does that mean? The war's over! What does that mean? How can the war be over?'"

Dani's voice was small and lifeless, "I guess he was wrong and you were right. They'll never let war be over. War. Always war. Guns, guns, guns. Everybody wants guns. Keep and bear arms. Wally's no exception. If you have a problem, just get your guns and let's solve it. Big war, little war, a couple of hundred million killed in the last century, give or take a few genocides."

He nodded. "Were the Gulf Wars just a proving ground for all the neat military equipment Reagan built? What happened? The Kremlin saw that their best weapons were just target drones. They threw up their hands and declared bankruptcy. There we were, all alone, all dressed up with nowhere to go. We didn't have a respectable enemy left on the planet! Thirty years ago the idea of invading Afghanistan would have been a bad comedy routine at Second City."

She nodded her head in begrudging concession.

He was on a roll. "So what are we going to do? Declare peace? Flood the unemployment office with pissed-off spooks and soldiers? Guys who've had their morality replaced with deniability? Guys with enough technical training to overthrow the government? I don't think so. They all got jobs working for Homeland Security. We'd have to invent people like Aldin if they didn't exist. Think what he's doing for the economy? They've dumped lots of money into Moraine, buying Cheetos and Pepsi at the convenience store. Can't get a hotel room within 50 miles when we're in court. Wally's better for business in Central Illinois than Homecoming at the University."

Dani shook her head slowly. "You're not buying into some conspiracy paranoia, are you?"

Carl sighed. "No, I guess not, but you and I grew up on Howdy Doody and the Beatles. Wally and his buddies grew up playing war with real guns. Put yourself in his place. Being paranoid doesn't seem as crazy as it would have been before I got into this case. And I've got a confession to make. I'm going to stick around and defend him through the trial. He's lunchmeat without somebody who cares. I also got paid, and that's always nice. Let's drive over to Katsinas and get a sandwich now that I can afford it. I'm hungry and we need to talk about some new stuff."

—————————————————————

The kitchen was closed when they got to Katsinas, but the bartender persuaded the waitress to find some cold chicken and make sandwiches for them. The staff knew that Carl was a good tipper.

They sat in the deserted dining room, away from the crowd in the bar and the noise of the juke box. Carl said, "I don't know if this is the right time, but I need to fill you in on Wally's latest tantrum. I got an offer from Gadsen to plead out for life."

She sat straight up and her eyebrows lifted. "Wow! That solves all our problems!"

"Not so fast. He's accusing me of selling him out. He insists on going to trial. Only thing is, he refuses to give me a chance to win. Says it's in God's hands."

She shook her head slowly, as if rediscovering the stupidity that seems to ooze out of cracks in the earth. "I can't believe it. Doesn't he know he's headed for lethal injection? Can't you make him understand?"

Carl exhaled in frustration. "Dani, I've done everything short of having them stick a sample needle in his arm. He just doesn't give a damn. I did my homework…strange way to put it…went over to the U of I campus and had a talk with a professor of religion. He explained that Wally is a Druze."

"What's a Druze?"

He replayed Professor Lebout's information, hoping he remembered all the important details. It felt a little like taking a philosophy exam.

She sat quietly for the ten minutes it took, and finally said, "I think I need a stronger drink."

Remembering her tastes, he asked the waitress to bring her a *Pinot Grigio*. He said, "I'm sorry if I've messed up your life."

She reached over and put her hand on his. "We're doing this together. That's the most important thing."

That made him happy until he remembered that he hadn't leveled with her about the near-miss disaster in front of the courthouse. And about the possibility that it would happen again and involve her.

Brother Bill took the lump of C-4 plastic explosive and kneaded it into a six-inch ball. He inserted the copper sheath of an electric blasting cap.

P. Michael Madden had suggested a bomb. Bill told him he had acquired C-4 explosive several years earlier from a patriot he met at a gun show. He had never known exactly why he bought it, but the chance to acquire such a rare item had been too tempting to turn down. Madden knew how to attach it to the electrical system of the car. The explosion would turn the Jaguar into twisted modern sculpture. Hardman and his ex-wife would die wrapped in the luxury car.

The car was parked in the lot outside Katsinas, the restaurant where Hardman spent most of his free time drinking and consorting with worldly insiders who profited from the sweat of ordinary people.

It was almost 11 p.m. and nobody was around. The lot was darker than usual because he had used a .22 Ruger Spartacus II, a silent target pistol, to pop the bulb in the streetlight high on the pole. It was an easy shot, bracing against the half-lowered window of his pickup.

Nobody near the campus paid much attention to things going on behind a place that sold liquor. He tried the door of the Jaguar and found it unlocked. He released the hood latch, being careful to avoid leaving threads from his work gloves on any part of the car. The hood popped open several inches. In just a few seconds he had the C-4 alligator-clipped to the leads on the starter. He nestled the clay-like explosive against the firewall in front of the driver's seat and carefully lowered the hood, snapping it closed, making almost no sound. Less than 15 seconds for the entire thing. Now he would park a block away and watch.

Madden had said there was only one thing to do, act without letting feelings get in the way. Then the Good Book said utterly destroy the accursed. That he would do.

— ·— ·— ·— ·— ·— ·— ·— ·— ·—

It was eleven minutes after midnight, and Brother Bill had been watching people through his 10 power binoculars as they straggled out of Katsinas'. A few were tipsy, most were noisy and laughing. Despite their lives of sin, he hoped they would all be clear of the Jaguar when the lawyer came out and started it.

Nobody was in the lot when the door opened and Carl and Dani exited the restaurant. Carl stopped, took a deep breath and stretched, looking up at the stars, absorbing the warm prairie night.

Good, thought Brother Bill. *They're alone. Hope he gets the most out of that stretch. It may be a little cramped down there in Hell.*

The lawyer and the woman took their time, making small talk as they strolled over to the passenger side of the Jaguar. He opened the door for her and she slipped into the passenger seat. He closed her door as she smiled up at him.

Bill swallowed hard. He took no pleasure in this.

The lawyer walked around the front of the car, opened the driver's door and sat down, searching with the key for the ignition. At last he leaned forward and twisted the key.

Brother Bill braced himself for the blast

A pause.

Nothing happened.

Bill blinked.

Hardman twisted the key again and again.

Brother Bill watched helplessly.

The restaurant door opened and a middle-aged couple walked out.

Brother Bill felt a surge of conscience. The shrapnel would surely kill these people. There had been no sign given that they should be killed. Then he saw Hardman get out of the car and slam the door in disgust.

"Son of a bitch! Hey, Rick! Mary! Can we hook a ride with you? Don't ever buy a Jaguar. The Lucas electric system crapped out again. Second time this month. I can't even get it to turn over. Battery must be dead."

"Sure, Carl. Leave it and we'll call for a tow on my cell phone. Didn't your Daddy ever tell you to buy American?"

"Jaguar's owned by Ford. What's American?"

Carl and Dani got into Rick's Cadillac and were driven away.

Brother Bill cautiously walked into the lot from the alley side. It took less than ten seconds to pop the hood, open it a few inches and snatch back the device. Utterly destroying Hardman was one thing, but harming a tow truck driver was quite another.

From the Ashes

Rick dropped them off at Dani's house. Instead of offering to drive him to his condo, she invited him in. There was a certain awkwardness at the front door. He sat across from her at the kitchen table. She made coffee to offset the drinks. A few minutes of small talk passed while he tried to decide what to do next.

He said, "Well…guess it's getting late." They both stood and she took her keys from the table and began to walk toward the garage to drive him to his condo.

Then it happened. She brushed against him and he savored the moment. She looked up at him with her dark eyes and touched his cheek. She sighed and seemed to surrender. She put her arms around him and buried her head against his chest.

Her scent dredged up deep memories of happiness and hurt. Her body was at the threshold of fifty, but was lithe and smooth. Her touch opened a treasure chest of sense memories from the years before the start of their cold war. The clean smell of her hair churned soft recollections of youth and hope. When he touched her cheek, tears welled up in her eyes, a distillation of the past. Afternoons of sensual delight in a vacation villa with a Caribbean breeze directing the filmy curtains in a ballet. The first night in the new house overlooking the Illinois River, permitting only tender intimacy to avoid waking the baby.

But there was also the memory of emptiness when only the husk of marriage remained. Nights when the distance across the bed was a canyon; days with pleasantness pasted on their faces for Susan's benefit.

The taste of her kiss was unique. It conjured up the first night he discovered Dani as a lover. They had been working late on a brief in the days before word processing, photocopying at midnight. They had touched and a pent-up force had flooded them. By morning the brief was still unfinished. Exhausted by the discoveries of the night, they had wheedled an extension out of their opponent and had spent the rest of the week at the Palmer House in Chicago. When they returned to the office on Monday, they were husband and wife as well as law partners.

Her kiss was what he remembered from that first night, her lips again melting from internal heat. A distant alarm was ringing. Was this smart? Hadn't he learned the first time?

She had her arms around him. He knew her dance. He overrode his misgivings and drifted into unfulfilled dreams and second chances.

Dani took his face in her hands and held it and looked at him as if he were a new object, unknown in all the universe. Then she took him by the hand and led him into her bedroom. The bed was a froth of white, a whiff from a movie about plantations and camellias. A ceiling fan with brass fittings and white blades was turning deliberately. He began to understand that the years had calmed her, revealing old-fashioned, feminine tastes. This was her place, filled with marshmallow softness and whipped cream garnish.

She slowly unbuttoned his shirt and ran her hands inside, along his waist. She pushed his shirt back from his shoulders. She loosened his belt. He was totally passive. She was determining the pace. When he stood naked before her, ready, far more ready than her tempo permitted, years melted away. The details of their present lives were forgotten.

Dani circled him, touching him with her body, still fully clothed. He was surprised how it excited, without the touch of her skin. She paused, facing him and unbuttoned her blouse. Her breasts were enclosed in black satin. The smooth black cloth teased his chest. She stretched her blouse around him, as if attempting to pull him inside with her.

He trembled with anticipation before this new creature that had evolved.

She placed his hands inside her blouse, and he freed her from the black satin. She leaned against his abdomen with her full breasts, forming the hidden cleft where his face had found sanctuary so many dreams ago. He slipped his her slacks down over her hips and she was free. Her abdomen and hips were smooth, her legs smooth and firm.

She ran the inner side of her left knee up his thigh and desire coursed through them. She clung to his neck, as if trying to climb higher. Her wetness was warm against his thigh. He fought to wait, to savor what was ahead, to pace himself to the ceiling fan's slow circular motion. They tumbled onto the white quilt and its chill caused them to race to completion.

It was a visit to old, familiar places with mouths and fingers and anything with a nerve ending. A sheen of perspiration covered him. He felt a pounding and a rush of confusion. She was the past and the present, but was she the future?

The last thing he thought as he surrendered to her was that he had rescued time from oblivion. The last thing he saw before it ended was a tear in her eye.

— · — · — · — · — · — · — · — · —

It was noon later that day. Dani was eating a veggie sandwich at the snack bar of the Krannert Art Museum across from the College of Law. She had been troubled since driving Carl home at daybreak, before Susan returned from her overnight. Through her lecture on Constitutional Law, emotions swirled. Feelings tumbled like clothes in a dryer. She lost track during a student's wandering report of *Mapp v. Ohio*. That had never happened before. At 11:30 she had given up revising a paper for an upcoming symposium on the *Constitution and the Presidency*. She walked across the street to the Krannert Art Museum, reaching for the serenity that usually came during a quiet half hour alone with the paintings. This time, it evaded her.

The night had been sweet and the intimacy was as comfortable as an old pair of slippers discovered in the back of a closet. But the dawn left her with the reality that nothing between them had changed except for the distance that separated his law practice from her new life in academia.

Susan had rushed through her breakfast over the rock station's morning drivel. Some rap group called *Nellie*, not Dani's way to start the day. She had been on the verge of raising a question with Susan about visitation or anything that would bring Carl's name into the conversation. A chance for Susan to say something positive or negative, to supply an omen. It didn't happen.

With a sigh she dropped the crusts of her sandwich in the trash and placed the juice bottle in the recycling basket. She wandered toward the main entrance, pausing to examine a display of student design projects.

It was a fact that she had strong feelings for him. Always had, always would. A fact she hadn't faced for a long time, but here it was. Funny how a night of sex could make you notice a person again. But it was also a fact that he was powerful and headstrong and committed to his own program. Calling and asking for help with the Motion to Suppress was the first concession he had made to her independent accomplishments. What did he really think of her? Obviously he still was attracted to her. But what about his daylight thoughts, high noon reality? Was there a chance for them to have a relationship that preserved their freedom? With Susan in the picture how could there be anything but surrender by one of them?

Dani crossed the street in the middle of the block, running the gauntlet of student cars trolling for a parking spot.

Then there was the Aldin case. Dani was troubled every time she thought about it. A right to be free from illegal search or seizure is the same whether the victim of the search is a saint or a sinner. Or a terrorist. But the thought made her shudder. Abstract principles strained against inner vibrations. She almost hoped they would lose and Aldin would be put away for life in some dark place where he could not infect others. If they lost, she would not lie awake grieving over Wally Aldin.

She entered the law building and smiled at several colleagues as they passed in the hall. Seconds later she couldn't remember who they were.

And what about Carl? Here he was, back in her life just when it felt normal to lead a life with or without men. A life with Susan and professional colleagues, with people of academic distinction and social grace. Then Carl came crashing through. What was he thinking? That she was easy? Was it just a nostalgic revisit? Did he think she was pining away for him? That it was going to be a regular thing? That she would become a way station? One stop on his route?

Her mind was swirling as she approached her office. She almost tripped over the small vase containing a single red rose.

Games

Carl paused in the doorway of State's Attorney Gadsen's inner office. Gadsen's desk was made of dented metal with a matching credenza that could only be seen between dangerously-balanced stacks of files. Hunting prints covered the walls, depicting noble retrievers pointing pheasants and fishermen landing largemouth bass.

Gadsen was warm and friendly, which roused Carl's suspicion. "Come in and have a seat. Let me clear off that chair. That other one is going to be picked up for repair."

Carl wondered what it would be like to dissipate his peak years in an office like this. He decided there must be a lot of personal satisfaction living in a town where making wild animals become dead passes as a fit subject for art. But Gadsen was not to be dismissed as a rube. According to what he'd heard, Gadsen was a threat when cornered. He could play rural jurors with the intuitive skill of a blues guitarist. Carl had spent thirty years dealing with downstate prosecutors. He knew not to be mesmerized by a hayseed dangling from their clenched lips. "Nice view," Carl observed as he wandered to the high window behind Gadsen's desk, pointedly declining the invitation to sit.

"Wait until they come back and park those TV trucks all around my courthouse. There won't be a square inch of grass left by fall. Honestly, the trash we picked up after the preliminary hearing..."

"The outside world invades Lincoln County. Better watch out or the Grease Pit will be serving bagels instead of donuts."

Gadsen forced a thin smile. "Not much chance we're gonna change that much. Good ol' boys get set in their ways. We're just kind of amazed at all this Star Wars media stuff. Big time case, big time out-of-town lawyer..."

"Come off it, Willard. You and your Dad both made Order of the Coif. Don't give me that overmatched crap. I'd just as soon crawl down an occupied badger hole as try a case against you in this county."

Gadsen's grin conceded the point. "Well, maybe I can get you behind a 12 gauge sometime. But this case will be over long before hunting season if your guy's not gonna testify."

Carl was grateful he was gazing out the window when Gadsen said it. The remark made his insides jolt.

How does Gadsen know Aldin's not going to testify? By the time he turned to face Gadsen, Carl had recaptured his poker face. "Who knows. Maybe he'll take a month on the stand."

The corners of Gadsen's mouth curled into tiny lines of disbelief. "Well, at any rate, I gather he's not interested in my offer. I thought he'd jump at the chance to avoid the death sentence."

Carl struggled to preserve a placid look.

This is bullshit! Either he's a great guesser or he knows what Aldin and I talked about.

Instead of demanding to be informed about Gadsen's source, Carl said, "Well, you never know about things like that. He's still thinking over what he wants to do." The response sounded weak.

Gadsen seemed pleased with two bullseyes for two shots. "I don't mean to press you, but if he's gonna change his mind, he'd better do it pretty quick. The offer won't be there after we go to the trouble of preparing for trial. There's a mountain of work to do, and this is a small county."

"Aided by the Attorney General's prosecution team and a horde of Feds beating the bushes, from what I hear. I'm the one who needs help. I'm a hundred miles from home and office." Carl was stalling to see if Gadsen would return to discussing Aldin's decision. If Gadsen were guessing, he'd come back to it and test his theory, trying again for a reaction. If he knew for certain what Carl and Aldin were going to do, he'd let it go.

And that's what happened.

The conversation drifted to Jury Instructions and which ones would have to be modified. This was an opportunity for Gadsen to mention the Instruction as to how to consider the defendant's testimony in cases where he elected to take the stand. Not a word. Carl watched for any signs of curiosity.

They finished by discussing a scandal involving a judge, always neutral ground for Illinois lawyers.

But nothing further came up that indicated Gadsen was fishing. It was clear he knew exactly what Carl and Aldin planned to do at trial.

Carl left the office and walked down the marble steps with apprehension. How did they find out what he and his client discussed? How much more did they know? He had always relied on the fundamental fairness of the police and the prosecution. This time had they invaded the attorney-client privilege? How could it have been done? Had the fury over domestic terrorism gone that far?

He cautiously looked around inside the Jaguar and carefully drove out of town, checking his mirrors and rejecting any thought of making a cell phone call.

It was almost midnight and the sparse crowd had trickled out of Katsinas, leaving only a couple Carl had gotten to know in the past few weeks. He didn't want to join them. The mental maze he was trapped in was overwhelming. A deep foreboding hung over him. For some reason, the attack in Moraine was vivid to him.

So how did Gadsen know? Was there a bug in the Condo or the County Board Room or the Jaguar or his cell phone? Was somebody leaking information? Did Wally have a cellmate trading away his sins by turning snitch?

Uncertainty eroded Carl's confidence. He felt like a relic from a time when law was practiced by honorable people. There had always been prosecutors who would hide exculpatory evidence, but they were rare. Never had he worried about attorney-client confidentiality. Was this an abuse by one of the nameless horde of government agencies that had sprung up, each created to deal with some special crisis? He didn't even know the acronyms for most of them. How could he try the case without knowing who or what was sucking up his defense and spitting it out to the opposition?

The thought of electronic eavesdropping gave him a chill. He had followed instructions and used the sweep, but he'd never really believed it was necessary. One thing was certain. If the government had sunk to penetrating lawyers' confidences, there was no chance of proving it.

Cellmates? Surely Aldin would not share his strategy with the common criminals he met in jail. If he didn't level with his lawyer, why would he share his innermost secrets with some bad-check artist?

The most likely possibility was betrayal from somebody close to the case. Someone he trusted was selling him out. But who could that be? He began to scribble names on a cocktail napkin. People who had access to Carl's notes or to his condo. The cleaning lady. The maintenance crew and the rental agent. But none of Carl's strategy had been reduced to writing. Letting his mind drift, he assessed more remote possibilities. Maybe somebody back at the Millington office. For sure it couldn't be Sheri. He may as well doubt himself. What about the associate lawyers? Almost as impossible as Sheri. No, he could all but eliminate the associates.

Then a lightning bolt hit home.

Oh no! Surely not Dani!

Carl had always had the utmost respect for her professional and personal ethics. She was committed to her beliefs.

But which beliefs?

She loved the Constitution but hated terrorism and guns and violence. He rolled it around in his mind. Her core beliefs were antithetical to what she thought Aldin stood for. Could she somehow have come to believe a higher purpose justified selling Aldin out?

He had always trusted Dani. She was the mother of his child. Now that their relationship had rekindled, he wanted to believe she was in his future. In all the years they worked shoulder-to-shoulder he had never doubted her integrity. Still, who else could have told Gadsen the things he knew? The thought was gut-wrenching. A cold shiver gripped him. He tried to play back the past few months, sifting his memory to isolate any strange incident or overlooked remark about the case made to anyone at all. Anyone other than Dani. What was twisting his stomach was the idyllic night and the work on the case and the long talks over coffee. Could those have been illusion spun out of betrayal?

It came down to Dani or the government. The government was frightening, but if it were Dani, a large part of his life was over.

How did I ever get into this?

Tin Soldier

Although he was a free agent and had to act on his own, Bill felt the need to speak to Madden, to go over the failure of the bomb and to devise a new plan. In their meeting in the pizza place, Madden had given him contact information. He was to place an open house ad for a commercial property on *PeoriaRentals.com*, a public website. The time was to be one day and one hour earlier than what was listed.

Bill went to the Urbana Free Library to use the public computers. The clientele of the library included many international students and campus types. Nobody would be able to connect him to its use. He pulled up the website and listed an open house time for a laundry in Tonada the following Sunday at 3 p.m. This tiny, all but abandoned town was located about thirty miles from Peoria and would be an easy place to spot strange cars or people. An offering to lease out a commercial building in Tonada was almost certain to be ignored.

On Saturday at 2 p.m. Bill drove slowly down the empty asphalt street. Tonada had withered since the last time he had been there. It had reverted to prairie grass. It was a typical Illinois bedroom-widespot, located close to places where people worked at real jobs, people who were willing to drive a few miles so that they could sleep with their screen doors unlatched on a summer night.

A crudely painted sign marked the laundromat. It wasn't hard to find. It was one of the few functioning businesses on a short street of derelict late Victorian buildings. Empty lots between them were like missing teeth in an insipid smile. Faded ads for Coke and Skoal were peeling off brick walls. Pots of stringy philodendron colonized a storefront window that said "Antiques." Three gnarled men in faded denim bib overalls sat on a primitive bench under the overhanging portico of an abandoned drug store. They stared at Bill until he nodded and smiled, then they nodded and returned to their conversation. He parked between puddles in the crumbling asphalt and wandered into the laundromat.

The only other person in the place was a woman with buttocks that were oozing out of the top of red shorts as she scooped underwear out of a dryer into a plastic laundry basket. She glanced at Brother Bill as she left without folding it.

By 2:10 p.m. on that Saturday afternoon, Bill was washing a load of work clothes. He looked out the window and saw a dented Ford Fairlane from the early '90s slowly driving down the street, P. Michael Madden's face staring through the windshield.

Bill went to the door and opened it wide enough to be seen as the car passed. Madden stopped a half-block away and walked back to the laundromat, carrying a paper bag. He entered and made no sign of recognizing Bill until he had walked through and looked out the back door. There was nobody in the building. Madden scanned the machines, looking behind them at the electrical outlets.

Bill reached in his pocket for a handful of quarters. Without a word he deposited four of them in each washing machine and dryer. The noise level in the room became uncomfortable, but would surely mask any electronic surveillance.

Madden smiled and leaned close to Bill's ear. "You're picking up on this sort of thing pretty quickly. My congratulations. This is an ideal meeting site."

Bill cupped his hand and said, "Thank you. Coming from you that's high praise. You must've learned to be very careful."

For the next half hour Bill recounted the strange failure of the car bombing. He explained his shock, but when he speculated about "Lucifer," Madden only smiled.

Bill asked Madden whether he should try the car bomb again. Madden simply shook his head and said, "Why repeat failure?"

They talked for several minutes. Bill suggested several alternative ways of taking out the lawyer. They ruled out staging an accident. That would fail to make a statement. It had to be definite and dramatic. A bonus would be to get Aldin at the same time. That narrowed the possibilities to a suicide attack or a sniper shooting. Suicide seemed to lack appeal to Brother Bill Carmichael. He told Madden about his marksmanship with a Mini-14. He described the Courthouse and the fact that the trial would be conducted in the first floor lobby.

Madden asked about line of fire.

The transom window popped into Bill's mind. The more he described it to Madden, the more he could visualize shooting through the transom window and taking out both of them.

Madden nodded. "You're going to need a vantage point. A sniper's nest. What's nearby?"

Bill thought for a moment. "The buildings across the street are mostly empty, at least on the second floor. Nobody rents places upstairs anymore because there's no elevator."

"You're going to need to check it out carefully. If you can find a good place that's empty, make sure you have a clear escape path that's out of sight. Oswald picked a place that was too high, but he still had a chance to get away because it took them several minutes to figure out where the shots came from."

They talked about details and cover stories. Bill had anticipated most of Madden's questions.

"I just want it to go right. I'm not wanting to throw away my life unless it's necessary. There may be other things for me to do."

Madden flashed a wry smile. "As smart as you are, you need to pass your seed to children. The mud people are out-breeding us. People like you will be needed if the White Race is to prevail."

This made Bill uncomfortable. He looked away.

Madden picked up on the embarrassment. "Hey, you better get used to hearing the truth with no varnish on it. I tell it like it is. They are the mud people. We are the true chosen people, the Children of Israel."

Bill nodded. Christian Identity doctrine held that the people who call themselves Jews are actually pretenders, and that cavasions are the true children of Israel.

Madden said, "I've got something for you. Something to give you courage when you put your plan into effect. It'll help you feel a connection with your race, with your people." He reached into the paper bag and drew out a CD titled *Das Heer.* Madden said, "Music is one of the most important motivators in the world. *Das Heer* is a collection of World War Two German military music. Play this when you execute your plan. You have a portable CD player, don't you?"

Brother Bill thought about the Sony CD player he kept in his truck so that he could listen to hymns while driving to Champaign or Decatur. Maybe it was time to let this new motivation into his life. But music of the Nazis seemed a step too far.

Madden watched him. "You're having trouble with this, aren't you?"

Bill was surprised to be read so easily. "I guess so…I've always been taught that the Naz…er…Germans were our enemies."

"My point exactly! You've been taught! Think of who taught you. The schools, television, the movies. All run by Zionists. You know that, Brother Bill! You've got to free up your mind. You'll find motivation in this music, comradeship. Imagine yourself marching with a million white

230

men, defending our way of life. You can draw on that image when it's time to remove the cancer."

On the drive back to Moraine, Bill rolled over in his mind all that had happened. It was clear that Madden was right. Bombing the car was out. The failure of the bomb must have been a sign. What did it mean? Hardman had said something about a Lucifer electrical system. Maybe the Devil had intervened to save him. That would make sense in terms of Madden's account of the Devil mating with Eve and producing the Mud People. He would be protecting them, and their lawyers.

Just as he had discussed with Madden, a long shot was the answer. A round from a Mini-14 with a scope. He would have to look for the right place.

Bill got out of the pickup and walked back to his machine shed. The birds were chirping and his golden retriever was asleep in the shade of an apple tree, sure signs that nobody was lurking nearby. He unlocked the padlock on the metal door. The hinges squeaked, waking the dog. Against the back wall was an old fashioned deep freeze the size of a burial vault, the standard size to store a butchered hog or two. It had been fitted with three hasps and padlocks. On close inspection, it was not plugged in.

He twirled the combinations and lifted the lid. On top were packages wrapped in white butcher paper. Each was marked to look like packages of meat. Instead they contained a variety of weapons and ammunition. Shotgun shells with double-ought buck, clips loaded with .223 factory ammo for what the enemies of the Constitution insisted on calling "assault rifles." There were loaded clips for .45 and 9 mm pistols and freeze-dried rations. There was also the C-4 explosive he had returned after the fiasco in the parking lot.

Under the packages was a false bottom made of white Formica, concealing a selection of weapons. His eyes drifted across the array. An AK-47, two Mini-14s, an M-16 and two Remington pump shotguns. He fondled the guns, loving them with his hands, feeling their power, protected

231

by the Constitution and protecting it in return.

He needed accuracy, but he would have to sacrifice the weapon after using it. A pang ran through him. It would be like losing the old dog. None of his weapons had been purchased at retail or at the infiltrated gun shows. Finally he took the Mini-14 he had purchased from a guy in the Michigan Militia who had said it had been in his family for about 10 years and was probably untraceable. It was fitted with a 4x30 illuminated scope, all he would need. He had a good eye and with that much scope he could put a dozen slugs from a 20-shot clip into a man a block away. Just to be sure, he took two clips loaded with Remington factory ammo, not the reload stuff he normally used for target practice. He also selected an old Colt Combat Commander .45 that his Uncle won in a card game while he was in boot camp. That should make it hard to trace. Three clips of hollow point should be enough backup.

He laid the weapons out on the hood of his pickup and said a little prayer they would be sufficient to do the work he had to do.

— ·— ·—·—·—·—·—·—·—

Carl had left Katsinas about twenty minutes earlier and had driven around with the windows open, trying to dissipate his gloom. Wondering whether someone you respect has sold you out does cast a shadow over things. He walked into his condo, still upset.

Dani was just shutting down Carl's Powermac at the kitchen table as he walked in. If he hadn't just discovered new depths of suspicion, maybe he would have felt something other than alarm.

She turned, startled. "Oh, you scared me! I didn't hear you."

His face must have betrayed him because she said, "Hey, I'm really sorry, but Susan needed a paper she wrote on your computer and the door was open."

"I assume you were able to find what you wanted." He couldn't conceal his sarcasm.

She wiped away her embarrassment by getting up and walking out the front door. "You're acting like an old fart. Don't worry. Your list of cyber-honeys is safe. I thought about you when I saw *Grumpy Old Men*."

— · — · — · — · — · — · — · — · —

When Sheri arrived at the front door of the office at 7:35 a.m. she was startled to see the figure of a man through the cut glass panel in the door of Carl's office sitting at Carl's desk. For a second a twinge of fear gripped her before she saw that it was Carl. Apparently he had driven up from Champaign very early. She walked into the office without knocking.

"OK, early bird, where's the worm?"

"You always seem to grasp the moment."

"Yeah? Well it's a cinch you're not up here checkin' on what time them kid lawyers show up. So what's the deal?"

He knew he would end up leveling with her, but wanted to hold out a moment more. "The deal?"

"Come on, Carl. This here's Sheri. I got x-ray thoughts. So what's eatin' you?"

"Loyalty? Being sold out? Double agents? Wire taps...or make that wife taps, maybe?"

"Do I get some kinda prize for guessin' what the hell you're talkin' about?"

He sighed. "Who the hell knows. I'm totally confused. The State seems to know as much about what I'm doing as I do. There's a leak somewhere."

Sheri stared at him. "Are you sure? I mean, Carl, you been readin' them spy books again? Are you really sure?"

He went on for almost ten minutes, laying out the information the other side seemed to have.

"So who's doin' it?"

He leaned back in his leather swivel chair and looked up through the

233

hole surrounding the fireman's brass pole.

"Come on Carl. I go home at five."

He exhaled and sat up straight. "I don't want to say it, but I think…it's gotta be Dani."

It was rare for Sheri to register surprise. "No shit! You think Dani'd sell out a client? Come on!"

"Who else?"

"Jeez, Carl, you might as well figure it's me. Dani's all lawyer. I know she's got her liberal thoughts, right down to them Birkemsuck sandals. She don't go for no violence and guns. But no way! She'd never do nothin' to sell out a client!"

"But is she more of a liberal than a lawyer? Don't forget we've got a terrorist killer here. She keeps talking about him as if he had a little mustache and a spasm in his right arm."

"Well, she's never gonna campaign for Bush, but she's got the same lawyer ethics you do. She's not gonna rat on nobody she's representing."

"What if she thought she was upholding some higher obligation? There are interpretations of the Canon of Ethics, you know, that make it permissible...even necessary...for an attorney to violate a confidence to prevent the commission of a crime. What if she thought that applied to Aldin? What if she thought he's in the middle of a conspiracy to blow up a whole string of judges?"

Sheri pursed her lips. "Maybe I just don't wanna think nothing bad about her. I always felt you two was great friends and gettin' married just screwed it up...maybe I shouldn't put it that way..."

"Hey, don't worry. I've felt that way many times. I probably miss her as my best friend more than anything else. Maybe you're right. Maybe. It's just that my mind's all wrapped around this case. I'm confused and upset."

"So what's that got to do with Dani?"

"Maybe nothing. But every time we get to discussing the case, she'll drift into how much she hates Nazis and racists and religious fanatics…and that includes terrorists, I guess."

"Carl, you gone nuts or something? She's just pullin' your chain like she done every day the two of you was married. She looks up to you. She bounces ideas off of you 'cause she respects you. She loves a good argument. You never saw that? It don't mean she's gonna screw over the client just 'cause she appoints you to the devil's advocate or whatever you call it."

"You really think so? I'd like to believe that. Doubting her is tearing me up. I'd like to believe there's still a basis for respect and friendship between us."

Sheri looked at her watch. It was a few minutes after eight. "Well, lighten up. Try on some other explanations. You're good at goin' back an' lookin' at a problem a new way. Meanwhile, that telephone's gonna start ringin' off the hook. The cops pulled off a beer raid over the weekend out at McPhederan's Falls. About a hunnert kids run away through the weeds. It was a birthday party for a doctor's kid. Rich people, Carl. That telephone's gonna sound like a cash register. So figger it out by yourself. I got a law practice to run."

— ·— ·— ·— ·— ·— ·— ·—

Gadsen was waiting for Carl in the hallway outside the State's Attorney's office. Judge Harrigan had called at seven to demand that they appear at the courthouse in Moraine immediately. Carl was tired. He had returned from Millington late the night before and was none too happy to be summarily jerked over to Moraine. Gadsen had expected an angry and frustrated lawyer and he was not disappointed.

Carl stormed down the hall and confronted him. "All right! What the fuck is this about?"

Gadsen held up his hands in a gesture of surrender. "Hey, this isn't my idea. Judge Harrigan called a couple of minutes ago from her car. She'll be here in about a half hour. You made pretty good time."

"Skip the travelogue. What's the emergency?"

Gadsen sighed. "Come in where we have a little privacy."

As they passed through the cluttered State's Attorney's waiting room, several of the local underclass began to wheedle Gadsen for just a moment of his time, hoping to bargain away their cases without having to hire a lawyer. Gadsen ignored them. After he closed the door and collapsed into his swivel chair, he leaned back and began to talk to the ceiling. "Your client is an asshole." He waited but got no argument. "He's the worst asshole we've ever had around here, and he's got a brand new stunt. Did you know he filed a complaint against Judge Harrigan with the Judicial Inquiry Board?"

Carl blinked. "What? He did what?"

"You heard me."

"When did this happen?"

"You don't know?"

Carl flared. "Look, Willard, stop playing games with me. I'm not in on this. Just tell me what the hell happened."

"OK, OK. I'll accept it was his idea...for now...but Judge Harrigan sounded like she has questions about whether you were involved. Anyway, she found out late last night. I don't know what your guy said in his complaint, but the judge sounded plenty ticked off."

"You really don't know what it said?" Carl was wary.

Gadsen shrugged. "Who knows? Aldin has a vivid imagination. He's surprised me too many times. If you're really in the dark, I suggest you trot on over to the jail and find out before she gets here."

"See you in half an hour." With that Carl got up and walked out.

—————————

"Jeez, Wally! What the hell did you do?" Carl was fuming as he entered the interview room. He slammed down his briefcase and towered over his client who was lounging in a folding chair.

Aldin was not intimidated. He was cool and controlled, as if he had anticipated a storm. "I assume you're referring to my complaint against that bitch."

"Let me hear it from you." Carl held his temper longer than he thought he could. Then he remembered that there was some sort of leak to Gadsen and this case was being tried under Moscow Rules. "Wait. Let me get out the Star Wars stuff." He opened the briefcase and did a half-hearted scan for electronic bugs. Nothing turned up. He sighed and confronted Aldin. "Now tell me what the fuck you did."

"I did what I have a right to do." Silence.

"Don't play games. Tell me or I'm out of here!"

"Do what you want. I'm a free man. I guess you are, too."

Carl forced himself to be patient with this client who had apparently painted another coat of self-destruction on his case. "Look, Wally. I'm still trying to get you a fair trial. Just tell me what new stumbling block you've placed in my path. I'm the one who has to jump over it. Isn't that fair, even in your world?"

Aldin stared at him with dark eyes smoldering. "OK. Just ask nice."

"Fine. Now please tell me what the fuck you did."

A look crossed Aldin's face which could have been amusement or self-congratulation. "What did you hear...oh hell, save it...I filed a couple of things against the bitch."

"Filed a couple of what?"

"Filed a complaint with the Judicial Inquiry Board. And I filed a Federal Civil Rights suit against her."

Carl had a sinking feeling. It was worse than what Gadsen had told him. Apparently the Federal Civil Rights suit hadn't reached Judge Harrigan yet. The second bomb was still falling. "What did you say?"

"Told the truth."

"And today's truth is...?"

"The bitch is against me."

"Go on."

"She ignored all your objections. She's staring at me. There's no way I'm getting a fair trial."

"So you sued her. And you charged her with...what? Prejudice?"

"Yeah. You got it. You're pretty sharp, you know that?"

"Lighten up, Wally! I'm on your side, but you don't know what you've done."

"I did what I've got a right to do. Complain to the authorities about somebody violating my rights and petition my government for redress of my grievances."

"Did it ever occur to you that I'm your lawyer and you ought to check with me?"

"Check what? Would you tell me I don't have a right to file a complaint? Do you think I give a shit whether it'll piss off the judge and screw up your chance to get her in the sack?"

"Hey! Back off, Wally! If you think I'm sucking up to Judge Harrigan, you're in another world. I'm walking on the edge of contempt, and that's beyond the call of duty. Wake up! I'm trying to save your life! At least you owe me the courtesy of letting me find out what my own client is doing from somebody other than the prosecutor."

Aldin thought about that. He seemed to sag into his chair as the tension was released. "All right. That's fair. What do you want to know?"

"Start with what you said in this lawsuit and in your complaint to the Judicial Inquiry Board."

"Just set out all the things she's doing in the courtroom. Here's a copy."

Carl did. It was handwritten, containing a list of remarks the judge had made and descriptions of her smirks and her derisive tone. Carl was impressed with its accuracy, but as an experienced trial lawyer, he had long ago learned that judicial pomposity and impatience was part of the game, not the subject matter of successful civil rights suits or complaints to the Judicial Inquiry Board, or even reversals on appeal.

"Wally, I wish you'd given me a chance to look at this and talk to you before you filed it."

"It wouldn't have changed my mind. I would've filed it anyway."

"Don't you realize this is the final piss off?"

"Don't you realize it doesn't make any difference? What's she gonna do, give me two death sentences? Buy one, get one free? Wake up, man! She got sent in here to take my life! I've gotta hit her with whatever I got! At least I can go down fighting."

There was a certain, desperate logic in what he said. From Aldin's perspective, total cynicism about the system of justice made sense. "OK, I guess I can see your side, but you've really blown up a shit storm, and I'm the one without an umbrella."

Aldin smiled at the thought. "Well, counselor, look at it this way. She's got a worse problem than you do. She's got to step down in this case, doesn't she?"

Carl's mind clicked onto the legal implications. A judge was supposed to be impartial, and Kirsten Harrigan certainly didn't seem to be. It was true that if a judge had a personal grudge or a relationship with a litigant, the Judge was supposed to recuse herself and let a neutral judge take the case. Being sued or being the subject of a complaint before the Judicial Inquiry Board would surely be enough to force the system to cough up a different judge if it were raised before the Judge ruled on anything, but she had already ruled on the Motion to Suppress. If Judge Harrigan didn't recuse herself, it might convince some higher court of her prejudice when reviewing a death sentence. Wally was dumb like a fox. "I suppose there's an outside chance she'll recuse herself to avoid what they call the appearance of judicial impropriety."

Wally's mouth took on an ironic twist. "Jeez, wouldn't that be awful? I guess they'd have to send in the second team."

"And if she doesn't step down, you've got a fascinating argument good enough for 10 years of appeals."

"Enough to keep me alive until they find the Constitution again."

— ·— ·— ·— ·— ·— ·— ·— ·—

Judge Harrigan was clicking her high heels across the gray marble floor in a rapid staccato. Her face was ready to explode. Carl nodded and let her go through the door first. She made no effort to acknowledge his presence, much less his courtesy.

They walked into the Clerk's private office that was being used as chambers. Gadsen was already there with his case file open on the chair next to him. Judge Harrigan slapped down her legal pad and took her seat. The court reporter entered the room out of breath. "We won't need a record for a few minutes. I'll call you." It sounded like a threat. The Judge turned on Carl and said, "Sit down!" He did. "I want an explanation!"

"Of what, exactly."

"Of what you're trying to pull."

"Of what I'm trying to pull? It sounds as if you're suggesting I'm involved in something improper. If so, I want a record of this conversation and I want to know what you're talking about. Give me my Miranda rights if I'm being accused of some impropriety."

Judge Harrigan blinked. Several seconds went by while they stared at each other. Then she said, "Let's start over again. What did your client do?"

"Mr. Gadsen told me a half hour ago that a complaint's been filed against you before the Judicial Inquiry Board. I can tell you I learned twenty-five minutes ago you've been sued in a Federal Civil Rights Complaint that apparently hasn't been served yet. I didn't have anything to do with either one. My client filed them on his own. I'm told he's been resourceful in the past."

She started to respond, then faltered. She looked at Gadsen, who presented a blank stare, then back at Carl. "You're telling me you didn't know about this...this shocking abuse of process?"

Carl set his jaw. "That's right."

She waited for more, but there was none. She seemed to be trying to rescue the moment. "We'll see about that. For now it's clear that at least Aldin filed these...scandalous documents. We're on the eve of trial. I am going to take this matter under advisement, perhaps ask for an investigation of who is involved. In the meantime inform your client he is under court order not to file any pleading in any court or board."

Carl heard more than he could ignore. "Your Honor, if you're making some ruling in a capital murder case, I respectfully demand that the defendant be present and that this proceeding be on the record. If you're going to enter an extraordinary injunction against an American Citizen restraining him from having access to the courts and disciplinary authorities, it needs to be argued in open court on the record, especially since he's doing it without the help of counsel."

Her eyes widened and her cheeks showed little red veins. "Are you mocking this court?"

He governed his tone and said, "No, Judge, I'm practicing law. Now tell me whether you are going to put this on the record or not. If not, I'm leaving."

Gadsen turned and looked out the window.

Judge Harrigan was trembling. "Sir! You are the most contemptuous attorney who has ever appeared before me! I've got a good mind to jail you for the duration of this case."

Carl didn't blink. "With all respect, Your Honor, that would be a welcome gift to my client on appeal. I think the Chicago Seven opinion of the Seventh Circuit covers that matter nicely. If you recall, it resulted in a complete reversal."

Judge Harrigan looked over to Gadsen. He was still staring out the window. She got up and stormed out of the room.

— · — · — · — · — · — · — · — · —

Brother Bill had never before stayed awake until 3 a.m. The day had always begun at 4 a.m. when his family had a cattle operation and raised

241

a few champion hogs mainly for county fair exhibition.

His pickup drove slowly past the sleeping Courthouse. During the day, there were too many eyes, too much of a chance of being accidentally photographed or recorded in the background of a television shot. He had heard about the astonishing technology that made it possible to blow up faces and license plates from small images in the background of photos and videotape. After it was over, there would probably be a massive effort to comb the images for a lead on who had taken out Aldin and Hardman.

Bill drove around the square, slowing as he passed the front of the Courthouse. He looked at the large transom window over the front door. It was a semi-circle, like the sun the moment the horizon cut it in half. Maybe that was a sign. The sun. Light on the evil going on in that makeshift courtroom. They would be holding the trial just inside that door, with the transom giving him a wide view of what was below. It would afford him an open line of sight to Aldin and Hardman.

He projected a ballistic path backward from the transom window across the street to a run-down Victorian brick building facing the Courthouse. The second floor windows were built above the high first floor ceilings old buildings had. They were at the correct elevation. The middle one would be perfect. It was grimy, but he could pick out the letters, *I.O.O.F.*, the abbreviation that stood for the Odd Fellows Lodge, a fraternal organization that had thrived in towns like Moraine many years ago. Nobody had spoken of this lodge, as long as Bill could remember. Without a doubt the space was empty, probably unoccupied for decades. What a perfect place! It would afford a direct line of fire from a high angle, through the transom window, to the defense table where Aldin and Hardman would be sitting.

Brother Bill turned the corner and scanned the street for any signs of activity. The block was deserted. He was prepared for being stopped or observed at this hour by having a plastic bag of trash in the bed of his pickup. He would claim he was looking for a garbage can to dispose of the bag. In the alley behind the building with the proper window there was an overflowing dumpster used by the convenience store fronting on the street. Selling coffee and sandwiches to the multitude in town to watch the trial had become a thriving business.

He got out of the truck, took the plastic bag, and scanned the alley as he walked along the back of the building. There was a modern, metal door, dented and scraped from the daily activity of the convenience store.

Next to it was a wooden door. Flaking green paint and a rusty door-knob spoke of years of abandonment. This must be the back stairwell to the second floor. He went back to the truck and located a can of WD40. After spraying the keyhole, the hinges, and the latch, he tried the door. It opened without a sound.

Bill slowly ascended the stairs, testing each thick oak tread for weak-ness and noise. He found none, which testified to the rock-solid crafts-manship of the past.

At the top of the stairs the window he had selected was about 10 feet directly in front of him. To the left and right were large open rooms that had once housed ritual and brotherhood. He walked to the window and hunkered down, approximating the angle his shot would require. Through the grime he could see that it was perfect.

He tested the floor. It, too, was solid and did not squeak. Everything was perfect, but it would require careful planning. There was plenty of time before the case went to trial, time to make all his preparations.

As he drove away, he put the *Das Heer* CD into his Sony portable player, inserted headphone buds into his ears, and reveled at the power of the German military music.

243

Fireworks

The Fourth of July had always been Carl's favorite holiday. He loved fireworks and bent the law that prohibited them, along with almost everybody else in the Midwest. The cops usually looked the other way except when it got out of hand, and then seldom did more than confiscate firecrackers from teenagers. Carl always wondered if there was a cop picnic someplace with a fireworks orgy. He had just returned from a trip with Susan to Turkey Run State Park in Indiana. They had stayed in a rustic cabin without any electronic connection to the world. He knew that when the trial started, time with Susan would become rare.

The cell phone rang three times and he answered. It wasn't hard to detect trouble in her voice. "Hello."

"Hello, Carl." It was Dani, and she sounded worried. His misgivings about her were immediately shelved.

"Are you OK?"

"I don't know. They just announced on TV that there were arrests of three, deep cover Al Qaeda men. Carl, what have we gotten into? Are we connected with these guys?"

He let several seconds go by while thoughts competed with emotions. "Don't you think you're jumping to conclusions?"

"I wish I could feel that way, Carl, but I don't. In my heart I know it's

244

the same bunch of screwballs. Why did I get involved in this accursed case?"

That was the second body blow. He reacted defensively. "Listen, Dani, we're lawyers and we defend..."

"Oh, Carl! I know that! I'm not second guessing you. I'm an adult and a professional. I went into this with my eyes open, but I was hoping for better. Maybe I'm just wishing I'd stayed in microbiology, where the germs are trapped under glass."

He would have smiled if he hadn't been hurting so much. Instead he said, "I guess you're talking about the arrest of the father and his two sons for being deep cover terrorists."

She said, "Yes."

He tried to think of something to say. Finally, the best he could do was "There's no indication they were Druze. They may be terrorists, but that doesn't explain Wally."

She said, "You're reaching Carl. You don't know he even believes in this Druze thing. He gives every indication of being a terrorist. Stop deluding yourself. We're involved with a committed killer who's pining away for the virgins in paradise."

He choked back an angry response. "So what if he is? We still owe him a fair trial. If you value my instincts, I think the Druze angle explains a lot."

"Does that mean he didn't do it?"

Carl shook his head, but she couldn't see that over the phone. "Dani...come on...would it make any difference if he did? He still has the same rights as the rest of us."

Silence for perhaps ten seconds. Then she said, "Alright, I had that coming. I'm sorry, Carl, I shouldn't be laying a guilt trip on you for doing what a good lawyer has to do."

"Accepted. You know I'm sorry I got us into this, but I can't see any way out. We're trying to fight the death penalty, even if he's not interested."

Her voice sounded as if she were trying to see the bright side of things. "You're supposed to be taking Susan to the fireworks later. Are you sure she'll be safe? I mean, there are lots of people who know you're representing Aldin."

"There'll be cops everywhere. I'm sure of that. Maybe the only thing I'm sure of right now, but we can't become prisoners in our own country. I'll call you later when I've had a chance to think."

"Ok, but be careful with her."

"Dani…"

"Yes, I know…but I've got to say that. See you later." She hung up just as his cell phone began to buzz again. The caller I.D. said "private." Carl let it ring three times, trying to decide whether to answer a call from an undisclosed caller. Finally, it crossed his mind that the caller might be calling to fire him. He snapped the phone open and said, "Who is this, please?"

The voice was cautious and said, "We met once before near Mahomet. Uh...I'm wondering whether you're celebrating the Fourth of July?"

"What?"

"I understand the fireworks show over near the stadium is supposed to be special this year. I want to talk about several kinds of fireworks. Check with the short order cook at Merry Ann's diner. I have reason to believe you know the place. He can tell you where the best vantage points are."

Carl felt a chill. How did this guy know he frequented the diner? Did he know of the midnight meeting at Merry Ann's with Dani? Had someone been listening to them pour out their most intimate thoughts? He broke the silence. "I'll be there with my daughter and a few of her friends."

———————————————————

The first aerial bomb went off a little after nine.

Carl was standing on the Illinois Central railroad bridge over Kirby Avenue, west of the stadium, where he had been directed by the short order cook. There were thousands of people sitting in lawn chairs or sprawled on blankets. Susan and three other eleven-year-olds were standing fifty feet down the tracks pretending not to watch some high school boys. A street light allowed him to keep track of the girls. The high school boys had been shooting firecrackers and holding Roman candles in their hands while waiting for the display to start. It didn't look safe. Carl worried whether Susan would take such risks in a few years.

A tall, swarthy man materialized out of the gloom. He looked around before asking, "Did you have any trouble getting here?"

"No. I'm getting to be a regular at Merry Ann's. They let me park in their lot."

They watched as the campus lit up with a succession of bursting shells superimposed on each other. Each new explosion was a burning flower, lighting the smoke patterns in the sky, the gray spiders left by faded shells. It was the kind of isolation in a crowd that guaranteed they could talk. The explosions would be a nightmare for electronic surveillance.

They chatted about the fireworks while the man scanned the tracks.

Finally Carl asked, "What's so important?"

He stared at Carl and said, "Are you losing faith in this case?"

Carl stared back and said, "No, but I sure as hell ought to be. I'm getting no cooperation from Aldin. He's rude, surly, and skeptical about me. How can I try to save this guy's life if he ties my hands?"

The man looked at him as if he were a child. "What does he say he wants?"

"He wants a trial. The problem is he refuses to testify."

"Doesn't he have that right?"

"Of course."

"Well, then, I don't see the problem."

Carl looked at the man as if he didn't understand why not. "I'm trying to save his life."

"You're assuming he will be convicted?" Immediately a series of aerial bombs went off, followed by the crackle of thousands of firecrackers showering down in a cascade of orange flashes.

Carl swallowed hard. "I suppose…yes…I guess so."

"Why? Isn't he presumed innocent? Don't you have any faith in the law?"

"I'm sorry. I've been around it too long. The law is a lot like an actress. On stage she looks great, but when you go backstage and see her scrape off the makeup, she's shopworn and disappointing."

A mammoth series of explosions ripped the sky and burning streamers lit the man's profile. He looked strong but serene. "That could be a description of the world."

"Well, it's the one I live in."

"Have a little faith. Refresh your belief in the goodness of God."

Carl had no response. He watched a ground display erupt with Roman candles and spinning corkscrews of fire.

The man said, "I came here to find out if you were still loyal to Walid. What is the answer?"

Carl said, "That's the first easy question you've asked. Of course I am. I'm straining every brain cell to try to come up with a way of winning…of saving him."

"That's all we can ask. As I said, the rest is up to God. Don't be cynical about that. He acts in all things. Just open yourself to His ways and don't try to take over His role. Do your job."

The thump of mortars and the crack of bursting shells punctuated what he was saying.

"How can I do my job if Wally insists on butting his head against the wall? It's frustrating when your client is an anchor instead of a sail. Why is he so…secretive?"

"Why do you ask that?"

"Why do I ask? Jeez, that's a hell of a question! I guess I'm asking because I'm a human being down under the lawyer coating and I'm a little afraid of what I've gotten myself into. The trial is about to begin, and I need some reassurance. Isn't that enough?"

The man looked up and watched three shells pop in rapid succession, making the sky a red, white, and blue bunting. "Enough of a reason." Slowly he looked around, casually stretching, checking to see whether they were still alone. "You have a picture of Walid as someone sinister, belonging to an organization something like the mafia. That isn't accurate. We are his friends, but we are not evil people. We have an obligation to help him."

"As fellow *Mowahhid?*"

The man wheeled and a frown passed over his face in the light of a starburst. He said nothing.

Carl's shoulders sagged. "Maybe I shouldn't have asked."

"Maybe."

They both stood and watched a ground display. There were enough explosions and rockets and Roman candles to turn the night into day. Carl looked past the man, trying to locate Susan and her friends. He saw them, but he also saw two men he had not seen before, standing in the bushes, watching the path up the embankment to the railroad bridge. Carl said, "What do you want me to do? Go or stay?"

The man said, "Stay in the case. You care about what happens to Walid, and that can't be bought. Just do your best, but don't treat his beliefs as if they were those of an ignorant person."

And he was gone.

Susan came running toward him and they stood and watched for several minutes until the last shell of the finale exploded with a huge orange burst, and dozens of sparkling arms reached across the sky, trailing golden fallout. They watched until the heavens cleared. At least something had cleared, even it was not Carl's mind.

― ·――·――·――·――·――·――·――·―

As Bill drove through Central Illinois, he could see flashes of light in the sky from all the points on the compass. Every little town was celebrating America's independence. Tears ran down his cheeks.

He had met with Madden in Tonada to give him the details of the Odd Fellows space across from the Courthouse. He felt like a student making a report. He was rewarded by a smile from Madden who said it sounded ideal.

Refreshed in his commitment, Bill cranked up the volume of *Das Heer* on his CD player while he watched America celebrate its independence on the prairie.

Laura showed up at the condo just as the local news was ending with a replay of the fireworks finale.

As he opened the door, Carl wondered why she would drop in so late. She was wearing a creamy white dress that was not suggestive of anything more than an ice cream social. Just cool and appropriate for the weather. He was conflicted by his emotions about Dani.

"I've been driving around trying to get the courage to barge in on you. Can I come in?"

He thought about it for an instant before he melted. "Sure. I always enjoy talking to you. What's up?"

She walked ahead of him. He motioned toward the kitchen because the living room was a mess, with legal papers strewn across the floor. The kitchen seemed safer to the part of him that recognized the potential for disaster that she posed.

Laura took a seat at the table. Without asking he took a pot of coffee from the warmer and began pouring two cups. "It's decaf, but I could make some high test if you'd rather."

"No, it's ok. Anything. I just came to talk. I was over here for a meeting at one of the churches about...well...you don't care about all that. Anyway, I was thinking it'd been quite a while since you and I had a chance to get together...and talk about Wally."

She seemed ill at ease. He thought about how close was the opening of the trial. A bad case of nerves goes with the territory.

He said, "I've been trying to get a Substitution of Judge based on some papers Wally filed. It's a desperate hope, but I have to try."

She smiled softly.

It warmed Carl. He asked, "How about you? How are you holding up?"

She shook her head. "Don't let that worry you. I'm all right. You've got enough on your mind. Just being here helps me. It feels good to know somebody smart and decent. I just wish I had known you before I met Wally."

He could feel a magnet pulling him toward her. It was getting stronger by the minute. He tried to think of his license and his position of trust. An impulsive act could twist his professional life in an instant. He tried to think of Dani and Susan. Carl wrested back control from his emotions. "Laura...Mrs. Aldin...you can't feel that way, much less talk that way. I'm just doing my job. But it does feel good to have somebody appreciate me." He smiled because it was the alternative to sadness.

She leaned across the table and put her hand on his. He stared at both hands. Then he got up and poured a refill in his cup and remained standing. "Listen, I've got a lot of reading to catch up on. It's going to be pure hell getting a fair trial, and I'd better get back to figuring out how to manufacture one."

She looked at him, perplexed. Her look lasted for a moment, then faded. She got up from the table and poured her coffee into the sink, then rinsed out the cup.

Carl watched, trying to keep from confessing the feelings that were coursing through him.

She stood close enough to let sparks leap the gap. She waited. Nothing happened. He was frozen by self-preservation and said, "It's really late, Laura. I'll walk you to your car."

Her eyes were wide open and the pupils were deep enough to drown the future. She tilted her face up toward him, but he ignored it and turned away from her and the temptation of paradise.

The next morning he threw together an emergency motion based on

Wally's filings. It asked that Judge Harrigan recuse herself or appoint another judge to consider Wally's charges. He also argued that the potential juror pool was prejudiced. He appended copies of newspaper articles and letters to the editor, along with affidavits from Dani's law students about vitriolic calls to talk shows.

His heart knew it was futile, but his head pretended there was some chance. The papers were faxed to Moraine for filing along with the request for an emergency hearing, copies faxed to the Judge and Gadsen. The answer came within an hour. A conference operator set up a call to the Judge and Gadsen.

Fifteen minutes later all the arguments had been made and rejected and Carl was told to be sure he was on time for the trial, so as not to inconvenience the jury or the state's witnesses.

By noon Carl was desolate. By evening he was worse. Through the afternoon, the impending disaster rolled closer and he felt tension taking over his body. He was prepared for a courtroom catastrophe, a real butt-whipping. No way to avoid it. Like trying to hold back a tidal wave. He got in the car, cranked up the air conditioning, and drove toward campus aimlessly. Normally this would relax him, listening to music and revisiting memories would give him new ideas or at least a fresh perspective. But tonight the opposite happened. Nothing happened. No inspiration. Nothing.

Vivid sense-memories of the rocking of the car and the crowd pounding on it. Acid-burn in his throat from the knowledge that he would have to drive to that accursed town for weeks on end. What awaited him when he would get out of the car and drag his heavy files into the courthouse? Would it be a daily gauntlet of picket signs and spitting or worse?

He drove through the warm summer night on the empty campus. It had an eerie quality. Fraternities and sororities stared with dead eyes.

Dorms looked like empty boxes. Neon beer signs lit bars lonely enough to have pleased Edward Hopper.

He wanted to be with Susan. He wanted to call her on the cell phone, to wake her up and tell her to get her jacket on and he'd take her for ice cream while she was still a little girl and that was still a treat. And teen-years hadn't coated her with anxiety.

Then there was Aldin. Fire behind those dark eyes. Did the men in the history books seem unbalanced to their contemporaries? Was it possible to give your professional best to a guy like Aldin who was terminally bitter? Carl welcomed the thought that he'd never have to speak to Aldin again after this was over. Why hadn't they come up with another lawyer to relieve him? He cursed the day he discovered the trial fee in his car.

Laura crossed his mind. He shook his head, trying to cleanse her from his brain. Nothing but frustration and disaster lay that way.

Don't Mess With Bill

"Action! The time of the Lord is near!" Brother Bill was in his glory, as he stood in the loft of his century-old barn.

He spoke out loud to the targets he had punctured with .223 slugs. Bill had set up two man-sized paper torsos at 30 yards, with old window sashes in front of each of them. He had fired from the second floor barn loft to get the same angle he would encounter with the transom window in the Courthouse. The only question in his mind, whether the first slug striking the glass at an angle might be deflected, had now been answered. Two shots and two shattered windows, each time he had been within an inch of the center of the chest.

The plan is perfect.

Brother Bill smiled the smile of a man who had discovered his answer. In celebration, he emptied the clip, pulling the trigger a dozen times so rapidly the rifle sounded fully automatic and pieces of the paper target flew like a swarm of insects.

— · — · — · — · — · — · — · —

It rained the day the trial was to commence. Not just a flatland storm, barrages of artillery shattered the sky just after 8 a.m., shaking loose curtains of rain. The cascade continued for almost twenty minutes. Almost a foot of water swirled down the gutter in front of the Lincoln County Courthouse. Television crews were in near panic, rescuing equipment and trying to elevate cables above the water. It was as if the judgment of Heaven was being handed down, a Divine cataclysm threatening the whole accursed thing with Old Testament vengeance.

Carl and Dani drove from Champaign in silence. They were pretending to listen to the storm warnings on the radio. The local news came on as the car waded through the torrent.

There was a chill between them, but they were doing their best to ignore it. The problems of Wally Aldin were far more pressing.

Carl was nauseated by the prospect of sitting next to Aldin for the next week or so, watching as evidence and prejudice rolled over him and choked the life out of him.

They parked behind the courthouse and they unloaded the two file boxes in a slackening of the rain.

The thunderheads told the whole story of what was yet to come. He had lived in the Midwest his whole life, but had never seen a more threatening sky.

At 8:10, a Sheriff's squad car with two deputies drove the short distance from the jail and appeared at the back door of the courthouse. Wally Aldin in leg chains, hands cuffed in front to a chain around his waist, was led into the Supervisors' room and was permitted to take his customary seat at the table, his blue suit drenched and rain water dripping from his hair.

As Aldin entered, Carl was overcome with misgivings bordering on dread. He was sitting on a chair at the big conference table, Dani next to him, away from Aldin who stopped to look out the window at the huge blue-black bruise on the western sky.

255

Aldin turned to Carl and gestured with his head toward the storm, "Let's see Judge Harrigan overrule the Almighty. They'll remember the day they killed an innocent man."

"You're not dead yet, Wally. If you'd let me..."

"Don't even say it. No deals. I told you that up front. I've got a presumption of innocence and that ought to do it. Just keep..."

"Right. Just keep objecting to hearsay and all those clouds will swirl down in a cyclone and sweep you into the Land of Oz, right?"

Aldin actually smiled. "You know, Counselor, your problem is you lost your beliefs. You've got no faith in the system you're supposed to be defending. You need a revival."

"Wally, this isn't getting us anywhere."

Dani said, "I quite agree."

Aldin had never warmed up to her and barely acknowledged her presence. Carl's suspicions about her triggered heartburn. He had considered calling her last night to make some excuse that Aldin didn't want her there. It would have been a coward's way out. Carl wanted desperately to believe in her, even though his mind ached with doubt.

Dani was not in a mood to spend time on small talk with Aldin. She turned to Carl, "Do you think we wasted a trip over here?"

"The storm?"

"Yes."

"Nope. These people live close to nature. You'll see rowboats tied to the courthouse steps before they cancel the big show."

It was almost nine when they were interrupted by Sheriff Burnett opening the door without knocking. Two burly deputies surged in and manhandled Aldin.

"Watch it!" Carl shouted.

Sheriff Burnett chested his way into Carl's path. "Watch it, yourself, mouthpiece! I got an extra cell for you." He glowered at Carl.

"One more crack and you're my first witness, fat boy! You're in my ballpark now. So let's see you disappear like you did at the Motion to Suppress. Go find some waitress who wants to shine your leather." Carl hoped Burnett would take a swing at him. The door was open and the press was watching. He would have been willing to take a punch to infect the record with grounds for reversal.

They were eyeball to eyeball for several seconds until one of the deputies put his hand on Burnett's shoulder and whispered into his ear, "It ain't worth it, Sheriff. Just bide your time."

The Sheriff's face was ready to burst. His collar was slicing a roll of pork from his jowls. He hissed, "I'm gonna watch fuckin' Aldin wilt when they squirt the juice in his arm. And I'm gonna think of you and that cunt with you! Fuck all three of you!"

Carl smiled and whispered, "And all three of you there in your uniform, Sheriff!" He left Burnett sputtering. Crossing the courtroom he caught the first glint of amusement from Dani in a week.

———————————————

Now it was 9 a.m. and renewed cascades of water ran down the side of the building, making a waterfall of the main entrance. But nothing succeeded in stopping the trial.

Carl sat with Dani and waited for the Judge to lead her retinue across the marble floor of the movie-set courtroom, where they would play out the scene as written.

Aldin sat like a stone. Carl was alone with his thoughts. They were locked in parallel realities.

All murders trials are gruesome, but something new and malevolent was hanging in the air. If the law could not dispassionately try someone accused of the ultimate insult to the law itself, then the Constitution was a broken promise, a colossal con job.

For the hundredth time he wondered what he could say to Aldin to convince him to accept a plea and save his life. Carl shook his head and leaned back in his chair. His gaze drifted upward into the space above the oval balcony. The deputies on the second floor followed his gaze upward with heightened tension, as if Batman might swoop down through the skylight and rescue Aldin.

The press began to stir, signaling the approach of the Judge. Carl waited until the incantation was underway and everyone else had risen. Slowly he stood, but he felt no respect.

Judge Harrigan took her seat and said, "Let me see counsel." Carl, Dani and Gadsen approached the bench. The court reporter had placed her machine near the bench, somehow knowing the Court would be calling for a sidebar conference before starting the trial. The Judge leaned over, her hand guarding her words from lip readers and from the television cameras peering down at them through the large transom window. "I want to make myself clear that there will be no political demonstrations in this courtroom. No speeches. No theatrics. Any violations will be dealt with harshly by direct civil contempt. I will not hesitate to jail the offender for the duration of this trial."

Never in his career had a judge started a trial by intimidating the lawyers, or more precisely, the defense lawyers, since Gadsen would be unlikely to protest anything but animal rights. "Is there some reason you're warning us, Your Honor? Has somebody done something wrong?"

She sharpened her stare. "Not yet, Mr. Hardman. Not yet."

"I've been practicing law for thirty years and haven't staged any contemptuous political demonstrations. Is there something I'm missing here? Why does the Court feel this admonition is necessary?"

"I'm running this trial, Mr. Hardman. This is a general cautionary."

"Well, Your Honor, it isn't necessary. I know how to act in a court of law. What concerns me is the mindset of this court. My client is entitled to a fair and impartial judicial officer. He has a right..."

"Mr. Hardman, don't lecture this Court!"

"Your Honor, I'm making a Motion, just as I have a right to do, if I may continue..."

"Well, put it in writing. We are about to start this trial."

"I will, but under the cases I have a right to move for a mistrial at any stage, and that is the motion I'm making. This Court harbors an animus toward counsel and Mr. Aldin."

Gadsen exploded. "How can you mistry a case that hasn't even started?"

She ignored him. "Mr. Hardman, you're treading a slippery slope. Just keep it up."

"Will the Court please rule on my motion to mistry this case and recuse yourself for prejudice?"

"Denied. There is no prejudice. Now go to your seat and proceed."

Carl shook his head at Dani as they strode back to counsel table.

The Judge barked, "Mr. Bailiff, call twelve prospective jurors." One by one names were drawn and small town people filled the two rows of chairs. Judge Harrigan interrogated them as a group from a canned set of questions. She asked no probing follow-ups. She ignored hesitant answers. She seemed satisfied with stiff, formal responses to superficial questions. She asked if each of them believed in the American system of Justice. Nods of heads. She asked if they would be fair to the State as well as to the Defendant. More nods. It went that way for no more than twenty minutes. Her voir dire of the panel came off more like a responsive reading from a pulpit. Then she turned to Carl and said, "Counsel may supplement the Court's examination with a few brief follow-up questions."

Carl began to probe answers given by an old man in the front row, Mr. Shurtz. He had been glowering at Aldin since he took his seat in the jury box. After the third question about his background, Judge Harrigan interrupted and said, "Mr. Hardman, wrap it up. You have two more questions of this venireman."

"Your Honor, this is a capital case..."

"Do not lecture the Court!"

"Please allow me to explore..."

259

"Two questions." She punched at him with two fingers in a vee. Carl recalled that the gesture was a British obscenity. Shurtz, who was old enough to have spent WWII in Britain, smiled a little too broadly. "Please excuse Mr. Shurtz." Carl glared at Judge Harrigan.

"Very well. Mr. Shurtz, you are excused with the apologies of the Court for taking your time." The Judge smiled at him. Shurtz beamed back a return smile as he left the jury box. He flashed a look of contempt as he passed the defense table.

The rest of the morning session had only one redeeming quality. It was over quickly. Carl exhausted all twenty of Aldin's peremptory challenges in under two hours, a new land speed record. He felt like a man with a six-shooter invited to a machine gun fight.

Guesswork substituted for inquiry. The jury was sworn. The posse had been chosen. The six-shooter was empty.

Gadsen gave his opening statement. It was laid back, as if he knew what the jury was thinking and felt he didn't have to inflame anybody. Carl followed, and kept it as short as he could. He wasn't sure what the defense would end up being, and merely told the jury of its obligation to keep an attitude throughout the entire trial that the defendant was as innocent of the charges as they were. And he ended by predicting that the evidence would fall far short of proof beyond a reasonable doubt.

Through lunch it continued to rain. Carl and Dani feasted on some granola bars she had in her briefcase.

The jurors were assembled and sworn at 1 p.m. and given instructions to avoid speaking with anyone concerning the trial. Judge Harrigan hinted that it was possible that she might sequester the jury. Carl knew there was no motel in Moraine. Sequestration would probably require busing the jury to Decatur or Champaign, or at least to one of the chain motels along the Interstate. He wondered whether any of the prospective jurors understood what sequestration meant and how long it could last. He had been through trials where a month away from home resulted in lost jobs and blossoming romances between jurors.

Judge Harrigan finished her admonition to the jury and said, "I want to see counsel at the bench." All the lawyers trekked to the makeshift platform.

The Judge took a deep breath, as if steeling herself for a distasteful duty. "I'm going to tell counsel once and once only. We are in the eye of the nation and there will be no second chances. Any deviation from classic textbook lawyering will result in contempt citations. You'll conduct your defense from a cell at the Sheriff Burnett Hotel. That should provide you lots of preparation time."

Carl had taken enough. He glanced to make certain the court reporter was taking the remarks. "Your Honor, the evidentiary portion of this trial is less than 3 minutes old. All counsel has done is sit through your admonition to the jury. Am I being accused of some kind of misconduct?"

The Judge's head snapped backward several inches. Her eyes narrowed, but she also glanced at the reporter. Her tone was steamy and dripping with venom, but her words were carefully chosen for how they would read from the written record in a higher court. "Why of course not, Mr. Hardman. Did I seem to single out the defense? That surely was a mere inadvertence. Please accept my apology. Of course what I said applies to Mr. Gadsen and his colleague, Ms. Powell, just as well as it does to you and Ms...it is Ms. Hardman, isn't it?"

Carl doubted that her sarcasm would come through when he argued the appeal. He had nothing to lose. "For the benefit of the written record, Your Honor's apology has been delivered in an ironic tone of voice. It seems the Court has made up her mind that my client is guilty and that his attorney must he intimidated into submission. Once again I move that the Court recuse herself from this proceeding immediately and request the Chief Judge to reassign this case. I ask for a hearing by another judge on these motions."

The Judge exploded without making a sound. She fumed but sat for a moment while the redness in her face reached full blossom. "Denied! This Court is not prejudiced against anyone. Now you will take your place at counsel table and we'll get on with it!"

Carl nodded without deference. He had gotten her goat and more. If made soon enough, Illinois requires a hearing by a neutral judge whenever a judge is accused of prejudice. The law is scrupulous in not permitting a judge to rule on his or her own fairness. Whether this was soon enough could be debated for years on appeal. Carl sat down at counsel table and scrawled a large "E" on the yellow pad in front of Dani. He whispered, "Error number one."

Dani shook her head, crossed out the "E" and wrote a "K" beneath it, the baseball symbol for a strikeout. She whispered, "Nice curve.

Where Were You?

The state's first witness was Hurshal Taylor. He strolled up the aisle, giving an occasional nod to a few of the faces in the audience. Regal in his false modesty, he marched up to the bench, nodded to Judge Harrigan, and snapped his right hand upward, as if demanding the right to tell the whole truth and nothing but.

Judge Harrigan administered the oath and Hurshal thanked her. He mounted the platform and thanked the clerk after she indicated that the witness chair would be a good place to sit. The courtliness of Hurshal's performance didn't seem to irritate anyone but Carl.

Gadsen and Hurshal exchanged smiles. After a calculated pause, Hurshal nodded to indicate his readiness to disclose the official version of reality. After preliminary background information, Gadsen established the setting in the courtroom on the morning Judge Esker had been killed.

"Please tell us what was taking place just before the event in question."

Hurshal's brow furrowed. "Something I'll never forget if I live a million years. We were trying an ordinary divorce case, just like hundreds I've tried before Judge Esker over the years. Wonderful man. Great judge. Fair beyond..."

"Objection. Judge Esker's unquestioned reputation is not on trial..."

"Overruled."

263

Carl had anticipated losing the objection, but thought he needed to crack Hurshal's porcelain tranquility. No lawyer likes to be interrupted.

Gadsen went on. "So you had known him over the years?"

"A colleague for a lifetime. When he was elevated to the bench, Central Illinois gained a learned and compassionate jurist. I had the honor of appearing before him perhaps a thousand times."

Carl made a note of that. It established that Hurshal was far less than a neutral observer.

Gadsen served up ten minutes of slow-pitch questions. Hurshal hit them all. He described Judge Esker as a veritable saint, a lawgiver of Old Testament proportions. Finally they got down to business. "Please tell us who was sitting where in the courtroom just before the explosion."

Hurshal said, "If I may, I believe there is a diagram which might help me illustrate my testimony. It's always difficult to keep 'right' and 'left' straight when you describe an event in court."

Carl thought about the irony of his remark. Judge Harrigan would have no trouble telling right from left.

Gadsen approached the witness with an easel and a large white display board holding a diagram of courtroom A. After foundation proof he asked Hurshal to come down from the stand and place variously colored markers where the participants at the trial had been sitting. Any demonstration always refreshes a jury's interest. Several of them leaned forward to try to read the lettering on the exhibit. Carl took his legal pad and stationed himself at one end of the diagram to make sure the jury didn't forget about him. Hurshal glanced at him, irritated at Carl's upstaging his performance. "I was here at the table in front of the bench." Hurshal placed a marker. "My client, a dear lady with an abusive husband, was sitting next to me on my right. The husband, a Mr. Yoder, was in the witness box right here. That other rectangle is the table where the husband's lawyer was sitting. He was out of the path. You can see the door and the aisle up to the gate just behind where I was sitting. The bomb flew right over my head." He paused, milking the moment. "I was standing up to approach the bench with an exhibit. I was certainly very fortunate I wasn't a second quicker."

"Please start just a few seconds before it happened and tell us what you saw."

Hurshal took a deep breath and let it out. "There was nothing special happening, then I heard the back door of the courtroom open. I can recall that now, but at the time I took no special note of it. People are constantly going in and out of courtrooms. Well, anyway, I was looking up at the Judge. I'll always remember his gold-rimmed glasses. They stared to glow, you know, reflecting the fire on the rag attached to the bottle. At the same time I heard this sort of roaring sound and smelled a strange odor and all of a sudden...shwoosh!...and there was a crash and there was fire rolling over Judge Esker. I'm truly fortunate that it didn't hit me right in the back of the head! Just goes to underline all the things you'd better be thankful for in your prayers. Well, anyway, it happened very quickly and the Judge was just frozen. When the bottle smashed, it coated him in flames, like one of those war movies, with napalm all over someone, burning him up. He couldn't run. He was writhing around in agony, screaming at the top of his lungs. There was no way to escape. The bench and his robes and the wall...were all on fire. The stench...it was awful! The poor man...finally fell behind the bench." Hurshal's voice broke several times as he testified.

"Did you see the person who threw the bomb?"

"Yes, I saw him clearly. That's the man right there!" Hurshal stabbed his index finger toward Aldin who stared back with cold eyes.

"Are you certain of your identification?"

"Absolutely! He's the man!"

Gadsen stopped and his eyes wandered down a yellow pad filled with questions. He toyed with settling for the short version. If in doubt, leave out details that might furnish a springboard for cross examination. Still, any prosecutor's temptation is to belabor everything he had worked to develop. He flipped a page on the yellow pad and continued. "What did the man do when he threw the bomb?"

Hurshal paused for a moment as if scanning his memory banks. Then he gathered himself and said with assurance, "He threw the bottle and stood there for maybe five seconds until it hit and then he turned and ran."

Carl wrote it down word for word. Was the bomb thrown as hard as he had said? If so, how could it possibly have taken five seconds to get to the bench unless it was rolled instead of thrown?

Gadsen drifted off the point, getting a description of the panic as everyone in the courtroom fought to escape the thick smoke and billowing orange flame. Hurshal described his escape through chambers in the wake of the husband and his attorney. Details consumed most of an hour. By the time Hurshal was done, much of the impact of his initial description of the bombing had lessened. Gadsen asked, "One moment, your Honor. May I have just a moment to examine my notes?"

"Certainly, Mr. Gadsen."

After a quick flipping of yellow pages, he said, "Your witness."

All eyes were on Carl. He let the moment sizzle for a few seconds. "Mr. Taylor, I wonder if I recall accurately something you said on direct examination...here it is...I think I wrote it down accurately...do you remember saying, 'He threw the bottle and stood there for five seconds until it hit and then he turned and ran?'"

Taylor made a great show of savoring the quote before he said, "I believe I said something like that. Anyway, that's what happened."

Carl made a show of slipping into Hurshal's contrived civility. He nodded gravely, as if appreciating Hurshal's exaggerated concern for accuracy. "You remember that clearly?"

Pause. "Yes. Very clearly."

Carl counted, "Thousand-one, thousand-two, thousand-three, thousand-four, thousand-five. If the bottle was thrown hard...hard enough to shatter...it couldn't have literally taken five seconds, now could it?"

Hurshal decided not to make a stand on the point. "Perhaps two seconds less. I don't see a significant difference."

Carl set him up. "You were facing the bench, not the back door when the bomb was thrown, isn't that right?"

"Yes, that would explain the small discrepancy of a second or so."

Carl leaned back and stretched. Several jurors took the cue and assumed a more comfortable position.

"I believe you said the moment sticks with you because when you looked up you saw the glint of the orange flame in Judge Esker's glasses from the burning rag on the bottle."

Hurshal seemed to be reliving the moment. "That's what I saw. I'll probably see the fire reflected off those glasses until the day I die. The bomb whizzed over my head. It was like...sort of a vibration, almost like a blowtorch."

Carl nodded. "It was close?"

"Yes. I could feel the heat. It's frightening to think it must have missed me by inches."

Carl tried to look sympathetic. "What you saw next was the bottle arcing toward the Judge?"

"It wasn't arcing. It was going full force. I saw that very clearly, Mr. Hardman. It hit the front edge of the bench and broke. I could see the liquid ignite, rolling like napalm in the old Viet Nam newsreels."

"You remember a lot of detail, then, about the instant the Judge was engulfed in the flames?"

Hurshal swallowed hard. "Unfortunately, I do. It was a nightmare in broad daylight. I can see every detail. The shock on his face, then the horror. The pain...one of the finest men I've ever known reduced to a...a charred waste." His voice faltered.

Carl was quick offer solace. "Do you need a moment? Perhaps a glass of water?"

Hurshal fought for control. "No. No, I don't think so." He sat a little straighter and cleared his throat.

Conventional wisdom dictated keeping a hostile witness from describing a heinous crime a second time, but Carl persisted. "When you saw this happen to Judge Esker, what did you do? Did you try to go up and help him?"

The jury was frozen. The news people were hanging on every word.

Hurshal's voice was full of scorn. "Go up to him? How could I? The bench was a fireball. I had to watch him scream and writhe in terror and pain. I had to watch him sink to the floor until there was nothing but a wall of flame and a huge cloud of foul smoke. That stench remains in my nose. I can still smell it at odd times."

Carl was nodding. "Pretty vivid experience."

"Worst of my life."

Carl bit his lip and seemed sympathetic. "Well, I imagine you have no doubts about the details, then, because you were glued to what was happening to Judge Esker?"

"Details? No, Mr. Hardman. Those details are as permanent as a tattoo. I relive them nightly."

Carl rose from his seat to create an emotional break for the jury. "Now, let me ask just a few clarifying questions to wrap things up. You said you had no doubt in your mind that you could identify my client as the person who threw the bomb. Wally Aldin? Is that right?"

"It most certainly is. He's the one." Hurshal nodded his head as he turned to the jury.

"Please describe what he was wearing."

"A gray sweatshirt."

"That was all?"

"No, of course not. He had on blue pants."

"What kind? Jeans? Cotton work twill?"

"I wasn't in the mood to examine the fabric that closely, Mr. Hardman. A wonderful man was dying at the moment."

Carl paused. He spoke softly but attempted to emphasize the remark. "A wonderful man was dying at the moment." He paused again. "That's what you said, wasn't it? 'A wonderful man was dying at the moment.'"

Hurshal bristled. "That's what I said, and that's what was happening. It's a bit distracting, Mr. Hardman. Pardon me for not memorizing the kind of trousers the killer wore."

Carl reacted as if he had been wounded by the remark. "I see completely. It certainly was riveting to see your lifelong best friend dying in a pillar of fire."

Hurshal looked up at him with raised eyebrows.

Carl pressed the point. "Your best friend since childhood, wasn't he?"

Hurshal seemed to be gauging where Carl was going, and why. "He was a wonderful Judge and a good man. We both grew up in this town and went to school together."

Carl had anticipated the evasion. From his briefcase he extracted a 1964 high school yearbook with a property stamp from the Moraine Public Library and opened it to a page containing candid photos from a long-ago Sadie Hawkins Dance. He casually walked toward the witness stand. "Does this refresh your recollection about how close you and Judge Esker were?"

Hurshal sat a little straighter as he recognized a picture of two boys dressed in a parody of farmer's work clothing. They were clowning for the camera, dancing together as their classmates laughed. Carl read, "The caption says, 'The Bobbsey Twins Cut A Rug.'"

Hurshal squirmed. Carl was in no hurry. He closed the annual and hugged it to his chest as he asked, "Now be fair with us, Mr. Taylor. You and Judge Esker were a good deal closer than just classmates, am I correct?"

Hurshal said, "I don't know why it makes any difference, but yes, we were friends."

"Just friends?"

Hurshal stared daggers. "Very good friends."

269

"Close enough friends that you two joined the same fraternity at the University of Illinois?"

"Yes." Hurshal's face had turned sullen.

Carl continued to drive the point home. "And you both attended Northwestern Law School together?"

"Yes, but we didn't room together."

"Ah, yes. But you did work together in Chicago at Isham, Lincoln, and Beale, isn't that right."

Hurshal flushed at the depth of Carl's probing. "There were over twenty young lawyers working there."

"Share an apartment in Chicago?"

A stare that could kill. "Yes, we did."

Carl nodded ironically, as if the clarification amounted to something important. "You and Judge Esker were golf partners on a weekly basis over the last thirty years, correct?"

Hurshal tried to relieve the pressure. "Even you couldn't call it golf, Mr. Hardman."

The jury snickered and Judge Harrigan smiled.

"To summarize, Mr. Taylor, isn't it fair to characterize you and the Judge as the closest of lifetime friends?"

Slowly he admitted, "Yes, I suppose so."

"You didn't tell us on direct how close you were to Judge Esker, did you?"

Hurshal pursed his lips and then responded, "Nobody asked."

"So when you watched that bottle burst and envelope him in flame, you were horror struck by the sight of your lifetime best friend burning to death?"

Hurshal squirmed. "Wouldn't you be?"

"But it's now clear you were deeply shocked and emotionally involved watching Judge Esker die?"

Hurshal swallowed before answering. His voice was fighting for control. "It was the worst thing I ever saw. What made it impossible to bear was the fact that I couldn't do a thing. There was simply no way to help him."

"You admit then, that you are not a neutral, dispassionate witness in this proceeding?"

Gadsen lurched forward as if absorbing a blow to the abdomen.

Hurshal mumbled, "I guess you…could say that." He looked down at his hands, which were trembling.

Carl lightened up, not wanting to torture the man and anger the jury. His tone was gentle. "I understand completely. If you need a moment or a glass of water, I'm sure we can take a short break." He glanced at Judge Harrigan, passing the decision up to her.

"Is that right, Mr. Taylor? Do you need a recess?"

Hurshal took a deep breath and recovered his composure. "That won't be necessary." He straightened his bowtie and rolled his shoulders to release the tension.

Carl had to press his point without creating a martyr. "So you were looking at the Judge, trying to find a way to help him. That's what you did from the time the bottle whizzed over your head and you saw the fire glow in Judge Esker's glasses, then saw it roll over and engulf him? I guess you must have looked away for a second or two."

Hurshal automatically took the opposite side. "A second or two? No, Mr. Hardman. A second! That was my best friend dying. I was frantic! It seemed like an eternity! Finally the flames and the smoke were just too much. I couldn't see any more. My eyes felt like they were on fire."

"Facing the Judge all through that?"

Hurshal's look was uncertain. "I suppose so."

"And you never saw the bottle until it whirred over your head and smashed, or you would have ducked, am I correct?"

"I suppose so."

Carl dropped his voice to little more than a whisper. "Well, if you saw all that, when could you possibly have turned around to see the perpetrator?" Carl could hear the jury stir behind him.

Hurshal swallowed hard and blinked. His voice became strident. "I don't know, but I saw him! It...it didn't happen the way you say."

Carl's eyebrows shot up and his tone reflected surprise. "I say? It's what YOU said, isn't that right, Mr. Taylor...or do you want the reporter to read back your answers?"

Hurshal exhaled. "That won't be necessary."

Quickly Carl bored in. "Then when did you see him?"

"I got a good look at him!"

"Wearing what?"

"A gray sweatshirt."

"With the hood pulled up over his head and the draw string cinched over his mouth and dark sunglasses over his eyes?"

"Yes. Yes. But I could see him."

"What did the sweatshirt say?"

Hurshal stopped and seemed to be trying to avoid a trap. "I don't remember."

"Didn't say anything at all, did it?" Carl picked up a police report and thumped it with his index finger.

"I guess that's right."

"Guess?" All lawyers are taught witnesses are never to guess in court. Hurshal grasped the point.

"All right, that's my best recollection."

"Now that you've been reminded of it, right?"

"That's what I recall."

"Are you going to tell me you stopped watching Judge Esker die and you turned and stared at the bomber?"

"That's the way it was." Hurshal thrust out his chin in anger.

Carl kept eye contact with him. "How long? How long did you stare at him."

Defiantly, "It must have been several seconds."

"We've already been through how well you estimate several seconds, Mr. Taylor. Did you estimate these several seconds in some different way?"

"You're distorting what happened."

Carl coldly appraised him. "For the record, Mr. Taylor, you appear to be a physically fit man of average weight in your mid fifties, is that fair?"

"Fifty eight," Hurshal snapped

Carl's stare never left him. "If you had several seconds why didn't you use those several seconds to try to capture the murderer of your best friend? There was a bailiff to help you."

The accusation landed like a bomb. Hurshal's composure was shattered. "I...I couldn't! There was no time!"

"But you just told us there was plenty of time, despite the horror, despite the smoke and the flame, despite the panic...to stand and watch for several seconds, enough time to make an accurate identification of a man whose face was covered. Is that the way it was, Mr. Taylor?"

Hurshal looked down and rubbed his eyes. He didn't answer. Carl paused for what seemed a long time and then said, "For the benefit of the record, I've just stood here waiting for an answer for several seconds. No further questions."

Judge Harrigan turned to Gadsen who was pinching the bridge of his nose as if to dispel a headache. He said, "No questions."

Judge Harrigan scowled and said, "Ten minute recess."

As the trial resumed, Carl wondered if he had actually done any damage on cross since Gadsen had waived his opportunity to rehabilitate Hurshal Taylor.

The next witness was Clancy Brown, the bailiff in Judge Esker's courtroom at the time of the attack. Clancy was at least seventy five. His food-stained brown suit looked as if it may have once belonged to his father. He mounted the stand with effort, took the oath and lowered himself into the witness chair.

Gadsen asked him routine foundation questions, pointedly failing to establish Clancy's age, then directed his attention to the minute or so before the bombing. "Mr. Brown, please tell us who was in the courtroom at that time."

Clancy's face showed the strain of remembering. "Uh...there was the Judge and the husband who was on the stand, testifyin'. I think maybe there was...yeah...there was Hurshal Taylor. He was askin' questions to the husband. The husband's lawyer was Harvey Barnes. He was sittin' off to the right. The wife...I can't remember her name...she used to be a cheerleader. Anyways, she was sittin' next to Hurshal." He stared at the ceiling, his lips silently mouthing the details again, to double check.

"Where were you sitting?"

"Uh...what?"

"Were you sitting in the Bailiff's chair when the bomber came in?"

"Uh...I was sittin' at the desk, right up against the rail on the audience side. I gotta be there so when people come in before court I can look at the list an' tell 'em they're in the right place."

"What else is your job?"

"Job? I'm retired from the police force."

"Yes, we know, Clancy. But what else were you supposed to do as Bailiff?"

As he began to answer, his face clouded over. "Security. I guess I was the one at fault. I guess I shoulda tackled him when he was gonna throw the bottle." He looked down at his right hand. His thumb rubbed his forefinger spasmodically as if he needed one of his cigars to dispel nervousness and guilt.

Gadsen went on. "What were you supposed to do if there was trouble?"

"Well, Sheriff Burnett don't want the Bailiffs to have no guns in the Courthouse, so we've got these here portable radios to call for help. If I'da had me a gun, maybe things woulda been different."

Carl silently agreed. *Probably two or three innocent people would have died.*

"What did you see when he came in?"

Clancy savored the question. He readjusted himself in the chair. "To tell you the honest truth, I gotta admit I didn't see nothin' till he already threw the bomb." He looked down at his hand, which was now twitching.

Gadsen didn't notice or didn't care. "Now tell us what the man looked like."

"He looked like Aldin there."

"Let the record indicate the witness identified the Defendant Aldin."

"So noted," Judge Harrigan droned.

"Now, Mr. Brown, what happened after you first saw him?"

"He was just followin' through on his throwin' motion. The bottle was on fire, and it was streakin' toward the Judge. I seen it, but there wasn't nothin' I could do. It was too late. Well, the bottle smashed, an' Judge was on fire, screamin' an' rollin' around, an' the whole room was full of smoke an' orange fire. You couldn't hardly see nothin', but I seen Aldin runnin' away. I tried t' get up an' chase him, but he was too fast. Then I tried t' help the Judge, but there wasn't no helpin' him. He was a goner."

Gadsen spent the next ten minutes at the diagram, getting Clancy to confirm the location of everyone in the courtroom. The testimony was a repetition of what Hurshal Taylor had said. Carl took the opportunity to lean over and examine Aldin's scrawlings on a yellow pad. Most of the comments were simply criticisms of Clancy. They huddled together for perhaps a half minute.

———————————

Before Carl could ask Clancy Brown any questions on cross examination, Judge Harrigan declared a recess. Carl followed Aldin to their broom-closet interview room. No sooner had the door closed than Aldin began to shout. He raged about Judge Harrigan, Gadsen, the government, and finally Clancy.

Carl tried to calm him, to get him to help. Without thinking what he was doing, he prodded Aldin for points to use against Clancy. Carl's questions implied that Aldin had a superior understanding of where Clancy had been standing and what he could have seen during the bombing. "You son-of-a-bitch! I told you I was innocent, so how would I know where that old bastard was standing? Quit asking me about what happened that day!"

Carl fixed him with a stare. "Look. I'm trying to help you. Don't testify if you don't want to. But this is the back room. Help me!"

Aldin scraped his chair back along the floor and shot to his feet. He pounded on the door for the deputy. When it opened a crack, he said, "This lawyer's coming out. Leave me alone until the trial starts."

Carl responded instantly. His chair clattered to the floor as he headed for the door. "You got it, Wally. See you in court."

———————————————————

The trial resumed and Clancy Brown was tendered for cross. Clancy swallowed nervously as Carl leaned forward in his seat and began a slow, patient interrogation designed to keep the old man from breaking down. The possibility of jury sympathy is always great with a fragile witness of any kind, but a retired Andy Griffith town cop was a potential disaster.

It didn't take long for Clancy to become comfortable. He warmed to his task and resumed his natural, friendly demeanor. Carl had lulled him with lollipop questions. Now it was time to dig in. "Officer Brown, will you think back to the last thing you were doing before the bomb hit?"

If Clancy didn't remember the moment, he should have gotten an academy award. He appeared tortured. Finally he began to open up. "I can't really put my finger on it, but I can tell you what prob'ly was goin' on. The divorce case was kinda nasty. Mr. Taylor was askin' this Yoder guy some questions. Then, like I said before, this here Aldin comes in and throws the bomb."

A repeated identification always makes a defense lawyer shudder, even when its basis is about to be challenged. Juries remember certainty, even when it is built on a shaky foundation. "Now you say you saw this man throw a bomb, right?"

"Yeah. I seen him." Clancy worked his mouth after he spoke.

"Saw him really well?"

"Real good."

"Watched what he did?"

"Yep."

"How did he throw the bomb?"

"Pardon?"

"Which hand?"

Clancy bobbed his head forward, straining to understand the question. "Pardon me?"

"Which hand did the bomber use to throw the bomb?"

Clancy stopped cold, his face transparent to his spinning thoughts.

"Come on now, Mr. Brown. You only have two possible guesses. Got a fifty-fifty chance of being correct."

Clancy moved his lips but nothing came out. Then it was a mumble. "...an' I seen it fly through the air."

"I missed what you said. The question was 'which hand did he use to throw the bomb?'"

Clancy was not clever. He cocked his head to one side while he considered what kind of a trick Carl was up to. It made sense. Aldin must be left handed if his lawyer was asking that question, to trick him into saying "right." But was the trick to make him guess left, and have it really be his right hand? Clancy opted for the middle ground. "I dunno." He looked embarrassed to be settling for the truth.

Gadsen gave a little start and looked up from his notes. Judge Harrigan looked over her half-glasses. Carl tried to keep from celebrating. It was just a tiny crack.

"How about it, Clancy, did you or did you not get a really good look at the person who threw the bomb?"

Clancy hesitated. "Well, I sure thought I did!"

Carl was on his feet now, stalking him. "If you clearly saw a man coming in through the door with a bottle that was on fire, why didn't you rush him, or shout a warning to the Judge, or at least use your radio to call the Sheriff's Office?"

The logic seemed unassailable. Clancy shifted to an excuse mode. His voice quavered and he pleaded, "See, there wasn't no time."

"No time? How long could it take to holler, 'Look out! He's got a bomb!' or 'Get down!'?"

Clancy was still desperate to defend his faded professionalism. "Well, it wouldn't have done no good by then."

Carl let the remark sizzle for a moment. "In other words from the time you actually saw the person until he threw the bomb, it was too short a time to even shout?"

Grasping at excuses, Clancy said "Yeah. That's right. Nobody coulda hollered that quick."

"And that's why you can't remember whether the bomber was right or left handed, am I correct? You watched it hit and Judge Esker was in flames."

Clancy swallowed hard. "Yeah. It was awful. When it hit I was sorta...like...helpless, you see? There wasn't nothing I could do but watch him burn. Then the courtroom went nuts, an' the guy was out the door."

Carl nodded as if granting Clancy absolution. He dropped his voice into a soothing tone. "Clancy, I know this is very difficult for you. Do you need a glass of water?" He was hoping he would refuse, letting Carl off the hook with the jury for being hard on the old man.

"I got a drink when we was in recess. I'm ok." He sat up straight.

"All right, then. What was the bomber wearing?"

"You know. You seen that composite picture."

278

"Yes, I know what some anonymous police artist thought he looked like, but I need to hear it from you."

"He had on one of them gray hooded sweatshirts."

"And?"

"Uh...dark glasses."

"I assume the hood was down around his neck?"

"Uh-uh..."

"That's a 'no?'"

"Uh...right. That's a 'no.' He had the hood up over his head."

Carl made a show of picking up the police report and tapping it as he took up a position only a few feet in front of Clancy. "Says here you described the bomber as being kind of short and slight of stature, maybe 5'7", and having a gray, hooded sweatshirt up over the head, the opening tied into a small circle up over the chin and mouth, covering all but a small part of the face, am I right?"

Clancy nodded. "That's what I said."

"And you said it right after the bombing, but before anybody went out and arrested Mr. Aldin, right?"

"Yep."

"The small part of the face you could see was pretty much covered with dark glasses, correct?"

"Uh...yeah, I guess so."

"Guess?"

"Well, that's what I said at the time." Clancy was starting to see where this was going.

"Mr. Brown, are you now saying you didn't get it right at the time, when it was fresh in your mind?"

He looked down at his fingers which were interlaced and flexing. "I ain't sayin' that. I guess I got it right when I give the statement."

Carl let up a little. "All right, then. Let's examine what you saw. For an instant too short to even shout a warning you saw a person whose body and face were covered by a hooded sweatshirt and dark glasses, right?"

"Yeah, that's right. It was too quick to holler."

"And you barely saw the hooded person as he threw the bomb, just an instant, can't even remember which arm, isn't that so?"

"Yeah. Sure. I never had no time to do nothin'."

"Then you watched the Judge burning and turned and saw the bomber's back headed out the door?"

"Right."

"Have you seen Aldin from the time of the firebombing until you just testified?"

"No. Sheriff Burnett took over as Bailiff. I guess I'm kinda retired again." Clancy looked at Sheriff Burnett as if betrayed.

"Now you testified that…I think this is exactly what you said on direct…'I seen Aldin runnin' away…' That makes it sound as if you recognized him at the time. Did you?"

Now Clancy was really fidgeting. "It was him. I seen him."

"If you recognized him at the time, why didn't you shout 'That's Aldin! He's getting away!', or tell the cops it was Aldin as soon as they showed up?"

Clancy said, "Huh?"

"So why didn't you identify the bomber as Aldin right there on the spot? That day you only gave a description."

"Yeah, that's right."

"So on the day of the crime you really didn't know it was Aldin or you would have told the Sheriff 'Forget the artist and arrest Wally Aldin!' Right?"

"Uh, what're you getting at?"

"What I'm getting at is who told you the bomber was Aldin? What made you sure it was him?"

Then Carl got one of those gifts that come along in court very seldom. Clancy said, "Well, they wouldn't have picked him up unless he done it, don't you see?"

Carl said, "NO, I don't see that at all. Do you, really see that? They never arrest the wrong guy?"

Clancy's eyes seemed to retreat into middle distance. Then for a moment he glanced at Aldin.

Gadsen quit writing on his note pad. His brow was furrowed. He plainly wanted Clancy off the stand. Judge Harrigan was looking at the clock mounted on the front of the oval second floor balcony. It said 11:05, too late for a second recess, too soon for lunch.

Carl bore down. " How long does it take to shout 'Get down!,' maybe a second?"

"Maybe."

"Then you said you watched the bomb hit. How long before you did anything to try to help?"

"Right away."

"Maybe another second?"

"Yeah. Maybe."

"Then what? Were you watching the Judge…watching the bomb explode?"

Clancy was still justifying himself. "Well, of course. You would, too. Then I turned around an' he was runnin' outta the courtroom. Wasn't no way to catch him, what with the smoke an' the fire, an' people screamin' an' bumpin' into each other an' such."

"So what you saw of the entire event..." Carl snapped his fingers, "was about two seconds?" Carl snapped a second time. "Just that long, am I right?"

"Yeah. Uh...yes. I guess that's right."

"And you were turned toward the Judge for part of that short time?"

Clancy knew when to quit. "I suppose."

Gadsen sighed and shook his head and looked down at his legal pad. The Judge was rocking slowly back and forth in her leather chair.

Carl paused and looked over at the jury to underline the timing. Then he walked back to the defense table to raise Clancy's hopes that it was over. Carl turned to him and asking, "What did it say?"

"Huh?"

"What did it say? The sweatshirt. What did it say on the sweatshirt?" Carl was boring in once again.

Clancy's voice began to waver. "In the police report? Is that what you mean?"

"You don't remember what it said on the sweatshirt?"

"No. What did it say?"

"You can't remember if it said Notre Dame or Budweiser or Monster Trucks or anything at all?"

Clancy was beaten. "Look. I'm just telling you what I remember. I didn't have no time to read it. I guess I really didn't really get a good look. It was too short a time."

"At the sweat shirt or the man?"

"Both, I guess."

"With the hood and the dark glasses, you really didn't get a good look in those few seconds, now did you?"

Clancy was willing to be led just to get it over with. "No, I guess not, now that you put it that way. The man run away too quick." He had stopped referring to the bomber as "Aldin."

Carl stood stock still for a moment, making eye contact with Clancy until he was sure the jury must be watching. "You said man."

Clancy blinked and asked, "What?"

"So how do you know it was a man?"

Clancy swallowed hard and said, "I just know."

Carl asked, "How? Are you psychic?"

Clancy said in resignation, "I s'pose it coulda been a woman, but from the way he...the way he threw it like a baseball player, it was like a man's baseball throw."

"Good form?"

Clancy brightened, "Yeah! Now that you mention it. Looked like a real good baseball throw."

Carl asked, "What about Wally Aldin? You said he was a soccer player and never played baseball. He didn't kick the bomb up there, did he?" Everyone looked at sullen Wally Aldin, who was chuckling. Clancy failed to answer.

Carl said, "Nothing further," and sat down. Aldin registered approval for the first time.

— · — · — · — · — · — · — · — · —

Bill found the satellite number of the Court Channel. He had memorized 120 for the History Channel and knew a number of Dish channels in the high 200's where a smorgasbord of religions made their pitches, but he had never been even slightly interested in trials, including the Simpson and Jackson carnivals.

His simple farmhouse encased some state of the art technology. Before buying his Sony big screen hi-definition television and installing the satellite dish, he had prayed on it, even looked at the Good Book as if there were some concordance that would guide him to God's position on lines of resolution and time shifting. Finding no prohibition, he went ahead and indulged himself. Having no children or dependents, no mortgage on the ancestral land, he could splurge on weapons and technology.

The analyst was droning on about the Aldin trial, making pointless chatter with a blonde woman who needed to dress more modestly. She seemed to be some kind of lawyer and the analyst was an ex-prosecutor, or so it said on the caption.

Here was an image of a street not five miles from where he sat, a street he had walked with his father as a child. He was being shown a twisted, big city version of the reality he had known for his whole life, live from a satellite in space.

283

They seemed to agree that the first day of testimony was surprising, that Hardman had poked a number of holes in the prosecution witnesses. That he had scored some points. The big city version of the trial was frightening, suggesting that the lawyer had created confusion in the minds of the jurors.

Bill was livid. Justice was being reported as if it were a sporting event. He was watching instant replay of the trial, taken through the transom window.

Hardman was gaining the respect of the TV people. What if he won? What if he loosed Aldin on the people? It was unthinkable.

One thing was certain. Watching the angle of the TV picture shot through the transom proved his plan. It rekindled Bill's fire.

Something had to be done.

Immediately!

Judge Harrigan had recessed for the afternoon following Carl's cross examination of Clancy, allowing Gadsen extra time to plan his redirect examination. It also had allowed Carl a sleepless night.

As they started up the next morning, Gadsen was holding a yellow pad crammed with scribbles. He leaned back in his chair and stretched his lanky body in an exaggerated attempt to appear untroubled. "Now, Clancy," he began. "You testified yesterday you feel a little guilty about not being able to rescue Judge Esker, am I correct?"

"Yes, sir. That's about it, Mr. Gadsen."

"It's been eating at you ever since, I suppose?"

Carl wasn't going to let Gadsen testify. "Objection. Leading."

Judge Harrigan reluctantly said, "I suppose he's right, Mr. Gadsen. Please let the witness tell the story."

Gadsen did his best look of mild frustration. "Thank you, Your Honor." He nodded in deference, then faced Clancy again. "Just tell me how you feel since the bombing?"

Clancy seemed to be editing several earthy phrases. Finally he selected "All tore up. That's about it."

Gadsen knitted his fingers together behind his head and stretched. Clancy followed the cue and seemed to relax. "Tell me if that's how you felt when you were answering counsel's questions about what you saw?"

The old man leaned forward in the witness box. His lip quivered. "You bet. I'da give the rest o' my life if I could go back an' stop him."

"Him? You're sure you know who it was?"

Clancy smiled. "Yeah, I'm sure. That guy right there." No quaver in the accusing forefinger.

"Anybody tell you the bomber was Aldin?"

"Nope. Figured that out on my own."

Carl sensed his cross of Clancy eroding. The jury seemed to be responding.

Gadsen said, "Let's go back and go over three or four points Mr. Hardman covered. First, the timing of the thing. Was it really just a few seconds?"

"Seemed like forever."

"How well did you see the bomber?"

"Real good. I know Mr. Hardman says I only glanced at him, but I seen him real good. I guess you see somethin' like that, you're gonna see it in your mind forever, kinda like gettin' shot. I caught one in the butt...uh...the backside...in Normandy. It don't take much time to get a real lively memory of those kind of things, you know."

Gadsen liked that one. He savored it, pursing his lips. "So how sure are you of your identification?"

Clancy turned to Aldin and stared at him. "Real sure. He's the one."

Gadsen then began a slow, skillful rehabilitation. He covered the identification problem of the sweatshirt and dark glasses by establishing that Clancy had often seen Aldin around town wearing sunglasses. He developed the failure to act or shout a warning as the frozen reaction of old age instead of proof the thing happened instantly. All the while Carl was in agony, absorbing body blows. He couldn't even muster a plausible objection.

Aldin leaned over to him and whispered too loudly, "Why don't you do something?"

All Carl could do was scribble on his legal pad "What do you want me to do? Make you testify and deny killing him?"

Aldin tore the page off and made a great show of angrily crumpling it into a ball.

Now Gadsen was asking Clancy how he felt during the fire.

The old man's eyes drifted upward. "It kinda felt like combat, but back then they let me have a rifle. I could do somethin'." There was guilt in his voice.

Gadsen exploited it. "And there was nothing for you to do but stare helplessly?"

Clancy shielded his eyes with his hand. "Right."

"Stare and memorize what you saw?"

The voice croaked out, "You bet!"

Gadsen slowly sat upright in his chair and clasped his hands as if in benediction. He said "That's all." The jury was very quiet.

Eyes shifted to Carl who felt helpless. If he probed the wounds on Clancy he would surely lose the jury. He did what he could to rescue the moment and said, "Your Honor, I believe the witness has been through enough. No further questions.

—·—·—·—·—·—·—·—·—

The first witness of the afternoon was Harvey Barnes, the lawyer who had been handling the divorce for Steve Yoder. After his interview with Harvey, Carl fully expected him to add another unequivocal identification.

As he walked into the courtroom Harvey looked ill at ease, perhaps a

286

little unsteady on his feet, as if his preparation included some liquid courage. Harvey took the oath and stumbled as he sat down in the witness chair. He waited for Gadsen to begin. The foundation questions seemed endless even though they consumed no more than five minutes. Carl wondered whether Harvey had settled on his story.

Gadsen stood in front of the witness. "Now, Mr. Barnes, after you heard the door open what did you see?"

Harvey took a breath and started. "Well, I...uh...I very clearly saw..." He stopped cold and shook his head, as if clearing an unpleasant thought.

Gadsen waited and said, "Go on."

"I'm gonna tell you exactly what I saw. And this is no kidding. I turned and I saw a blur. It was gray and I guess it was the sweatshirt of the guy...uh...the person who threw the firebomb. There is a memory of something dark, and I guess that's sunglasses. There was a lot of shouting and screaming and almost instantly there was a sound like glass breaking and then there was intense heat and a huge fireball. I turned and ran. I'm not proud of that, but I sure wasn't the only one. I don't think anybody else in the courtroom..."

"Objection. Non responsive." Gadsen seemed to feel betrayed.

"That's my objection on cross, Your Honor, not his on direct."

Judge Harrigan looked as if she had never heard of that. "I'm directing the witness to answer the questions and not to volunteer information."

Carl thought, *Yeah, we don't want the whole truth to sneak in here.*

Gadsen asked Harvey to describe the bomber.

"I'm sorry, Mr. Gadsen, I can't do that with any degree of accuracy."

Gadsen seemed about to come unglued. "Didn't you give a statement..."

"Yes, I did, but I've been thinking about it and I'm just not sure it was Mr. Aldin, although his body type is similar to the bomber."

Carl silently applauded an act of courage from a person who had a lot to lose, an act of conscience that was sure to expose Harvey to ostracism in this small, closed world.

Carl made a futile objection that half the population was consistent with the description, but Judge Harrigan said it was for the trier of fact to determine how much weight to give to the statement. Nevertheless it weakened the identification linking Aldin with the crime.

The State tendered the witness.

Carl mused for a few seconds, rolling his pen between his thumb and forefinger. "Mr. Barnes, you say you can't identify my client, Mr. Aldin, as the perpetrator?"

Harvey hunched his shoulders and said, "That's right."

"You've thought about this quite a bit, haven't you?"

"Every day since it happened."

Carl nodded and said, "Sometimes it's hard to tell the truth as your conscience dictates, isn't it?"

Harvey said, "You got that one right."

"But that's what you're doing today when you're telling us the event went by so quickly all you saw was a blur, am I right?"

Harvey's hands were clenching the armrests of the witness chair, squeezing hard, to muster the last of his integrity. He sighed and said, "I honestly don't see how anybody could identify the guy who did it...what with the hood...and the glasses...and how fast it happened."

Carl was proud of his profession for the first time in months. His eyes met Harvey's and saw integrity. Carl nodded, as if a salute, and said, "No further questions."

Gadsen let several seconds go by while tapping his ballpoint against his legal pad. He shot Harvey a look that could have scolded a puppy for messing the carpet. He shook his head in disgust and said, "No redirect."

Judge Harrigan broke the mood. She said, "We will be in recess for a chambers conference to discuss jury instructions." Carl suspected it was to cover some problem the prosecution encountered in having another witness ready to testify, but he welcomed the break. They met for a dull hour, organizing piles of legal forms containing statements of the law, or what passed for it in Judge Harrigan's court.

— · — · — · — · — · — · — · — · — · —

Soon it was five o'clock and Carl was in the Jaguar. He held his breath as he turned the key, but the engine roared to life as if it were eager to leave Moraine behind.

As Carl drove out of Moraine, he thought back on his last chat with Aldin. He hoped the force of the firm identifications might soften Aldin's blind faith in the presumption of innocence and his refusal to testify. No way. He seemed more unshakable than ever. No, he would not consider finding out if a deal was still possible. No way. In the end Carl had to promise Aldin he would not discuss the point with Gadsen even if Gadsen raised it.

Carl was bruised. He had never learned to take refuge in booze or tonight would be a binge of classic proportions. He reached for the cell phone because he needed a friendly voice. Sheri was elected. Although it was after five, he knew she'd be puttering around, finishing up something or other. A couple of rings. She answered, "Hardman Law Offices. We're closed."

She had a unique sense of discipline that she tried to impose on the clients. "Can you open up again for me?"

She didn't miss a beat. "Depends. Who'd you kill?"

He smiled for the first time all day. "I'd like to price exterminating a judge. How much to defend me."

"We got a group rate on that."

"Sheri, you're one of a kind."

"And if you're callin' after five, some kinda shit hit the fan, right?"

"You got it."

She sighed. "Carl, Carl! When you gonna grow up and take the money and give 'em a good defense an' let it go without losin' a piece of your soul every time?"

"What do I win if I guess the answer?"

"Maybe a couple of extra years on the far end of your life. So what's botherin' you?"

He thought about the question. "Hell, I don't even know how to describe it. I've been the guest of honor at an ass-kicking lots of times, but this is ridiculous. It's kind of like the whole system is coming apart. I've never represented a jerk like Aldin before. He's got a fire burning inside that cold exterior. He keeps talking about the Constitution and his rights. Sometimes I think he doesn't give a damn what happens to him. At first I thought he just didn't understand. Now it seems like he just doesn't care."

Sheri's tone softened a little. "I know you're really into this thing, Carl. But maybe he's got some bigger thing going on in his mind."

"What could be bigger than defending your life? He won't let me cut a deal for him. Won't testify in his own behalf. It's gotta be his strange religion but if I brought that up, he'd explode for sure. Do you think the jury is going to follow the law and set aside their feelings against somebody who won't at least get up and deny he did it? It just isn't possible for ordinary people. Their minds haven't been warped by law school."

"That's too much for me after five o'clock, Carl. You need to buy me a drink first if you're gonna spray me with your bullshit."

"Wish I could. I'm still down here."

"Buy one for Dani. She likes to talk about that stuff."

"Come on, Sheri. We went over that. I've thought it over and I can't trust her, and that hurts."

"Carl, I'm tellin' you, there's somethin' twisted here. Dani would never sell out a client even if you wasn't involved. Hell...she might piss and moan to your face, but she'd never sell you out."

The sprawl of Champaign was spilling over the horizon. He wanted to find his bed and sleep until time for the next day's disaster in Moraine. "I'm too zonked to argue with you."

290

"Then do it. Just trust me, if you need an excuse for trustin' her. It'll work out."

"We'll see. Call you tomorrow."

"Yeah. I got a bunch of offers on some of your personal injury cases. You need to call the clients. But none of them injury clients are goin' to die if you screw up, so spend them gray cells on your problem child down there."

"Thanks!"

"Don't mention it."

In The Wee Small Hours

Brother Bill entered the back stairwell of the Odd Fellows building about 4 a.m., when small towns are at low ebb. The few charged with being awake—the town cop, the cashier at the Marathon gas stop out on the highway—all had the awareness level of a potted fern. Sleep was still being hoarded by those who would soon drive to other places to work at mega-stores or to type words they could not define into computers at the University.

It had not been a sleepless night for Bill. The plan was clear and he had slept the sleep of the just. Now he was fresh and ready to be alert for however long it took.

The stairs made no sound, nor was there any creaking of the floorboards. It didn't matter yet because the little store downstairs wouldn't open for several hours, but Brother Bill was grateful the Lord had made a quiet escape possible. There was no other human presence in the entire block, except for one apartment over the drug store three buildings away, inhabited by a stone-deaf old man.

Because the muzzle would be back at least a foot from the open window, the report of the rifle would be baffled within the room, muffling it and making its source difficult to locate. Bill thought about the JFK assassination, and the decades of debate and testing to pinpoint the direction and number of shots. He thought as many as four shots could be fired before discovery became a risk. Nobody would begin checking buildings for several minutes. Their first thoughts would probably center on the hydraulic lifts next to the transom window, serving as camera platforms. In that time he would have the plastic drop cloth rolled around the disassembled rifle, the empty shell casings, the gloves, and the Handi-Wipes carrying away the superficial gunpowder residue from his exposed skin. Removing the barium isotopes and the antimony residue left by the shell primer, which only neutron activation scans could detect, would have to wait until he could scrub off a layer of skin. What he would have to carry to his pickup would be a small, chubby package, looking not at all as if it contained a rifle. He had on denim bib overalls covering chino work pants. Inside the button pockets of the bib were his bud earphones and Sony CD player loaded with the German military music given to him by Madden. It would consume his time until the shooting.

His pickup was parked perpendicular to the alley, between two empty buildings, on a concrete driveway that ran through to a side street a block from the Courthouse. There would be just fifteen feet of alley to cross without being seen. He had muddied the pickup and its license plates, making it look like a typical work truck in Central Illinois. In its bed were shovels, coils of used rope, bags of fertilizer and a 55 gallon barrel lashed to the side of the cab, to permit high speed driving. It was half full of fuel oil, but had warning labels that it contained concentrated pesticide. That was where he would hide the package containing the rifle and evidence. He could quickly seal the lid. No rural deputy would ever consider reaching into a container of pesticide to see what else it contained.

The driveway had been washed by the incessant rains. He had swept the few spots where light mud remained and had discarded the broom in a dumpster at the end of the block. No tire tracks or footprints would be left behind. His bib coveralls and the plastic-wrapped evidence would be dropped down a well at an abandoned farmstead a mile out of town. The entire escape should take less than one minute. Driving at legal speed, he would be at the well in three more. If he had time, he would run a raspy steel rod down the rifle barrel to confuse its ballistic characteristics, but it would be painful to deface a beautiful instrument of Almighty Justice.

The ammunition was cold and beautiful. The .223 rounds were stark and sleek. Their 55 grain, full-metal-jacket copper points gleamed in the 20-shot clip, like tiny spears ready to pierce window and bone and muscle; their high velocity slugs were ready to tumble and twist unpredictably after touching the body, dissipating enormous energy while opening paths through the lawyer and the terrorist. The 55 grain bullets had been on target when he simulated the shot through window glass. He had rejected the thought of using more powerful special ammunition that might jam. Besides, the second and third and fourth rounds would find no glass to deflect them.

He took no pleasure in the thought of killing other humans, no matter how evil they might be. This particular lawyer was no worse than many and probably had done nothing wrong in his own mind. On TV, Hardman even seemed pleasant in a big-city-liberal way. Were it not necessary for the protection of America, Bill would find it abhorrent. But duty it was.

Bill walked across the room and laid the rifle on the sheet of plastic, just under the window. Then he swept an exit way to the door with a whiskbroom. He even Handi-Wiped the soles of his worn military surplus boots. Any recognizable footprints could create a problem. Except for the coveralls, his clothing would be deposited in a Salvation Army drop box in one of the bigger towns. At worst, his boots would be discovered on some homeless man, creating a false lead to waste the time of the Feds and conspiracy people.

His plan was detailed, perhaps over-cautious, but Brother Bill didn't feel a call to become a martyr.

He took a small pinch bar from a pocket of his coveralls to pry the window open, but it proved unnecessary. The casement made a sharp pop and then a small squeal, but there was nobody in the street to hear it. The window slid up and stayed open about 4 inches. He had brought with him two pieces of cardboard, one about two feet wide and the other about a foot wide. They were six inches high, and he folded them to fit into the opening, to mask it. He had spray painted them dull gray, about the same color of the outside of the window sash, using paint purchased at a Super K-Mart in Champaign. The empty paint can had been discarded in a dumpster behind the Farm and Fleet in Urbana.

He jammed the cardboard into the open space below the window sash so the smaller one could be slid aside seconds before the shot. In the gloom of the rainy day there was little chance the open window would be spotted, even if security forces scanned the nearby buildings.

The inside windowsill was wide and about thirty inches above the floor. Across the room was a battered wooden chair, probably abandoned by the Odd Fellows. He moved it in front of the window and waited, occasionally leaning forward to look through the tiny, clean patch on the glass. He was careful not to extend the rifle barrel anywhere near the window. When time came, the rifle barrel would rest on a small Ziploc bag filled with sand when he fired from a kneeling position, as if in prayer.

The Jaguar entered Moraine slowly. It was just before eight. Carl was nauseated at the prospect of sitting next to Aldin, watching him slowly die as the evidence buried him.

Dani was not with him today. The intensive summer session at the Law School would not yield another day no matter what. Or so she said.

Carl wondered if it was an excuse to avoid the tension between them, along with Aldin's attitude toward her. At least it gave Carl breathing room.

Bill waited...waited as the janitor opened the courthouse...waited through the sounds of the little convenience store opening for the day...waited as he smelled coffee brewing.

Carl parked the car behind the courthouse and unloaded the two file boxes of papers. They were a flimsy barricade against prejudice and blood lust.

The swirling sky made him wonder if a tornado was trying to form. He had lived in the Midwest his whole life, but had never seen a more threatening cloud mass.

———————————————

Bill watched as Hardman loaded boxes onto a small hand cart and entered through the back door, away from the TV people. Boxes of legal papers. One book should do. One Bible to replace boxes of lies.

Bill sat patiently despite the boredom. It was difficult. He was made for farm work and detested the sitting that people did in offices.

Heavy clouds were rolling in from the west and the birds in the trees in front of the courthouse were taking wing. Early morning spectators formed a background for television reporters doing stand-ups in front of the Courthouse, their images being pumped into the menacing sky by the big satellite dishes that lined the street.

He checked the rifle, pulling back the slide to chamber a round from the 20-shot clip loaded with only 16 rounds to prevent jams. It worked smoothly. He pulled back the fingerholds on the .45 and a fat cartridge popped into the chamber. He released the clip and reached into his pocket for a loose cartridge, filling the clip to seven, making the weapon ready to speak 8 times. Extra clips for the pistol were in his shirt pockets, only a second away.

He waited. Waited and listened to the sounds in the convenience store below. Heavy rain was on the way, but it would destroy any footprints and tire marks he might make while leaving. Bill wondered what effect a deluge might have on his shot. He decided to take no chances on firing when rain on the window might obscure his target or deflect the slugs. The answer was to wait until it cleared, no matter how long.

At 8:15 a Sheriff's squad car with two deputies drove the short distance from the jail and appeared at the back door of the Courthouse. Wally Aldin, hands cuffed in front to a chain around his waist, was led into the County Board room and was permitted to take his customary seat at the table, showing a partially obscured left quarter-profile to Brother Bill.

He waited for Hardman to appear in the window with Aldin.

———·——·——·——·——·——·——·——·——

Carl didn't react when Aldin entered the room and took his seat. Neither did Aldin. All that had been said between them still hung in the air. Carl took the opportunity to scan the discovery material, hoping to find some tiny flaw that might be enlarged into an opening.

It was more like a library than a conference room. A silent truce, despite the rumbling of thunder getting closer by the minute.

———·——·——·——·——·——·——·——·——

A half-hour passed and the Courtroom was filling up. Aldin and Hardman entered from a side door and strolled over to their table. Hard rain was driving against the transom window, obscuring Brother Bill's line of sight. Lighting flashed and was followed only an instant later by ear-splitting thunder. He began to recheck his weapons, not so much because there could have been some demonic rearrangement of their working parts, but simply for the touch of them; to fondle them and feel their power.

But conditions were wrong. The time was not right.

Patience.

———·——·——·——·——·——·——·——·——

The next witness was Cathy Yoder, who had been winning her divorce case at the time of the firebombing. When the bottle was thrown, Cathy was at counsel table, sitting next to her lawyer, Hurshal Taylor.

She was of medium height, in her late thirties, dressed in a white nurse's uniform that enhanced her youthful figure. Her dark hair was cut short, with blonde highlights that looked costly but cheap. Despite the packaging she looked as hard as nails as she fixed Aldin with a blazing stare. Carl silently complimented Gadsen for toning her down with the uniform.

Without warning, the rain began to slacken and heads turned to look out the transom window. It had lulled to an ordinary downpour.

Across the street, Brother Bill relaxed his grip on the rifle and forced himself to breathe deeply. The time was at hand. Now the rain had died down, but there was still the problem of the television cameras making the shot difficult. One of the camera booms shifted its position to scan the jury. It partially obscured the transom window and the line of fire. Through the scope he could see the witness in a nurse's uniform in front of the lawyer and Aldin, at risk from a missed shot. He was frustrated and was tempted to become angry, but that kind of feeling was his enemy, not to be tolerated. This was a holy quest, and his chance would be provided.

— · — · — · — · — · — · — · —

The next few minutes passed like water torture. Cathy Yoder was intelligent and well prepared. She missed no opportunity to refer to Aldin by name as the bomber. She recreated a vivid picture of terror and panic in the courtroom. She insisted she had observed the firebomber carefully.

Gadsen asked, "Why did you watch him that closely?"

"Because I thought I was gonna die and I wanted to know who killed me. I wanted to know who was gonna burn in hell." She looked at Aldin as if she wished she had a match

"How do you know it was Mr. Aldin?"

"I know him. He was a little older than me, but he ran with some of my cousins. He's a skinny little sh...er, uh...he's built real slight, like you see him now. Not too many guys around here built that way, plus he's shorter than average. He's in good shape. Ran real good after the fire. Mr. Aldin was a soccer player. Plus it was just one of his typical sneaky..."

"Objection!"

"MS. YODER!" Judge Harrigan seemed to resent Cathy Yoder. "You will refrain from making comments of that kind!"

Cathy Yoder leveled a scorching stare at the Judge. "Let's just say I recognized him for sure."

Gadsen apparently decided to end it there and not risk another chance the Judge would intervene and appear to be siding with Aldin. "Nothing further from this witness, Your Honor."

Judge Harrigan looked at Carl and said, "Cross examination," in a voice that erased any illusion of sympathy for the defense.

— · — · — · — · — · — · — · —

Across the street, Brother Bill was stabilizing his rifle. The Judge had just said something and Hardman was moving around in his chair, picking up papers and a yellow pad. The shot was possible, but surely it would become better.

— · — · — · — · — · — · — · —

Carl stared at Cathy Yoder for a moment, trying to decide what he could possibly do to tone down her fiery attitude.

"Mrs. Yoder...is that the way you'd like to be addressed?"

She found a way to take offense at the question. "What do you mean by that?"

"Nothing at all. It's just polite to inquire what form of address a woman prefers."

"Call me Miss Yoder. I earned it."

"You sound a little bitter over your divorce."

299

"Objection, irrelevant." Gadsen was testing how far the Court would let Carl go.

"What's the purpose of your inquiry, Mr. Hardman?

"I believe I'm permitted to establish that she is angry or that she holds a grudge against the defendant because he messed up her divorce."

Judge Harrigan said, "I don't see any bias against your client."

"Maybe you would if you let her answer the question, Judge. If there is none, surely there will be no harm to the State."

"Get to it, then. I warn you that we are not going to allow this to deteriorate."

He wanted to slap down the yellow pad and make the jury aware that he was being handicapped by tight rulings, but decided to adopt an exaggerated tone of friendliness instead.

Carl could see that Aldin was angry. Not that this was anything new, but Carl didn't need the burden of his client giving the jury free samples of fury. Aldin was focused on Cathy Yoder. He had been making eye contact with her while Carl and the Judge were clashing. Aldin whispered, loud enough to be heard, "THAT BITCH! SHE'S FROWNING AT ME!" With that he threw down his ball point. It bounced once and rolled off the table. As the pen fell to the floor Carl reflexively grabbed for it, like an infielder trying to prevent an error. He bent over and retrieved it from under the table. The entire play didn't take more than the three most important seconds of his life.

— · — · — · — · — · — · — · — · —

Brother Bill's rhythm hit the last exhale and his finger was tense on the trigger, squeezing it smoothly when the head disappeared from the scope as Hardman bent over for the ballpoint. Bill sucked in air and caught himself as he began to curse. Even if he had to start the shot all over again, it wouldn't do to pollute this holy thing with a profanity.

Hardman's head reappeared from under the table and he handed the pen to Aldin as the camera gantry moved and made the shot difficult.

He knew he needed to calm himself. To accept the discipline necessary to do this thing the right way. Bill pushed the button on his Sony CD player and *Das Heer* began to play again. Its stirring music reached the depths of his soul.

— · — · — · — · — · — · — · — · —

Brother Bill began the litany again.

"Mrs. Yoder, when the fire bomb hit, you were winning, weren't you?"

"What?"

"The divorce case. You were winning, weren't you."

"Winning? You bet I was winning. My lawyer was makin' hamburger out of the drunken bum."

"And after the case was tried all over again with a new judge, you didn't do as well, did you."

She couldn't restrain herself. "It was unbelievable! I don't see how that judge could do what he did! There was something funny going on!"

Judge Harrigan was squirming in her chair, looking at Gadsen, inviting an objection. None came. Gadsen was staring at the witness, fascinated.

Carl stood and reached in his briefcase and got out a copy of the decree in the Yoder divorce case. "It says right here in your decree that your ex husband got the farm and you were denied alimony, right?" He walked over to the end of the jury box, hoping the witness would continue to stare daggers and that the jury would catch a few.

She reddened. "Mr. Taylor is taking that up on appeal. He says Judge Esker would never have made the mistakes the new judge did...some guy they brought in from Champaign."

Judge Harrigan seemed ready to intervene.

Carl decided to come in on the side of the angels. "Couldn't it just have been that the new judge simply saw the evidence in a different light?" Carl counted on her coming right out of the water.

301

"He must have been paid off."

This was too much for Judge Harrigan. "MISS YODER! Be very careful what you say about the Court! You are an inch from being held in contempt!"

They glared at each other, neither yielding that inch.

Carl broke the stalemate, "You feel that Judge Esker was about to give you a lot more?"

"Aldin cost me around seventy five, maybe a hundred thousand dollars, the way I figure it."

Carl tossed the Yoder decree down on the witness stand and leaned forward, "You think it was Mr. Aldin's fault you didn't get that money?"

"Who else? We were winning big time until that jerk threw the bottle." She jabbed a finger at Aldin.

"Should he be punished for what he did to your divorce case?" Gadsen stirred but apparently couldn't name an objection.

Cathy Yoder narrowed her eyes and fixed them on Aldin. "He ought to pay me for what he did to me."

Carl decided to quit while he was ahead and collect his small winnings. "No further questions." He returned to his seat next to Aldin.

Judge Harrigan said, "Redirect?"

Gadsen thought for a moment, appraising the charming Ms. Yoder and said, "No questions."

Aldin had written on the legal pad, "What a bitch!" Carl wrote beneath it "For sure, but the jury probably thinks she hates you enough to identify you correctly."

––·–··–··–··–··–·–

Hardman and Aldin were leaning over a yellow pad, writing on it. Their heads were inches apart. They were clear of the TV camera. It was a gift!

Brother Bill forced himself to relax. The German Military music was playing in his ear buds, and it helped him to focus. He used it to coordinate the required breathing to stabilize the shot. He imagined his heartbeat merging with that of the military band. Slowly he let out the last breath and moved his index finger toward the trigger.

From the top of the stairs came three sounds no louder than coughs.

Two men, dark men with heavy brush moustaches, dressed in coveralls, were nestled on the top of the steps, ten feet from where Brother Bill was taking aim. They, too, had taken advantage of the silent stairway treads. The shorter, slighter of them was bracing a semi-automatic Ruger 10/22 rifle against the top step. It was equipped with a small, homemade silencer, looking like a miniature automobile muffler. The rifle's clip had been loaded with 10 rounds of 40-grain RN long rifle target ammunition, selected for its accuracy and impact, but mostly because the slugs would not exceed the speed of sound, making them almost noiseless except for the tiny "splat" they made when they entered the base of Brother Bill's skull.

The first shot disconnected the nerves required for Bill to pull the trigger on his rifle. It was so accurate that the second and third were surplus. The spent shells would bear distinctive tool marks that a forensic lab could connect with the rifle. As they were ejected, the second man picked them up immediately.

The slugs entered Brother Bill's skull and fragmented. They caromed off the inside of Bill's skull like pool balls on the break and blenderized enough gray matter to erase a lifetime of prejudices, plans, and beliefs. Bill's trigger finger went slack. He slumped over his weapon and began his journey through the dark tunnel toward the bright light.

The two men exhaled. The tall one turned to the other. "We must wrap him in that plastic. There has been no sound, so there is no hurry. We must take our time and collect anything he brought. When it is dark we will leave." He said it calmly, as if he had waited through other acts of violence or combat. He took a *Partagas Série P* Cuban cigar out of his inner jacket pocket and put it in his mouth, chewing on it to calm himself.

The other nodded his head and said softly, "I will wrap him. You disassemble his rifle and close the window. One day Walid will know that we have kept faith with him, and that God has delivered him from these fanatics."

The first said, "When it gets dark we can bring the van through the alley and take this man back to his farm for disposal."

They broke down both rifles, cut a piece of plastic and packaged Bill's rifle with his .45 pistol. The .22 rifle would have to be destroyed, but the firearms of the dead man, since they had not been used, were perfect for some future use. If captured, their history, if any, would trace to the right-wing and would constitute a false lead. They cut a segment of the plastic sheet and rolled Bill in it.

What remained of the plastic they pulled over against the wall. They sat on it and mused about how events had proceeded so smoothly it must have been the Divine Will. The taller of the two thought back to Beirut in the '80s, and the day he had lost his brother, Walid's father, to the mortar blast. It had been the final blow, and he had moved to New Jersey and had bought a store in a bad neighborhood. A year later he had brought Walid to America to recover from injuries. Now he was keeping faith with his obligation to guard and protect a fellow *Mowahhid* who was also his nephew.

The second man said, "You were right. Watching and waiting is our way. These American people lack the discipline. They think Walid is an Islamic fundamentalist terrorist. This dead man is a Christian fundamentalist killer. But they will never know that." They sat quietly until Moraine closed down for the night.

Riders On The Storm

It was morning again in Moraine, but the sun was still missing, as it had been for days. *More rain*, Carl thought. The weak humor failed to dispel the gloom, but it was one more day that Wally Aldin was still alive and unconvicted. Carl felt a surge of stomach acid.

The morning trip to Moraine had become routine. Carl was musing about two weeks in London if this hellish case ever ended. The Oldies station shifted into the 8 a.m. local news. Carl's attention was drawn at the mention of Moraine. "...late yesterday a body, tentatively identified as Lincoln County farmer and lay minister, William Carmichael, was found after being caught in a grain auger on his farm. The machine was over 40 years old, according to Ag Extension Advisor Dave Berg, and lacked modern, protective devices to prevent being pulled into the movable parts. The extent of the injuries has delayed confirmation of the identification, pending DNA testing. Known as Brother Bill in various conservative political causes in Central Illinois, he was apparently cleaning and adjusting the machine..."

Carl snapped off the radio as he winced in horror. *Being sucked into a machine with nobody around. What a horrible way to go!*

305

Gadsen was standing under the overhang of the back door to the courthouse with his arms folded, looking grim. Fossum slouched in the doorway behind him with a brooding look, examining his fingernails. A few large drops of rain were spattering on the parking lot, announcing the arrival of a fresh mass of thunderheads. Most of the press was scurrying into the television vans or taking refuge in the little convenience store.

Carl closed the driver's door and began to open the trunk to remove a fresh file box to supplement those left in the courtroom.

Gadsen called out, "Counselor!"

Carl looked up to see Gadsen motioning him to join him. He felt a twinge, wondering what new disaster awaited, but his curiosity overcame his apprehension. He hurried across the courthouse lawn, covering his head with the file box. As he started up the steps to the courthouse, Carl's mind began to sift through the reasons the prosecutor would be ambushing him. "What's on your mind?"

"Can we find a place to talk?" Gadsen glanced around, looking for cameras. He saw concern in Carl's eyes. "Don't worry, it's nothing bad involving you personally."

Carl decided to keep quiet and play along. They walked through the Courthouse, into a small alcove behind the clerk's office. Gadsen led Carl to a clear space behind rows of ancient filing cabinets filled with dead disputes, out of sight from the hall. Fossum blocked the narrow entrance to the alcove. Carl's warning lights were flashing full alert. "Ok, Willard, what the hell's going on?"

Gadsen seemed to be trying to digest something unpleasant. Then he pursed his lips and babbled, "This isn't easy for me, you know, but I guess I've got a professional obligation to discharge, you know." Discomfort played across his face. At last he selected the simplest thing to say. "Okay, it looks like you win."

They stared at each other for several seconds.

"You've got a piss poor sense of humor, Willard."

Gadsen squirmed. "I wish this was just a bad joke, but it's not. Last week, a secretary at wholesale fuel distributor in Douglas opened up for the morning and found his manager slumped over his desk in a pool of blood. One bullet hole in the forehead, back of the skull blown away. There was a .38 snub-nosed Smith on the desk with his right thumb in the trigger guard. Looked self-inflicted. A suicide note was lying on the desk with blood splashes indicating it was there when the shot went off. Anyway, this note confessed to the murder of Judge Esker." He stuck his hand out and Fossum gave him a photocopy of the note with a photo clipped to the front.

Carl's eyes became saucers. It was the haunted face he had seen several times in the crowd around the Courthouse. The same sunken eyes of the gaunt man in the mob, but this time the haunted look was gone. Replacing them as a point of interest was a small, dark hole in the man's forehead.

Carl's stomach clutched into an acidic knot formed around his assumption that his client was guilty. Others had labeled him a terrorist, or worse, condemning him because of his national origin.

Gadsen continued. "According to the clerk...and we're still checking out details...this guy, Clifford Collins...well, for years he's had a hard-on for Judge Esker. The docket sheet in Collins' divorce indicates he lost a real gut-wrenching custody battle about 5 years ago. Judge Esker awarded the kid to the wife."

Carl nodded. "Let me guess. Her lawyer was Hurshal Taylor, right?"

Gadsen looked annoyed at being interrupted. "Yeah...I guess so...Hurshal. So anyway, she was screwing half the bikers in Central Illinois. Her double-wide was open house for anybody with a Harley. Apparently the kid woke one night from the noise of two guys banging his mother. He wandered into the kitchen and turned over a pan of water she was boiling for humidity. He got second and third degree burns all over his face. I guess he's had all kinds of skin grafts and plastic surgery, but he's gonna be a real mess for the rest of his life."

The image made Carl wince.

Gadsen went on. "You know how bad a burn hurts? Well, they took him to the burn unit in Springfield, but he's looking at a lifetime of disfigurement. The kid's face is like a hockey mask. Collins got to be like a broken record about how Judge Esker never gave a damn about the kid, how he must have been paid off, that kind of crap. Nobody could say hello to him without hearing how much he hated the courts. Even more than he hated his ex wife."

Carl was still trying to absorb the details. "Is this on the level? If this is some cheap trick..."

Fossum couldn't stay out of the conversation any longer. He bristled and interrupted Carl. "Listen, Hardman, I've got kids of my own! This tears me up!"

Carl ignored Fossum and asked Gadsen, "So what happens now?"

A look of genuine pain crossed Gadsen's face. "About twenty minutes ago we went into chambers and dismissed the case."

Swirling emotions churned within Carl. He was nauseated by visualizing the little boy's injury. He felt the outrage that must have haunted Collins and pushed him into violence. He was shocked that the Court would enter a dismissal order without him and his client being present, shock at the unceremonious dumping of the Aldin case. But the feeling that burned hottest was shame that he had come to believe that Aldin had thrown the firebomb. Remorse for losing faith in his client simply because Aldin refused to take the stand and deny the crime. He felt perplexed. *Why would Aldin refuse to testify? Why wouldn't he demand to tell the world?*

Fossum broke through the thought. "We're not quite done yet, Counselor." He ignored the frown that Gadsen was leveling at him. "Don't give me hard looks, Willard! I'm not your lackey. There's more, Hardman. This is from me. It's been bothering me for a couple of weeks, and I'm gonna get it off my chest. Time for true confessions all around."

Carl was about to tell him to save it until he could break the good news to his client, but Fossum was intense, looking as if he would relish an excuse to take a swing at somebody. "I really don't have to tell you this according to the way we run the world these days. *Catch me if you can* seems to be the standard for cops and politicians. So you can write this off to outmoded ideas of fairness I learned on the ball diamond. I've spent my life in law enforcement, but there are a few things that just don't set right with me. Maybe it's a good thing I'm retiring."

Gadsen was on the edge of interrupting, but Fossum held up his palm to shut him off. "I'm gonna tell him, Willard! Just stay out of it!"

Carl listened.

Fossum went on, "Once in a while something happens in this job that violates the retch and gag standard, and that's a pretty high threshold anymore. So here goes. If you repeat this, I'll deny it." He glanced at Gadsen.

Carl waited.

Fossum was struggling. "Here it is. You've been sold out. We've been getting intelligence from a confidential source since the very beginning."

Gadsen started to speak. Fossum growled, "Just keep your mouth shut, Willard! I don't work for you, and I don't go along with the way you've played your hand."

Gadsen looked at Carl, then back at Fossum, but said nothing.

Fossum said to Carl, "Somebody very close to you has been selling you out. A real insider. You probably think it's somebody we infiltrated, or electronic surveillance, but it isn't. I wouldn't be telling you except there are a few things law enforcement shouldn't be messing with."

Carl narrowed his eyes, "Like what?"

Fossum snapped, "Stuff like marriage and family."

Carl was now inches from Fossum's face. "So you're gonna tell me you've been getting information from my ex wife?"

Fossum stared at Carl for a few seconds. Then his look shifted from anger to perplexity, finally to mild amusement. "Your ex wife? That's the woman lawyer you've been bringing to court?" Fossum was smiling broadly.

"What's so funny about that?" Carl's fists wanted to double.

Fossum shook his head. "Now there's an angle for you! I guess lawyers have something in common with human beings after all!"

Carl flushed, but found himself speechless.

Fossum continued, "You poor, dumb son of a bitch! The leak is Aldin's wife."

Carl blinked and pursed his lips to speak, but nothing came out.

Fossum bored in. "Yeah, your client's beautiful little dark-haired sweetie! Really cute, isn't she? Wouldn't say shit if she had a mouthful. Well, she's been selling out her husband since day one." Fossum paused.

Carl said quietly, "Go on."

"Think about it. Where would Sheriff Burnett get a tip about a gas can and groceries in Aldin's trunk? That call had to come within minutes of the firebombing. Remember the testimony? Deputy Otto, the big blimp? Burnett told him to go out to Aldin's place and serve a civil paper and try to get a look in the trunk, right?"

Carl nodded.

"So who would know right after the crime what was in Aldin's trunk? There's a real short list, beginning and ending with little Laura. There was a lot of other stuff we knew about. It wasn't illegal for us to listen to her betraying your trial secrets, but I sure as hell didn't feel real good about it. I mean, a guy's wife flipping on him. That just rubs me the wrong way."

Carl had a sinking feeling. The scenario was compelling. "But why would she do that? I mean, she seems like..."

"...like what? Like such a pretty little thing? Like somebody you could go for if you were 20 years younger?" Fossum rubbed salt into Carl's wound.

Carl said, "Now that's none of your fucking business."

"Bullshit. It's exactly our business. It's the Bureau's business to convict terrorists. We're dealing with killers here, not dope smokers. Fight fire with fire. She's been playing you and that's our business. What's a little marital intrigue compared with a scorched body? If you've got the hots for your client's wife and that blinds you, so be it. Or at least that's the way they see it in Washington."

Carl wanted to walk away, but it was like being transfixed by the horror of a bad traffic accident. "You still haven't explained why she would do that."

Fossum continued, "Real simple. This whole case is about people caught up in their beliefs. They're prisoners of their own bullshit. You, too. You're hung up on saving every worthless mope from the death penalty. Well, anyway, little Laura is no exception. Did you ever ask her what religion she is?"

Carl stammered, "I...I don't see..."

"Catholic. A real old-fashioned Catholic. Did she tell you what an asshole Aldin was? The things he did to her?"

"Kind of hinted at it."

"Well, she told us plenty, and we checked it out. He's been beating on her since they got back from the honeymoon. Deputies been out there on domestic calls eleven times in the last six years. He spends all their money on guns and screwball books and big computers. She'd dump him in a minute, except she's an old-fashioned Catholic and doesn't believe in divorce."

Carl was overloaded by the new picture of Laura, no longer gentle and weak. He was forced to see her as tough and devious and driven by a belief system as hard and unforgiving as a Midwestern ice storm.

Fossum watched the transformation in Carl. "Oh, she really believed Wally killed the Judge, alright. It popped into her mind right after she heard the news on the local radio station. She called Sheriff Burnett and told him Aldin had a gas container in his trunk. She thought her hubby finally lost it. In her own way she felt justified...free to turn him in. I guess today's word would be 'liberated.' Anyway, it only took her a minute to decide to rat on him. She said it was because she believed in law and order and saving lives. Personally, I think she just figured it was a good way to get loose. If he got executed, she'd be free."

Carl had been staring through the window. He turned reflexively and stared at Fossum. "You really think...she wanted him to die?"

"Yeah. Sure, she wanted him to die. Wouldn't you? The bastard's been beating her black and blue. Apparently she thought it's okay for the state to execute him, even though it's not okay for the state to divorce him. She's been taught there's no excuse for a divorce. Like I said, a very old-fashioned Catholic. So she volunteered to help drag Wally off to get his needle. The Sheriff tried to cover up her information about the gas can in the trunk by inventing grounds for the search warrant. That's the reason he had the deputy serve the civil paper and get a peek into Wally's trunk. It worked. Go figure."

It figured, all right. Carl felt the truth of it in his bones. But the knowledge sickened him. It leeched at the small measure of idealism that had survived 30 years of tinkering with shattered lives. "It's plausible," he said, weakly.

"Plausible, hell! It's true and you know it."

"Is nothing sacred anymore?"

"Sacred? That's a good one coming from a criminal lawyer. You've been making shit out of the cops and courts since your student days."

Carl said, "Listen..."

Fossum cut him off. "No, you listen! I don't give a damn what you think of me, or the Bureau, or that Andy Griffith Sheriff, or the Barbie doll judge or anybody else. But I want you to know one thing. For the last month or so, I've been trying to tell the big guys in the Bureau...and Gadsen, here...that there was no proof your client did it. And that's long before the suicide."

Carl blinked.

Gadsen said, "Now listen, Fossum..."

Fossum ignored him and pointed his finger at Carl's chest. "This is important. You might learn something. But if you ever quote me on this, so help me I'll scorch your ass!" He shot a threatening stare at Gadsen, "Both of you!"

Carl said, "Agreed. Go on."

"About a month ago a guy in the Bureau who shall remain nameless called me up to tell me the testing wasn't checking out. This was well into the case...weeks after that bozo sheriff made his arrest and looked brilliant for the cameras. Anyway, the guy called me and told me the hydrocarbons in the ashes, in Esker's clothes, on the bottle fragments...they don't check out with the gas can in Aldin's car."

Carl's face began to color. Gadsen's face was ashen.

"I know. You're gonna start hollering about why didn't somebody tell you. Well, if you remember in your discovery, the lab tests go on and on with raw computer stuff, and at the end there's no real conclusion. It's all there, counselor. If you were a Ph.D. in chemistry with a desk reference manual for chromatography, you might have spotted the fact that it doesn't match. Nothing held back, mind you. It's all there so nobody on appeal could claim this violates *Brady versus Maryland*. But it's in a form you weren't likely to understand." Fossum looked accusingly at Gadsen.

Carl exploded. "You mean you guys were playing with Aldin's life when you knew perfectly well he didn't do it?"

Fossum fought for control. "That's bullshit! Nobody thought he was innocent! Everybody thought he did it, all right, but we just didn't get the right gas can. We thought he threw us a curve and put a phony where we would find it. You think we'd try to pin something like this on an innocent man? Fuck you!" He was quivering.

"But it was ok to play God and warp the evidence because you thought he was guilty?"

Gadsen said, "Now Carl..."

313

Fossum cut him off. "Ok. In hindsight you can twist it around so it looks like that. But, for the record, there was a big debate about how we should handle the test results. Your friend Gadsen, here, wanted to wait to see whether you picked up on them. He knew if you did we'd find out from little Laura. You won't believe me, but I was on the verge of tipping you to get somebody to review the raw data. An anonymous call, if necessary. Everybody was convinced he was guilty and we wanted to make an example of him. There are some real hard-asses in Homeland Security, and your prosecutor, here, isn't exactly Mother Teresa."

Carl shook his head. He had discovered a new sub-basement in the system. He stared at Willard Gadsen with contempt.

Gadsen responded with a matter-of-fact tone. "Don't be so pious, counselor. We did make you an offer."

"The offer to drop the death penalty?"

"Right. We war-gamed it a dozen times. Aldin is trouble. And you've got to remember, our job is to keep trouble away from the American people. He's been messing with the courts for years. Everybody figured we had the right guy, but we just didn't have the right gas can. If that moron Sheriff Burnett would've let the Bureau investigate this thing before he made an arrest, none of this ever would have happened. This case wouldn't have been dropped in my lap like a hot potato. We would have plodded along, like we usually do. Maybe we would have gotten this Collins guy before he did a Kevorkian."

Carl exploded at Gadsen, "You would've done that except for the fact Aldin was as innocent as the driven snow and you jumped to the conclusion he was guilty! You bastards! The only reason you sat down and fed me donuts and offered to plead him to life was because you had no laboratory evidence against him, but you thought he'd jump at a deal for life and that would prove he really did it."

Gadsen had recovered a certain self confidence, apparently having calculated how the story would play with the public if it came out. "Kind of. And if you think about it long enough, you're gonna find a sort of primitive justice in that."

"Did it ever cross your mind that an innocent man might plead out just to save his life? This is beyond belief!"

Fossum took over again. "Yeah? Well, you better believe it. One more thing, counselor, I've got my neck stuck out a mile for you and that screwball. I want you to think about that. Think about how somebody in the government was trying to be straight with you. My boss is gonna be in the Bureau long after I retire. He's a real prick. His type is what you've got to worry about. I thought they should tell you up front. I thought we should just get our butts in gear and find the real accelerant. But I sure never thought Aldin was innocent."

"There! You just said it! You never thought he was innocent! Who are you guys? Don't you think the presumption of innocence is part of the law? I thought you held up your hands and promised to defend the Constitution!"

Fossum's face went scarlet. His index finger dented Carl's sternum and his voice lowered to a rumble. "I defended it, buddy. While you were out on some picket line, I was walking point in Viet Nam! I'll tell you another thing! Some of us in the Bureau have a hero, an agent named Danny Coulson. You never heard of him because he's responsible for something that didn't happen. Remember in '85 those four Neo-Nazi fugitives who killed the radio guy in Denver? They took refuge in that Christian Identity compound in Arkansas?"

Carl nodded.

"Well, Coulson was in charge of surrounding the place. The whole damn bunch of them were itching to become martyrs. They had enough ordnance to defeat Saddam. Coulson kept cool and called a truce. He got one of the nutcases to come over and persuaded him that nobody from law enforcement was gonna fire the first shot. Danny was a patient man and it worked. Eventually the religious fanatics expelled the Nazis. Coulson

315

said, 'If you kill a terrorist you create a martyr. If you arrest him and let the jury decide, you create a criminal and Americans don't care about criminals.' That's the way I tried to play it."

Hardman didn't yield an inch. They were nose to nose. "Let's go back to that picket line remark. On that picket line I defended what this country stands for. You guys think you've got some divine insight into who the bad guys are, that you've got a charter to pin something on them. You ought to start with the idea that you're there to find the truth of what happened. All of it. Both sides. You're supposed to be completely fair, even to the people who hate you."

Fossum pursed his lips. "I've been on the edge of retiring. I think maybe this whole thing just pushed me over. But right now there's one more thing."

"Yeah?"

"The testing profile for the gasohol and diesel from Collins' job was identical to the accelerant. Complete match, right down to the contaminants." Fossum stared at Gadsen who was eyeing the path out of the alcove.

Carl's eyebrows went up. "If that's true, then all your moralizing is bullshit! You guys just hit a dead end on technical proof. You had to dismiss it or walk in there without a witness and get beat in public!" He leveled his finger at Gadsen. "You're fresh out of lab experts to put on the stand. This is unbelievable!" He could feel his pulse throbbing in his temples.

Gadsen stepped back and turned toward the door. "Yeah? Well there's no talking to you. Anyway, it's over."

Outside the window, a score of reporters with umbrellas were doing stand-ups. Apparently news of the dismissal had leaked. Half the world already knew that Wally Aldin had been cut loose, but Aldin was still in the other half. Telling him about the dismissal became far more important than whatever could be accomplished in the alcove. As he stormed into the hall, Carl wondered what would have happened if Fossum had another ten years of career ahead of him. Or if he had retired six months ago.

Oz

Wally Aldin was lounging in the broken swivel chair, wrinkling his cheap blue suit. He was unaware of his fate, much less that millions of people already knew it. He stared out the window at the armada of television trucks, their satellite dishes connected to the world, oblivious of the tornado that was about to suck him into Oz. As Carl came in, Aldin nodded his head with a listless "Morning, Counselor."

Carl set his briefcase on the table and stuck out his hand to Aldin, who looked at it for a moment, but didn't offer to shake. "What's that for?"

"That's to say good-bye. You're outta here."

Aldin stared at him. A beat went by. "I'm what?" Surprise registered for the first time since they met.

"Outta here."

Aldin fixed him with a bayonet of a stare. "What the hell are you coming up with now?"

"You're a free man, Wally. We won. You can get up and leave right now." Carl's smile could not be contained.

Aldin mutated from perplexity through skepticism and ended in what seemed akin to disappointment. "You're shitting me!"

Carl was stunned. Nevertheless, he rambled through Gadsen and Fossum's disclosures, except the part about Laura.

Aldin sat motionless through the first several minutes, leaning forward, listening. Then he came alive, eyes blazing, slapping both arms of the chair. "No! They can't do this!"

Carl's shock broke into exasperation. "'No?' You're saying 'no'? 'No' to what? Just what the fuck are you telling me 'No' about?"

Aldin clenched his jaw and sprung to his feet. "I'm telling you 'No' to your little plan to get a mistrial in this bullshit joke of a trial. What are you doing? Playing footsie with them?"

This was the final insult. What was left of Carl's elation gushed out like water from a burst pipe. Numbing weariness was all that was left. He slumped into one of the chairs, feeling a throbbing, physical threat to his body. "There's no mistrial! It's a complete dismissal!"

"Doesn't make any difference! This is some kind of trick." Aldin's jaw was set, his eyes ablaze.

"I guess I'm too old for this. I bust my ass for you and come in here telling you we won and you're a free man and..."

"I always was a free man, Hardman, and don't you forget it! One of the few still left in this country."

Absolute silence. Perhaps a half-minute went by as they stared across the chasm between their worlds.

At last Carl said, "I don't get it. I just don't get it, Wally. Are you worrying about being tried on Federal charges? The Feds admit you're the wrong man..."

"Fuck the Federal charges."

"Well, then, what's the problem?"

"You tell me. You're in on whatever it is."

Carl shook his head in perplexity. He hadn't been this confused since they tried to explain quadratic equations to him back in high school. "Wally, I've invested a lot of my life in your case."

Aldin cocked his head, apparently listening, even if he would not avert his gaze from the window, watching the media in its feeding frenzy.

Carl seized on the tiny concession. "Wally...please...be a gentleman and hear me out. I just don't get it. I can't understand you failing to find joy at the prospect of walking out of here right now. Wally, you've dodged a bullet!"

Aldin looked down at his shoes, then turned away.

Carl softened. "Why are you climbing up my ass for telling you the case is over?"

"They'll never let it be over. This has got to be some kind of a trick. If you're not on their side, then you're just not seeing it."

"I think I'm beginning to understand why you never thought it mattered what defense we put on. You really thought you were going to get a needle jammed into your arm no matter what we did! And you think they've got more in store for you down the line...somehow."

"That's what I've been telling you from the beginning. You deaf or something?"

"No, I'm not deaf, but it never sunk in how far apart we really are."

"Hey, I meant everything I ever told you about being innocent! But you never believed me! I figured it was just a game for you, just collecting your money, so I decided to keep the faith and defend what's right..."

"You decided to prove that you could keep your mouth shut? To die bravely and be a martyr so you'd be revered in convenience stores all over New Jersey?"

Wally mumbled, "Something like that. I didn't want to die in vain."

Carl smiled. "As long as you were a goner, you might as well die standing on your feet..."

"Well, it's true, isn't it? I mean...I knew I had caused them lots of trouble in all those Court cases. Where's that Aldin guy from the Middle East? Go find him! He's been messing with us long enough! I mean, after all, us guys are all Islamic fundamentalists, aren't we? You know, Hardman, you only heard one side of what I did to mess with their system. You never asked me why I did it. For years I was a good boy...showed up on time…showed respect…and every time I went to Court in this worthless little town, Judge Esker treated me like a leper. I'm an American citizen! I chose to be one! Esker…he got born American. His parents probably made the choice by accident. He got to be a judge by family connections and backroom deals. He used his office like a club to take care of the people who count. The rest of us were just spare parts. Want some cream in that coffee, sir? That'll be thirty dollars for the gas. Esker…he was the terrorist…not me! Jerks like him sit on the little people and keep them paying the banks and credit card companies. He deserved to die. Maybe it was God's will. The guy who did it should have a statue in the Courthouse Square."

"So when it comes right down to it, Wally, you were embarrassed you didn't kill him! You were willing to accept being a martyr!" The idea was so strange it bounced off Carl's beliefs like a handball.

Aldin mumbled, "That's pretty close, I guess. After he got taken out, I wished I'd thought of it."

What he was hearing undermined everything he had spent a career defending. "That's bullshit, Wally. Nobody tried to…"

"Set me up? Is that what you were going to say? You just told me they knew I didn't do it for at least a month! They didn't tell you, they didn't tell me! They kept on trying to get me executed. Isn't that called lynching?"

Carl sat dumbfounded. What could he say? He put his hand to his forehead and rubbed it, but he could not remove the words Aldin had put into his head.

Aldin looked up at him, almost pleading. "They're going to play this up as a triumph for the system! The guy who did it was found. Justice triumphed. An innocent man was released. The system works! That's tomorrow's story. There won't be a word about trying to railroad me. Nothing about why the Collins guy was driven to take out Esker."

In the west, a new wave of clouds had rolling in. Lightning flashed. They waited for the thunder. Then Aldin said, "Maybe somebody will listen. Maybe…despite all of you."

"Me, too?"

"You too. From the beginning you assumed I did it, like all the rest. Why? Because I'm an Arab? You preached in Court about the presumption of innocence, but you never gave it to me. All you wanted to do was attack capital punishment. This case was never about me, it was about you and your beliefs!"

Carl stood mute as he watched Walid Aldin walk through the open door and exit onto the Courthouse lawn. Reporters and cameras jammed against him. He wondered how long it would take for Wally to wonder about Laura. And then what?

Click Clack

Carl walked through the deserted mock-courtroom, drained. Judge Harrigan was exiting the Circuit Clerk's office carrying a brief case in her right hand, a black judicial robe draped over her left arm. She was moving rapidly toward the rear door and her heels set a brisk tempo.

Carl stepped in front of her and said, "Excuse me!"

When she noticed it was Carl, her face became impenetrable. "Yes? What is it?"

"Well, that's kind of what I'd like to know. Are we going to have some sort of a hearing or something? I've been told..."

"Mr. Hardman, the case has been dismissed." With that she began to walk away.

"Dismissed?"

"Is there some acoustical problem here? The case has been dismissed!"

It was ending with a whimper. Carl wanted closure. Motions and a formal ending. Cases didn't end with a revelation in an alcove, the judge high-tailing it out the back door. "Don't we have to put something on the record here?"

"Mr. Hardman, your case has been dismissed by Mr. Gadsen. As you know, the State has an absolute right under Illinois law to bring a case or dismiss one. Since you and your client have nothing to say about it, I went ahead and dismissed the case." Her look would have brushed off a New York panhandler.

"That's it? Is that all there is?"

"That's it. The case is over."

His smile registered derision. "You and Gadsen just sort of put it to sleep like an old dog, right?"

Judge Harrigan stiffened and glanced around the imitation courtroom, apparently looking for a witness. It was strangely empty. The deputies had melted away, perhaps to cope with the press, perhaps to avoid seeing Aldin walk out a free man. At any rate, the Judge and Carl were alone. She took a breath and shaped it carefully and then said, "Mr. Hardman. This is a courthouse and I am a Judge. You'd better watch your tone!"

An attorney who had survived many years of trials once told him it was a lawyer's obligation to get held in contempt at least once in a career. He said, "Damn! That fact escaped me someplace along the line. Thanks for making it crystal clear that what we've been involved in was some sort of a judicial proceeding."

"Just keep it up. I'm counting and I'm up to a week."

"Better get a reporter and make a record, Judge. This is the equivalent of a chambers conference. Nobody's publicly holding up the system to display its unwiped butt. This is just us. So tell me why it was so important to dismiss this case without facing Aldin? Did it trouble you to look him in the eye and concede he truly did nothing wrong? To admit that for the last four months you assumed an innocent man was guilty? That you cheated on your oath?"

She flared and abandoned her shell of judicial detachment. "You're a fine one to be preaching to me! You were hired by these...these terrorists! Maybe Aldin didn't get around to committing this particular crime, but we won't be so lucky next time..."

"I can't believe I'm hearing this! You're admitting the presumption of innocence is a parlor game? An illusion? What do you really believe, Your Honor? Tell me. We're off the record. I'd be fascinated to know what you think about when you put on that robe. What is it, something like, 'Well, here's a troublemaker who probably did something wrong? Hold the bus for Joliet!'"

Her face was crimson. "I'm charged with responsibilities you will never understand! You're out there playing footsie with forces that want to bring us down. The polite game is over, Mr. Hardman. Get real! We're in a war..."

"And the first casualty was the Constitution!" Now they were toe to toe. "You've abandoned all pretense of judicial restraint, haven't you? He was guilty from day one, and now you feel cheated."

Her eyes snapped as cruel irony crossed her face. "Tell me you believed he didn't do it! Tell me you didn't choke a little when he told you he wasn't going to testify!"

The remark stung. "Maybe you're right. This is a wake up call for me. But I'm not a Judge. I'm just an ordinary country lawyer who operates on the reality that people like you are biased."

Her eyes narrowed as she fought for control. "This conversation is over. I'd advise you to think about it for the next few days while I sleep on what I'm going to do about your attitude."

"Judge, you've just done wonders for my attitude. I've re-learned a valuable lesson about believing in my client. Thank you for the insight. You can go ahead and hold me in contempt right now if you want. I'd love to tell this story to the higher courts. In fact, I'd love to tell it to that gang out in front of the building."

He walked over to the counsel table that held the file boxes of trial preparation and started to put them on the hand truck. They represented months of work created to keep the hollow promises the system made. Carl's stomach turned. These boxes of dead paper would remind him of Aldin's last words to him, words he could not face, at least not yet. He stood the hand truck on end and walked away from the files. They would be somebody else's problem.

Out on the lawn, Aldin was holding forth in a thicket of microphones. Cameras studied him from every angle. Carl shook his head and wondered how long it would take for the glare of publicity to nurture bitterness into a more mature form of sabotage than filing bogus pleadings and faking heart attacks. Four months had been stolen from Aldin; for that, somebody owed him. He would forever be convinced the system spat him out not because of his innocence, but because he was indigestible. Hitler had written *Mein Kampf* while serving time. Malcolm X had become a charismatic leader while in prison. Would Wally Aldin become the next man on horseback, rallying the scattered elements of his people into a phalanx?

Carl couldn't watch. He headed for the back door to escape from stupidity on stupidity. As he walked out of the Lincoln County Courthouse he was alone. The front of the building was teeming with the camp followers of celebrity. Ants on a fresh glob of confection. A surreal swarm, devouring Aldin's every word. But the back of the court house was empty, deserted. He found a certain irony in that.

—·——·——·——·——·——·——·—

The Jaguar started the first time. He drove slowly through the puddles. Light rain dotted the windshield. He looked back at the Lincoln County Courthouse and fantasized that the hundred year old structure was dissolving in the incessant rain. He felt as if he had survived a pointless bar fight. He inserted a favorite jazz cassette tape and scanned until he heard Ben Webster playing *You're My Thrill*.

The case had ended like an explosion, with shrapnel blasting in all directions, scattering jagged fragments that were yet to come down. Acid boiled into his throat.

Webster's throaty tenor captured the sad futility of the Wally Aldin case.

By now Judge Harrigan was driving back to her home county. On her desk would be a mundane stack of files waiting to be decided. She would climb to the higher branches of the judiciary, rewarded by her peers for her firm handling of this tough case. At bar meetings and civic dinners, she would claim that blind Justice had freed Walid Aldin. Phrases that masked the fact that a pre-determined result was accidentally derailed.

Gadsen would slip back into rural obscurity and permanent electability. Hunting seasons would come and go marked by empty shotgun shells and executed fowl. In the end he would lie under a granite monument after the Bar President delivered a high-flown eulogy and the Methodist choir sang an off-key recessional.

Carl needed a large shot of normality. Perhaps he could talk Dani into letting him take Susan someplace for a week. He wished that somehow they could all take a family trip like they used to.

In the rear-view mirror Moraine's faded houses and shabby storefronts receded. He hoped he would never see them again. The Jag held the puddled road in a cat-like grip. Through the streaked windshield he saw a familiar Jeep Cherokee in the oncoming traffic. It was Dani. He flashed his lights and pulled into a parking lot in front of a grain elevator. She did a double U-turn and pulled up next to him, driver's windows facing each other. The rain splashed into both cars as they lowered the windows. He turned down the music to background level.

Dani said, "I heard about the dismissal on the radio. I figured maybe you'd want to talk about it. They made it sound like Gadsen decided to give him a break for some reason. What the hell is going on?"

"The only break was that Gadsen finally had the decency to tell us Aldin didn't do it, after keeping it a secret for too damned long. A guy named Collins shot himself and left a suicide note confessing to the bombing. They were hoping Wally would cop a plea for life, just like I tried to get him to do. Worse yet, the lab testing proved the gas can didn't match the accelerant. They actually let us go on with this case without telling us! One other little nugget...Aldin's wife has been selling us out, spying for the prosecution. I'm just floored by this, Dani. What would have happened if Aldin had followed my advice to plead guilty for life? What's tearing at my gut is the simple fact that Aldin was right, in his twisted way. The system spent the last four months covering up...trying to convict an innocent man."

Dani tried to find a middle ground to placate him. "But they eventually told you..."

"Only after the suicide of the guy who did it! If that hadn't happened, Aldin would be marching to the death chamber, surer than hell. I'm gonna have nightmares about this one. I thought he did it just because he refused to testify. I'm just as bad as the Judge or the reporters or the rabble..."

"Carl! Just shut up! You're drilling for a new ulcer."

He stared at her rain-streaked face. It was smiling. He tapped his fingers on the wooden steering wheel and asked, "Sheri call you?"

Dani smiled, "You ask too many questions. Just like a damn lawyer!"

He asked, "So what do you want to do about it?"

She looked straight ahead while the windshield wipers slapped several measures of two-beat rhythm. Then she turned toward him and said, "I don't know. I surely don't."

He felt a twinge. Was it despair or hope? The raindrops felt clean. He said, "Want to talk about what happens next?"

She smiled and said, "Sure."